THE BLUESTOCKING

BY THE SAME AUTHOR:

THE BLACK UNICORN
THURSDAY'S CHILD
A TIME TO SPEAK
A CAGE OF HUMMING-BIRDS
WELCOME, PROUD LADY
CABLE CAR
THE SABOTEURS
THE GANTRY EPISODE
THE PEOPLE IN GLASS HOUSE
FAREWELL PARTY
BANG! BANG! YOU'RE DEAD
THE BOON COMPANIONS
SLOWLY THE POISON
FUNERAL URN
THE PATRIOTS
I SAW HIM DIE
SUCH A NICE FAMILY
THE TROJAN MULE

THE BLUESTOCKING

A NOVEL

by

JUNE DRUMMOND

LONDON
VICTOR GOLLANCZ LTD
1985

First published in Great Britain 1985
by Victor Gollancz Ltd,
14 Henrietta Street, London WC2E 8QJ

© June Drummond 1985

For Lindsay

British Library Cataloguing in Publication Data
Drummond, June
　The bluestocking: a novel.
　I. Title
　823 [F]　　PR9369.D7

ISBN 0-575-03598-6

Photoset by Centracet
Printed in Great Britain by
St Edmundsbury Press, Bury St Edmunds, Suffolk

I

ON A MORNING late in February, 1816, the members of the Wakeford family assembled in the red drawing room of Wakeford Hall, the home of the late Mr Henry Wakeford, to discuss the implications of that gentleman's last will and testament.

Although the broad terms of the documents had been known since his death eleven months earlier, it had taken the authorities the whole of that time to unravel the threads of Mr Wakeford's business affairs. He had been a scholar of note, respected throughout the academic world, but certain quirks of character had made him wholly unreliable in matters of finance.

It was for this reason that the family had requested their solicitor, Mr Thomas Shedley, to travel down from London and explain to them just how they stood with the world. He had arrived the night before, bringing his senior clerk with him, and the two were now busy at a table in one corner of the room, sorting through papers and occasionally conferring together in low voices.

Henry Wakeford's interest had lain in books and artefacts of the mediaeval period. During his lifetime he had amassed one of the largest collections in Britain, and made his house the Mecca of collectors and antiquarians.

The original Manor of Wakeford, like the Abbey it served, had long ago fallen to ruin, and the Palladian mansion built on the site by Mr Wakeford's grandfather provided more than enough space for bookrooms. No expense had been spared in equipping these with the best heating-systems available. Books, declared Mr Wakeford, must be kept at precisely the right temperature if they were to remain in prime condition.

Unfortunately, he cherished no such conviction about the human frame. The ten main living-rooms and thirty-odd bedrooms of the present building were inadequately warmed by wood and coal fires. The vast entrance hall, conceived by Leoni and executed in white marble by a team of Italian stone-masons, enjoyed for most of the year the climate of an ice-house, while a walk along any of the corridors put one strongly in mind of the rigours endured by Napoleon's army during the retreat from Moscow.

By reason of its being situated directly above the main stackrooms, the red salon was relatively cosy, and Miss Davina Wakeford had decided that the day's discussions should take place there. She now stood as close to the fireplace as was safe. One wrist lay on the chimney-piece, and her head was bent over a small leather-bound volume which she had propped against the side of a Sèvres clock. She frowned slightly as she read, as if she were trying to close her ears to what went on about her.

She was a slender young woman, a little above average height, with a neat waist and narrow, delicate hands. Although only twenty-one years of age, she was often taken for more because of her composed, reflective manner. Her mode of dress was austere. She wore a quakerish gown of grey kerseymere, with a plain white collar and long tight sleeves. Her dark brown hair was twisted in a knot on top of her head, and her only ornament was a cameo locket on a thin gold chain.

Despite this somewhat old-maidish apparel, Miss Wakeford was by no means ill-favoured. There was something very pleasing in her countenance—a look of candour and intelligence. Her eyes were large and of a clear grey, under fine dark brows, and her mouth, though too wide to conform with current standards of beauty, suggested a lively sense of humour.

The room at her back was lit by three tall windows, and opposite the centremost, in a wing-chair placed to catch whatever thin sunshine might filter through, sat Henry Wakeford's widow, Davina's step-mama.

Eulalie Wakeford was a large woman, with strong features and a high complexion, but she liked to pretend to a frail constitution. She was much given to fads of diet, the latest being nettle tea, a dish of which fumed gently between her hands. Her hair was auburn, and arranged in elaborate puffs, over which she had drawn a cap of point lace. Her lilac gown, cut in the very latest style with a high bodice and balloon sleeves, was too youthful by far for her forty-five years. The fine wool shawl round her shoulders was secured by a gold medallion embellished with a coat of arms. Mrs Wakeford liked to remind people that her first husband, Mr Septimus Foote, had been brother to the Marquis of Alverford.

Her complaint that she had, in her second marriage, come down in the world, was not taken seriously in Rigborough, or anywhere else. It was common knowledge that Septimus had wasted his fortune, and left his wife and young son without a feather to fly with. As to rank, the Vicar, Mr Standish, pointed out that the Wakefords could trace their line unbroken to the days when there was still an Abbot on Hagg Hill. The first Henry of Wakeford had taken part in two crusades, as testified by the inscription on his tomb in the village church. By comparison, even the Rowans of Rowanbeck must be counted parvenus.

Unable to make any impression on Rigborough society, Eulalie turned her attention to the London scene. Each summer, she hired a house in the fashionable part of town, and spent several months there. She declared that only this spell among people of taste made it possible for her to put up with life in the country. The fear that this annual respite was now to be snatched from her, had honed her temper to a dangerous edge. She was spoiling for a quarrel. Her eye fell on her nephew, Mr Mortimer Foote, who was snoring gently in the chair next to hers.

Mortimer was an unremarkable young man, in looks and mental capacity very like a duck. His manners were graceful, but self-effacing. He must have passed unnoticed in any crowd but for his sense of dress, which was unerring. His aunt, glaring at his beautifully-cut coat, the immaculate fawn pantaloons encasing his plump legs, the exquisite set of his cravat and the unbelievable glossiness of his Hessians, was forced to admit that sartorially speaking, Morty was a pink of the ton.

The same could not be said of her own son, Roland, who had flatly refused to dress for the occasion, and was wearing the buckskins and riding-boots he affected every day of the week.

Irritated beyond reason, Mrs Wakeford leaned forward in her chair.

"Mortimer!"

Mr Foote jerked awake and goggled at his aunt. "Ma'am?"

"You do not take snuff, Mortimer?"

"No, ma'am."

"Never?"

"Never. Don't care for it. Gives me the headache, truth to tell."

"Aha!" Mrs Wakeford struck her hands together in triumph. "Then will you tell me, pray, why my husband left you all his snuffboxes? Twenty-seven valuable boxes, many of them exquisitely jewelled, and one said to have belonged to King Louis himself—bequeathed to a man who does not intend to make use of them. Why?"

Mr Foote cast about desperately for an answer. "Thought I'd take good care of 'em," he offered.

"Could not the same be said of my own dear son?"

"No," said Mortimer simply. "Roly don't look after things." He was about to add that Roly was far more likely to pop the lot, when he chanced to catch his cousin's eye, and lapsed into uneasy silence.

Baulked of her prey, Mrs Wakeford turned to consider Roland. He was her only child, and the apple of her eye. In his heavy build and florid colouring, he resembled his mama, but he lacked her driving energy and shrewdness of mind. He had never thought it worth his while to learn to please others. The spoiled child had become the spoiled young man, who put his own wishes first.

He leaned now in the window embrasure, staring moodily at the road that led up past the house to the crest of Hagg Hill. Mrs Wakeford tapped his elbow.

"Are they in sight yet?"

"Not a sign." He jiggled his shoulders impatiently. "We may count on Aunt Sophy to be late."

Eulalie craned her neck round the wing of her chair.

"Davina," she said, "we should begin without them."

Davina glanced up, blinking. "I beg your pardon, Mama?"

"I say, the Tredgolds are unpunctual. It is most discourteous in them. My nerves are quite worn down by all these delays." Mrs Wakeford noticed that her step-daughter was marking her place in her book with a finger, and added pettishly, "Be so good as to pay attention when I am speaking to you!"

Davina laid aside the volume of Lord Byron's verse, and studied the clock on the mantel. "They're not so very late, it still wants ten minutes of eleven."

Eulalie pursed her lips. "I declare, I cannot imagine what concern it is of the Tredgolds, how my husband chose to divide his estate."

"Some concern," said Roland glumly. "Uncle Murray is our chief creditor, ain't he?"

"That may be so, but he's unlikely to dun us. He has more money than he knows what to do with. It's monstrous to see his tribe roll in wealth, while we totter on the brink of penury."

Davina gave her a measuring look. "Hardly fair, Mama. We may have to pinch a little, but we don't lack the necessities."

"Pinch a little?" Mrs Wakeford spoke with loathing. "Let me tell you that at my age a female is entitled to expect some comfort, some little luxuries. I do not expect to have to scrimp and save, nor do I intend to join the ranks of the shabby-genteel."

Roland swung round to face the room. "Quite right," he said loudly. "It's all very well for you, Davina. You're content to frowst among books all your days, but we deserve something better. Why, one need only visit our stables to see how low we've sunk! I swear I'm ashamed to ride out on the slugs we own. The Squire's huntsmen are better mounted than I—and it's all because of your father's lack of foresight and management."

This was going too far. Miss Wakeford advanced on her brother with a look of sparkling anger. "You've no right to speak so, Roly. We may have problems, but we're far from being paupers. If you don't believe me, ask Mr Shedley."

"I don't require Shedley or anyone else to tell me what the whole county knows already—that you were made heir to the estate, over my mother's head and mine. We're no more than pensioners in this house. We've been cheated of our dues."

His face was dark with fury. It seemed that a royal quarrel must break, but Mortimer, who had been listening to the dispute in growing alarm, was inspired to say that he rather thought he heard a coaching-horn.

This brought the two ladies hurrying to the window. The horn sounded again, and a moment later a handsome carriage, drawn by four bay horses and accompanied by liveried postillions, rolled from behind a belt of trees and advanced towards the house. In its wake came a chaise piled high with baggage. The Tredgolds, Sir Murray and Lady Sophia (as she was known), had arrived.

II

It could be seen at a glance that the lady who alighted from the carriage and hastened into the shelter of the Hall was not only well-to-do, but of the first stare of modality.

Lady Sophia's sea-green pelisse was cut in the latest style, with a high rolled collar and full gigot sleeves. She carried a muff of sable fur, and her dashing bonnet, with its high poke and finish of ruched taffetas, was unquestionably the creation of a London modiste.

She was the twin sister of the late Henry Wakeford. Cynics held that in apportioning gifts, the gods had given Henry the wits and Sophia the looks, but that was unjust. Sophy Tredgold might not possess a powerful intellect, but she had a great deal of common sense. Her charm and vivacity made her well-liked in all quarters, and even those who thought her a trifle high in the instep—a little too inclined to dwell on her Wakeford ancestry—were bound to admit that she was a model wife and mother.

Now she embraced her niece warmly. "Davina, my dearest! Did you quite despair of us? We thought to be here an hour since, but you can't conceive of the state of the roads."

"Our factor warned there'd been heavy snow on the tops."

"An understatement!" Sir Murray Tredgold handed his beaver hat and many-caped coat to Hoby the butler, and advanced to drop a kiss on Davina's cheek. "Must have snowed all night by the look of it, and then this morning it thawed. You never saw such mud! The carriage rode it well enough, but the chaise came near to foundering. I shan't risk my cattle on Hagg Hill again. We'll take the long route home, through Ivinghoe."

"I hope that won't be for a month at least. We've seen too little of you since the funeral."

"I know," said Lady Sophy contritely, linking her arm with Davina's, and moving with her to the stairway. "It was very bad in us, but there was Lizzie's wedding, and Margaret's lying-in, and then all of John's brood went down with the scarlet fever, and were so ill that I had to remain at Luton for seven weeks, helping Emily nurse them. Which reminds me—how is dear Eulalie's health?"

"She complains of spasms of the stomach."

"Indeed? It sounds distressing. What does she take for it?"

"Hot nettle tea, every four hours."

Lady Sophy shuddered. "I had rather endure the spasms. Do you tell me Dr Sampson advised such a remedy?"

"No. Mama dispensed with his services some months ago. After he told her her pains were imaginary. We have Dr Burrows now."

Lady Sophy reflected privately that no doubt Dr Sampson was delighted to be rid of a patient whose ills sprang from a surfeit of rich food, wine, and ill-temper; but it would be improper to say as much to Davina. She turned instead to giving news of her grandchildren, and when the party reached the red salon, greeted her relations with every expression of goodwill, apologised for keeping them waiting, and begged Mr Shedley to proceed at once with the day's business.

Thomas Shedley was not enjoying the task of administering Henry Wakeford's will.

Though he was now a senior partner in the London firm of Shedley, Rathbone and Monk, he was Rigborough-born, and could count many of the local gentry among his clients.

His friendship with the Wakeford clan was of long standing. He had known and loved Henry's first wife, and recognised that she had absorbed whatever affection that eccentric man was capable of generating. After Serena's death from consumption of the lungs, Henry turned his back on society, and devoted himself entirely to his collection. He neglected his family and starved his lands in order to cherish and feed his bookrooms. As his eyesight failed, he employed his daughter, still a child, as his amanuensis.

By the time Davina Wakeford was sixteen, she had acquired an extensive knowledge of mediaeval literature, including certain writings that were, in Mr Shedley's opinion, totally unfit for the eyes of a delicately-bred female.

Henry's unwise marriage to Eulalie Foote took place in 1810. Mr Shedley ascribed it to a temporary loss of sanity on his friend's part. The union was unhappy from the start. Though it was impossible to like Eulalie, one could not help feeling a sneaking sympathy for her. Only a wise and generous woman could have borne with Henry's foibles, and she was neither. She craved company, and an outlet for her social ambitions. They were not to be found at Wakeford Hall. She was envious of the reliance her husband placed on his daughter, and of the easy popularity the girl enjoyed among local folk. Her own son Roland was no solace to her, for he lacked talent, and his erratic temper constantly led him into sordid scrapes and unseemly quarrels.

Mr Shedley knew—none better—that even the most devoted of families can come to loggerheads over the division of property. The Wakefords had never been devoted, and from the day of Henry's death, when the terms of the will became known, the animosity between them had mounted daily.

Over the past eleven months Mr Shedley had been at pains to make it clear, to the widow at least, that Wakeford Hall, its contents, and the lands attached to it, belonged to Davina, and that no one would be suffered to defeat either the terms or the intent of the will.

Today he was striving to drive home a second lesson—that only stringent economies could lift the estate from the quagmire into which it had sunk. Having explained the details of the financial statement, he was now reaching his conclusion.

"As you know," he said, "at the time of Mr Wakeford's death, this house was already mortgaged, and there were debts which I can only describe as crippling. Luckily, there were also assets which your executors have been able to realise. The farms at Eston fetched an excellent price, and that money has been used to reduce the mortgage. The sale of certain stocks has allowed us to settle the worst of the debts, with the exception of the very large sum still owed to you, Sir Murray."

Sir Murray waved a hand. "No need to worry about that for the moment."

"It's generous of you to say so, sir."

"Not really. I'm being practical. No point in redeeming the loan if it destroys Wakeford's chance of recovery. Let's set the place to rights, and the rest will follow."

"Fine words," said Eulalie tartly, "but what's to become of

us, I'd like to know? How does my son stand, how do I stand, what are we supposed to live on?"

Mr Shedley considered her over his spectacles. "The situation is better than we at first feared, ma'am. You are assured of six thousand pounds a year for your personal use, without encumbrance of any kind."

"Six thousand?" Mrs Wakeford's face turned a rich beetroot hue. "And what, pray, can be done with that paltry sum?"

"A very great deal," answered Mr Shedley with acerbity, "especially if you remember that you are able to live at Wakeford without having to bear any of its expenses. You will not be called upon to contribute to the maintenance of the buildings, or the care of the grounds, or the feeding of livestock."

"I should hope not, since I own none of them."

"What about me," interrupted Roland. "What do I get?"

"You are to receive an allowance of five hundred pounds a year, Mr Foote, until you reach the age of twenty-five."

"Be damned, man! That's years away!"

"Less than five years."

"And when I'm twenty-five, what then?"

"There will be an adjustment, according to the funds then available—and your own situation."

"What's that mean?"

"It was your step-father's hope that you would attend one or other of the universities, and qualify yourself for some useful role in life. If that should happen. . . ."

"Well, it won't," burst out Roland in a furious voice. "What should I do at university but grub along like some half-pay soldier?"

"It's for you to choose, of course. If you dislike the idea of an academic training, there's plenty to occupy you here."

Roland scowled. He had no intention of kicking his heels in Rigborough, but he knew better than to say so. Shedley was an old woman. He'd prose on and on about the need to set one's shoulder to the wheel, and so forth. He might even find a way of cutting off the dibs. Roland agreed with his mama. A certain position was due to him. Five hundred a year, scaly sum though it was, would pay for a little fun and gig in London. It was certainly not going to be spent on patching roofs, or fencing pigpens.

Mr Shedley had talked for close on an hour. He paused, removed his spectacles, examined them against the light, and put them on again.

"We come now," he said, "to the urgent question of how to restore Wakeford to prosperity. The land is in poor heart. It has, I'm afraid, been neglected for years."

"True enough," agreed Sir Murray. "I warned Henry time and again, but he paid me no heed."

"Naturally, he would not," said Eulalie, "since all he cared about was his books, and his fusty old papers."

"We may yet be thankful for it," answered Mr Shedley. "The Wakeford Collection is unique. It's been kept in prime condition, and has appreciated in value over the years. It will find a ready market."

There was a moment of stunned silence. Then Sir Murray said sharply, "No, no, impossible. Henry's books were his life. We can't have 'em put up to auction—scattered through the length and breadth of Britain. We must find some other solution."

"I entirely agree," said Lady Sophia. "It would be wicked to destroy what my brother built up at such sacrifice."

"*Our* sacrifice," muttered Roland; but no one so much as glanced at him.

"The alternative," Mr Shedley said, "is for all of you to sit with hands folded while Wakeford sinks to ruin, and the family becomes bankrupt."

"Surely," said Lady Sophy in distress, "it cannot be as bad as that?"

"It is, Lady Sophia. That is what I've been trying to explain to you today."

Mortimer Foote, who had been sitting spellbound at the back of the room, suddenly rose and came over to Davina.

"Tell you what, Dav," he said, "sell the snuffboxes. I don't want 'em. Sell 'em for whatever they'll fetch."

Miss Wakeford smiled at him gratefully, but shook her head. "It wouldn't serve, Morty. The boxes are a drop in the ocean."

"Why can't we do as everyone else does?" demanded Roland. "Why can't we sell off a parcel of land?"

"We've sold too much already," Davina said. "I've spoken to the executors and to . . . to people who understand farming.

They say that to make Wakeford pay, we shall need all the land that's left, and we must develop it at once. That's why I'm resolved to dispose of papa's collection." She rose and crossed to the table, rummaged among the papers on it, and selected a calf-bound catalogue. "I've marked the things that I think must be sold. Uncle Murray?"

She held out the book and he took it, scanning the pages rapidly. After a while he glanced up, his face troubled.

"The Rigborough Missal?" he said. "My dear child, you can't mean it?"

"I do."

"But ... it was Henry's pride. It's Rigborough's pride. It belongs here, it's part of the history of this village."

Mr Shedley cleared his throat. "One might also say, Sir Murray, that it's a national treasure, and deserves a wider audience."

"Humbug sir. Henry would never have sold it. Never!"

"One cannot know what he might have felt in the matter. Surely he would not have wished to see Wakeford go under—which is what will happen if we don't act with despatch. This house, the lands, the tenants' farms and cottages, everything will be lost. The collection will go too, in the end. It's best to make a partial sacrifice at once."

Sir Murray sighed and shook his head. Mrs Wakeford spoke imperiously. "I am for selling," she announced. "I've no use for books. But it's my opinion the money must come to us—to the members of this family—to permit us to live as we ought."

"I take leave to remind you, Eulalie," said Sir Murray with an angry gesture, "that your opinion counts for nothing. Davina owns the collection. She will do as she sees fit."

Lady Sophy intervened hastily. "The Vicar? If we consult him?"

"I've already done so." Davina sounded tired. "Papa used to say Mr Standish was the finest scholar in the south, and there's no one more anxious than he to keep the Missal in Rigborough. But when he'd considered, he advised me to sell. He feels some important collector—perhaps even a Royal personage—will pay us a handsome sum for it."

*

Soon after this the company removed to the small dining-room to share a light nuncheon, and a glass or two of wine, before Mr Shedley and his clerk set out on their journey to London.

The little solicitor took the opportunity to have a quiet word with Lady Sophia.

"It will be a long, hard haul," he said, "but I make no doubt that in ten years or so, Miss Wakeford will find herself the owner of a prosperous estate."

"Ten years!" Lady Sophy laughed. "Good God, man, Davina will be married long before then, and lay the load on her husband's shoulders."

"I hope she may marry," said Mr Shedley with a sharp look. "I've the highest regard for her, and I'm sure she would make an admirable wife for the right man; but let us be honest, she has little chance of finding him in Rigborough."

"What makes you say so?"

"A bluestocking, my lady, is seldom the quarry of a hunting squire . . . particularly if she can offer her groom nothing but debts as a dowry."

"You told us Wakeford will make a recovery."

"In ten years' time. By then your niece will be an old maid."

"You're blunt, sir!"

"I'm an old friend, and extremely fond of the child." Mr Shedley hesitated. "You know how deeply I revered her mother. If Serena were alive, there would be no need to address you."

Lady Sophy stared unhappily across the room to where Eulalie Wakeford sat. Her gaze returned to Mr Shedley.

"I'll give the matter some thought," she said.

"I beg you will, ma'am, for no one else will."

After Mr Shedley and his junior had departed, Mrs Wakeford and Lady Sophia retired to their bedrooms to rest, Sir Murray fell to snoring before the drawing-room fire, and Roland and Mortimer rode off to visit the Hunt kennels.

Left to herself, Davina made her way to the library. She planned to add one or two items to the catalogue she was preparing for the agents, but instead found herself standing in front of the cabinet that held the Rigborough Book of Hours.

For as long as she could remember, she had loved it. The

richly illuminated letters, the delicate illustrations of the mediaeval scene with its knights and yeomen, pilgrims and serfs, were a world in which she could seek refuge from the irritations of her daily life.

Her father had always believed the artist to have been a Rigborough man, taking his inspiration from the Rigg Valley and Hagg Hill above it. Probably he had worked in a cell of the monastery that stood on this very ground; and for four centuries his masterpiece had rested in Wakeford hands, their trust, and their most precious possession.

Davina moved to the window. On the crest of the ridge she could see the last ruined arch of the old Abbey—all that was left standing by Tudor Henry's vandals. It was in his reign that the fine house on the far side of the river passed into the possession of the Rowan family. Was that when the ancient feud had begun? The Wakefords holding by the Plantagenet line while the Rowans came out for Henry? Whatever the source of the rift, it had continued down the years, the Wakefords espousing the Stuart cause and the Rowans rallying to Cromwell, the Rowans for German George whom the Wakefords cordially loathed, the Wakefords staunch Tories, and the Rowans doughty Whigs. Not until the time of the fourth Earl of Rigg was there any sort of accord between the two households.

How foolish it seemed now that she was faced with such real and pressing problems. And how lost she would have been, without the support and advice of the Rowanbeck coterie!

It was now past three o'clock, and Davina, hoping that fresh air and cheerful company would drive out the megrims, decided to stroll over to Rowanbeck. She went to her bedchamber to change into stouter shoes, and was tying the strings of her cloak when there was a tap on the door, and her aunt's abigail, Rebecca Bracket, appeared on the threshold.

At Davina's smile and nod, she advanced into the room.

"Lady Sophia's compliments, Miss Davina, and she'd like to know what she should put on, this evening."

"Oh . . . Becky, love . . . whatever is comfortable. We shall be just the family for dinner. And will you tell my aunt I'm going over to Rowanbeck, but won't be late home?"

"Very good, Miss." Rebecca paused, then said, "If you'll show me what you mean to wear, I'll give it a press for you."

"There's a blue crape gown at the end of the closet. The flounce is a little torn. If you will set a stitch in it?" Davina checked long enough to give the tall woman a swift hug. "We must talk tomorrow, Becky. I wish to hear all your news."

She was gone, running along the corridor and down the broad stairs. Becky advanced on the closet with a grim expression and made a rapid examination of its contents. In her view not only the blue gown, but the whole of Miss Wakeford's wardrobe, was fit only to be parcelled up and sent to the deserving poor. When, a few minutes later, she arrived at her mistress's room to deliver Davina's message, she was in a mood to speak her mind.

"Just look at this objick, my lady," she said, shaking the dress at shoulder-level. "Four years old, I know for a fact, and not worth ten shilling, even when it were new! Shoddy goods, as I told Mrs Wakeford when she went for to buy it. Nothin' but a waste o' good money. It's a cryin' shame, my lady, that one so pretty as our Miss should have nothin' fit to wear, while others I could name strut about as fine as peacocks!"

Lady Sophy could not find it in her to rebuke this outspokenness. Becky enjoyed a position of privilege. Raised on the Wakeford estate, she had known Henry and Sophia from their cradle days, and been present at Davina's birth and christening. Although she had left Rigborough with Sophy, at the time of the latter's marriage, she retained for Henry's daughter an affection she never tried to conceal.

It was Becky who had persuaded the Tredgolds to invite Davina to join their own children for holidays, and who had cajoled Henry into sending her to Miss Pinkerton's Academy with Eliza and Margaret Tredgold.

Now it seemed, she was about to embark on a fresh crusade. "What we need," she declared roundly, "is a husband, your la'yship, and how we'll find such in this wormy ol' dump, the Lord alone knows."

Hearing this advice twice in one day put Lady Sophy on the defensive. "You know, Rebecca, I did tell my brother years ago, that Davina should have a proper come-out, but he paid no attention to me."

"Course he didn't. Wanted her here, to read to him, and pay his bills, and look after the house, which his own wife didn't care to do. Wicked, I say, that the poor lamb was used so, when she should a been spreading her wings, and enjoying herself like the rest."

"I doubt if she'd have left Henry, once his health became so frail."

"Mr Henry's gone now, and she's free to do as she pleases. Been free a year, come to that."

"There was the mourning period, Becky. It quite ruled out parties, and balls. . . ."

"Mourning's done. Reckon we'll have to fetch Miss Davina to Lunnon now, my lady, so we will."

Lady Sophy sighed. "There are certainly few eligible gentlemen in Rigborough."

"Aye," said Becky sombrely, "and that's the danger. I was talking to Hoby, not an hour ago. Not that I make a habit o' gossip, my lady, but Hoby's been at Wakeford man an' boy, and he's that fond of Miss Davina, he felt bound to speak up. He says Mr Edward Clare, that lives at Rowanbeck these days, has been most particular in his attentions to Miss Davina. Comes over here most days, Hoby says. I know it's not my place to say so, but Mr Clare ain't suitable, not by a long chalk."

"Of course he isn't. Davina wouldn't contemplate marrying him, not for an instant. We certainly need not be anxious on that score."

"There's some that think different, my lady."

"Ridiculous. A Rowan cannot presume to marry a Wakeford. Why, Edward Clare is son to Hugo, that was a gambler and a bankrupt. He's brother to Jocelyn Clare that nigh ruined himself a few years ago. He's first cousin to Talbot and Lucas Rowan, and I need not remind you what a scandal they raised."

"I know it, but folk are sayin' Edward had no part in what happened. They hold that for the past two year, he's been of service here, pullin' Rowanbeck together. They say that without him, Talbot Rowan wouldn't of kep' his head above water as long as he did."

"It was not water that drowned Talbot Rowan," said Lady Sophy tartly, "it was brandy. The fact is, Rowan blood is bad blood, and Edward Clare is as tainted as the rest."

"What you're sayin' is, you wouldn't wish him to wed Miss Davina."

"Precisely."

Rebecca met her employer's eye. "My lady, when a young girl don't see any birds in the bush, she'll like as not latch onto the bird in hand. That's what I'm afeared of, my lady, that she'll take whatever she can get!" So saying, Rebecca bobbed a curtsey, gathered up the torn blue gown, and retired with it to the sewing-room.

Lady Sophy sat for some time deep in thought. Becky often went beyond the bounds of what was permissible, but she was seldom out in her judgements.

It was true that the Rowans had an unsavoury reputation. It had not always been so. Lady Sophy could remember how, in her girlhood, Rowanbeck had seemed the seat of all that was romantic and delightful. There was George, Fourth Earl of Rigg, bluff and swaggering, a bruising rider to hounds, a capital fellow all round; his Countess, frail and timid but endlessly kind; his dashing sister Charlotte, Sophy's own particular friend; the two small boys, Talbot and Lucas, young gods born to inherit Olympus.

How quickly the illusion had faded! Lady Rigg died, and George fell into raffish ways. Charlotte, having refused all the eligible gentlemen who offered for her, suddenly made a runaway match with a very vulgar person, a merchant who had amassed a fortune in the East India trade, and was not accepted beyond the limits of the City.

George Rowan got himself killed in the hunting-field, and Talbot, then eighteen years of age, succeeded to the title. It soon became plain he was unequal to the position. Indeed he left Rowanbeck to look after itself, and removed to London, taking up residence at Rowan House with his brother Lucas. The two of them entered upon a life of unbridled dissipation, lost fortunes at the gaming-tables, raced their horses or their curricles at risk to their necks, brawled, consorted with the birds of paradise of the theatre and opera-house. Behaviour, one could say, that was common among young bloods sowing their wild oats; but those closest to the Rowans saw in them something that challenged reason, and predicted they would come to no good end.

The final scandal erupted when the ravishing Amabel Sears

arrived in London, in the spring of 1812. Such a beauty, remembered Lady Sophia. Within a month she'd become the toast of the town. True, her fortune was no more than respectable, but she was of good stock, being niece to the Marquis of Avonmore, and daughter to Graham Sears, who'd distinguished himself as a diplomat.

Even Miss Sears's critics predicted she would make a brilliant match; but to the chagrin of her parents and well-wishers, she chose to cast her favour on the rakehelly Rowan brothers. No one could be sure which of the two she preferred, for she flirted outrageously with both, and both were infatuated with her. Bets were laid in the Clubs, which she would have. The cognoscenti said it was Lucas who had captured her heart. The cynics replied that the chit had a fancy to be Countess of Rigg, and would take the elder brother. The cynics proved right. Just before the season ended, a notice appeared in *The Times*, announcing Amabel's betrothal to Talbot, Fifth Earl of Rigg.

The wedding had been ill-omened, the groom arriving at the church half-drunk, and having to be supported by his bride as they returned down the aisle. Lucas Rowan did not show his face at the ceremony. It was reported he had gone to Ireland for an indefinite stay.

The happy couple set out on the customary round of bride-visits to relatives and friends, returning to Rowanbeck in April of 1813. Two weeks after they were installed, Lucas Rowan arrived at the house. That same night, he and Amabel Rowan left it together. Talbot was informed next morning they had taken the road north. He pursued them, but they had a long start, and the roads were bad because of the spring rains. It was not until three days later that he came up with them, at a coaching-house near Doncaster.

Precisely what occurred there, Sophy had never learned. It was said that the landlord of the inn admitted Talbot to a parlour set aside for the runaways. Soon after, voices were heard in furious argument. There followed the sound of a shot, and a cry of agony.

The landlord and his ostler pounded on the door, demanding entry. After some delay, it was thrown open, to reveal Lucas Rowan with a pistol in his hand, Talbot lying bleeding in a corner, and his bride kneeling beside him, half-fainting from shock and grief.

Amabel Rowan maintained, when she was later questioned by doctors and magistrate, that the pistol was Talbot's own. He had threatened her with it, she claimed, and Lucas, in trying to wrest the weapon from his brother, had accidentally triggered it.

Lucas confirmed this story. It was known that the brothers owned identical sets of duelling-arms, given them by their father.

The landlord, however, had a sharp eye, and noticed that there were no powder-burns on Talbot's coat, such as would have resulted from a shot fired at close quarters. The brothers' bitter rivalry and recent quarrels were recalled. The rumour grew that Lucas had fired at Talbot deliberately, and from a distance of two or three yards.

If Talbot died, the pundits said, it would be a case of murder.

For days the young Earl's life hung in the scales. During this time, Lucas Rowan slipped quietly out of London, made his way to Tilbury, and took ship for India.

London, of course, buzzed with lurid tales, but the Sears family rallied to Amabel's defence. They insisted that Talbot's drunken rages had put his wife in fear of her life, that she had written to Lucas begging for help, and that he had merely been trying to bring her safely to her parents' home in Yorkshire.

Talbot slowly recovered of his wound, and returned with Amabel to Rowanbeck. They lived in close seclusion, seeing only their near relations. The Rowan clan preserved a discreet silence. No child was born whose paternity could be called in doubt. In time, the London scandal-mongers wearied of the topic, and found fresh meat to feed on.

In Rigborough, it was otherwise, society being deeply divided on how to treat the young couple. The more stiff-backed would have nothing to do with them. Talbot, they said, was no better than a sponge. To dine at his house was a penance, because of the insulting language he used to his wife, and because more often than not he had to be carried insensible from the dinner-table.

The more generous pitied Amabel, saying she had erred through youth and inexperience. They pointed out that since the tragedy, she had remained at her husband's side, and nursed him devotedly.

It must have been a year after the shooting that the Clare cousins moved in. Talbot suffered an apoplectic stroke, the doctors were convinced he would die, and sent for Jocelyn and Edward to attend the deathbed. But to everyone's surprise, the sick man survived, though afflicted with paralysis of the right side of his body.

Somehow it came about that the Clares took up residence at Rowanbeck. While it was true that Jocelyn was often away in London, Edward seldom moved from Rigborough. He busied himself on the Rowan lands, directed the repair of barns and fences, planted crops and brought in new bloodlines to improve the stock. As Talbot's incapacity became more marked, Edward took over the handling of all accounts.

In short, he ran the estate. He was an excellent farmer, everyone agreed. The labourers came to him for their orders. The local gentry declared him to be a thorough good sort. The Vicar held him up as an example of Christian charity.

Nobody asked what Talbot thought. He had become a wraith, hunched in his chair before the fire, seen by no one save the members of his household. When in the summer of 1815 he suffered a second and fatal stroke, his going was hardly noticed.

Edward Clare stayed on. Jocelyn was a frequent visitor. No one queried their presence. Lucas Rowan, the heir, was in some godforsaken part of the world, and seemed in no hurry to come home. Things were allowed to drift.

But, decided Lady Sophia, they must be allowed to drift no further. Her brother Henry had been neglectful and selfish, but he would not have allowed his only daughter to make an unsuitable marriage. He would not have allowed her to marry a Rowan.

Lady Sophy rose, and went in search of her husband.

"My dear," she said, settling herself in a chair opposite his, and fixing him with an earnest stare, "I have made up my mind that we must do something for Davina. Mr Shedley and Rebecca are both agreed we have been neglectful in our duty to her."

"Neglectful? Shedley? Rebecca? What in the world are you talking about?"

"London," replied his wife. "We must invite Davina to make her come-out this year, with Jane."

"But why? She seems perfectly content, here in Rigborough."

"She must have a Season."

"Why?" persisted Sir Murray, who regarded the London Season as a foretaste of hell.

"In order that she may meet people."

"Won't meet anyone in Town but a set of bores and fribbles."

"I refer," said Lady Sophy patiently, "to suitable prospects."

"If by that you mean bachelors," Sir Murray replied, "I must say I don't see why that entails postin' up to London! Most girls spend a fortune there, then go straight home and marry some oaf they've known since he was in leading-strings. Meg did, Lizzie did."

"You know quite well, my love, that a Season is desirable."

"I know mamas and their daughters desire 'em. Papas don't. Papas merely comply, because if they don't life ain't worth the living."

"Rebecca informs me," said Lady Sophy, changing tack, "that Edward Clare is laying suit to Davina. I'm sure you won't approve of that."

"No feeling either way. Never clapped eyes on the fellow."

"You have met him on a number of occasions."

"Don't recall. Fellow must be eminently forgettable."

"Then do but call to mind the family history!"

"What history?" Sir Murray frowned, then brightened. "I remember George, all right. Cracking horseman. Broke his neck, at a wall-and-ditch, out with the Quorn."

Lady Sophy chose to ignore this irrelevancy. "I fancy you are acquainted with Sir Jocelyn Clare, are you not?"

"Well, yes, I am, and I can't say I like him. Don't like any of the Great-Go men, come to that. Somethin' idiotic in playin' so high. But I'll say this for Jocelyn Clare, he's everywhere accepted. Friendly with the Prince Regent. Member of White's and Watier's."

"I'm told he has gambled away a fortune, and only came to live with Edward at Rowanbeck in order to make a recoup."

"No crime in that, that I can see, m'dear."

"Surely it's plain that if Jocelyn has lost all the Clare money, Edward's expectations cannot be great?"

"Don't know about that," said Sir Murray thoughtfully. "May have money from his mother's side. Maria Clare was a Wyverne. When Hugo Clare cashed in his chips, she went back to live with her father, somewhere in the West Country. Perhaps, later on, this Edward will come into something through her."

"Rich or poor, I do not intend Davina to marry a Rowan. They're a ramshackle lot, everyone agrees."

"Well, but it ain't for us to say whom she marries. Why don't you speak to Eulalie?"

"Because," said Lady Sophia in exasperation, "I have a strong suspicion that Eulalie does not wish Davina to marry at all."

"Then there's nothing to worry about."

"There is, of course there is. Of course she must marry, but not some rapscallion, without a penny to his name! Tredgold, I wish you will give the matter your immediate attention."

Sir Murray knew that when his wife called him "Tredgold", the time for argument was past. He smiled at her reassuringly. "My love, if you wish to offer Davina a few months in London, by all means do so. I'll be happy to foot the bill. Fond of the little puss. But I doubt if you'll be able to persuade her to leave Wakeford. She's committed to the place, hook, line and sinker. Anyway, she ain't one for town gig, is she? Bit of a bluestocking, bless her!"

"She is no such thing!" cried Lady Sophy, in the tone of one denouncing nameless vice. "She is a pretty young female who's been condemned to live like an aconite. . . ."

". . . anchorite. . . ."

". . . and I propose to take her to London with Jane and bring her into society."

"If she'll go."

"She will go," promised Lady Sophy. "I will contrive it somehow. Wait and see."

III

AT APPROXIMATELY THE same time that the Wakefords were gathering in the red salon, a rowboat left the shelter of London's West India Docks, and began to make its way over to the New Surrey Docks on the south side of the Thames. It was manned by two oarsmen dressed alike in dark blue livery, and it carried a single passenger.

This man might at first glance have been taken for a French émigré. There was a certain flamboyance in the style of his dark blue coat, his skin-tight dove-grey pantaloons, his high-crowned beaver hat, that spoke of Paris. However, it could be observed that his cravat was faultlessly tied in the Oriental knot made popular some years earlier by the unfortunate Mr Brummell; that his shirt was of the finest Irish linen; and that his boots had certainly been fashioned by an English craftsman.

He wore neither tie-pin nor fob-chain, his only ornament being a signet ring set with an onyx, on which was engraved a rowan tree.

In build he was above average height, with the good shoulders, flat waist and muscular thighs of a horseman. It seemed he must have lived for some time in a sunny climate, for his skin was burned as dark as any gipsy's. His features were strongly marked, the nose aquiline, the cheekbones rather high. He looked like a man accustomed to go where he pleased, and do as he chose. His eyes, under straight black brows, were of a brown so light as to be almost amber. At the moment they gazed with lazy amusement at the river scene.

At this time of day the Thames was crowded with craft. Bum-boats laden with fresh fruit and vegetables nosed in and out of every creek. Lighters carrying salt, fish, pork, and barrels of water nuzzled the bellies of the larger ships along the wharves. Fishing-boats forged upstream to Billingsgate market, and wherries scuttled like water-spiders to cross the Limehouse reach on the flood-tide.

Further downstream, the Margate steam-packet could be seen threshing along, her great wheel churning amidships, and smoke belching from her tall, striped funnel; while far to the south a three-master barque, her mizzen rigged fore-and-aft, swung from her anchorage and slid between the steeps of Greenwich and the great tongue of the Isle of Dogs.

By the time the barque was out of sight, the rowboat had entered the main basin on the Surrey bank.

It was less than ten years since these new docks were opened, but the demands of war had ensured their rapid expansion. The quays were crowded with goods, with cranes and hoists, with drays and horses and shouting, toiling men. Further back stretched a line of warehouses, and across the largest of these, in letters a yard high, appeared the title: JOSHUA TURNBULL & SONS.

The boat bumped against the foot of a flight of stone steps and the younger of the two boatmen gripped a mooring-ring to steady her. The passenger, picking up a leather valise, stepped ashore, then felt in a pocket and produced two gold coins which he handed to the older boatman.

"Thank you, Silas."

"Want us to bide a while, Mr Lucas? Milord, I sh'ld say?"

"No. My uncle will see me conveyed anywhere I wish to go."

The old man screwed up his eyes. "Reckon they'll be lookin' fer yer at Rowan 'Ouse, 'fore long, sir."

"I doubt it." The amber eyes were cold. "I've not informed them of my arrival. I prefer to leave them in ignorance. Is that clear?"

"Aye sir, it is." Silas rubbed his nose, stowed the coins in the depths of his pea-jacket, and took up his oars. The dark man gave him a smile and a nod, and turned to climb the steps.

As the boat pulled away into deep water, the young boatman spoke for the first time.

"Proper mumchance you are! Never let on it were 'is lordship we was fetchin' over."

As Silas afforded this challenge no more than a grunt, the young man persisted. "Reckon there's some might come down 'andsome fer word o' that gennelman's whereabouts."

Silas spat over the side of the boat. "Don't try to chouse Luke Rowan, cully. 'Twouldn't be 'ealthy."

The young man squinted at the tall figure striding along the quay. "I did 'ear tell 'e were a werry wicious cove. Run orf wiv 'is bruvver's mort, and wellnigh killed is pore bruvver."

27

Silas sniffed. "None o' yer business, wot 'e done. Just you remember, young Jem, that's Josh Nabob's nevvy. If yer aimin' ter work on the River, keep a still tongue in yer 'ead."

This caution seemed to impress Jem, for he muttered that he meant no harm, and refrained from further comment until the boat reached Wapping.

Lucas Rowan—sixth Earl of Rigg as he had been since the death of his brother Talbot in the summer of 1815—reached the top of the quay to find himself facing a barrier of sawn logs, piled several feet high. A gang of stevedores was busy adding more timber to the stack, which by its colour and smell Lucas judged to be Burma teak.

It reminded him sharply of earlier visits to the Turnbull yards in Cheapside. Joshua had owned a house in Great Tower Street then, between Eastcheap and the massive walls of the old fortress, but he had since removed to a new residence, one built to his own specifications in Russell Square.

Charlotte Turnbull had written to tell Luke of the move. "Your uncle has decided to cut all ties with the East India Company. Josh Nabob is to be buried, and Josh Bull raised in his stead. There is a deal of bustle among all the City men, these days. So many new manufactories are being set up in the Midlands and to the North. It is all power-looms and spinning-machines, and the country weavers are migrating there to seek work, there being none to be had in their own villages. Joshua says that once we have Old Boney safe under lock and key, the ships we have employed to bottle him up will be free to carry our goods wherever we choose. He has plans to increase our enterprise in America and the West Indies. As to the new house, it is not so large as Blenheim, nor so poky as St James's Palace! It is time you came home, dear Lucas, to see how we prosper, and to curb our pretensions before we become quite above your touch!"

At thought of the Turnbulls, the Earl's expression softened. Without Joshua, he might well have starved in the first month of exile. Without Charlotte, he would certainly have lost touch with his family. Her letters, reaching him in a dozen different lands, had brought him news of home. Few of his one-time cronies had thought to pen him so much as a line over the past three years.

Turning, Luke walked along the quay until he came to a break in the stacked timber. As he stepped through, the main door of the warehouse burst open. A bulky figure emerged and lumbered to meet him, a great voice boomed above the clangour of the port: "Lucas, dear lad! Dear lad, welcome home!"

Joshua Turnbull's private eyrie was in an upper corner of the building, and overlooked the wharves and a glittering stretch of river. Every inch of the room seemed to be crowded with ledgers, bolts of silk, trusses of tobacco, tea-chests, spice-canisters, way-bills, maps and charts.

Mr Turnbull, rummaging like a porker after truffles, at last lifted a bottle by the neck.

"Yon's un," he said. "Brought in under exciseman's nose, and saved for this very day!" He drew the cork and lovingly poured brandy into two goose-necked glasses. Raising his own high, he smiled. "Here's to you, Lord Rigg!"

Luke shook his head. "We could find a better toast, I think."

"Nay, we could not. I'm reet glad you've come to your own. You'll do better by the title than that loose fish Talbot." As he spoke he was running a critical eye over his nephew. "I must say you've everything fine about you. Burbage gave you my draft in Paris did he? I told him to be sure you weren't short o' brass."

"Burbage was most attentive, but I didn't buy much. I don't care for the French cut, to be honest. Thought I'd rather wait till I could call on Weston . . . that is, if he's still top of the trees?"

"Oh aye, he's that, to judge by his prices, though they do tell me some o' the military men favour Schultz." Joshua patted his own old-fashioned brocade weskit, and grinned. "Don't look at me, lad. I'm none o' your dandy set! Your friend Robert Clintwood will come nearer the mark. Always bang up to t' nines, is young Bob."

The Earl glanced up quickly. "Is Clint in London?"

"Why yes! Posted up from Evesham, soon as I sent word you was expected home. He'd have been on the dock to greet you, only I explained you was wishful to travel incog. That's a good friend you have there, Lucas. True blue, and will never stain."

"I know it. I'm surprised, though, to find him in England. When last I heard, he was with the Army of Occupation."

"He bought out, three months ago. You know his brother Clement was killed? Got his head blown off at Genappes, poor lad, so Robert's the heir now. This autumn old Mr Clintwood took a congestion of the lungs. The doctors sent for Robert to come home. With the war ended, and nowt to do but mope around Headquarters, he decided to buy out."

During this exchange, the two men had remained standing by the window, but now Joshua took his nephew's arm and drew him to a chair. "Sit down, Luke. We mun talk, you and I. I know you won't take it amiss if I speak of what I know best—which is brass."

As the Earl seemed about to protest, Mr Turnbull held up a hand. "Nay, hear me out. I like things in the open. You know, when you was forced to quit England, I made you a member of this firm, same as my own boys. I've not regretted it. You've done sterling work for Turnbull & Sons, no error about that. We've been fair 'mazed at the cargoes you've secured for us. What I want to say is, we've kept close score, the boys and I, and your share of the takings is there, any time you want it."

"I'd as lief see it ploughed back into the firm," said Luke carelessly. "I'm not short of funds."

Joshua pulled a long mouth. "Don't speak too soon. That brother of yours nigh burst his britches, trying to bankrupt the estate."

"He didn't succeed. It seems I'm still offensively rich."

"You're sure of that?"

"Yes. Shedley sent me full reports to Boston, and Paris. There's ample shot in the family lockers."

"I'm reet glad of it. Still, lad, we mun face facts. You can't be buying and selling and jostling in the market place, now you're Earl of Rigg."

The Earl tilted his head. "I see what it is, Uncle. You're trying to give me the hint I'm not quite up to Turnbull standards."

The old man refused to be diverted. "I'm telling you plain,

Rowans and Turnbulls ain't birds of a feather, and a Cit you'll never be. A gentleman don't sully his paws wi' trade."

"Nor does he abandon the folk he holds dear, merely because his circumstances change. Reconcile yourself to having me about the place for the rest of my life."

"I'll do that. But it don't alter the fact you mun take your rightful place in the world." A sharp glance accompanied these words. "That is what you aim to do, eh, Luke?"

The Earl regarded him thoughtfully. "If I did," he said, "how would you rate my chance of success?"

Joshua shrugged. "Hard to tell. There's things in your favour."

"Such as?"

"The title. The money."

"In short, I may count on the support of toadeaters who love a lord, and cadgers with pockets to let!"

"Come, that's not all. You've some good friends."

"A short list, I fear. Well, so much for the pros. How about the cons?"

This time Mr Turnbull took longer to answer. At last he said quietly, "Reckon your brother's the greatest."

"Talbot? He's dead!"

"Aye, and you shot him."

"He didn't die of it! Tal drank himself into his grave!"

"I know that, lad, but there's folks will claim you were the death of him, none the less."

"Very well. Let us accept that society casts me in the rôle of fratricide. What else must I contend with?"

"Your cousin Jocelyn Clare does his best to blacken your name."

The Earl made an impatient movement. "Envy. He learned the vice of his father, and I can do nothing to cure him of it."

"Don't dismiss him too lightly, Lucas. Sithee, Clare's a man of consequence. Runs with the Carlton House set, belongs to all your smart clubs—and there's nowt he'd like better than to climb into your shoes and be Rigg of Rowanbeck."

"That I'm aware of. Is he there now?"

"No, in London, I think. I heard reports he lost five thousand at faro, last week. He's bought a house in Grafton Street that must have cost him a pretty penny." Joshua's scowl deepened. "While you were overseas, he made free of your property. Lived at Rowanbeck, visited Graydon, hunted from your place in Leicestershire."

"Did he, indeed?" Luke sat quiet for a moment, then said, "What puzzles me is how he contrived to worm his way into Tal's good books. In the past they were barely on speaking terms."

Joshua shrugged. "After you had to skip out, Talbot changed. Scared of his own shadow, seemly. It was on his sayso the Clares moved into Rowanbeck. Edward's a fixture there, now."

The Earl gave a sudden crack of laughter. "Edward too? Poor old Tal! He must have been at ames-ace to invite that dummy into his house. We used to call him The Effigy, at school."

"Edward may be thick gruel, but he's better than his brother. He did write your Aunt Charlotte a very proper letter, when Talbot died."

"I'm sure he did. He was always a very proper fellow."

"He's taken good care of Rowanbeck, that I'll say. Saved it from going to rack and ruin."

The Earl nodded almost absently. "What of Amabel?" he said abruptly. "Is she at Rowanbeck, too?"

"Where else would she be?"

"I thought perhaps she might have gone to live with her parents."

Mr Turnbull grunted and set down his empty glass. "Nay, she's there—and I'd like to know how you'll feel about meeting her. She's a beautiful woman, more beautiful by far than when she was a lass o' seventeen. It's in my mind how she used to wind you round her little finger."

Luke's face was expressionless. "She won't do so again."

Joshua looked unconvinced. "There's bound to be talk, you know. What will you do when th'old cats start sinking their claws in you?"

"You mean, will I be able to curb my notorious temper?"

"Aye, that's about it."

"I give you my word, I shan't put my neck at risk for Amabel, or any other woman."

"Or for your Cousin Jocelyn?"

As Luke remained silent, Joshua said urgently, "Don't try to level old scores, lad. No good ever came of it."

Luke got to his feet. "I'll see justice done, no more."

32

Joshua sighed. "That being so, reckon it might help if my agent Hawkins were to ask a few questions, like."

"Hawkins? Fellow with yellow eyes?" The Earl frowned. "I think not, uncle. Let's find the snake-hole, before we loose the mongoose."

Mr Turnbull did not press the point. "When do you go to Rowanbeck?" he said.

"In a day or so. There are people I should consult here—Shedley, for one."

"You'll not reach him this week. He's gone out of town. Won't be back till Thursday next, so old Rathbone told me."

"The business will keep." The Earl was eyeing his reflection in the glass above the fireplace. "Really, I shall have to buy a coat," he said. "I'm damned if I'll enter the bosom of my family dressed like a French dancing-master."

IV

AT THE TURNBULLS' new residence in Russell Square, an earnest discussion was taking place between Lady Charlotte Turnbull and Mr Robert Clintwood, a tall, ruddy-complexioned young man with the fine moustachios and ramrod bearing of an ex-captain of Hussars.

Lady Charlotte was a handsome woman in her late forties. Her carriage was graceful, and her style of dress quietly elegant. She had inherited the strong Rowan features, but there was a warmth in her regard, and a friendliness in her smile, that was not to be seen in the male members of her family. In youth she had shown signs of the rebellious nature that was the Rowan hallmark, but time had taught her to curb it, and her manner now was equable.

She sat on a straight-backed chair with a pile of household mending on the table at her side, but she was making no attempt to deal with this. Her hands were clasped in her lap, and her gaze fixed on Mr Clintwood, who was engaged in reading the letter she had just handed him. When he reached the end of the closely-written page, he folded it, and returned it with a shake of his head.

"Not very encouraging, I'm afraid."

"No," agreed Charlotte with a sigh, "and I'd reposed such hopes in Lady Bessborough. She herself has known the anguish of an ill-chosen love. I believed she must feel sympathy for Luke's situation. Indeed, I'm sure she does, but I must suppose she doesn't wish to fall out with the Devonshires. The present Duke always took Talbot's part in the quarrel, and it seems he won't relent. Mr Clintwood, if Devonshire House sets its face against Luke, who in society will dare befriend him? I live in dread of his being snubbed, or insulted. He has not the disposition to bear such treatment. He'll commit some new folly. That is why I prevailed on you to come here for this quiet chat. Be frank with me. How do you think Luke will fare in London?"

"Well, ma'am, you know you may rely on my family to do their possible for him . . . as will his own particular friends. I've spoken to Wisbech, the Lumleys, the Skevingtons. They're with him to a man, but they constitute the younger set. I can't vouch for the older folk. It's the high sticklers he'll have to get round —the club martinets, and the ladies with daughters to marry off."

"And the Clare coterie. I wish I could think of some way to deal with them. They've done all they can to poison public opinion against Luke. I happened to meet with Sally Jersey, a week or so ago. You know how she lets her tongue run on, and she's forever rehearsing *on-dits* fed to her by Jocelyn Clare. She revived all the old scandal about Luke, until I was hard put to it to be civil to her!"

Mr Clintwood did not at once reply. He'd heard the rumours that were going about, but they were the least of his worries. What concerned him was how his friend would stand in the eyes of the law. Could Luke be charged with some crime? Brought to trial, sentenced to prison, or worse?

He didn't know the answer, and he certainly did not intend to convey his fears to his hostess, so he merely said, in a rallying tone:

"I think, ma'am, you must not underrate your own influence. I'm persuaded you have many friends who will support your cause."

"Friends like Lady Bessborough?" said Charlotte drily.

Mr Clintwood shifted uncomfortably. "It may be the poor creature can't absorb any more public opprobrium," he said. "They say her daughter Caroline Lamb is mad as a March hare now, and William Lamb suing for a formal separation. That will have put Devonshire and Melbourne House at sixes and sevens. But they're not the be-all and end-all of society. There must be others to whom you can appeal?"

"You mistake the position," said Charlotte quietly. "I'm not at all the thing, you know. My marriage was at one time named the *mésalliance* of the century."

"You still have the entrée, everywhere."

"Yes, but my husband does not."

"Times are changing," said Clintwood. "Why, many of our City families are now held in considerable esteem."

Charlotte gave him a direct look. "Joshua is not of such a family, sir. He's the tenth child of a Leeds schoolmaster. At the age of eleven, he was orphaned and thrown on the parish. He ran away to London and found work in Billingsgate fish-market. He told me once that even on the coldest winter nights, he and the other children had to lug the baskets from the gutting-tables, and clear away the slime from round the gutters' feet. Only one thing saved him from a life of misery, and that was that he could read and write. Because of that, he was able to find employment as clerk to a ships' chandler, and later, to travel to India as a writer for the East India Company. He rose to become a Factor, then a Junior Merchant, and at last the man people call Josh Nabob—with wealth, fine houses, carriages, power and influence.

"Nowadays you may hear him called a patron of the arts, a philanthropist, a patriot. One title only is withheld—that of gentleman.

"I will not beg favours from people who hold up their noses when Joshua enters a room, as if he still smelled of the fish-shop. Do I make myself plain, sir?"

"You do." Mr Clintwood regarded his hostess steadily. "You've been open with me. May I be so, with you?"

"Of course."

"When you found your husband was not accepted by the ton, you learned to live without 'em. Cannot Luke do the same? He'll have Rowanbeck, and good friends to bear him company. In the course of time one may hope that. . . ."

"No!" Charlotte interrupted with some vehemence. "Luke's too impatient, too arrogant. Can you see him creeping about town like a leper? The first time some counter-jumper thinks to insult him, Luke will lay him flat in the dust. We shall be lucky to avoid pistols at dawn!" She encountered a frowning glance from Mr Clintwood, and said quickly, "I'm sorry. I ask too much of you. You've your own career to think of. Pray forget what I've said."

"No such thing," said Clintwood with a smile. "It's come to me, there's more ways of capturing the castle than by direct assault. What we need, ma'am, is a friend within the walls, and the name's to hand. Holland. I make no doubt you're acquainted with Lord and Lady Holland?"

"I knew Lord Holland, years ago. I'm not on close terms with his wife."

"No matter," said Clintwood cheerfully. "My mama and Lady H. are bosom bows. What's more, Lady Holland's a divorced woman. Eloped from her first, with Lord Holland. Knows what it is to face public censure. Bound to feel kindly towards Luke, on that score."

"By the same token, as a divorced woman she's not received by the high sticklers."

"They're vastly in the minority, I assure you. No one can deny she's a famous hostess. Drawing-rooms crowded to the roof, any night of the week, and every guest a flower of the modality! As for Lord Holland, he's a prime gun, liked by all, the doyen of Whiggery, besides."

"That's true," agreed Charlotte, brightening. "I recall I met Charles Fox at Holland House—and Sidney Smith—and Mr Sheridan. Yes, if his lordship gives us the nod, then we're halfway home. But Lady Holland. I've heard her described as something of a quiz."

"Oh, she has her eccentric quirks, but she's sharp as a needle, and can talk the hind leg off a donkey. What's more, she backs her fancies. If she takes a liking to Luke, she'll sponsor him to Hades and back."

Mr Clintwood's enthusiasm was infectious, and Charlotte found herself smiling.

"Dear friend," she said, "will you write to your kind parents, and ask their help?"

"This very day." Mr Clintwood rose, and Charlotte with him, but at the door she laid a hand on his sleeve.

"There is one more thing I must say." She seemed to search for words, and at last said simply. "It's Amabel. Luke has never once referred to her in his letters. So far as I know, he's not sent her a single line in two years. Dare one hope he's put her out of his mind?"

"No," said Mr Clintwood flatly, and Charlotte sighed.

"I agree, it's too much to expect. Then, what are we to do?"

"In that regard, nothing. I shan't even mention her name, unless Luke does so first. If he thinks we're on that tack, he'll cut line and run."

She nodded. "You're right, I'm sure. Will you dine with us tonight? The family will all be here. We'll look for you at six, that will give you time to talk to Luke before dinner."

He thanked her, and hurried away. Charlotte stood for some minutes, thinking over what had been said, then went to see that the house stood ready to receive an invasion of Turnbulls.

Russell Square, where Mr Turnbull's new mansion stood, had been laid out in 1801, and was the largest square in London, with the exception of Lincoln's Inn Fields.

A great many lawyers and well-to-do merchants had made their homes there, and Mr Turnbull informed the Earl of Rigg, as they travelled northward, that his nearest neighbour was Sir Thomas Lawrence, at No. 65.

"Nice place he has, too," conceded Joshua, "as you'd expect of an artist that's made his name. Still, it's nothing to mine. I told my architect at the start, 'I want summat bang up to t'minute, none o' your old-style notions'. So we've got piped water to proper bathrooms, and indoor water-closets, and I mean to install gas-lighting, just so soon as I can persuade your Aunt Charlotte it won't blow us all to smithereens. Yes, I flatter meself I've built a house where a man may be comfortable. You'll see for yourself, soon enough."

Soon after two o'clock, they reached their destination. The wintry sun shone upon a massive facade of lemon-yellow brick, on a white marble portico soaring two storeys high, and above that, crowning the roof, a marble balustrade. The effect was of an immense Christmas cake trimmed with marchpane and heavily iced.

As the carriage turned into the short curve of drive, a sudden commotion broke out. A large woolly mastiff bounded from the back yard, barking vociferously. Windows were flung up at every level, heads poked out, kerchiefs fluttered, voices shouted. The front door burst open, and out rushed two small boys in nankeen trousers, frilled shirts, and blue jackets. They were followed by a butler, two footmen, three spaniels, and finally by Lady Charlotte herself.

The carriage halted. A groom ran to let down the steps. The boys raised a lusty huzza.

"Home," said Mr Turnbull with the utmost satisfaction. "Out you get lad. I don't know how it may be with you, but for my part, I'm fair famished!"

*

The next few hours passed in cheerful confusion, as more and more members of the Turnbull clan arrived to greet Luke. By three o'clock the reception rooms were crowded, the press being aggravated by the number of servants who found it necessary to pass among the guests with trays of refreshments, stoke the fires, remove the used dishes, and linger long enough to catch a glimpse of the new Earl.

Henry, Mr Turnbull's heir and already counted a coming man in the City, brought his wife and four children from Highgate. James, the next brother, had travelled posthaste from Bristol, with his brood. The two young men cornered Luke and peppered him with questions about trade in the West Indies; the extent of development of New York and other American ports; and the likelihood of there being renewed hostilities over the Right of Search on the High Seas. Luke answered as best he could, promising more intensive talks in a day or so.

Next to arrive was Joshua's elder daughter, Amelia Hedley, with her country-parson husband and their three-week-old son. The hopeful infant having been displayed and generally admired, he was handed to the care of his nurse, while his mama plumped down on the sofa next to the Earl, and demanded an instant account of his travels over the past three years. Mrs Turnbull's warnings that a nursing mother should rest after a long journey were dismissed out of hand.

"Lord, Mama," cried Amelia, "you know I'm as strong as a brood-mare, and take it all in my stride!" She turned with a wink to Lucas. "I can tell you, the day Simeon was born, his papa was in far worse case than I! Such suffering you never saw! But with prayer, and fasting, and a dose or two of laudanum, he pulled through, and was fit to preach a rousing sermon the very next day—on the joys and duties of fatherhood!"

The Reverend Ralph Hedley took this banter in good part, merely saying that he and his wife would esteem it an honour if his lordship would consent to stand godfather to their boy.

Charles Turnbull now approached to shake Luke's hand. Aged twenty-two, he lacked the boisterous spirits of his siblings, resembling his mother both in his dark good looks, and his serious, intense manner. He confided to Luke that he had decided against joining Turnbull & Sons. "I've no flair for commerce," he said. "Pa knows it. That's why he agreed to let me go to Cambridge."

"And now you're down, what will you do?"

"Try my hand at politics. Do you know, there are towns in the north, like Manchester, that don't return a member to Parliament?"

"And villages in the south that return two." Luke regarded the younger man with some amusement. "Tell me, Charles, do you mean to be rid of me and my kind?"

"Not at all. I shall need your help. Money's no problem, and a candidate needn't be gentry, nowadays, but I must be sponsored by a man of rank and standing."

"I fear my sponsorship would sink you without trace. However, should I come about, be sure I'll back you."

"Thank you," said Charles tranquilly. "I'll hold you to it."

Miss Emily Turnbull, who had recently become engaged, begged leave to present her fiancé, a jovial youth whose father was a City goldsmith; Miss Amanda, not yet released from the school-room, came forward to make her curtsey; and it was not to be expected that her younger brothers, Herbert and Frederic, would allow themselves to be excluded from the general excitement. They dogged the Earl's footsteps, rushed to perform his lightest request, snubbed the pretensions of their country cousins, explained the principle of the pneumatic hoist that their papa had installed between the first and second floors, and could only be dislodged when their mama announced that it was long past five o'clock, and time everyone dressed for dinner.

Mr Turnbull's cook was accustomed to catering for guilds, corporations, and worshipful companies. Warned to concoct "a neat little dinner for twenty or so," he produced a banquet that included: Rich turtle soup, removed with fillets of turbot and followed by ducks served in a sauce of tarragon and sweet basil; a sirloin of beef with artichokes; roasted swan; three home-cured hams; a dish of veal cooked with mushrooms and salsify; a couple of raised mutton pies; and numerous vegetables, dressed and plain. The second course presented such an array of creams and pastries, jellies, cakes and candies as must daunt the keenest appetite; and as the wines had been selected by Mr Turnbull to match the occasion, the conversation around the table was soon very lively.

Mr Clintwood had joined the company at six, and was placed at Lady Charlotte's left hand during the meal, facing the Earl, who was on her right. The two gentlemen quickly fell to exchanging tales of their travels, adding such wild embellishments that their audience vowed there was no knowing which was the greater romancer.

After dinner, the company repaired to the sitting-room at the back of the house. Two tea-chests, which had been brought by dray from the docks, stood open in the centre of the floor, and from these Luke produced gifts for every member of the party.

For Mr Turnbull there was a pottery horse of the Yung Chen period, and for the other gentlemen chessmen carved from jade or ivory, ancient maps, and buttons of filigree silver. The ladies received bolts of embroidered silk and muslin, and jade or coral trinkets. Charles by his own choice was awarded an Indian flute from which he managed to coax a warbling sort of tune. Herbert, who had lived in hopes of a shrunken Borneo head, was compelled to make do with the head-dress of a Mohawk chieftain, while Frederic expressed himself satisfied with a walrus tooth, marvellously engraved with mystic symbols by the Esquimaux of Hudson Bay.

While these treasures were being compared and admired, Luke strolled over to Lady Charlotte, and dropped a silk purse in her lap. Opening it, she discovered a magnificent string of pearls of even colour and size. She stared at it in dismay.

"My dear Lucas, you can't give me such a costly gift! Why, these must be worth a king's ransom!"

"A maharani's," he said.

"How did you come by them?"

He gave her a glinting smile. "I won them for services rendered. Don't put me to the blush by further questions, I beg."

"You're incorrigible." Charlotte slipped the necklace back into the bag, and held it out to him. "You must keep them."

"Why? I shan't wear 'em!"

"Your wife will be glad to, some day."

At once, his smile faded. He said stiffly, "I've no plans to marry, yet. When I do, it will be for the succession. I'll find some female with a virtuous nature and a flat chest, and the Rowan parure will do very well for her. These are for you. I wish you will accept them."

Charlotte knew it was no use to argue. The pearls were a token of the gratitude and affection he felt for her. It would be churlish to refuse them.

She had seen little of her nephews during their early childhood. After her runaway marriage, her brother George forbade her to visit Rowanbeck. His poor timid Chloë never dared to challenge this ukase, but wrote often to Charlotte, giving news of her sons, and bewailing the ramshackle way they were being raised.

Talbot was twelve and Lucas ten when their mother died of a putrid infection of the throat. Their papa, far from mourning her death, lost no time in filling his house with hunting and drinking companions, and fly-by-night women from London. Unpleasant stories of debauchery reached Charlotte, and when she heard that the boys were allowed to share in the drinking and gaming, she drove down to Rigborough, and offered to take them both home with her for the Christmas holidays.

George, who found children a dead bore, replied that the boys could suit themselves. Talbot opted to stay at Rowanbeck, but Luke made the journey to the house in Cheapside, and from that time on, looked on it as his second home.

Without doubt he had learned much from the Turnbull family, their commonsense views, their loyalty, their dislike of ceremony. But nothing would ever undo the damage done to his character during his early years. A child born into the nobility, and surrounded from birth by people anxious to flatter and indulge him, required firm handling. The Rowan boys had had no such discipline, but had been treated to alternate bouts of spoiling and neglect, which had made Talbot weak and wayward, and bred in Luke a cynicism, and an arrogance, one could not approve.

On the other hand, Charlotte knew that Luke's few close friends loved and trusted him. He was capable of deep and lasting affection. His despair at losing Amabel had been dreadful to watch. Though he had never once spoken about his quarrel with his brother, nor its violent, terrible climax, Charlotte guessed his silence covered a sense of bitter betrayal.

In those days, with every man's hand against him, he had

turned to her and to Joshua for support, and found them ready. The pearls were his way of expressing his thanks.

She took the necklace from its wrapping, and fastened it carefully about her neck.

Later that night, as she and Joshua were making ready for bed, she told him of her anxiety about Luke.

"I wish with all my heart," she said, "he'd given me a few loving words, or a warm hug, as any of our children would have done. It's our cursed Rowan pride in him. He can't reach out, and he won't allow others to reach him."

"Eh, give him time, love. He's been home nobbut a few hours! And think on't, he's three years older than when last we met, and he's seen a plaguey lot o' the world meantime. You heard him talk tonight, the close shaves he's had wi' bandits, and Frenchies, and those red pagans in Canada. I reckon it must blunt a man's sense o' fun, to know someone is after his scalp!"

"Danger has nothing to do with reticence," said Charlotte. "I daresay Mr Clintwood has run into just as much peril, but he's as merry as a grig, and finds no difficulty in saying just what he feels." Charlotte extinguished the candles and climbed into the four-poster. From the dark, she said, "It's Amabel that's the root of the problem. Luke still adores her. I know it in my bones."

Mr Turnbull was aware that sweet reason was no match for his wife's bones. He took refuge in counterfeit snores, which soon became genuine.

It would have cheered Charlotte greatly to know that her nephew and Mr Clintwood were at that moment engaged in frank and easy discussion of the future. They were in the library, where a good fire burned. The Earl leaned comfortably against the chimney-piece, nursing a glass of cognac. His friend lounged in a wing-chair, puffing on an evil black cigarillo, a vice he'd acquired in his Peninsular days.

"The first thing we must do, Lucas," he said, "is buy you a new coat. We'll visit Weston tomorrow."

"No, we won't. I don't want it going the round that I'm back in town—at least, not till I'm ready."

"No one would recognise you, dressed like that. Take you for a bum bailiff, most likely."

"In your company, it's very probable." The Earl bent to toss a couple of logs onto the fire. "I thought we might ask Weston to call at your house in Clarges Street."

"That's a good notion. I shall say it's my father wants to place an order. He knows the old man is frail, and can't go about much. The mountain shall come to Mohamet."

"I'll need carriages. A curricle, a travelling chaise, perhaps a high-perch phaeton. And tits to pull 'em all."

"Venner's your man for coachwork. Excellent craftsman, and he's close as an oyster, too, won't blab. As to horseflesh, my advice is, do nothing till you know what's in the stables at Rowanbeck. I'll say this for Talbot, drunk or sober he was the best judge of a prad in the shires. I'm sure you'll find his carriage cattle are just what you'll like. Don't know about hunters, though. He couldn't hunt at all the last two years. You may have to stock up a bit, there. In the meantime, I've a nice six-year-old that's up to your weight. Sweet goer and a kind eye. You're welcome to use him till you're suited."

They continued to discuss what was necessary to set up Luke's wardrobe. Mr Clintwood ran through the catalogue. Coats and weskits for morning, afternoon and evening wear; knitted breeches for town, and buckskins for the country; at least three caped overcoats; shirts, boots, hats and gloves, and those accessories such as snuffboxes, walking-sticks, fobs and cravats that distinguished the top sawyer from the mere counter-coxcomb.

The Earl acquiesced meekly on all points save one. He refused absolutely to purchase satin knee-breeches.

"Have to!" insisted Clintwood. "Still *de rigueur* in some circles. Grant you, only the old fogeys like 'em, but what if you should receive a card for Almack's my dear chap? Couldn't show up in pantaloons. Not at all the thing."

"Nothing will induce me to visit Almack's. I've vivid memories of the place. Insipid girls with tigrish mamas, and nothing to drink but warm lemonade. What's more, you know as well as I do that not one of the patronesses will dream of allowing me across the sacred threshold. An adulterer and home-breaker may be forgiven, but to shoot one's brother is to go too far."

"Doing it too brown, Luke! The fact is, people have had time enough to learn the truth about Talbot. Not to put too fine a point on it, he was a welsher."

The Earl's eyes narrowed. "Gammon. I never knew Tal to renege on a debt."

"He did so, after you left. Used to invite men down to Rowanbeck to play cards. Lost a fortune, but didn't always pay. In the end, no one cared to accept his chits or his invitations. Only reason he wasn't called to account was that everyone knew he was a sick man."

"Tell me, who were his companions, of late?"

Mr Clintwood looked embarrassed. "Oh, there was Franchot . . . Cleveden . . . that fribble Whitstaple, who always got in deeper than he should."

"What you're saying is that Tal took up with Jocelyn Clare's set."

"That's about it. All much older than Tal, and looking for lambs to fleece. You know, Luke, you should keep an eye on that cousin of yours. He's not above dealing you an underhand trick, if he sees the chance."

"He's already done so." The Earl returned to the fireside. "The night I left Rowanbeck with Amabel, I wrote Tal a letter. I told him I was taking Amabel north to her parents, until he was well enough to discuss the future. I left the letter on the table beside his bed. He never received it. What he did receive was the tip to the road we'd taken. He was hot on our heels, all the way north. He'd have come up with us sooner, save for the state of the roads. It was a very wet winter, if you remember."

"You think someone stole the letter?"

"It's possible. The Clares were staying in the house at the time."

"But . . . why would they raise the hunt?"

"Simple. Tal and I might easily have killed each other. In fact, it was pure good fortune we did not."

Clintwood shook his head, appalled. "My dear fellow, there must be some other explanation."

"That is what I mean to discover."

"You won't do anything foolhardy?"

"I won't shoot anyone, if I can help it."

"When do they expect you at Rowanbeck?"

"I wrote to Amabel from Paris, saying I'd be in England

shortly. I gave no date for my homecoming. Clint, what precisely were the circumstances of my brother's death?"

Mr Clintwood moved uneasily in his chair. "An apoplexy, I believe, brought on by the news that Boney was back on French soil. The first reports caused a furore, as you may imagine, and the stocks on 'Change came tumbling down. Talbot had money in the funds, and thought himself ruined. Fell down as if pole-axed. Couldn't move, or speak. Of course, three months later we had the Frenchies rolled up, and the stocks went up again, but by that time Tal was dead. Thing is, Luke, if that shock hadn't killed him, it would have been another. His health was all to pieces. He'd lived too hard, for too long."

"Was Amabel with him when he died?"

"So I'm told." Mr Clintwood frowned. "It was the wonder of us all she stuck with him so long. Her mama told mine in confidence that the Sears begged her to leave him. Feared he might do her some injury, in one of his drunken fits; but she stayed to the end. Strange creatures, women."

"There's a good deal I find strange," murmured the Earl. "A good deal I shall want explained."

Clintwood tossed the stub of his cigarillo into the fire. "It's late. I'm for home and bed. Tomorrow I'll arrange for Weston to meet with you at Clarges Street."

As Mr Clintwood had foreseen, London's tailors, hatters, haberdashers and boot-makers lost no time in beating a path to his house in Clarges Street, once they understood that his mysterious visitor was the Earl of Rigg.

After all, what more could a purveyor of fashion ask than a client who was rich, titled, possessed of a physique that must display their wares to best advantage, and whose recent involvement in a notorious scandal was bound to make him the cynosure of every eye?

It may be supposed that tradesmen familiar with the pecuniary frailties of the late Talbot Rowan made discreet enquiries about how the new Earl stood with the world; but on its being learned that his lordship's credit with the bank was excellent, and that he was moreover Josh Nabob's favourite nephew, all doubts were stilled, and his custom was eagerly invited.

As to his lordship's oft-expressed desire for privacy, not a man but promised to honour it, and not a man but hastened to pass the word that Rigg of Rowanbeck was in London.

Mr Clintwood, coming to dine at the Turnbull home some five nights after Luke's return, complained bitterly of this situation.

"The clubs are buzzing with your name," he said. "I daren't set foot in Brooks's, or White's, for fear of being quizzed by some rattle. Skevington tells me he's being hounded in the streets by people wanting to know if the rumours are true. Wisbech says the same."

The Earl gave a soulful sigh. "Human frailty, Clint! It's the melancholy truth that the surest way to attract vulgar attention, is to travel incognito."

"I believe that's been your intention all along," said Mr Clintwood crossly, but the Earl's only answer was a smile.

He himself spent most of his time within doors at Russell Square, but he did venture out on two occasions.

On the first, he drove in a closed carriage to the Magistrates' Court in Bow Street, where he remained for two hours in private conversation with the Chief Magistrate, Sir Nathanial Conant.

That same afternoon, Mr Samuel Hibberd, butler at Rowan House in Berkeley Square, was roused from a comfortable postprandial snooze by an out-of-breath footman, who announced that a bang-up rig, druv by a cove wiv military whiskers, had that very moment stopped at the front door, and set down none other than Lord Rigg hisself, lookin' as fine as fivepence in a greatcoat wiv sixteen capes to it.

When Hibberd replied that this was impossible, his lordship being still in Paris, the footman informed him rudely that that was all gammon; that he, Croker, could reckernise the Rowan fizz anywheres; and that Hibberd had best stir his stumps, for it wouldn't please his nibs to be kep' standin' on his own doorstep in a nasty east wind.

Hibberd contrived to open the front door at the third peal of the bell, and thereafter endured one of the unhappiest hours of his life.

Lord Rigg, after the most perfunctory of greetings, desired to be conducted over the house. The tour was swift, but thorough. His lordship missed nothing. He drew Hibberd's attention to sins of omission and commission; sent for the inventories of china and glass and studied them with a cold eye; enquired the whereabouts of pictures that were missing from the walls; and when Hibberd tried to gloss over the glaring gaps in the racks of the wine-cellars, treated him to a look of quelling contempt.

The outcome was inevitable. Hibberd received a month's pay and his notice.

Lord Rigg then repaired to the drawing-room, summoned Mrs Dubbleday the housekeeper, and told her that Hibberd was dismissed.

"I've appointed my cousin, Mr Charles Turnbull, as my secretary," he said. "He will arrive here tomorrow, and help you to engage new staff. I want the place set to rights. The guest rooms are to be refurbished. Provisions, coal, and so forth must be laid in. Discuss your requirements with Mr Turnbull."

Mrs Dubbleday, a servant of long standing, who detested Hibberd, ventured to speak her mind.

"You'd best be warned, my lord," she said, "Hibberd will carry tales. I'll be surprised if he don't run straight to Sir Jocelyn. They're thick as thieves, and held some parties in this house that fair made my hair stand on end."

"You may leave me to worry about that," said the Earl repressively, and she bobbed a curtsey, and withdrew.

Lord Rigg gazed about him. The drawing-room was on the first floor of the house, and overlooked Berkeley Square. Recent redecoration had not changed it much. It was as he had always known it, dove-grey brocade on the walls, delicate white woodwork picked out in gold, the ceilings and doorways embellished with pastoral medallions by Angelica Kauffmann.

Over the tall Adam fireplace hung the portrait Thomas Lawrence had made of Amabel, shortly before her marriage. She was depicted as Spring, standing on a gentle hillside against a lightening sky. A posy of wild flowers lay in the grass at her feet. Her head was turned a little from the viewer, as if she were about to hurry away down the slope to the valley below.

The Earl stood for a long time studying the picture, and the expression in his eyes was anything but cold.

Mr Clintwood arrived to collect Lord Rigg soon after four o'clock. He was in a mellow mood, having passed a pleasurable hour or so with old cronies at the Horse Guards, refighting the Spanish campaigns.

He was about to recount an excellent joke he had heard during this visit, when a glance at Luke's face made him change his mind.

"Blue-devilled, old fellow?" he said. "What's wrong! Things go badly at Bow Street this morning?"

"No, on the contrary, Sir Nathanial assures me there's no charge standing against me. The case is closed."

"That's capital news."

"Rowan House has been plundered," continued Luke. "I've had to dismiss Hibberd, the butler."

"Pig-faced fellow, with mean eyes? I never cared for him."

"No more did I, and he's been thieving for years, but it's never pleasant to turn a man off without a reference."

"His sort always survives, don't worry."

"Mrs Dubbleday says he'll hotfoot it to Jocelyn Clare."

Mr Clintwood looked perturbed. "And Jocelyn will bleat to your family. You should forestall him there."

"I wrote to Amabel yesterday, saying I shall travel to Rigborough on Friday. Do you care to come with me? It will be very dull, I'm afraid, but I'd be glad of your company."

"Count me in," said Mr Clintwood.

V

On the Wednesday following that on which Mr Shedley had visited Wakeford Hall, Miss Wakeford received a note from the Countess of Rigg. Amabel's writing, always deplorable, was more illegible than usual, but her message was clear. Would her dear, dearest Davina please come at once, as disaster was about to strike?

Davina, who knew Amabel of old, raised no alarm, but told Hoby that she would be out for an hour or so, and strolled over to Rowanbeck.

She did not take the road down the hill and through the village, but chose instead the path that led along the top of Hagg Ridge. This commanded the whole of the Rigg valley, with its fields and scattered farmsteads, as well as Rigborough itself. The hamlet was an island, being embraced on three sides by a wide bend of the river, and on the fourth by an old canal-cut, no longer in use but still full of water.

Miss Wakeford walked briskly, for the air was frosty. She crossed the stile that divided Wakeford from Rowan land, and made her way down through a belt of the woods. A stream traversed this, to feed the river, and she forded it on the stepping-stones that were said to have been placed there in Saxon times. From the stream it was an easy walk up the far slope of the valley, to Rowanbeck's kitchen garden.

The sun was westering, and she stood at the gate for a moment to admire the burnish it put on the house. The ancient brickwork glowed dark red, the fountain in the central court spurted living flame, and rose-coloured doves circled down to the dovecot under the roof.

Rowanbeck had none of the grandeur of Wakeford Hall. Generations of Rowans had added a wing here, a courtyard there, with no thought for the overall design. Yet somehow the whole was harmonious, and surprisingly comfortable. The chimneys never smoked, the windows trapped all the available sunlight, and the hill behind provided shelter from the cold north winds.

Miss Wakeford entered the house by a side door, hoping to find Amabel without troubling any of the servants; but as she walked through the Great Hall that formed the core of the building, she heard her name called, and turned to see Miss Cornelia Finch hurrying towards her.

Miss Finch was a distant relation of the Rowans, and had come to Rowanbeck after Talbot's death, Amabel's own mama having ruled it improper for her daughter to remain in the house without female companionship.

Whether Miss Finch was companionable was a moot point. She was a nervous woman, one of those spinsters who, finding themselves in straitened circumstances, must earn their bread as governess or duenna. A townswoman, she had never become used to country life, where every hedge seemed to shelter things damp, dangerous, or unfit for maiden eyes.

Now she advanced on Davina with her mittened hands raised, looking for all the world like a panic-stricken hare.

"My dear Miss Wakeford!" she cried. "I am so glad you are here! I have been wondering all afternoon whether I dare send word to you! I would have done, had I not feared to exacerbate the problem."

"What problem?" asked Davina, pulling off her gloves and bonnet.

"Alas, I don't precisely know." Miss Finch shook her tight grey ringlets, "But it must be something dreadful to cast poor Lady Rigg into such despair. Ever since Sir Jocelyn returned from London . . . he travelled all through the night, you know . . . the poor child has been as a doe wounded unto death! Not a morsel of food has passed her lips all day! I have taken her the hartshorn, and bathed her temples with lavender-water, but it is truly shocking to see how pale and distraught she looks!"

"Where is she now?"

"In the library. She and Mr Clare have been closeted with Sir Jocelyn for above three hours. Dear Miss Wakeford, I entreat you not to leave without speaking to her. You are so commonsensical, so steady of mind, perhaps you may be able to prevent her falling into one of her feverish starts."

"I'll do my best," said Davina cheerfully, handing Miss Finch her bonnet and gloves. "No need to announce me, I'm here at Amabel's invitation."

She crossed the Hall to the library. This was large, with a high ceiling picked out in Tudor red, blue and gold. Two roaring fires, one at each end of the room, made the air pleasantly warm. The long crimson curtains had been drawn against the gathering dusk, and numerous branches of candles cast a comfortable light.

Sir Jocelyn Clare and his brother Edward had moved to the farthest window embrasure, and were so deep in conversation that they did not notice Miss Wakeford's entry. She advanced quietly to the figure seated on a sofa to her right.

She could not help reflecting that for a wounded doe, Amabel Lady Rigg looked to be in excellent trim. Indeed, she seldom looked otherwise. Nothing ever seemed to dim Amabel's incredible beauty. Pallor only accentuated the symmetry of her delicate features. Tears deepened her eyes to amethyst, without in the least reddening their lids.

She was dressed this evening in a plain round gown of blue crape, for she had given up wearing mourning. Her hair, the pale silky gold of a willow-catkin, was arranged in curls at the back of her head, with a single tendril falling on each side of her face.

She sprang from her place as Miss Wakeford approached, and ran to embrace her. "Oh, Davina, how good it is to see you! Do say you'll stay, and raise our spirits a trifle."

"Are they so low? Is it bad news?"

"The worst!" Amabel clasped her hands together in an attitude of despair. "It is what I've been dreading, ever since Talbot died. Lucas is in London!"

Miss Wakeford blinked. "But my dear, that's hardly unexpected. I recall you told me, as long ago as October, that he'd been traced to New York."

"Yes, but then he took ship for Genoa, and we heard nothing. My hopes were quite raised that he had changed his mind, or even been lost at sea! Then last week I received a letter from Paris, and today one from London. Davina, he may arrive here at any moment!"

Davina was puzzled. She knew how Amabel loved to enact a Cheltenham tragedy, but she sensed that this time the panic was real. Taking her friend's hand, she said soothingly:

"Come, how can you fear to meet Lord Rigg? What harm can he possibly bring you?"

"All the harm in the world. Oh, it's all very well for you to smile, but you don't understand. Luke is . . . a spectre from the past. His return will revive all the old unpleasantness, all the wicked gossip, that is so repugnant to me. I shall be miserable beyond description."

"I suppose there'll be some talk," Davina agreed, "but I dare say it won't be directed at you. Lucas Rowan is the villain of the piece, and you the innocent victim. You have everyone's sympathy."

"What good is sympathy, may I ask?" Amabel sank down into a chair, and tears welled in her eyes. "What's to become of me? Where will I find a place to lay my head? He'll cast me out, I know it. He'll cast us all out."

"I expect he may offer you the Dower House. It's the obvious solution."

This remark was unfortunate. Amabel's tears flowed still faster, and she said in a choking voice, "I do not wish to be a D-Dowager! It is so elderly! And I don't wish to live in a horrid, cramped little house like a p-poor relation!"

"The Dower House isn't horrid. It's delightful. A fine garden, orchards, an orangery, besides being convenient to the church and the village. I only wish I might occupy something as comfortable."

"Rigg will never let me have it," said Amabel unreasonably. "You'll see, Davina. I'll be anathema to him!"

"I'm sure you couldn't be anathema to anyone."

"Yes, I could. Luke will take revenge on me for all he's been made to suffer."

"Oh . . . fustian!" Davina turned to the two gentlemen, who now came up to greet her, Sir Jocelyn giving her a formal bow, Edward a beaming smile and warm clasp of the hand.

"Sir Jocelyn," she said, "surely you don't credit that your cousin will sink to such melodrama? The Vengeance of the Wicked Earl?"

He gazed at her sombrely. He was a tall man, aged about five and thirty, with narrow shoulders and long, slender hands. His features were handsome, very much in the Rowan mould. He put Davina in mind of a portrait of his grandfather, dressed in satins, powder and patch, that graced the long gallery of Rowanbeck. There was the same air of languid elegance, the same withdrawn, watchful expression in the deepset eyes. It was impossible to feel quite easy in Sir Jocelyn's company. He never appeared to lose his temper, or break into spontaneous laughter. He missed nothing, and gave nothing away.

"I cannot discount Amabel's fears," he said now. "Lucas feels no kindness for any member of his family. He has never written to us about Talbot's death. He has given no hint when we might expect to see him here. Apparently he has been in London for some days, staying with the Turnbulls, but I only learned of it by chance . . . from a servant Rigg dismissed, who turned to me for help."

"Yes, that is all very bad, very unfeeling, but even so, I can see no reason to fear him."

"One hopes you may be right, but one is not over-sanguine. Rigg's nature is violent and vindictive. He has never shown the smallest regard for the rules of ordinary mortals."

Davina turned to Edward. "Mr Clare, what is your opinion?"

"I think," he said gravely, "that we must be on our guard."

"Against what? What can Rigg do? Surely he won't try violence? Having had one brush with the law, he'll never risk another!"

"Oh, I agree with you there."

Davina went over to take Amabel's hand. "I'm sure you're fretting about nothing," she said, "but you know if you're unhappy here, there's room and to spare at Wakeford. Come to us whenever you wish, only do, I beg, bring your warmest clothes with you."

Amabel only shook her head mournfully. Nothing could be said to comfort her, and at last Davina conducted her upstairs, and with Miss Finch's help, put her to bed, with a hot brick at her feet, and a cloth soaked in vinegar on her forehead.

Returning to the Great Hall, Davina found Edward Clare waiting for her.

"I've taken the liberty of ordering the carriage brought round," he said. "With your permission, ma'am, I'll drive to Wakeford with you."

"You're very kind."

He smiled at her gravely. "No. There is something I particularly wish to discuss with you."

He handed her into the carriage, took his place beside her, and signalled the coachman to drive on. Davina, leaning back on the cushions, thought how reliable Mr Clare was, and how considerate of her comfort.

He did not speak until they were past the gates at the foot of the park, and then said abruptly: "I'd no wish to alarm Amabel, back there. When I said Rigg won't try violence, I meant he will have no need to. He can find better ways of evening the score. He'll have us out of Rowanbeck in a trice, for a start."

"Would you wish to stay?" asked Davina, diffidently. "If it's true that Lord Rigg dislikes you, would it not be a very awkward thing to remain in the same house with him?"

Edward answered at a tangent. "We've known all along the present state of affairs couldn't last. Perhaps we shouldn't have come to Rigborough, but Talbot was in such bad case. Amabel had to put up with abuse, and worse, from him. She begged us to stay."

"I know she did—and that you've worked miracles with Rowanbeck. Everyone says so."

"The devil of it is, Miss Wakeford, that in setting Rowanbeck to rights, I've become far too attached to the place. I've come to think of it as my home, which I've no right to do."

The carriage slowed to negotiate the humpback bridge over the stream, and the sharp bend beyond. Now they could see the village about half a mile ahead, its church spire black against frosty stars.

"One thing is certain," said Edward, "I shan't run out before Rigg arrives. I mean to hand things over to him and none other, and all in apple-pie order. If the man has a shred of proper feeling for his land, he'll want an account of what I've done, and what's still to do. When I've said my say, I'll quit. Not before."

"Where will you go, Mr Clare?"

"Perhaps to my mother. She resides with my grandfather, near Bath. He has sizeable estates there."

"We'll miss you."

He turned his head to smile at her. "I hope so, indeed. Miss Wakeford, you must know by now how warm a regard I cherish for you. If I have not declared myself formally, it is because my situation has been . . . unsettled. However, I am not without prospects. My grandfather is old and infirm, and he has been good enough to make me his heir. When he goes, I shall inherit a respectable acreage. The house is nothing as splendid as your own Wakeford, of course, but it's a pleasant building with a pretty outlook across the Avon, and we have both arable land, and pasturage. The income, while not princely, is extremely comfortable.

"I mention these things because it has been in my mind for some time now to ask you to do me the honour to become my wife. Had your father been alive, I should naturally have asked his permission to address you. As things stand, I give you the facts, in the hopes they may go some way to persuade you to look with favour on my suit."

"Indeed," said Davina, "I'm conscious of the honour you do me. Your friendship means a great deal to me. But there's been so much on my mind since Papa died—so many legal tangles, and problems with the estate—I've had no time to consider marriage."

"No matter, no matter. I've no wish to hurry you. It must in any case be some time before I'm established at Bath. I shall possess my soul in patience till you can give me your answer. Now let's talk of something else. I've not seen you since old Shedley was down. What news did he bring you? Good, I hope?"

They were driving through Rigborough now, past the green with its pond and clumps of chestnut trees. The canal-cut lay to their right, and to the left was the Grey Goose Inn, from which flowed sounds of singing and laughter. Davina looked up at Hagg Hill, where Wakeford stood in its parkland.

"We'll survive," she said. "There's a shortage of ready money. I've decided to sell papa's collection." She paused. "Including the Rigborough Missal."

Edward nodded. "Very wise of you."

Perversely, Davina found herself irritated, and he seemed to sense it, for he said kindly, "Books, I believe, can never be held more precious than land, though I know you think much of them. Tell me, what have you been reading this week?"

"A tract by Mr Coke," she replied, "on the rotation of crops.

I've been wondering if I should plant cattle-feed in the east fields, instead of wheat."

Edward chuckled indulgently. "My dear Miss Wakeford, why do you bother your head with such nonsense? Farming is not learned by reading, but by long experience."

"Is not Mr Coke experienced? I'm told his own farm is a model of all that is to be admired. I have been thinking it would be interesting to drive down there, and consult with him. I believe he will draw up a programme, for a very modest fee."

Mr Clare shook his head firmly. "I cannot advise that. One should not go jauntering about, these days. The roads are full of discharged soldiers and sailors, dangerous ruffians, I promise you. May I speak frankly?"

"Of course."

"I could wish that that brother of yours did more for Wakeford, instead of lolling about with his hands in his pockets."

"Roly has no feeling for farming. He doesn't want to be tied. He's only twenty-one."

"The same age as yourself! It goes against the grain with me, to see you carry such heavy burdens. Well, perhaps one day you will let me lift them from your shoulders."

When they reached Wakeford Hall, Davina asked Mr Clare to set her down at a side entrance, from which she could reach her room unobserved. She wished to be alone a little, to think over his words.

Although it was not the first offer of marriage she had received, it was by far the most flattering. She could not rate very high the proposal made by the last curate, who soon afterward was found to be suffering from acute religious mania; nor the stammered pleas of the Squire's son Tom, just turned eighteen; nor the approach of Mr James Rourke, thrice widowed and the father of seven daughters, all of them older than herself.

Edward Clare was a good friend, who had proved himself staunch in adversity. He was well-born, hardworking, and a good-looking man. He loved Rigborough. He had asked for her hand in the knowledge that Wakeford was going through hard times. Davina felt sure that hadn't weighed with him at all.

So why, she enquired of her reflection in the pier-glass, did she feel reluctant to give him an answer? She couldn't claim to have been taken by surprise. For months, he'd been showing her marked attention, sending her posies, remembering her likes and dislikes, remaining at her side at every gathering they attended.

The whole of Rigborough expected him to propose to her and she had done nothing to discourage him. Why then did she feel so . . . lackadaisical?

She took off the kerseymere dress she was wearing, and moved to the washstand. The water in the can was nearly cold, and as she bathed her face and arms, she wondered how it would feel to be mistress of a good plain house such as Edward described. She thought she might like it very much. It would be a pleasant change to live among amiable people who never carped, or prosed, or accused one of being a monster of selfishness.

She drew on a fresh gown, and was struggling with the buttons at the wrists when there was a tap at the door, and Lady Sophy entered.

Her ladyship wore amber silk, which admirably set off her fair Wakeford looks. Her hair was skilfully arranged, and crowned with a ravishing little cap of Brussels lace. A silk shawl was looped over her elbows, and she carried a small beaded reticule. It was a toilette at once simple and modish, an effect that Lady Sophy had been at pains to achieve.

"Nearly ready?" she enquired, coming to fasten the wayward buttons. "I saw you drive up the hill with Mr Clare. How are they all, at Rowanbeck?"

"Sunk in gloom," said Davina. "Lord Rigg is in England."

"And if he is?"

"Amabel is convinced he will cast her on the parish."

"That is the last thing she should fear! He's far more like to urge her to set up house with him!"

"Jocelyn Clare is down from London."

"What has he to say for himself."

"That Rigg is violent, and vindictive, and will cause trouble."

"Jocelyn always had a viperish tongue."

"You dislike him, don't you?"

"I think him highly unscrupulous. He's ruined more than one halfling at the tables." Lady Sophia moved away to sit on the chaise longue. "You know, my love, that you have your mother's beautiful hair? So fine and thick, and with a natural wave."

"I can do nothing with it."

"That's only a matter of cutting. When you come to London, my coiffeur shall try what he can do for you."

Davina shook her head. "I'm afraid I shan't be in London this year."

"No? I made sure you'd come up to arrange for the sale of the collection."

"I'll do that through an agent, I hope."

"All agents are brigands," said Lady Sophy with conviction. "It's been in my mind that you should consult some private collector—someone who knows what he's about, but won't try to bamboozle you. There is Mr Angerstein, for instance—and Sir John Fleming Leicester, a great patron of the arts." Lady Sophy paused for a moment, then went on. "You know Davina, it is in Wakeford's interest that you spend a week or two in Town. Your uncle and I have talked it over, and we would like you to come to us for at least part of the Season. We're bringing Jane out this year. You would be such good company for each other."

"Aunt Sophy, I'm long past being a débutante!"

"Oh, yes, at your last prayers, I've no doubt! My dear child, please hear me out. There would be no expense to you or to Wakeford. It would be our gift to you, one I've long wanted to make, not only for your sake, but for the sake of your parents. Henry was very dear to me, and so was Serena. They would have wished you to make your come-out. There is another point to consider. Eulalie tells me she means to hire a house for herself and Roland. She has heard of something in Curzon Street. You know what that will cost! Much better if you all three come to us in Park Street. It will be a saving for Eulalie, and you may put up the shutters here for a while. I beg you won't refuse out of hand."

"I shan't. I shall think it over very carefully. And thank you with all my heart." Davina came to sit beside her aunt. "Do you know, this is the second promising offer I've received in an hour?"

"I take it the first came from Mr Clare?"

"Yes."

"Did you give him your answer?"

"No. I asked for time to reflect."

"Good. It does no harm to keep a gentleman waiting for a little. Tell me, what does your mama think of him?"

"Truly, I don't know. She's said nothing for or against him. She seldom notices what I do. Her attention is fixed on Roland you see. She worries about him a good deal."

"On what score?"

Davina looked uncomfortable. "Trivial things, that were better ignored. Mama can't accept that Roly is full-grown. She watches him, and questions everything he does. It makes him resty and bad-tempered."

"I've noticed he spends a great deal of his time at Rowanbeck. Does Amabel Rowan encourage him to do so?"

"Not exactly. She's . . . lonely."

"And is Roland in love with her?"

"He imagines he is. It's only calf-love, and quite harmless."

Lady Sophy was not so sure. She had vivid memories of Lord Rigg's passion for Amabel, and his ruthless handling of any challenger. Between his arrogance, Amabel's stupidity, and Roly's quick temper, an explosive situation might develop, one that could arouse the old feuding, and cause much distress to Davina.

Her fears intensified when the ladies descended to the drawing-room, to find the rest of the family embroiled in heated argument.

Roland at once rounded on his sister. "Why the devil didn't you tell me that Rigg was back in England?" he demanded.

"I only heard of it an hour or so ago. How came you by the news?"

"How d'you think? Morty and I called at Rowanbeck. That Finch female told us the whole house is in an uproar, and Amabel beside herself because Rigg is due home any time." He turned to his mother. "Will you please bespeak dinner at once? I must get back to Rowanbeck as soon as may be."

"You'll do nothing of the sort," declared Mrs Wakeford. "I'll not permit you to go where you're not wanted, and that is final!"

"I'm going," cried Roland, "and no one shall prevent me! I mean to be on hand if Amabel needs me."

"And why should she, pray?"

"To protect her from Rigg, of course! She goes in terror of him. Told me so herself. Well, she may count on me for aid. If Rigg harms so much as a hair of her head, he shall answer to me for it." He glanced at his cousin. "You'll come with me, eh, Morty?"

"Not on your life," said Mortimer fervently. "Dashed if I'll make a cake of myself, sittin' on the Rowans' doorstep all night! 'Sides, Rigg won't arrive. Too sudden. Wouldn't be decent."

"That is precisely what he'd wish—to take us all by surprise."

"Well, he ain't goin' to surprise me."

"You're craven!"

"Yes, I am, where Rigg's concerned. He's a dead shot, and handy with his fives, as well. Saw him level three Mohocks in the Strand, once. Laid 'em all on a row in a brace of shakes. Take my advice, Roly. Don't mix with him."

But it took some pungent words from Sir Murray to damp the flame of chivalry that consumed Roland.

"Your mother's right," he said. "If you make a nuisance of yourself at Rowanbeck, you won't be invited there again. Far better to pay your formal respects, once Rigg's in residence. And now if you don't mind, I've had enough of this caterwauling, and would like to sit down to my dinner."

Lady Sophia was far too worldly-wise to comment on Roland's behaviour to his mama. Instead, she contrived to draw Mrs Wakeford aside, later in the evening, and discuss her plans for the coming Season. She expressed her desire to present Davina at court, and said how agreeable it would be if all three members of the Wakeford family were to stay in Park Street for the summer. She pointed out the advantage of that address over one in some less fashionable part of town, and remarked casually that it would help Roland to receive a little guidance from Sir Murray, who had already launched two sons into the ton.

Mrs Wakeford was never slow to see which side her bread was buttered; without committing herself completely, she agreed that there was much in what her sister-in-law said.

As soon as the tea-tray had been removed, her ladyship excused herself from the company, and retired to her bedroom to write two letters.

The first was to her housekeeper in London, warning her to expect three guests from the end of March. The second was to her old and trusted friend, Lady Holland. After some polite generalities, Lady Sophy wrote that her niece Davina Wakeford, being anxious to dispose of some of her late father's books (many of them rare and precious items), wished to make the acquaintance of the librarian, Mr Allen. If at any time during the next few weeks Miss Wakeford was able to come to London, might Lady Sophy bring her to Holland House, to meet Lord Holland and perhaps Mr Allen as well?

These matters attended to, Lady Sophy climbed into bed and slept the sleep of the successful strategist.

When Edward Clare returned from Wakeford Hall to Rowanbeck, he found the butler, Gooden, waiting at the door for him.

"Sir Jocelyn's compliments, sir, and would you be so kind as to step up to his apartments?"

Edward climbed the stairs unwillingly. He disliked these fraternal invitations, which all too often turned into inquisitions.

He found his brother changing for dinner. He had donned shirt, stockings, and tightfitting dove-coloured pantaloons, and now stood before the looking-glass, fastening his collar. A valet waited at his side, a dozen clean muslin neckcloths draped over his arm. Sir Jocelyn took one of these, wound it deftly about his throat, twisted it, and then very delicately arranged three transverse folds at the front. Onto these he slowly sank his chin, thus setting them into permanent creases. He studied the effect in the glass, pursed his lips, sighed, and said, "By no means perfect, but it will have to do. My coat, Brawne."

The valet came forward with a jacket of dark green Bath superfine, and held it so that his master could insert his wrists; then, with a strong, smooth pull, he drew the coat up and settled it across the shoulders. Next he handed Sir Jocelyn a lace-edged handkerchief, a snuffbox, and a quizzing-glass on a black ribbon. Finally, he set a pair of evening slippers ready, and supported his master while he stepped into them.

Sir Jocelyn nodded dismissal. The valet left the room, closing the door after him, and for the first time Sir Jocelyn seemed ready to acknowledge his brother's presence.

"Good evening, Edward. I trust you are going to . . . ah . . . spruce up a little, before we dine?"

"Why? Do we expect company?"

"Your cousin Lucas may arrive."

"Not he. No prudent man would drive over Hagg Hill in such cold. The road's like glass."

"Lucas was never a prudent man." Sir Jocelyn sat down in a chair near the fire. One slim hand signalled Edward to take the chair opposite.

"This may be our last opportunity for some days to talk privately," he said. "Did you address yourself to Miss Wakeford tonight?"

Edward's handsome face showed a fleeting resentment. Then he shrugged. "Yes, I did."

"And did she accept you?"

"She gave no definite answer. I did not expect her to. She is too well-bred a female to wish to appear forward, or over-eager."

Sir Jocelyn sighed. "She did not reject you, though?"

"Certainly not. She asked for time to consider. I told her I will not be in a position to marry until I'm settled at Bath."

The older man picked up a china ornament from the table at his side, and examined it frowningly. "Edward, do not imagine that you have time on your side. The girl may be an easy mark while she's buried alive here in Rigborough, but if I'm any judge, that frivol Sophia Tredgold will do her damnedest to bring the chit into society this Season. I warn you, if Miss Wakeford reaches London, anything may happen."

"Oh, I don't fear competition," said Edward airily. "Miss Wakeford's mind is of an elevated tone. She won't wish to compete in the vulgar marriage-mart, I assure you. Besides, most of the girls presented at Court are several years her junior, and many have handsome fortunes."

"A Wakeford may look a good deal higher than you, my dear." As Edward continued to look mulish, Jocelyn leaned forward in sudden irritation. "May I remind you that our situation leaves no room for complacency? Once Rigg is home, we will have to fight him every way we can."

"I don't know why you say that. I concede he'll want us out of Rowanbeck, but beyond that, what can he do? He'll have no pull with people of quality. It's plain as a pikestaff he won't be received in any polite home. Edgebaston told me, only last week, if Rigg dares to set foot in White's, or Brooks's, he'll quickly be shown the door."

"If you believe that, then you're a greater fool than I thought!"

Edward's face reddened. "I happen to know they're laying bets that Rigg will be drummed out of London within the month. He put himself beyond the pale when he ran out of England. It proved his guilt. I don't know how many times I've heard you say his star is set."

"I said so when he was plain Lucas Rowan. Now he's Earl of Rigg. I don't underestimate the power of the title, even if you do. Added to that, he's rich as Croesus, and has address enough to charm the devil, if he puts his mind to it. Accept that if we are to hold our place, we shall need all the allies we can muster —and that includes the Wakeford coterie."

Edward merely shrugged. Sir Jocelyn studied him under his lids, and said at last, "What's this talk of settling in Bath?"

"Mama wishes it. So does grandfather."

"Grandfather won't give you a brass farthing. He refused to buy our father a miserable cornetcy—or to save him from the moneylenders. He's never made the least push to help me out of my difficulties."

A gleam of malice showed in Edward's eyes. "He doesn't like you," he said, "but he does like me. He'll pay me to manage his lands for him, and I'll inherit one day, see if I don't!"

"Ah, now I understand. You'll hire yourself out as a jobbing farmer, and wait for dead men's shoes!"

"I prefer that, than to seek my bread at the faro-table, as you do!"

For a moment the two glared at each other. Then Jocelyn chuckled. "Well, well, each to his own poison. But don't let Miss Wakeford elude you, dear boy. Her property may be encumbered, but that is a temporary thing. In time, it will be one of the richest in the south. Take my tip and drive the girl over to Bath some day, to meet mama. It will lend respectability to your suit, and raise you in mama's judgement. She always had a liking for dowdy, bookish females."

Sir Jocelyn stood up. "And now, I shall go and talk to dear Amabel. I have very little time left to put her in the proper frame of mind to welcome our illustrious cousin."

VI

It had been the intention of Lord Rigg and Mr Clintwood to drive themselves to Rowanbeck, but Mr Turnbull vetoed this plan out of hand. The weather, he said, was by far too harsh for them to be tooling about in an open curricle. They must take his travelling-chaise, with Bowker to drive it, and a groom to see to the horses, carry the yard of tin, and repel any would-be highway-robbers. His bays, he said, were solid goers that would get them to Jericho and back, rain or shine, and he'd already sent his courier ahead to arrange for as many changes of team as might be necessary.

Mr Clintwood, whose time in the army had given him an aversion to closed carriages, tried to argue the point, especially when he found the chaise to be an enormous affair, upholstered in dark blue suede leather, emblazoned with Mr Turnbull's personal crest, and fitted with fur rugs, foot-warmers, and a set of silver-topped decanters.

All his objections were swept aside, however, and at dawn on Thursday, the travellers set out for Rigborough.

From the start, the journey was plagued by misfortune. Five miles outside Beaconsfield they came up with a train of wagons that was lumbering along as though time had no meaning, and causing a long line of traffic to bank up behind it. The driver of the lead-wain was not only in his cups, but bellicose. He refused to allow anything to pass him, lashing out at all challengers with his stockwhip. On the outskirts of the town, he succeeded in locking wheels with an oncoming dray, and the two vehicles entirely blocked the road, bringing the whole caravan to a halt.

The drayman addressed the wainman in Anglo-Saxon terms. This was a sign for the other wagoners, most of whom were in no better case than their foreman, to jump down and begin an internecine argument that soon led to bloodied noses. Only when Lord Rigg and Mr Clintwood banded together with two burly farmers was order restored and the highway cleared. By the time they entered Beaconsfield, nearly two hours had been lost.

From there on, the weather deteriorated sharply. A wind toothed with sleet was running across the lowlands of the Thame, and several times threatened to topple the carriage. The ruts in the road were like iron, and made it impossible for Bowker to spring his horses. Frequent changes of team were necessary, and they climbed the rise that dominated the Rigg Valley only as night was approaching.

Once over the crest, they faced a splendid prospect. A full moon rode above Hagg Hill and lit all the terrain below. The church steeple, the gable of the Grey Goose Inn, the river and the canal-cut were bathed in pallid fire. Few lights showed in the cottage windows, but to their right Wakeford Hall glittered in its park like a crouching dragon.

The Earl lowered his window, and called to Bowker to halt a moment. As he leaned out, gazing towards the high ground on the far side of the valley, the light of the coach lanterns fell across his face. Clintwood saw on it an expression both eager, and apprehensive. However, all Luke said was, "The woods have encroached somewhat. One used to see more of the house from this point."

By now the horses had picked up the smell of warm stables and oats, and were anxious to be off. The Earl raised his hand. Bowker touched the reins lightly, and the carriage rolled down the slope into Rigborough.

They had cleared the village and were nearing the bridge when they caught the sound of another vehicle coming towards them. It was on the far bank of the river, and still hidden by the woods, but they clearly heard the rattle of its wheels, the drumming of hooves, and a man's voice shouting on a high, urgent note.

"The fool's at full gallop," Clintwood said. "He'll meet us head on!"

Luke swung the door open and jumped down to the road. "Bowker," he shouted, "pull off, man, there's flat ground to your left." He ran to the horses' heads, forcing them sideways. Clintwood and the groom sprang down to join him, and slowly the heavy chaise was edged off the road.

They were just in time. An instant later a high-perch phaeton burst from the shelter of the trees and careered across the bridge. It dashed past the stationary carriage, its wheels churning up a pate of pebbles and mud. They saw the driver, eyes glazed, mouth twisted in a grimace of drunken laughter. Seated next to him, and clinging to the handrail like an organ-grinder's monkey, was a chubby young man who cast Luke an anguished glance, and mouthed something inaudible. Then the phaeton was gone, rocking away up the track that led to Wakeford Hall.

Mr Clintwood brushed mud off his face and coat. "If this is a sample of country quiet," he said, "give me Piccadilly every time. Who was that Jehu?"

"I fancy the driver was Roland Foote," the Earl replied. "The son of Henry Wakeford's second. I'm unacquainted with his unfortunate passenger."

They set about easing the chaise back onto the road, and a short while later, turned through the gates of Rowanbeck.

As may be guessed, the news of Lord Rigg's imminent return had thrown the household into a frenzy of preparation. Gooden the butler, and Mrs Hobbs the housekeeper, had between them reduced the indoors staff to near-hysteria. In the kitchens the French chef Daudet raged like a berserker, and in the gardens an army of workmen tidied the already immaculate borders, and shaved the lawns to an even smoother finish.

Finally, at dusk, the great flambeaux that lined the driveway from the gates to the front doors were lit and lamps placed in all the many windows, so that the whole house blazed with light.

Mr Clintwood was moved to say that it made a splendid spectacle.

"Very," agreed the Earl drily. "Better than Vauxhall on fireworks night."

"Come now, would you have preferred darkness?"

"Oh, much! Pomp and circumstance is to Jocelyn's taste, not mine."

"Brace yourself, Lucas. I suspect there's worse to come."

Mr Clintwood was right. Within the Great Hall, no effort had been spared. The walls and the two massive fireplaces were decked with evergreens. Bunting hung in loops from the screen of the musicians' gallery. On each step of the stairway stood one of Mrs Hobbs's underlings, while at either side of the entrance a row of footmen in scarlet livery stood stiffly to attention.

Gooden himself came forward to wring the Earl's outstretched hand, and reverently relieve him of his coat and hat.

"Welcome home, my lord. May I say it warms my heart to see you back?"

"Thank you." His lordship's gaze moved over the ranks of watching faces.

"I don't see Hunsdon," he said. "Is he ill?"

"Mr Hunsdon died, my lord. He . . . left Rowanbeck a little over two years since . . . and died not long after."

Lord Rigg studied the women on the staircase. "And Mrs Tidbold?"

"Retired, my lord, at the same time as Mr Hunsdon. Mrs Hobbs is housekeeper now. She came to us from Bath—on the recommendation of Mr Clare's mother."

There was the faintest note of warning in Gooden's voice. The Earl nodded.

"Well, it's too late in the evening for introductions. Tell all these good folk I look forward to meeting them tomorrow. And request Winkler, if you please, to see that my uncle's coachman and groom are given a hot meal and toddy, and comfortable quarters. Their names are Bowker and Tickle."

"Very good, my lord."

"Now to my family. Where shall I find them, Gooden?"

"In the green drawing-room, my lord." The butler hesitated, then said without change of expression, "Sir Jocelyn said I should announce your lordship."

"Announce? In my own house? I think not." The Earl smiled to take the edge off the words. "We'll talk later, Gooden."

So saying, he linked an arm through Mr Clintwood's, and the two sauntered away towards the green salon.

Luke would have been hard put to it to say precisely how he felt about meeting Amabel again.

He had once loved her with all the ardour and idealism of youth. He had shared with her the happiest and the saddest moments of his life. To win her, he had been ready to sacrifice good name, liberty, life itself. The bitterest pain he had ever endured was the knowledge that her heart was set on something far more commonplace, his brother's title, and vast estate.

In the long years of exile, he had done his utmost to put her from his mind. He believed he had succeeded. Yet, as he stepped through the open doors of the salon, he felt his mouth go dry, and his heart pound painfully. There were four people in the room, but he saw only her.

She rose from her chair and came towards him. She was wearing a gown of some pale wheaten shade. It gave her an ethereal look. She seemed taller ... more slender ... more beautiful than he remembered.

Halting before him, she made him a formal curtsey, and gave him her hand. It was cold as ice, and trembling. He bent to kiss her cheek, but she turned her head away, so he kissed her fingertips instead, drawing them to his chest so that she was obliged to look up at him.

The expression in her eyes shocked him. Indifference, or aversion, he could have understood, but not fear! All the careful speeches he had prepared vanished into thin air, and he said in a low voice, "Amabel, my love! What in the world is the matter?"

"Nothing!" She dragged her hand free and took a step backward. "I'm sorry, Luke. I cannot accustom myself ... it is all too sudden!"

"Sudden?" Luke strove for a lighter note. "It seems to me I've been travelling home for an eternity! I wrote you from Genoa ... Vienna ... Paris. Had you not my letters?"

"From Paris only." Reproach darkened her eyes. "Nothing else, in all these years. Nothing, even, when Talbot died."

"I wrote, I assure you. Frequently."

The sound of a step made him turn. Jocelyn Clare stood smiling at him, extending a long white hand.

"Rigg, my dear fellow! My felicitations on your accession. And Clintwood? Your servant, sir. I confess I'm astonished to see *you* here. I quite thought you to be in Austria, playing the gallant Hussar."

"I bought out," said Clintwood shortly. He made his bow to Amabel. "Your ladyship's most obedient."

Amabel, still struggling for composure, managed to summon up a smile. "Mr Clintwood, I vow it's an age since we met! I read in the Gazette, how your troop distinguished itself at Waterloo. But such dreadful casualties. It made my heart ache!"

"Yes. We lost many brave lads. James Kerr-Lewis, Rodney

Cranko, Leo North. You remember Leo? A great tall buffoon with a laugh one could hear the length of a parade-ground?"

"Yes, indeed. He took me to watch a balloon-ascent in Hyde Park. How long ago that seems. I've hardly left Rigborough you know, in three years."

"That's been society's loss, ma'am, one I hope may soon be repaired. Do you mean to come to London, this year?"

"Perhaps." Amabel glanced quickly at Sir Jocelyn. "That is . . . we shall see." She turned to Lord Rigg. "Lucas, I'm sure you do not need to be reminded of our dear Cousin Cornelia Finch, who has been my companion since Talbot's death?"

"Certainly not." Luke moved across the room to shake hands with the elderly lady in the outmoded black gown, whose uncapped ringlets marked her as a spinster. "You are the kind friend who came to look after us whenever we were down with the measles and I think, ma'am, you read to me from *Gulliver's Travels*. The Houyhnhnms, was it not?"

"Yes, and you said there was nothing wonderful about them, for horses were always cleverer than people." Miss Finch was pink with pleasure. "Fancy your remembering, my lord! You can have been no more than five or six at the time."

He smiled down at her. "Pray don't call me 'my lord'. 'Cousin Luke' will be much more agreeable."

He turned to the last occupant of the room.

"Edward, my uncle Turnbull tells me you've wrought miracles for Rowanbeck. I stand in your debt."

Edward shrugged ungraciously. "It was no burden to me."

"No, I know how fond you are of the place. Still, I'm much obliged to you. I hope you'll find time to drive about with me—put me in the way of things? I've everything to learn about estate management."

This speech seemed to mollify Mr Clare, for his features lost their sullen cast, and he greeted Mr Clintwood with something like friendliness.

"Never thought you'd come through tonight," he said. "Made sure you'd put up at some inn t'other side of Woodstock."

"Oh, it was none too bad," said Clintwood cheerily. "The last few miles were a toboggan run, but we suffered no spills—except that some local charioteer near did for us, just the far side of the bridge. Missed us by a whisker. Luke says it was someone from Wakeford Hall?"

Edward frowned, evidently unwilling to carry tales, but his brother laughed.

"I expect you mean Roland Foote," he said.

"Whoever he is, he's rats in his rafters, and shouldn't be let loose."

"Foote's only wild when's bosky," said Edward gruffly. "That ain't so often."

"He wasn't drunk tonight," Sir Jocelyn said. "He was here with us until half an hour ago, and perfectly sober, though in a very ill temper." The thin smile switched to Luke. "You see, my dear cousin, the poor fellow is head over heels in love with Amabel—and convinced that now you're home, you're bound to cut him out."

Dinner was served at eight o'clock.

Despite the excellence of the food and wines, it was an uncomfortable meal, marked by none of the easy conviviality that had obtained in the Turnbulls' home.

Amabel sat stiffly, her eyes downcast, replying in monosyllables to whatever was said to her. Edward Clare, after delivering a few observations on the weather, and giving it as his opinion there'd be no hunting this week or next, devoted his attention to his plate and his glass. Sir Jocelyn, though he plied Mr Clintwood with questions about the recent war, barely listened to the answers, and managed to suggest that these military matters were hardly a fit topic for intelligent beings.

The evening was saved from complete disaster by Miss Finch. Her hobby, it appeared, was genealogy, and when by some happy chance the Earl asked her how the Finch and Rowan lines were connected, she launched into an explanation that carried her listeners back to the Norman Conquest. Between the first and second courses she ranged through several female sublines, and over the dessert was able to prove to her own entire satisfaction that the Rowan family was linked (albeit on the wrong side of the blanket) with several of the crowned heads of Europe.

When at last the ladies left the dining-room, the gentlemen did not linger over their port. The Clares repaired to the library and the backgammon board. Mr Clintwood, declaring himself to be burned to a cinder, went off to bed. And Luke strolled out to the stableyard to talk to the Head Groom, Winkler.

This wizened old gnome had been at Rowanbeck for over fifty years. He greeted the Earl without surprise, informed him that he looked blacker'n any gipsy, and led him over to the horseboxes.

As Mr Clintwood had foreseen, Talbot's horses were magnificent, the pick of them being the team of matched greys, which Winkler displayed with consummate pride.

"Prime blood 'n bone," he said, running a hand over a leader's glossy flank. "Sixteen-mile-an-hour tits. Nobbut me grandson and me lays 'ands on 'em. You won't find much in the 'unters' boxes, but no doubt you'll be buyin' what you fancy. They do say Squire Birkett, over to Banbury, is off to sell 'is bloodstock, 'count of the artheritees got to 'is backside. You couldn't look for better 'osses, m'lord. As to 'acks, them I can do you, an' we don't want for work-a-day prads." Winkler sighed happily. "Ah, it'll be sweet to see a real Rowan back in the saddle—one that won't take no nonsense from no Johnny-come-lately, neither."

The master bedroom at Rowanbeck was in the oldest part of the house, that built in 1396, and boasted a vast stone fireplace carved with the arms of Sir Tristram de Rohan and his wife Elinor. It had last been refurbished by the third Earl, Luke's grandfather, whose taste ran to French wall-tapestries, and gilded furniture.

The fire had already been lit, and burned with the scent of apple-wood. Branches of candles illuminated every corner, and on the buhl table near the door was a silver tray, set with decanters and glasses.

As Luke entered, he saw that a portly man in black was engaged in laying out a set of nightwear on the bed.

"Gooden," he said, "surely there's someone less august to perform these chores?"

The butler inclined his head gravely. "From tomorrow, my lord, my nephew John will attend you, but tonight I wished to assure myself all is as it should be."

Luke looked about him with a somewhat rueful smile. "You

know, until this moment, I had not fully realised I'm Earl of Rigg."

"Also tenth Baron de Rohan," reminded Gooden, advancing across the room. "It is an impressive apartment, and the chimney does not smoke, even when the wind is in the east. If your lordship will be so good as to sit down, I will remove his boots."

Luke settled in the nearest chair, and the old man drew off his muddied Hessians and placed them outside the door. He fetched a brocaded dressing-gown from the closet, laying it over the back of a second chair. Luke stood up and allowed himself to be eased out of his coat, then slipped on the gown and tied its belt.

"Did you keep all my rig?" he said curiously.

"Down to the last handkerchief," said Gooden firmly. "Your lordship will find the clothes a thought out-of-date for Town wear, but very suitable for Rigborough."

Luke dragged off his cravat and tossed it aside. "Drink a glass with me, Gooden, to celebrate my return?"

"Gladly, my lord."

Walking to the side-table, Luke poured brandy into two glasses, carried them back and handed one to the butler.

"Your very good health," he said.

"And yours, my lord."

"Nectar," said Luke, after an appreciative pause. "You wouldn't credit the witches' brews I've been forced to swallow, these past three years."

"You will find your cellars well-stocked." Gooden's face was impassive, but some emphasis in his words made Luke look at him sharply. "You will find a full inventory in the muniments-room. I've kept tally of every bottle bought, stored, and consumed. I thought it expedient . . . after Mr Hunsdon left and there was no new steward appointed to deal with the accounts."

"Yes, let us talk about Hunsdon." Luke returned to his chair and waved Gooden to another. "Why did he leave? Was he dissatisfied, was he ill?"

"He was dismissed, my lord."

"Dismissed?" Luke stared in disbelief. "In God's name, why?"

"He had a disagreement with his late lordship."

"Talbot? Talbot dismissed him?"

"Yes, my lord."

"Was my brother drunk at the time?"

"I believe on that occasion he was sober, my lord."

"What was the cause of the disagreement?"

"I am not precisely sure. Mr Hunsdon was in such distress after the encounter that he could barely frame his words. He did speak of the books, and used the word 'misappropriation.'"

"Whose?"

"That I can't say."

"When did this happen?"

"Two years ago—in January of 1814."

Luke considered. "That was six months after Tal suffered his first seizure, was it not?"

"It was, my lord." Gooden turned his glass slowly in his hands. "Your brother was never himself, after the attack."

"Were my cousins—Sir Jocelyn, and Mr Clare—in the house by then?"

"They were. They came soon after his lordship was taken ill."

"And Lady Rigg?" said Luke. "Surely she spoke in Hunsdon's behalf?"

Gooden's only answer was a slow shake of the head.

"You say Hunsdon's dead?"

"Yes, my lord. He bought a small property in Witney, but never lived to enjoy it. I went to see him, once, and found him very low. Not eating, not sleeping. In the spring he contracted a chill, and it settled on his lungs. He died in May of 1814."

"I see. Tell me, were others dismissed at that time?"

"Yes. Marriott, who your lordship will recall was Head Gamekeeper. His lordship's valet, Bryce. Mrs Tidbold left of her own accord and went to her daughter in Taunton. She ... wasn't happy here, my lord."

"And you, Gooden? Was there any attempt to remove you?"

"There was, for a while, my lord. But his lordship, setting such store by his cellars, was loth to let me go. I was careful to give no cause for complaint—and I let it be known in certain quarters that I'd kept good account of all in my charge, and would send it to Mr Shedley, if need be."

"You did excellently, Gooden. I'm grateful to you."

Gooden smiled and inclined his head.

"Thank you, my lord. Will there be anything further?"

"Nothing. Except . . . warn my uncle's coachman that I shall have a letter for him to carry, tomorrow."

"Very good, my lord. Goodnight."

Carrying the used glasses, the butler quietly left the room, closing the door after him. Luke went to the writing desk in a corner of the room, sat down, and drew pen and paper towards him. He sat for a moment thinking, then scrawled a single line: "Set on your mongoose. L."

VII

Luke was woken next morning by the crowing of a cock on the home-farm. The fobwatch hanging at his bedpost informed him that it was a little after six o'clock. He could hear faint sounds of the servants moving about in the lower rooms, sweeping and riddling the grates.

He climbed out of bed, crossed to one of the casements and threw it open. Icy air struck at him. He could see in the early light the pearly fields rising to the ridge, and the woodlands, ghostly under mist, that separated Rowan from Wakeford land.

He felt a sudden wish to ride out alone, to enjoy for a short while the cold purity of the morning, and let it wash away the sour taste of his homecoming.

He washed and dressed in buckskins and boots, a thick woollen shirt, belcher neckcloth and heavy jacket. No one was astir in the upper regions of the house, and he made his way quietly down the back stair, and out into the stableyard.

Mr Turnbull's chaise had already been drawn out of the coachhouse, and Winkler was helping Bowker and Tickle to harness the horses. The Earl waited until the task was done, then handed Bowker a purse containing money for the return journey, and also the letter he had written.

"Thank my uncle for all his kindness," he directed, "and say I shall write more fully in a few days' time."

When the chaise had lumbered away, Luke turned to Winkler.

"I've a fancy to ride before breakfast," he said. "Find a mount for me, please."

Winkler rasped his jaw. "You'd best take Sentinel," he said. "Nice paces, and good off his hind legs, too."

The stable clock was striking seven as Luke rode out through the rear archway and took the track up to the ridge. The sun had turned from blood-red to rusty gold, drawing steam from the river.

There were no ploughlands on the crest of the ridge, only sheepgrass that ran for several miles in a wide arc to the peak of Hagg Hill. Luke turned Sentinel eastward and gave him his head. The beast responded eagerly, keeping up a fast, effortless stride, and clearing several low stone walls like a bird.

At Hagg Hill, Luke slowed and turned homeward. Much of the territory that now lay to his left, was Wakeford land. The area close to the great house lay fallow. Lower down, there were a few cattle grazing, but no sheep. To Luke's inexpert eye, it seemed that Wakeford had been neglected of recent years. He sighed a little, envisaging what it was going to mean, to administer Rowanbeck.

His father had been only fifty years old when he died, and had given no thought to training his sons in the management of a vast estate. Talbot at least had expected to inherit, but Talbot was gone to an early grave, and it was Luke who must cope with the problems he left.

He was pondering these matters when he heard a distant halloo, and turned in the saddle to see two riders cantering in his wake. They waved to him. He stopped to allow them to come up with him.

The first horseman was a plump young man astride an equally plump roan. He was immaculately clad in riding-breeches, glossy boots with snowy tops, a coat of black Bath suiting, and a fresh white neckcloth. A curly-brimmed beaver adorned his head, and York tan gloves his hands. His long, leveret's face was pink with cold. Luke recognised him as the passenger in the phaeton that had nearly run them down the previous night.

The other rider, a young woman mounted on a nondescript mare, was as grubby as her companion was clean. Her dark blue riding-habit was kilted up to show a boot caked with mud, and a fringe of mudstained petticoat. Round her shoulders hung a thick frieze cape, also mud-spattered. It was impossible to tell if her complexion was good or bad, for it was streaked with brown and green. From this mask shone out a pair of eyes that were large, and of a light, sparkling grey. She was smiling, but the smile quickly faded to a look of consternation.

"Oh, I beg your pardon! I'm afraid I took you for Edward Clare."

Luke removed his hat. "Do we look alike?"

"No, not at all." She smiled again. "It was the horse, you see. Mr Clare always rides Sentinel."

"Does he? Then I fear I'll be in his black books again."

The girl held out a gloved hand. "My brother told me you were home, Lord Rigg. I'm Davina Wakeford."

"Yes," he said. "I . . . er . . . recognised you as soon as you spoke."

Her hand flew to her face, and she laughed. "Am I so very dirty? I took the short-cut across Turner's field, and it proved to be a bog. May I present my cousin, sir. Mr Mortimer Foote."

Mr Foote leaned over to shake hands. He seemed to be in a state of acute embarrassment, for he stared meaningly at the Earl, murmuring quickly, "Should be glad of a word with you, my lord. Not now, later." He then reined in his horse, and allowed the other two to ride side by side on the narrow road.

The Earl felt it incumbent on him to make some attempt to converse with his companion: but some unexceptionable remarks about the weather, and the fine view to be obtained from this elevation, drew no more response from her than an abstracted nod. Clearly Miss Wakeford was struggling with weightier matters. The Earl waited, in the gloomy certainty he was soon to be informed of them.

"Lord Rigg," she said at last, "what do you know about drains?"

"Drains?" He stared at her in astonishment. "Nothing whatsoever."

"No more do I," she said regretfully, "though I've been reading a treatise by Mr Piers Mandeville—the architect, you know? He says that if one does not provide a damp-course under the foundations of a house, underground seepage will occur."

"One can see that that might very well be the case."

"Yes," continued Miss Wakeford, "and then, you see, damp will rise into the walls and weaken the entire structure. At the first high wind, or flood, down it will all tumble. I suppose that is what is happening to our riverside cottages." She caught his blank look, and shook her head. "Don't tell me you're not aware that the watermeadows are flooded."

"I'm afraid no one thought to mention it."

"It only happened last night," she explained. "The canal froze, and the water spread across all the lower fields. My factor arrived at five this morning to say that two of our cottages have collapsed. I wished to warn Mr Clare to have an eye to yours. If you can throw up a dyke, they may be saved."

"Thank you, that is very thoughtful of you. I'll see Edward gets the message."

They had now drawn level with the five-barred gate that led by way of a lane to the kitchen gardens of Wakeford. Miss Wakeford reined in her horse. "If you should wish to study Mr Mandeville's book," she said, "I'll be happy to lend it to you."

Luke leaned from the saddle to open the gate, and with a final smile of thanks, she rode through it. Mr Foote, however, lingered to speak to the Earl.

"Couldn't broach it before," he said, "didn't wish to distress Davina. Enough on her plate already. Thing is, I'm deuced sorry for what occurred last night. My cousin Roland . . . sound fellow, excellent bottom, bruisin' rider to hounds, but all thumbs when it comes to handlin' the ribbons. Addle-pated, too, when he's a trifle in alt. What I mean to say is, hope you won't regard it? Accept my sincere apologies on his behalf?"

The Earl smiled. "Of course. Say no more, Mr Foote."

But the young man was not disposed to take this advice. "Fact is," he continued confidingly, "I don't altogether blame old Roly. Not for puttin' you in the ditch, of course. Shockin', that. But for wantin' to lash out a bit. Feels thwarted, don't you know? Doesn't enjoy bein' tied to his mama's apron-strings, but can't cut loose because the dibs ain't in tune. Pinched for cash. Pockets to let. Devilish situation for a man to be in."

The Earl murmured assent, edging his mount towards the road.

"What's worse," insisted Mortimer, "the poor fellow's in love. Makes him act the numskull, if you catch my drift?"

"I understand perfectly. Love doth make asses of us all. 'The ruling passion conquers reason still.'"

"Eh?" said Mortimer, momentarily thrown off-course.

"To quote the great Pope," supplied the Earl.

Mr Foote's brow cleared. "Ah! Just so, sir. Knew you'd understand. So we can consider it settled, can we?"

The Earl bowed his head. "Absolutely. The book is closed. Honour is satisfied."

Mr Foote gravely returned the bow, saluted Luke with a flourish of his riding-crop, passed through the gate, closed it punctiliously, and cantered away after Miss Wakeford.

Luke turned homeward once more, reflecting that his neighbours appeared to be a rum lot. Roland Foote he took for a mannerless Yahoo, who would never apologise for his misdemeanour. Mortimer was an amiable clothhead. And Miss Wakeford? He thought he had never met a female less careful of her appearance, or less blessed with polite small-talk. Did she know no better? Or was it that the Wakefords were so high in the instep that they considered themselves above the ordinary rules of conduct?

Granted she had a pleasant laugh, and quite speaking eyes, but there was precious little else to commend her. Taken all round, a bookish, draggled article, doomed to spinsterhood; a female to be pitied, and scrupulously avoided.

Lord Rigg would have been intensely annoyed to know that his opinion of the Wakefords very closely matched theirs of him.

Davina, over a large helping of ham and baked eggs, gave her family a full account of the encounter on Hagg Hill, and expressed the view that Lord Rigg was much to be pitied.

"He's very cold in his manner," she said. "I think he doesn't know how to converse, except on trivial topics. And he has the look of a man who's suffered a great deal."

"If he has, he's brought it on himself," said Sir Murray. "My advice to you is, avoid him. He's a profligate, like all the Rowans."

Davina's sense of justice was outraged. "Uncle, you can't accuse Mr Clare of profligacy."

"No, he's a dull stick," agreed Sir Murray unreasonably. "But Luke Rowan's a gambler and a rake. I could name a dozen birds of paradise he's had in keeping, prime articles that must have cost him a fortune!" He caught his wife's warning look, and waved a deprecating hand. "All right, all right. But leave Rigg alone. Observe the courtesies, of course, but go no further."

To Davina's surprise, Mr Foote, who up till now had been concerned with demolishing a dish of devilled kidneys, took up the cudgels for his lordship.

"I liked the cut of his jib," he said. "No side. Nothing in the least top-lofty about him." He frowned. "Must say, I never knew the Rowans were of the Roman persuasion."

"They aren't," said Lady Sophia. "Why, they were for Oliver Cromwell, Morty. One cannot be more Protestant than that."

"Must have converted," said Mortimer flatly. "Quoted the Pope to me."

"The Pope? You must be mistaken."

"Well, I'm not. Nothing wrong with my ears, Aunt." Mortimer closed his eyes, thought a moment, then recited, "'The ruling passion conquers reason still'. Nicely put, I thought."

"That's Alexander Pope," said Davina.

"Told you it was," said Mortimer, sounding hurt. "And even if Rigg's a papist, I shan't let it count with me. I liked his style, and when he comes to London, I shall do my possible for him. Introduce him to the Vanbrughs. Staunch Catholics. Bound to take him up."

This reduced the Tredgolds to stunned silence, and Miss Wakeford to such an attack of giggles that she found it expedient to excuse herself from the table, and go upstairs to see how her mother did.

Eulalie Wakeford never left her bedroom before noon, and Davina found her propped up on her pillows, a boudoir cap on her head, a glass of hot chocolate in her hand, and the morning mail scattered over the quilt.

That her mood was peevish was at once apparent, for without so much as a good morning to her step-daughter, she picked up a letter and brandished it angrily.

"Imagine," she said, "that wretched house-agent has sent me the most odious, insulting letter! He begins by demanding payment in advance, as if one was the veriest nobody. Then he offers me a villa in Bayswater. Bayswater, indeed! As if I should ever contemplate anything so shoddy. I shall write to inform him that if that is the best he can suggest, then he need not keep my name on his books. Where is Roland?"

"Still asleep, I think." Davina sat down on the bedside chair. "How are you today, Mama?"

"Far from well. I scarcely slept a wink. I have been worrying all night over what Roland said—that he will pick a quarrel with Lord Rigg."

"I'm sure Rigg won't let him do any such thing. It would be quite beneath his dignity to squabble with a stripling."

Mrs Wakeford bridled, unsure whether to take offence at this stricture, or ignore it. Finally she decided to revert to her original theme.

"I'm sure I don't know where I will find accommodation in London," she complained. "The prices are so high, and the demand so great." She glanced at Davina under her lashes. "Your Aunt Sophia wishes us to stay with her, in Park Street."

"I know, but it's impossible for me. I can't leave Wakeford."

"Nonsense, of course you can. You may make your come-out in the best style imaginable, and your uncle will foot the bill. That is a very handsome offer, and I must say, if you refuse it, I shall hold you to be selfish past belief."

"Whether or not I go, you may accept—and take Roland."

"That won't fadge," said Eulalie with an angry jerk of the head. "Sophia has made it plain that the invitation is conditional on your coming to Town. And while I think such favouritism deplorable, I am ready to disregard it, for the sake of my dear boy. And in case you are going to say that the Tredgolds' home is not large enough, may I remind you that they have raised five children of whom only Jane is left in the nest, and there will be ample space for us all. Sophia suggests we travel up to London towards the middle of March, but I suppose we may be flexible in our dates."

Seeing Davina begin to shake her head, Mrs Wakeford played her trump card. "Your Aunt," she said casually, "tells me she has written to Lady Holland. She hopes to arrange for you to meet with a Mr Allen, whoever he may be."

"Mr Allen? The librarian?" Davina sat up, her eyes shining. "Oh, that would be beyond everything wonderful. He's the most erudite man, and with the best knowledge in England of the book-market. He could do more for me than all the professional agents put together. How good of Aunt Sophy to think of it. I must thank her at once." She sprang from her chair, and was about to run from the room when Eulalie's hand closed on her skirts.

"Do I take it, Miss, that you mean to go to London, after all?"

"Not to stay. But for a day or two, oh yes, it's a chance not to be missed."

Davina hurried away. Mrs Wakeford, left alone, regarded the letter in her hand with revulsion.

"Bayswater!" she said. "The man is all about in his head! I'd as soon reside in Wimpole Street!"

On returning from his ride the Earl bathed, shaved, donned fresh clothes and strolled to the breakfast-room, where he found Mr Clintwood consuming roast beef and ale. When Luke asked if anyone else was yet down, he shook his head.

"Edward Clare was asking for you, though. He seemed miffed not to find you."

Luke inspected the contents of the dishes on the sideboard. "I took his horse," he said.

"*His* horse?" Clintwood's tone was innocent. "Does he keep his own here, then?"

"The horse he's accustomed to ride. I suspect Winkler gave me the beast on purpose to annoy Edward."

"Good for Winkler!"

"All very well, Clint, but I've no wish to provoke unnecessary battles."

"The provocation has not so far been on your side."

"That may be, but I'll call a truce if I can."

Clintwood looked unconvinced, but merely said, "Clare left a message for you. He'll be in the south fields until noon. If you wish, you may seek him there."

The south fields of Rowanbeck lay alongside the river. Luke, arriving there soon after eleven, found Edward Clare's horse hitched to a post at the head of the slope. Edward himself could be seen splashing through the shallow floodwater, directing a gang of men armed with mattocks and shovels. Catching sight of the Earl, he broke away, and came striding up the hill. His face was thunderous, and while he was still some distance away he said in a blustering voice, "Where the devil were you this morning? Here was Strickland searching high and low for you, and none could say where you were."

"I'm sorry," said Luke contritely. "I should have given Winkler my direction. I'd no idea there was this crisis. What are we doing to meet it?"

"I've told the men . . . that is, I suppose you will wish them to cut ditches, and drain off the surplus water?"

"By all means, if that's what you advise."

Edward nodded. He turned and signalled to the waiting men, who moved off. Then he made towards his horse. Luke rode after him.

"I owe you an apology for taking Sentinel," he said. "I wouldn't have done so, had I known you are accustomed to ride him."

"The horse is yours, not mine."

"True, but there are other hacks I can use when I ride for pleasure."

This brought him a look of contempt. "I don't keep animals for pleasure. There are far too many beasts, eating their heads off in the stables. I've told Shedley time and again they should be sold, and the money put to better use." Edward shot Luke a kindling look. "But I suppose you've other notions."

"Why yes, I have, but they don't include letting horses stand idle. I shall put them to good use."

"Tooling up to London, I make no doubt."

"Certainly, once the Season begins."

Edward snorted. "I have better things to do, than to play the town-smart."

He swung himself up to the saddle, and the two started back along the bridle-path.

"You mentioned the name Strickland," Luke said. "I don't remember to have heard of him before."

"Your bailiff. He's been at Rowanbeck two years. I took him on as Head Keeper, after Marriott left, but soon promoted him. He's too good a man to beat coverts. I rate farms above pheasants, any day of the week."

"Gooden tells me Marriott was dismissed. Also Hunsdon and Bryce. And Mrs Tidbold quit of her own free will. Quite an exodus, was it not?"

Edward reddened. "I'm surprised Gooden spoke of it. It's not his place to prattle about the staff."

The Earl glanced up lazily. "It is Gooden's place, my dear Edward, to answer any question I care to put to him. Naturally I enquired about these people, whom I would have thought were our most trusted servants. I was particularly shocked to learn of Hunsdon's dismissal. He was far more than a steward, he was a friend of the family."

"You may say so. I found him both stubborn, and incompetent."

"Stubborn, I grant you. But incompetent? I never hope to find a more efficient man."

"What do you know of what has passed here, these last three years? I tell you, I've had to stand by, and watch your brother waste his patrimony, and ours! He was no more than a toss-pot, drunk before noon, never making the least shift to attend to his estate. It stands to reason the servants were out of control, and took too much on themselves. I told Talbot to his head he should think shame to leave Rowanbeck in the hands of hirelings, when there were members of the family able and willing to play their part. I'm glad to say, Talbot saw I was in the right of it. He told Hunsdon that if he couldn't take his orders from me, or Jocelyn, then he'd best pack his bags. And so he did."

"And died of the disgrace!"

"Mere vaporising. The man was well compensated for his long service."

"I doubt if there's enough money in England to repay that sort of loyalty. But let it pass. Quarrelling won't bring him back." Luke was silent for a moment, then said, "I met Miss Wakeford while I was out, this morning. She asked me to tell you that two of Wakeford's riverside cottages have collapsed because of the flooding."

Edward looked concerned. "Did she ask for help?"

"No. Merely offered me advice about drainage."

"How came it that you met?"

"I was passing the Hall. She was out with her cousin, Mr Foote. She mistook me for you, as I was riding Sentinel."

"I see." Edward's tone was stiff. "I think I should tell you, Rigg, that I take a particular interest in Miss Wakeford's welfare, not only because we are neighbours, but because I hope that she may one day do me the honour to become my wife." He cast Luke a glance that was half-embarrassed, half-defiant. "I suppose you will tell me I aim too high!"

"I will do no such thing." Luke was becoming heartily sick of the conversation. "It's no business of mine whom you marry, nor do I care a jot for Miss Wakeford's cottages. It's my own I'm concerned for. Are they in danger?"

"No immediate danger. But they're old, and the fabric is rotten. It's only a matter of time before they crumble."

"Then I suggest we rebuild them at once."

"There's no money for that sort of thing."

"Rubbish. If it's needed, I'll find it."

"Where?" Edward gave a sneering laugh. "At the end of the rainbow? Or do you mean to tap your rich Uncle Joshua?"

"That won't be necessary. I'm not yet at *point-non-plus*."

"You don't know the facts! I asked Talbot more than once for money to make urgent repairs. I was told there was none."

"Then he was in error. I assure you I can and will fund whatever work you wish to do. It won't put me in dun territory."

As he spoke, Luke saw his cousin's expression range from flat disbelief, through astonishment, to resentful acceptance.

"What I should like," Luke said, "is for you to draw up a list of the most pressing needs. Leave me to worry about payment. We'll start with Rowanbeck, and move later to Graydon. I imagine that must be in poor shape. Or have you been keeping an eye on that, too?"

Edward shook his head. He seemed to be conducting a debate within himself. After a moment, he said grudgingly, "It will cost you a packet to set all to rights, but if you're game to try, then so am I."

During the days that followed, the Earl and Mr Clare put this plan into effect, visiting a different part of the estate each morning, and returning home to discuss what action was necessary. It did not take long to establish in both their minds that Luke was woefully short of the training needed to manage so vast a property, but he was as anxious to learn as Edward was to impart advice, so the tension between them very soon eased, and they established some sort of rapport.

Within the walls of Rowanbeck, Luke's efforts at peacemaking were less successful. His first step was to do away with what he considered unnecessary formality. He gave orders that as long as the house party remained small, meals were to be served in the small dining-room, rather than the immense banqueting-hall on the first floor. He informed Gooden that he did not care to have a footman breathing down his neck at dinner, and was quite able to pick up his own handkerchief, should he drop it.

He made a point of speaking to every member of the staff, and found a few who had served him in the past. It disturbed him to find that even these were guarded in their attitude towards him.

"They watch me," he told Clintwood, "as if I were a pugilist, about to take on the ruling champion. I get the feeling they are trying to decide where to place their bets."

He had no doubt that it was Jocelyn Clare who was leading the campaign against him. Jocelyn, after all, had ruled the roast for two years, and probably had his informants in every department of Rowanbeck. Jocelyn, though, was not fond of Rowanbeck. He said often that he abominated country life. He never rose before noon, and when he did appear, could barely stifle his yawns. Invited to make up a table for whist, he replied that he did not care to play for such paltry stakes. And his manner to Luke was a mixture of patronage and malice that roused Mr Clintwood to fury.

"Why don't you plant the fellow a leveller?" he demanded, after an especially tiresome evening. "Here he is living off your bounty, and can't bring himself to show you common courtesy. I don't know why you put up with him."

"I'm giving him enough rope," said Luke placidly.

In truth, he was more disturbed about Amabel's behaviour, than his cousins'. The nervousness she had shown on the night he returned, did not diminish. She seemed anxious to avoid him, and if he came upon her by chance, she speedily bethought her of something she must attend to elsewhere. She made private talk impossible by keeping Cornelia Finch constantly at her side.

She was more at ease with Robert Clintwood, who set himself to amuse her, recounting anecdotes of people she had known in London, strolling with her in the garden, and making her such outrageous compliments that she felt bound to laugh at them. Something of her old, flirtatious charm revived. Yet watching her, Luke saw that under the raillery and the soft, speaking glances, lay misery and fear. Often, when she felt Jocelyn's gaze on her, she would break off what she was saying, and sink into silence.

Her attitude hurt and puzzled him. It was one thing for her to treat him coolly, but quite another for her to go over to the enemy camp.

One evening, she consented to sing for them. Sitting at the pianoforte in her pale gown, with the candlelight shining on her wheaten hair, she looked, Luke thought, like a beautiful ghost, a shadow of that past he had lost forever.

Contrary to the general expectation, Mr Roland Foote did not appear at Rowanbeck in that first week. Late one night, however, as Luke was going upstairs, he saw from the landing windows a lonely figure standing on the terrace, and gazing with great intensity at Amabel's casement. It was Mr Foote, blue-lipped and red-nosed with cold, and looking so forlorn that Luke was half minded to call him in for a reviver. Before he could do so, Roland caught sight of him, and at once disappeared into the darkness of the shrubbery. Luke continued on his way to bed, feeling very much like a character from a Sadlers' Wells melodrama.

VIII

RIGBOROUGH WAS SHARPLY divided on whether or not to extend the hand of friendship to Lord Rigg.

The Sotherbys and Barrables were firmly against calling. The Montagus were known to have adopted a wait-and-see attitude.

On the other hand, Squire Osmund, who was a popular Master of the local hunt, lost no time in driving over to Rowanbeck with his lady, to pay the new Earl his respects. And on Sunday the Vicar, Mr Standish, took as his text the parable of the prodigal son, speaking with so many weighty pauses, and sharp glances in Luke's direction, that no one could be in any doubt of his meaning.

Without precisely killing the fatted calf, many of the local people did make Luke welcome. He found his work at Rowanbeck constantly interrupted by callers. The gentry bowled up in their carriages, the tenant-farmers arrived in their pony-traps with their plump wives perched beside them, and the commonality strolled up from the village to shake Luke's hand and wish him well.

Mr Clintwood was delighted, and when one day the Sotherbys' card was found to top the pile on the hall tray, he exclaimed in triumph, "Now, you see, Rigborough is solidly for you."

"And where Rigborough leads," murmured the Earl, "London must surely follow."

At Wakeford Hall, no less than elsewhere, argument raged. Mrs Wakeford was of the view that there was no need for haste. "We must be guided by the Montagus' decision," she said. "If they feel Rigg is beyond the pale, we cannot be faulted for thinking the same."

"What," enquired Davina innocently, "if the Montagus are waiting to see what we do?"

"Don't be frivolous," said Eulalie sharply. "This is a serious matter. A little judicious coolness may be salutary to Rigg's conceit, which was always excessive."

"Shouldn't think he'll care what we do," said Mortimer,

"Doesn't seem the sort to worry what others think of him. Own master, if you ask me."

Roland said hotly, "I suppose that means you will kow-tow to him, like the rest of the toadeaters?"

"Greet him civilly," said Mortimer. "Already have, come to that. As for calling at Rowanbeck, that don't come into it. I'm leaving for town tomorrow. Expect I'll see Rigg there. Hope I do."

Before Roland could raise any further dust, Sir Murray folded his newspaper and said decisively, "I shall call. For one thing, it's the proper thing to do, and for another Rigg owns the best pheasant coverts in five counties, and I shall like to be invited to shoot over 'em, this autumn. Sophia, my love, we will visit Rowanbeck on Wednesday morning. The rest of you may accompany us, or not, as you choose."

A week after the arrival at Rowanbeck, Mr Clintwood drove over to Evesham to visit his parents. He was absent for three days, returning with the expressed intention of avoiding his family for the rest of the summer.

"Not that I ain't fond of 'em," he told the Earl, "but a little of one's nearest and dearest goes a long way. M' mother's a darling, but bent upon seeing me leg-shackled to some dashed wholesome female with buck teeth. M' father may be frail, but he's stubborn as a mule, and if I so much as lift a finger to help him, he wishes me at the Devil. Mary is staying in the house with her dolt of a husband and four children under six—and when Mary leaves, Harriet is to move in with her brood. I promise you, Lucas, I'd as lief storm Badajoz again as endure one more day of family life." He lit one of his cigarillos with a sigh of contentment. "Can't even blow a cloud at home," he said. "The ladies won't stand for it."

Luke smiled faintly. "I think you fortunate in your relatives."

"My dear fellow!" Clintwood was contrite. "I spoke off the top of my head!"

"Don't apologise. I should have known better than to hope for domestic harmony. My uncle warned me my cousins had dug themselves in—but I tried to believe it was done to oblige Talbot."

"If Tal offered 'em a finger, no reason for them to swallow

the whole arm. I've said before, and I say it again, get rid of the pair of 'em."

"Easier said than done. Edward's taken good care of Rowanbeck."

"And made himself a handsome living in the process!"

"I don't grudge him that. What does get under my skin is the thought that he may have intercepted the mails. For two years I received not a single line from Talbot, or Amabel. Letters are taken to the mail office by Strickland—and he's in Edward's pocket."

"Why would Edward set himself up as a censor?"

"Because if I'd known what was afoot, I'd have come home, whatever the risk—and it suited him to remain at Rowanbeck, running the farms. It's what he's always wanted." Luke got up and began to pace restlessly about the room. "The third point that troubles me is the dismissal of so many of our trusted employees. Marriott ... Bryce ... and especially Hunsdon. Hunsdon would never have stood for any sharp practices. That's why he was given his marching orders."

"Have you examined the ledgers?"

"Minutely, and found everything in good order. The accounts relating to Rowanbeck, the farms, Graydon—even Amabel's pin-money—are exactly as they should be. No doubt Shedley checked them, after Tal's death."

"Then what is it that troubles you?"

"Tal's private income. It was enormous, and no one had the right to question how he spent it. He did spend a very large portion of it. How, is in some doubt."

"Drink?" said Mr Clintwood succinctly.

"My dear Robert, there's a limit to what the most confirmed toper can absorb. We're speaking of many thousands of pounds. Gooden kept a record of all that passed through our cellars. It covers only a fraction of what Tal spent over two years."

"In other words, your charming cousins bled him."

"Jocelyn did, I'm sure. I'm inclined to exonerate Edward. He hasn't the head for embezzlement—could never add two and two but he made five."

Mr Clintwood's normally cheerful features took on a grave cast. "And Lady Rigg?" he demanded. "What was her part in all this?"

Luke shook his head. "Amabel's no more than a pretty widgeon. Such stratagems would be quite beyond her."

"That for a tale!" Mr Clintwood pitched his half-smoked cigarillo into the fireplace. "No woman is so shatterbrained that she will stand by and watch her husband fleeced, without breathing a word to anyone. For God's sake, Luke, stop acting the part of Amabel's whipping-boy, and look to your own interests."

For a moment it seemed the Earl would return an angry answer, but after a moment, he nodded.

"I know," he said. "I'll talk to Amabel, and make her tell me the truth."

The chance to speak to Amabel arose next morning. Seeing her cross the fountain court, Luke met her at the door of the house, and brushing aside her protests, marched her into the morning-room.

"Sit down," he said sternly, "and let's have no more of your Banbury tales about laundry, and still-rooms! I pay servants to attend to such matters."

She sank down onto the chair he set for her, and sat staring up at him with frightened eyes.

"Come," he said more gently, "don't look so woebegone. Don't you know by now that I'm your friend?"

She turned her head away.

"Believe it," he said. "Believe that in three years, you've seldom been out of my thoughts." He sat down facing her. "I wrote to you, many times. I prayed for an answer, but none ever came."

"I had no letter from you."

"And felt no surprise at it?"

She looked at him fleetingly. "Jocelyn said . . . he told me that because of the war, many letters went to the bottom of the sea."

"Did you write to me?"

"At first. Once or twice. Then they said I should not . . . that it would give you a false idea of my sentiments . . . that it was best to make a clean break."

"What of Tal? Did he write to me?"

"He may have done. He used to scribble sometimes, at night.

He could have franked his own letter, and sent it to the mail." Amabel made a weary gesture. "He could as easily have thrown what he wrote on the fire. He was ill, his mind destroyed by brandy."

"You never thought to leave him?"

"Often. But if I tried to leave the house without him, he would send after me, and rage and weep like a maniac. I felt . . . I felt he'd become what he was, through my fault. I tried to atone for it by staying here with him. I tried. . . ."

Luke saw that she was trembling and turning her head from side to side, as if her memories were too much to bear. He said quickly, "Forget the letters. Tell me something else. Did Talbot ever stint you for money?"

Her violet eyes widened. "Stint? Why no! My allowance was more than generous, though sometimes he would take some wild start about economy." She added sadly, "There was little to spend on, in Rigborough."

"Did Tal handle the accounts himself?"

"No. You know how he hated to be troubled with bills. At first he would turn all over to Hunsdon, and say, 'See to it'. Later . . . after he was taken ill. . . ."

". . . after his first seizure, you mean?"

"Yes. After that, his whole nature changed. He was sometimes very low in spirit. At other times, he suffered such morbid imaginings, he terrified me! And the estate was neglected, because he could not see to anything. I was at my wits' end, to know how to manage."

"So you wrote to Cousin Jocelyn?"

"Yes. He came at once, with Edward. It was to be a short visit. The doctors said Talbot could not live long, but he survived the attack . . . and our cousins were so kind . . . everything was so much more comfortable with them to advise me . . . that it became a permanent arrangement."

"I see. What were Mr Hunsdon's views about the . . . er . . . new dispensation?"

For the first time, Amabel could not meet his eyes. "I did not seek Hunsdon's opinion," she said haughtily.

"Then you were in error. How long after our cousins arrived was Hunsdon given his *congé*?"

"Not long. A few months."

"Did you ever know Talbot to complain of his work?"

"I've told you, Talbot could no longer judge of anything save whether the bottle at his elbow was full or empty!"

"And you, Amabel? Were you dissatisfied with Hunsdon?"

"How should I know? Jocelyn said he was becoming too full of his own importance."

"Did you dislike him?"

"Dislike?" She put up her chin a little. "He was a servant. I neither liked nor disliked him."

"In fact, you never thought of him at all?"

Amabel caught the angry note in Luke's voice, and shrugged. "He was a dry old stick," she said petulantly. "I suppose he had grown too old to manage the accounts. I . . . I was sorry when Edward said he was to be turned off, but there was nothing I could do."

"You could have told the Clares to leave, and kept Hunsdon."

"No! I could not! I could not! You don't understand!"

Luke sighed. "After Hunsdon left, who handled the accounts? Was it Jocelyn?"

"I think so. He helped Talbot decide what should be paid, and what might stand over."

"Did Tal give money into Jocelyn's hands? Drafts on the bank, for instance, or coinage, or bills?"

"I don't know." Her voice rose. "I know nothing of such things, it's no use to question me."

"Quite right. I shall question Jocelyn, instead."

Amabel paled. "Luke, you won't offend him? He . . . he has been good to us. He used to sit with Talbot, late into the night. When Tal took an inflammation of the lungs, it was Jocelyn that insisted on bringing doctors from London, and took us off to Leamington Spa, and nursed Talbot with the greatest devotion!"

"No doubt," said Luke harshly, "he did not want to lose the goose that laid the golden eggs."

"You're wrong. Jocelyn wished to help us."

"What happened after Tal's death? Who paid the bills?"

"The . . . the lawyers gave us what we needed."

"Shedley gave money directly to you, did he?"

"Yes, for the household, and my pin-money."

"And you, Amabel? Did you ever give money to the Clares?"

"Of course not!" The reply came too pat, and Luke was sure she was lying. He put a finger under her chin so that she was forced to look at him.

"Tell me, my dear, are you afraid of Jocelyn?"

"No! Please let me go!"

"Then, do you fear me?"

She shook her head dumbly. Tears welled in her eyes and trickled down her cheeks.

"My pretty," Luke said softly, "how can I slay the dragon, if you won't tell me where he's hiding?"

She tried to smile, but could not. After a moment, she found her handkerchief and dabbed at her eyes, saying in a muffled voice, "I beg you won't regard this. I beg you won't speak of it to anyone."

Luke straightened. "Let's forget the past and talk of the future. I want you to understand that you need never worry about material things. You will have an ample income. It only remains to settle where you will live."

"I don't wish to leave Rowanbeck."

"Not at once, naturally. Later, though, when the Clares leave, it would be inadmissible for you to remain. Just think what the old cats would have to say!"

"Why must the Clares go?" She stared at him with feverish intensity. "Why cannot we just continue as we are? For my sake, Lucas, will you not permit it?"

"My child, it wouldn't serve. Much as I'm grateful to Edward, I intend to run my own property, just as he'll run his, some day. And you will like to have your establishment, will you not?"

"No. I prefer to stay here. I will be happier here."

"And when I marry, what then?"

"Marry?" Amabel stared at him bleakly. "Do you plan to marry?"

"In time, I must come to it, if only to secure the succession. You'll hardly like to live at Rowanbeck with some other female in charge! Perhaps you may like to have the Dower House? It's a respectable size, but not so large that it's burdensome to run. Gooden says it needs refurbishing. I expect you'll enjoy that? And it's so close to this house that you may stroll over and visit us whenever you feel inclined."

Amabel jumped to her feet. Her tears flowed faster than ever and she said in a choking voice. "I see how it is! You are determined to be rid of me."

"Nonsense, I'm merely. . . ."

"I was warned it would be so, but I dared to hope that after all that has passed between us . . . all we have m-meant to each other . . . you would not c-cast me off like an old shoe!"

Luke took a step forward and caught her by the shoulders "Amabel, what fustian! Who has been priming you with such a pack of lies? If it was Jocelyn, I make you a promise, you will soon be rid of him!"

"I will never be rid of him! Thanks to you, I'm tied to him for the rest of my days. You ran off and abandoned me, without a friend in the world, without protection. . . ."

He shook her. "You know damned well, it was to protect you I left England. For heaven's sake quit this play-acting, and tell me the truth!"

"You would not relish it, if I did."

"What do you mean?"

"I mean that between you, you have destroyed me. You, Talbot, Jocelyn—you have crushed my hopes to ashes!"

With this she wrenched free of his grasp and rushed sobbing from the room. Luke strode after her to the door. "Amabel! Come back here. Come back at once, I say!"

It was wasted breath. She was already flying across the Great Hall, making for the stairs. Moreover, Luke saw to his chagrin that he was not the sole witness to her flight.

Close to the main entrance stood a junior footman, his arms piled high with overcoats and hats. Next to him, frozen like the figures in a *tableau vivant*, and wearing expressions that ranged from the faintly embarrassed to the deeply censorious, were his cousin Cornelia Finch; Sir Murray Tredgold and his lady; Mrs Eulalie Wakeford and her son; and Miss Wakeford.

IX

Miss Wakeford had always found morning visits to be boring beyond words. One arrived, drank a little weak tea or a glass of mediocre sherry, exchanged a few perfectly insipid remarks with one's hosts, and as soon as the statutory twenty minutes was up, thankfully took one's leave.

On the other hand, such visits presented no social hazards. Morning callers did not slide under the table in a drunken stupor, did not flirt desperately with the parlour-maid or enter into inflamed political arguments. The rules were clearly defined to promote decorum and goodwill.

The sight of Amabel dashing headlong up the stairway filled Davina with foreboding. When guests surprise the lady of the house in a fit of strong hysterics, two courses are open to them. They may retreat unseen, or remain and pretend to have noticed nothing out of the way.

On this occasion, neither alternative was possible. Lord Rigg was already advancing towards them, his face ominously set; while one glance at her step-brother's flushed countenance showed that he would not let the incident pass without comment. Indeed, he stepped to meet the Earl with fists clenched, and demanded in the most peremptory tones what the devil his lordship had done to upset Lady Rigg.

It was an appalling effrontery, and Davina waited with a sinking heart for the expected setdown. But after a moment's icy silence, Lord Rigg said calmly, "My sister-in-law and I were talking of my late brother. I fear it put too great a strain on her sensibilities. You will forgive her if she does not come down to meet you."

He then directed a curt nod of dismissal at the footman, offered his arm to Mrs Wakeford who was closest to him, and led the party into the Long Drawing-room.

Even Mrs Wakeford was conscious of the awkwardness caused by Roland's rudeness, and she tried to mask her discomfort by talking effusively about Talbot Rowan.

"What a tragedy," she mourned, "that a career of such

promise should be brought to an untimely end. How well I understand dear Lady Rigg's sentiments. It must ever be painful to a widow to pronounce the name of a Loved One Gone Before. Why, it is close on a year since I lost my own dear husband, yet the slightest reference to him strikes a pang in my heart."

She then began to catechise the Earl on his plans for the future. He answered her with a cold courtesy that would have daunted anyone less thick-skinned than Eulalie. Yes, he said, he intended to remain in residence at Rowanbeck for some weeks to come. Yes, he proposed to ride to hounds, and would join the local hunt just as soon as he was able to pick up one or two likely mounts. (Roland's glower grew more furious still, at that.) Yes, he hoped to visit London during the Season, and yes, he would certainly open Rowan House.

However, when Mrs Wakeford tried to ask insinuating questions about the Clares, and enquired how long they would stay in Rigborough, Lord Rigg blocked her queries quite bluntly; and Gooden soon after appearing with the tray of sherry and madeira wine, he took the opportunity of moving away to sit with the Tredgolds.

Lady Sophia found herself in something of a dilemma. She held strong prejudices against the Rowan clan, terming them rakehelly and ramshackle. She certainly had no wish to strengthen the links between Wakeford Hall and Rowanbeck. But she also felt the need to compensate for Roland's lack of breeding, and therefore spoke to Lord Rigg with warm kindness, offered her condolences on his brother's death, and said she hoped Rowanbeck might now enter a happier era.

"When I was a girl," she said, "I spent many pleasant hours in this house. I was bosom bows with your Aunt Charlotte, you know. How does she do, these days? I vow it's an age since last we met."

"My aunt goes little into society, ma'am. Her interests lie in other directions—in her family, and her charitable work. She's patroness of I don't know how many worthy organisations."

"Well, it's a great shame, for I never knew anyone prettier, or with a livelier sense of fun, than Charlotte. Charity should be left to dull, pug-nosed females, don't you agree?"

Sir Murray then remarked that he had met Mr Joshua Turnbull several times during the campaign to end the slave rade. "I thought him an excellent man," he said. "Fox was high in his praises, for the way he stood out against slavery when most of the Cits thought only of their profits, and pressed for the slave-running to continue. Was it your aunt that interested him in the matter?"

"No, quite the reverse. My uncle was orphaned and suffered great privations as a child. It has given him a sympathy with others in like case, and what he feels to be wrong he contests."

Miss Wakeford, listening quietly to this exchange found herself revising her early opinions of his lordship. Up till now she had quite failed to see how Lady Sophy could describe him as a breaker of hearts. His features were too harsh to be called handsome. There was a coldness, an indifference in his regard that was repellent. Though his physique was splendid, and his style of dress admirable, there was something in his bearing that suggested he held the world in contempt. What is more, she felt that his air of detachment concealed a dangerous temper. When they had interrupted his quarrel with Amabel—Davina was sure it was a quarrel and not a discussion, as he claimed—there had been a look of fury on his face. It was easy to see how Amabel might go in terror of him.

Now, though, he displayed a different side of his nature. It had taken more than good manners to ignore Roland's gaffe. Davina suspected that Rigg was not the man to score off a weaker opponent. His expression, too, when he spoke of his Turnbull relations, quite altered. His smile was attractive, lighting his eyes. She liked the way he had defended his uncle. Nothing in the least snobbish about that. She began to see that Lord Rigg's character was more complex, and more interesting, than she had supposed.

Her attention was now diverted by Cornelia Finch, who had worked herself into a perfect panic, because the Wakeford party had witnessed the scene with Amabel.

"Such an embarrassment for you all," she lamented, "and it is all my fault! I should not have admitted you to the house! I should first have enquired if Cousin Luke was receiving. But it was the circumstances, Miss Wakeford! The chance of my being in the Hall just as your carriage drove up to the door. I simply told James to admit you. I pray that Lady Sophia will not think me quite without conduct. . . ."

"Of course she won't," Davina said, "and I don't see how you could have left us standing out in the cold. Don't fret, Miss Finch. Everyone knows that Amabel takes these starts. By now she'll very likely have forgotten all about it, and so must you."

Miss Finch was not to be consoled, and continued to apologise until Davina diverted her thoughts by asking the history of the portrait above the fireplace. Miss Finch's passion for genealogy was stirred, and when Lord Rigg turned to speak to Miss Wakeford he found her gazing at the likeness of a gentleman in an unbecoming black hat, and a white quaker collar.

"Nicholas, the second Earl of Rigg," Miss Finch was saying, "fought with distinction at the Battle of Naseby, and later served as a member of Oliver Cromwell's exchequer. Have I that right Cousin Luke?"

"Word perfect," said the Earl, "though I fear the old devil robbed the poor to feed the rich. Consider those close-set, beady eyes, Miss Wakeford. Note how they seem to follow one about the room. Wouldn't you say the fellow knows to a farthing what each of us is worth?"

"Undoubtedly. There is a description of Nicholas in our library, at Wakeford. A political satire. It refers to him twice as Nick Nipcheese, and once as Nick Clutchpenny."

"Oh, I cannot think that true," said Miss Finch, much shocked. "The slander of an enemy, no doubt! There is no mention of pennypinching in the New Guide to Rigborough which the dear Vicar has recently compiled."

"If guide-books spoke the truth," said the Earl, "then ancient monuments would be visited much more often than they are at present." He looked challengingly at Davina. "And twice as many pilgrims would come to wicked Rowanbeck, as did to virtuous Wakeford Hall, I'll lay odds."

"Not at all," retorted Davina. "You have Nicholas. We have John Wakeford, who tried to steal the succession from his brother, by smuggling a male baby into his wife's lying-in. The child was concealed in a warming-pan, but cried so lustily that the fraud was discovered."

"Errol Rowan," countered the Earl, "was beheaded on Tower Green, for treason."

"Cuthbert de Wakeford was hanged, drawn and quartered, for the same crime."

"The third Baron de Rohan," said his lordship, with the air of one producing a sure winner, "was accused of practising the black arts, and burned at the stake. His spectre is said to walk the gallery on Walpurgis Night."

"At Wakeford," said Davina smugly, "we have two ghosts, and one of them drives a carriage drawn by six headless horses."

The Earl spread his hands. "For the time, I give you best! But I shall make a recover, never fear."

At this moment, the stable clock beginning to chime the hour, Lady Sophy said that they had taken up enough of Lord Rigg's time, and led her party away. In the carriage she leaned her head against the squabs with an exhausted air, declaring that never in her life had she endured a more uncomfortable visit, and that if Roland could not behave with common politeness when he was abroad, he'd best remain at home.

Roland replied that he was not a whit sorry for his words. "I meant everything I said, and in any case, Rigg didn't care. It's nothing to him that we know how brutally he uses that poor defenceless angel."

"I saw no brutality," said Sir Murray.

"You heard him shout at her. The whole of Rigborough must have heard."

"If I had to live with a weeping willow like Amabel Rowan, I'd shout. Might even deal her a slap or two, for good measure."

"You may crack jokes, sir, but it's plain that Rigg has been forcing his attentions on her, that he plans to dishonour her!"

"It's not plain to me, and if you talk in that fashion, my lad, you'll soon land in the suds!"

"I shall speak my mind at all times. If Rigg calls me out, I shall meet him."

"Don't be a fool! Rigg might give you a bloody nose, but he'll not demean himself by calling out a stripling that can't hit a house at ten paces! Come to that, I wouldn't care to feel the weight of his hand. He'd strip to advantage, I'd say. A hundred and eighty pounds, if he's an ounce, and muscles hard as teak."

Roland seemed disposed to argue, but his mother put a hand on his arm.

"Hush, my dear," she said. "Whatever you may feel in your heart, it's better to hide it, for if you don't, people will say you are jealous of Lord Rigg."

"Jealous? Why should I be? Amabel detests the man. She told me so."

"As to that," returned his mama, "I can't agree with you. don't think Amabel finds Rigg's advances at all distasteful. S welcomed them in the past, when he was no more than t second son. Now he's an earl, and owns a fortune as well. No doubt but Amabel will wish to take up with him. Perhaps sl hopes to be his Countess, who knows?"

"She could not!" Roland's face twisted. "She could not sir so low!"

"If Rigg offers for her, she'll be a fool to refuse him."

"I'll not listen to you," Roland shouted. "And I'll not allo Rigg to lay a finger on her. If he tries, I swear to God, I'll ki him."

When the carriage drew up at Wakeford Hall, he sprang ou at once and dashed into the house. Sir Murray, watching hi go, shook his head at his sister-in-law.

"That was not well said, Eulalie."

Mrs Wakeford bridled. "Roland is my son, and I shall sa what I like to him. I won't have him dangling after a widov years older than he is, and of dubious reputation! I intend t nip that little romance in the bud!"

"Do as you please, but don't set Roland up against Luk Rowan. It's downright madness."

"Oh, tush! Roland is all talk. It means nothing."

"I sincerely hope you may be right, but remember, at tha age a man is guided by impulse, not reason. I suggest you rid Roland on a light rein, for if you don't he may bolt, and come real cropper."

"Roland is not a horse, and I'll thank you not to talk c him as one." Mrs Wakeford flounced into the Hall, and sai imperiously to Davina, "I am going to my bed. I feel one of m spasms coming on, and I'm chilled to the marrow. It's a pity w cannot have better fires at Wakeford. I suppose it is one of you new economies, to freeze us to death in order to save a fev shillings on firewood. You may help me upstairs, and the instruct Eliza to fetch me up a hot posset, with nutmeg."

When Mrs Wakeford and Davina had gone, Sir Murra turned to his wife. "That woman," he said crossly, "is infallible She's always wrong!"

Lady Sophia drew her fur pelerine more closely about her shoulders. "She's right about one thing," she said. "This house is miserably cold. Did you notice how yellow the sky is, to the north? I expect we shall have snow within a day or so."

As soon as the Wakeford party had driven away from Rowanbeck, Lord Rigg went to his study, where a pile of correspondence awaited his attention. He had sorted through this and was busy trimming a pen, when the door was flung wide, and Jocelyn Clare strode into the room. He advanced to the desk and stood glaring down at Luke.

"I have been speaking to Amabel," he said abruptly. "She has told me how harshly you have treated her!"

The Earl laid aside knife and pen and leaned back in his chair. "You are the second person in an hour to accuse me of brutality," he said, "without having the smallest right to do so."

"Right? It is a question of common compassion, Rigg! The child is distraught. She was weeping so, she could hardly frame her words."

"Indeed?" Luke shook his head. "That is serious. Amabel's tantrums do not in general last more than ten minutes. A full hour is something of a record."

"You may make light of it. Society, I think, will not."

"And you, of course, intend to acquaint society with my infamous conduct?"

"I shall certainly make it known that you have banished Amabel from her home."

Luke studied his cousin's countenance. It was pale, and shone with points of sweat.

"I have not banished her," he said mildly. "I've offered her the Dower House, but if she prefers another of my properties, I'll arrange it."

"Provided she leaves Rowanbeck?"

"I fear her reputation would not benefit if she attempted to live here alone with me."

"Aha! Now we come to it! What you mean is that you are evicting Edward and me!"

"'Evicting?' A strange word, Jocelyn. I never understood you to be in permanent residence here. Edward speaks of removing to Bath. And as I remember, you own a house in London and a shooting-box in Leicestershire. I don't wish to pry, but perhaps you will find one or other place congenial."

"The shooting-box was sold years ago."

"Then it must be London, for you. Really, you know, I never thought you would be anxious to remain at Rowanbeck now that it is . . . er . . . under new management."

"I can't say I'm surprised at your attitude, Rigg. Common gratitude was never your forte. Evidently you wish to forget all my family has done for you and Talbot, over the past few years."

"There you mistake, Cousin." The Earl's voice was silky. "I shall forget nothing that either you or Edward has done. That is a promise."

Sir Jocelyn glared at the Earl for a moment or two, then said softly, "I don't think, Lucas, that you can have considered all the arguments against such a decision."

"I have tried to. I'm prepared to hear fresh ones, if you know of any."

Again Sir Jocelyn hesitated. Then he moved away from the desk, and sat down.

"It is a delicate matter," he murmured. "One which, as a gentleman, I have hesitated to raise."

"My feelings are not so nice. Pray continue."

"Then . . . I must tell you that I know the truth of what happened on the night Talbot was shot. I had the facts from Amabel herself. I am sure you will agree she is in the best possible position to know them. I am also sure that you will not want the story to go any further."

Luke picked up the penknife and turned it slowly in his fingers, so that the blade caught the firelight. "I think you should know," he said, "that before I came down here, I visited Bow Street, and talked with Sir Nathanial Conant. He told me that the matter of the shooting is closed. No charge will ever be preferred, against . . . anyone."

"Ah, but we are not talking of the process of law, my dear fellow. We are not discussing the views of a magistrate, or even of a Judge on his bench. We are talking of our peers, of society, a body which you well know is apt to condemn or condone on the lightest of whims. I ask myself how society will regard the facts of this case."

"I neither know, nor care."

"Ah yes, you were always arrogant. But what of Amabel? She, poor girl, won't wish to put things to the test." Jocelyn's tone became suddenly sharper. "Come, let's have done with fencing, Rigg. I know it was Amabel and not you that shot Talbot. She had good reason to kill him. His drunken ways, his physical abuse of her—motive for murder, many will say."

"There was no question of murder. It was an accident."

"Who will swallow that tale? And what will be Amabel's chance of being accepted by the ton? Of remarriage to any decent man?"

"Are you threatening to accuse her of murder?" Luke's voice held such a deadly calm that Sir Jocelyn glanced at him quickly, under his lids.

"I have uttered no threats," he answered smoothly. "Merely, I paint the picture of what may befall if I tell what I know."

"Blackmail, Jocelyn?"

"An ugly word, Luke. Let us rather call it bargaining. I admit I find it hard to be tossed out of Rowanbeck in this fashion. I can, as you so kindly point out, go to London, but you must know that my purse is not at all plump at the moment. I've suffered reverses of recent times, and my fortunes have only just begun to mend. I leave it to you to consider how I may be helped over my difficulties. As for my brother Edward, you will have heard that he is anxious to fix his interest with Miss Wakeford. He has asked her to marry him, and awaits her decision. He will hardly like to leave Rigborough, at this present. However, you must talk to him about that. Our main concern —our joint concern—must be Amabel. We must plan for her peace of mind, her comfort, in fact her entire future happiness. It rests in our hands." Jocelyn rose from his chair and sauntered towards the door. "Don't think I am trying to force your decision, my dear Lucas. There is no need to act hastily. I'm sure that in time we shall work out a modus vivendi that will suit us all!"

Luke said coldly, "You have until the end of the week to quit this house, Jocelyn."

"Oh, certainly. It is, in any case, against my nature to live where the atmosphere is unfriendly, and the manners farouche."

He left the room, closing the door gently after him. Lord Rigg sat for some time deep in thought. Then he drew a sheet of paper towards him, picked up his pen, and began to write.

It was about an hour later that there came a knock on the study door, and Edward Clare appeared. He stood uncertainly on the threshold until Luke invited him in, and once seated, seemed unable to say why he had come.

Luke put him out of his misery. "Well, Ned. Come to tell me my fortune?"

"No, of course not!" Edward looked uncomfortable. "I gather . . . Jocelyn told me . . . that there've been ructions. You wish us to leave Rowanbeck."

"I don't remember having said anything of the sort to you."

"But you do wish it?"

"I think it inevitable, in the long term. Don't you?"

Edward met his eyes, and after a minute nodded. "Yes. It wouldn't fadge, for us to stay. Can't have more than one bull in a herd. When do you want us to go?"

"There's no hurry. Rather the contrary. I'll be going to London on business soon, and would much prefer to know you are here, seeing to things. But as I said, we must think of the long term. I've heard you speak of going to your grandfather's place, at Bath?"

"Yes."

"A smallish place, is it?"

"Respectable. Nothing like Rowanbeck, of course."

"Your talents deserve better. I've been wondering whether you might not prefer to manage Graydon for me."

"Graydon?" Edward's face lit up. "Do you mean it?"

"Certainly I do. I imagine it must be in pretty poor shape, is it not?"

"Oh . . . tol-lol, you know. I've kept an eye on it, but that's not the same as living on the acres, and being able to direct things aright."

"We'll drive over, some day, and see what needs to be done. Is the house habitable?"

"Lord, yes, nothing that a lick of paint can't cure. The

pasturage is in excellent heart, too, having lain fallow so long. I think your main problem will be to recruit labour."

"Your main problem," corrected the Earl. "We'll come to some financial arrangement. I've a fancy to be paid a nominal rent—a barrel of Rhenish, say, or a cheese a year. It will be up to you to make what you can from the farm."

"You're more than generous." Edward's expression had clouded a little. "Luke, why are you doing this?"

"Self-interest," said the Earl promptly.

"You could find any number of men who'd leap at the chance of running Graydon."

"Not of my own kin. I've always thought your father should have had the place."

Still Edward hesitated. "There's something you should know," he said. "It's been on my conscience. The night you left Rowanbeck with Amabel, I saw you go. I sent one of the stable-lads after you, to see which road you took, and next morning I told Talbot. I . . . I believed it to be my duty. I never dreamed it would come to bloodshed."

Luke shrugged. "What happened was an accident, a gun mishandled, no more. That's all you need remember."

"Talbot said the same. He never thought ill of you. He often spoke of you, and wished you'd come home." Edward was watching Luke with anxious eyes. "I thought, sometimes, of sending you a line, but I feared to meddle in what didn't concern me. Now you know the truth, I suppose you'll wish to reconsider your offer."

"No," said Luke matter-of-factly. "We'll visit Graydon when the weather eases, and next time I'm in London, I'll have old Shedley draw up a formal agreement."

Mr Clintwood, who had spent the day at Oxford with friends, returned late to Rowanbeck. On being told the full history of the day's events, he voiced the opinion that Jocelyn Clare should be publicly denounced.

"The man's a thief," he said, "a scoundrelly, blackmailing shabster. He's terrorised that poor girl for years. Hanging's too good for him."

"Agreed, but we have to think of Amabel. If I expose Jocelyn he'll spread it abroad that she shot Tal because he discovered us abed together."

"Then we'll counter with the truth—that Talbot flew into one of his rages and threatened her, that she snatched up the pistol to warn him away, and it went off."

"It's my experience that society invariably chooses to believe the more salacious tale. Amabel could never face another scandal, Clint. Public approval means everything to her. Why else do you imagine I gave out it was I that shot Tal? If you could have seen her that night, so desperate, so terrified of the consequences—I had to do what I could to spare her."

"All I know is that you can't let that dog Clare get away with this. If you do, he'll batten on you for the rest of your days."

"No. I won't allow that." There was so much quiet menace in the Earl's voice, that Mr Clintwood was alarmed.

"No violence," he warned. "You couldn't stand the racket. Raise a hand to Jocelyn, and you'd have the law down on you like a wolfpack."

Luke shook his head. "There's more ways than one to skin a cat," he said. "My uncle Joshua is busy delving into Jocelyn's affairs. I've no doubt he'll be able to furnish enough material to fashion Jocelyn's shroud."

X

LADY SOPHIA'S PREDICTION that the weather would worsen proved correct. The day after the visit to Rowanbeck, bitter winds began to sweep in from the north-east, snow blanketed the hilltops, and the local shepherds made haste to bring their flocks from high ground to the shelter of the valley.

The intense cold continued for two days, confining all but those with essential tasks to their homes. Tempers at Wakeford Hall became querulous. Mrs Wakeford found endless fault with the food, her family, and the servants. Roland, unable to go out riding or meet his cronies, fell into a fit of the sullens, rousing himself only to crab about his neighbours in general and Lord Rigg in particular. Even Lady Sophy, whose nature was sunny, complained of the headache, while Becky said flatly that if that pesky wind didn't drop soon, she'd be fit only for Bedlam.

Luckily, during Friday night, the storm blew itself out. Davina woke to a silence so complete she was sure there must be snow on the ground; but when she stepped from her bed and went to the window, she saw that Rigborough and the surrounding countryside were in the grip of a white frost.

It was a landscape transformed that stretched about her. Every tree was traced with fire, every reed a drawn sword, and every pebble a diamond. The early sun struck bursts of brilliant scarlet, blue and gold from the frozen canal, and the aspens near the house gave off a continual tingling music, like Chinese bells.

For a moment she could only marvel at the beauty of this world, but she was soon reminded that to farming folk, frost is no friend. Hoby brought a message to say that the pipes in the kitchen were frozen solid, and like to burst. The head stockman next appeared, with urgent pleas for fodder to be carted to the high crofts, as the animals were unable to graze. To cap all, as Davina was snatching a hurried breakfast, Sir Murray brought the news that her aunt was running a high fever, and he thought the doctor must be summoned immediately.

Dr Burrows arrived at eleven, and pronounced Lady Sophy

to be suffering from the influenza, which was very prevalent at the moment. He prescribed bed-rest and promised to send round a paregoric to help reduce the fever. By the time he left, and the patient had been comfortably settled, it was nearly noon, and time for luncheon.

This was an uncomfortable meal since Sir Murray and Mrs Wakeford chose to fall out over the proper treatment of *la grippe*, and by the time the table was cleared Davina was heartily sick of her relations, and glad to escape to the bookrooms.

She was working on a catalogue of the paintings in the house, several of which had been brought to the library because they stood in need of repair. She found herself thinking, as she sorted through these, that it would be exceedingly pleasant to sell Wakeford, and purchase some quite small house where she might live a life of peace and seclusion. She would have her books, and would keep two cats and a fat spaniel for company. Friends would visit her, and from time to time a learned professor from Oxford or Cambridge would come to discuss a mediaeval text, or debate a point of scholarship.

It was a pleasant enough scenario, provided one was inured to being a spinster. Davina was not sure this was the case. The alternative was to marry Edward Clare. If she did, how would her life be altered? She would enjoy security, the pleasures of a shared existence, companionship, perhaps love in time, and children.

Yet somehow, she found the prospect of marriage to Edward daunting. For one thing, he would insist on residing at Wakeford. He had said more than once that it was a fine house, just the sort of place for a gentleman's family. For another, he was not a man who thought highly of the pursuits of the mind. His own understanding was narrow, and though he chaffed her now about her passion for reading, might he not prove a good deal less tolerant, once they were married?

Davina sighed. With the exception of the Vicar, who was seventy and a grandfather, Rigborough men were not bookish, and they certainly did not wish for bookish wives.

That was why it had been so delightful, last Wednesday, to converse with Lord Rigg. He had not lectured her, nor condescended to her, but had chatted as does one intelligent being to another. He had shown considerable knowledge of

Rigborough history, but treated it with a refreshing lack of respect. Talking to him, she had glimpsed that brilliant world in which music and the arts were held as important as hunting or the state of the crops, where one might attend a scientific address, a concert, and a dress ball all in one day, and where females were positively encouraged to take as much interest in politics and poetry as in the housewifely skills.

This bright image was shattered by the sound of Roland's voice, calling her name with some urgency. A moment later he burst through the door, his eyes shining.

"Dav," he said, "the most famous thing! The ice is holding on the pond and the canal, too. The whole village is down there, playing the goat. Dashed if we shouldn't look out the old skates, and go and join 'em!"

Rigborough had succumbed to the spirit of winter carnival. At several points on the village green, water had been poured to make slides for the infant brigade, while their elder brothers and sisters could be seen on the pond, the timorous pushing chairs before them, the bold striking out alone, or spinning round and round in a long rat's-tail. Their shrieks of excitement rang on the frosty air.

The innkeeper of the Grey Goose, ever quick to scent the chance of gain, had fetched several iron braziers from his stable-yard, and set them up on the grass. His cook and his kitchen-maid were busy roasting chitterlings, chops, and whole potatoes over the coals. Meantime his tapman was rolling barrels of ale from the main tap to a makeshift trestle under the elms, and his wife, Mrs Tucker, was dispensing flagons to a steady stream of customers.

Davina and Roland made their way past the edge of this crowd. A number of people were already skating on the canal, which ran in a straight cut from the village to the river some half a mile distant. Their antics were attracting a large audience, some of whom stood on the gently sloping banks, while others enjoyed a grandstand view from the line of carts and wagons drawn up along the road.

The Rowanbeck party could be seen further along the cut. Amabel, looking radiant in a cherry-red pelisse trimmed with winter ermine, was seated in an open carriage, holding court to a group of gentlemen who stood alongside. Davina recognised

Robert Clintwood, Mr Quintus Sibley, and Squire Osmund among them. There was no sign of Edward or Jocelyn Clare. Lord Rigg was already on the ice, executing a series of neat figure eights.

Seeing him, Roland gave a snort of disgust. "Coxcomb!" he said. "We can do without such dandified airs in Rigborough!" He then announced that he felt he ought to enquire how Lady Rigg did, and thrusting a pair of skates into Davina's hands, went hurrying off.

Davina made her way to a quiet stretch of the canal, tied on her skates, and edged gingerly onto the ice. It was years since she had skated, and at first she felt most insecure, but the trick of it soon came back, so that she was bold enough to join the crowd on the widest part of the cut.

She discovered at once that survival lay not so much in watching her step, as in steering a course through the skaters, many of whom were well-charged with Mr Tucker's best home-brewed. She had made several successful circuits, and was beginning to feel quite confident, when disaster struck in the form of four-year-old Master William Tucker.

This hopeful infant had been given a bag of baked potatoes by his doting mama. Unwilling to share the loot with his peers, he was hot-footing it along the towpath when he missed his step, and fell. His solid form, swathed in numberless coats, gaiters and scarves, rolled like a puffball down the bank and shot onto the ice, straight in Davina's path. Unable to change course, she was knocked off her feet. Willie's bag of potatoes burst, discharging its contents like cannonballs to fell two or three more skaters. Yet others sprawled over them.

Master Tucker, more shocked than hurt, set up a banshee wail. His mama rushed to enquire what ailed her darling. His papa adjured him from the bank to stand up like a man and not act the looby. Mr Smithers the greengrocer, who was nursing a bloodied nose, said bitterly that what the lad needed was a sound slapping, while Mr Venable from the smithy roared out that his breeks was split from stem to starn, and he'd want the price of a new pair from someone.

Onto this field of carnage stepped the Earl of Rigg. He assisted Miss Wakeford to her feet, then seized Master Tucker by the slack of his trews, lifted him like a puppy and said brusquely,

"Well, young varmint, what will you have, a sound slap, or a shilling?"

"Shillun'," said Master Tucker, ever his father's son. The Earl dropped a coin into the child's paw and set him on his feet again, then turned back to Miss Wakeford.

"Are you all right, ma'am?"

"Perfectly, thank you." Miss Wakeford straightened her bonnet, which was canted over one eye. "Did you really give that horrid boy a shilling?"

"Yes. It seemed cheap at the price. Do you think I've ruined his character?"

"No—only the going rate in bribery."

He smiled lazily down at her. "Ah, but you see, I have to redeem my family's reputation for stinginess. 'Nipcheese', I think, was the word you used?" He offered his arm. "Come, take a turn or two with me. It's best to make a quick recoup, when one's taken a toss."

Davina allowed him to lead her onto the ice. She felt a little shaky, but the muscles under Lord Rigg's sleeve were reassuringly solid. After a few circuits, she found she was able to forget about her feet, and look up into his face.

"You're an expert, sir."

"No, I assure you. The Canadians, now, are truly masters of the art. In Montreal, where the winters are very harsh, even urchins as young as Will Tucker dart about like dragonflies."

"When were you in Canada?"

"From October of last year, until Christmas, when I moved south to Boston."

Davina heaved a sigh of envy. "I suppose you must have seen a great deal of the world?"

"Yes. Rather more than I care to remember."

"I don't see how that's possible. Have you been to the Far East, my lord?"

"To India, Java, and Ceylon." Lord Rigg increased his speed slightly, and Davina clutched at his arm.

"Pearl-divers," she said giddily. "In Ceylon, there are pearl-divers, I believe?"

"There are," agreed his lordship. "The best of them can hold their breath for as long as four minutes at a time, but there's no need for you to emulate them. If you wish to slow down, just say so."

"No!" She gave him a sudden, sparkling smile. "I never enjoyed anything so much."

At that he extended his left hand to take hers in the skaters' crossgrip. Arms linked, they began to skim along the canal at what seemed breakneck speed. Cottages and fields, and pollarded willows spun past, the bright air stung, their skates rang on the ice. Soon no other person was in sight. One part of Davina's mind warned that it was quite improper for her to be skating alone with Lord Rigg, and that she would certainly be castigated for such fast behaviour. Another replied that for once in her life she was doing precisely as she wished, in the company of her choice. A delightful recklessness possessed her.

"Tell me about India," she said.

He obliged her by describing the Coromandel coast, the monsoon jungles further north, and the great deserts beyond. He spoke of hunting tiger from the back of an elephant, and told her of the peoples of India, their intricate religious customs, their many tongues and diverse costumes.

It seemed to Davina that they reached the end of the canal all too soon. There their path was blocked by the embankment and lock that separated the cut from the river, and they turned homeward, but skating slowly, pleasantly at ease with each other.

"Some day," Davina said, "I shall travel. It may be difficult for an unattached female to do so, but if Lady Hester Stanhope could go as far as Arabia, surely I may aspire to Italy, or even Greece?" She added thoughtfully, "I must say, I would *not* wish to live in a Bedouin tent. It must be an excessively sandy sort of existence, don't you think, as well as attracting a great deal of notoriety?"

"Quite right. Notoriety is extremely wearing."

She glanced up quickly. "I'm sorry. I wasn't digging at you."

"I know you weren't." He looked at her consideringly. "You will marry, you know, and your husband may then take you abroad, with all the panoply of couriers, maids and valets."

"Somehow that would not be an adventure. And from what I've learned, English husbands do not like to leave England. I should have to marry a diplomat, or a serving officer, and I don't know how it is, but at present I can't seem to lay hands on either."

She spoke lightly, but there was an undertone of regret in her voice. Watching her, Lord Rigg reflected that Miss Wakeford was an odd sort of girl. She seemed to possess no artifice. No one had taught her to blush, to pout, to flutter coy lashes. She seemed prone to say whatever came into her head, and her speech was as plain as her deplorable garb. She was in no way awed by his consequence, but appeared rather to pity him for not being a Wakeford. Although she was certainly aware of his history, she was not in the least perturbed by it. Above all—and this piqued a man who was used to securing instant attention from every female in his vicinity—she showed not the smallest disposition to flirt with him. At the moment she had apparently forgotten him completely, for her grey eyes were fixed on space, and her thoughts were evidently miles away.

Lord Rigg cleared his throat. Davina turned to smile at him. "I was woolgathering," she said, "or rather, I was thinking of something that might interest you."

"I am all attention."

"I could not but notice," she said, "when we examined the portraits of your family, that there was none of your Aunt Charlotte among them."

"No." He sounded regretful. "When she eloped with my uncle, my father ordered all pictures of her to be destroyed."

"One survived," said Davina. "Your steward sent it to Wakeford for safekeeping, and we have it still. It depicts the Three Graces, Lady Charlotte being one of them."

"I can't remember ever to have seen it. Who is the artist?"

"A Mr Bridgeworthy—a pupil, I think, of Sir Joshua Reynolds."

"A pupil?" Lord Rigg's gaze became thoughtful. "May I ask who are the other two subjects?"

"My mother Serena Wakeford, and my Aunt Sophia Tredgold."

"So you may lay claim to two Graces, over my one. I imagine that gives you the superiority."

"No, because the work was commissioned and paid for by your grandfather. It belongs at Rowanbeck."

"Umh. Tell me, Miss Wakeford, what do you consider to be the artistic merit of the painting?"

Davina cast him a doubtful look. "That's hard to say. Not having known Lady Charlotte in her youth, I can't swear to its being a good likeness. It may be that Mr Bridgeworthy somewhat exaggerated the cast in your aunt's eye. As to the flesh-tones, I am not myself fond of those rather purplish hues, but you may think them lifelike. In any event, they are bound to flake away. The pigment is badly cracked in places."

"Ah! And how large is the picture, ma'am?"

"Oh . . . I suppose . . . not much above ten foot long, and six deep."

Lord Rigg fixed her with a kindling eye. "I tell you what," he said, "we'll make it even-steven. I will take your Graces, and you may have my Massacre of Saint Bartholomew. It's about of a size with your work, and the bloodstains are as bright as the day they were painted. What do you say?"

"Impossible, sir. I could not ask such a sacrifice of you."

"You drive a hard bargain. Yet I don't despair. I can offer you a fine Saint Sebastian—stuck full of arrows as a pincushion, but still addressing the soldiery in the most uplifting way! Or if you dislike religious subjects, how about a deathmask of Robespierre, done in yellow wax? Or the Delhi epergne, of brass in the form of six elephants with trunks upraised? The whole may be made to revolve, and play 'Rule Britannia'. I see you are tempted by that!"

The banter continued until they reached the village. The sun had by now gone down behind the ridge, and the pond and surrounding green lay in deep shadow. Most of the skaters had retired to the warmth of the inn, and those who remained on the banks of the canal were much the worse for drink.

"We've had the best of the day," Lord Rigg said. "Shall we quit the field in good order?"

He helped her to take off her skates and climb the bank. The Rowanbeck party had vanished, and Roland was sitting some way off, huddled over a fast-dying fire. When he caught sight of Davina, he beckoned furiously. She waved, and then held out her hand to his lordship.

"My brother will see me home," she said. "Thank you for a delightful afternoon." She started along the tow-path, but turned to call back to him, "I'll have The Three Graces delivered to you tomorrow. It's really a charming picture."

Before he could answer, she was gone, running across the grass to join her brother. Lord Rigg stood looking after her for a moment, then set off homewards through the woods.

Roland began to berate Davina as soon as she reached his side.

"What the devil do you mean by going off with Rigg in that hoydenish way? You've been warned against him often enough, yet you disappear into the blue with him for well-nigh an hour! I dare say every tongue in the village is wagging by this time. Lady Rigg was quite in disgust of your conduct."

Davina flashed him a look. "Was she indeed? Did she tell you so?"

"Certainly not. She has too much breeding, but I could see how she felt. I tell you, I was ready to sink! How do you suppose I'm to fix my interest with her, if my own sister is going about behaving like some demi-rep?"

Davina wheeled to face him. "Be so good as to mind your language, Roly. And what do you mean, 'fix your interest'?"

"What I say, damn you! I hope to marry Amabel, some day!"

"Don't be absurd! She'll never so much as look at you!"

"And why not, pray?"

"For one thing, she's years older than you."

"Not so many, and what does age matter, when there's true love, true devotion?"

"Oh . . . nothing, perhaps! But you know you can't even think of marriage, yet."

An evil glint appeared in Roland's eyes. "You mean I have nothing to offer . . . no property . . . no fortune. And whose fault is that, may I ask? I'd be flush enough if your father hadn't treated me so scaly. I have him to thank for my empty pockets, and as if that ain't enough, here's Rigg come back to spoil my chances. Amabel was glad enough of my company, till he arrived to flaunt his wealth and title. Now I can hardly get so much as the time o' day from her. And you make things worse for me. Oh, it's too bad! You shan't get off light, I warn you. Mama shall know of your behaviour, and then we shall see!"

He snatched up his skates and rushed away up the slope towards Wakeford Hall, leaving Davina to follow as best she might.

XI

WHEN ROLAND BURST into his mama's boudoir, he was in a state bordering on hysteria. He flung himself on his knees beside her chair, and poured out a diatribe about his love for Amabel, his loathing for Lord Rigg, and his fury at Davina's lack of conduct.

Mrs Wakeford was not a perceptive woman, except where her own interests were concerned, but the events of the past few days had convinced her that her son's passion for Lady Rigg was not a passing thing, as she had hoped.

It was essential to engineer a breach between her own family and the Rowans, before some disaster occurred.

Amabel herself would present no obstacle. If she had encouraged Roland at all (which Eulalie very much doubted), it was out of boredom and loneliness. Now, with Lord Rigg home, and her period of mourning at an end, Amabel would waste no time at all on a penniless boy.

Roland, too, could be handled. It should not prove hard to lure him to London. Once there, he could be left to sow his wild oats with the other young bloods. Let him drink, gamble, and mill, above all let him pursue pretty women, whether virtuous or not. He would soon forget Amabel's charms.

Davina's case was different. Mrs Wakeford felt quite faint with annoyance at the thought of her step-daughter. Never could there have been a more stubborn, cross-grained creature! To refuse the Tredgolds' offer of a season in London was pure selfishness, born of a desire to spite her own kith and kin.

Mrs Wakeford dismissed out of hand the argument that Davina wished to remain in Rigborough on Edward Clare's account. Anyone with half an eye could see that the handsome lobcock bored Davina to tears. There was no danger there.

But one must give very serious attention to the rapport that seemed to be building between Davina and Lord Rigg. Eulalie had watched with deep misgiving his manner towards the girl when they visited Rowanbeck. That man-of-the-world air, that easy, frank, teasing way of talking were just what would appeal to a young woman with no experience of life. Even Rigg's scandalous reputation was to be feared. It was well known that young girls adored a rake. Lord Rigg was quite capable of setting up one of his casual flirtations, merely to keep in practice; and if Davina was to fall for the lure, then nothing would make her go to London, and all their hopes would be destroyed.

Mrs Wakeford allowed Roland to talk himself to a standstill, and then told him bracingly that he must leave all in her hands. "Don't nag at your sister," she cautioned. "Least said is soonest mended! As for your sentiments towards Lady Rigg, I advise you to keep those to yourself. Don't show your disappointments, for if you do, people will only laugh at you behind their hands, and take you for a mooncalf."

As soon as Roland had left her, Mrs Wakeford rang for her maid, and ordered her first to make up the fire, and then to go and fetch Miss Wakeford.

Davina received the summons without surprise. She was used to Roland's tale-bearing, and had learned to deal with her step-mother's scolds by listening meekly, saying nothing, and afterward continuing on her own chosen path.

Tonight, however, she was surprised to find herself received with the utmost friendliness. As she entered the room, Eulalie extended a welcoming hand, invited her warmly to sit down, and remarked that she hoped she was not encroaching too much on Davina's time.

"I wish to have a little cose with you, my dear. To be honest, I don't know whom else to confide in. I am gravely worried about Roland, you know. The poor boy has been pouring out his heart to me, this past hour and more. His emotions are quite overset. I fear he may do something desperate, and all because he fancies himself to be in love with Amabel Rowan."

"I don't think Amabel takes Roly seriously," Davina said.

"Exactly my view, but I cannot make Roland see it. You know how headstrong he is. He cannot bear to be thwarted. If I'm to wean him from this very unsuitable affair, I shall need your help."

"Mine? Mama, Roland won't heed what I say!"

"He might, my love, if only you would not provoke him! Allow me to give you a little hint. You should avoid putting a man upon his high horse, for then you will get nothing from him. Roland told me you two had crossed swords this afternoon, because you went skating with Lord Rigg. Now I must say that that was not wise in you, my dear, not wise at all."

As Davina started to reply, Mrs Wakeford held up a minatory hand. "No, let me finish. I do not reprove you. I am sure you saw nothing wrong in accepting Rigg's invitation, indeed it may have been hard to refuse. While there are folk who contend that Rigg must be kept outside the pale—certainly he will not be admitted to decent London homes—we all know that Rigborough is not London. No doubt you did not wish to appear standoffish. But though I don't wish to distress you, I feel it to be my duty to warn you that Rigg's motives for paying you such particular attention may be . . . well . . . unprincipled."

"I assure you, mama, you are making too much of this."

"I hope you are right, Davina. I believe you acted in innocence, just as I am convinced that Rigg did not."

A coldness began to enter Davina's mind. "I don't understand what you mean," she said.

"Of course you don't, because you are a straightforward sort of girl, and not familiar with the ways of the ton. Among them, philandery is common-place, in fact it is almost *de rigueur* for a gentleman to flirt with every personable female in sight. No, don't fly out at me, I beg! I have seen too many girls sink into a decline because they have been deceived and cheated by just such practised rakes as his lordship."

"Lord Rigg," said Davina in a firm voice, "did not flirt with me. We talked of his travels—of India, and North America. If Roly hadn't formed the ridiculous notion that he can marry Amabel, nobody would have noticed the incident, and we wouldn't be sitting here making a to-do over nothing!"

Eulalie smiled sweetly. "You have missed the point," she said. "Roland did not object to your skating with Rigg. I daresay he would not have thought twice about it, had not Amabel drawn his attention to it."

"I fail to see. . . ."

"It was Amabel that protested, Amabel that took offence! Surely you can see what that portends?"

"I'm afraid not. I don't see why Amabel should suddenly become so old-cattish."

"She's jealous," said Eulalie. "Jealous of you, as Rigg intended her to be."

"Oh, that's gammon!"

"It is not gammon." Eulalie leaned forward. "Tell me, did Rigg invite Amabel to skate with him?"

"No. She did not skate at all, she stayed in the carriage."

"Just so. Rigg invited you, to pique her ladyship. You saw how things stood with them on Wednesday. They have had a lovers' tiff, and he means to show her he is not at her beck and call. It's the oldest trick of all, and it always succeeds . . . as it did today. Of course Amabel vented her feelings on Roland and you, but my guess is that by now, she and Rigg will have kissed and made up."

As she talked, Eulalie was watching Davina keenly, and was gratified to see a shadow of doubt in her eyes.

"It's not to be wondered at," she continued, "if those two make a match of it. It will solve many problems for them."

Davina spoke stiffly. "I don't believe Lord Rigg's sentiments towards Amabel are . . . are such as you describe."

"My child, you can know nothing of his sentiments. He will hardly discuss them with you! What you have to think of is what he feels about you, and I promise you it is nothing at all. Rigg has a heart of stone. He has always been able to take his pick of women. From the day he came on the town, they've been falling at his feet. I can't remember a time when his name hasn't been linked with one or another bird of paradise. You can't imagine the lengths to which some females will go to gain his attention. Why, poor Miss Beresford-Whyte allowed herself to be thrown from her horse right outside Rowan House, so that Rigg would be obliged to carry her indoors! And all that came of it was that when her mama came to fetch her, Rigg advised her in the coldest way to send the girl for riding lessons. Everyone laughed themselves into stitches about it. I know you would not like to become such a target for vulgar gossip!"

Davina sat staring straight before her, her face scarlet. Mrs Wakeford judged that the moment had come to soften her approach.

"Come," she said, "don't take it to heart. I spoke in your own interest, for I don't wish to see you hurt. There is someone else you should keep in mind, too, and that's your loyal friend, Edward Clare. I'm sure you don't wish to sink in his esteem."

Standing up, Eulalie placed a hand on Davina's shoulder. "There, I have said my say. I'm glad we were able to speak frankly. As I told you at the outset, I count on you to help me save Roland from his own folly, and you can do so very easily, you know—by persuading him to go with us to London for a few weeks."

"I have not decided to go," said Davina in a low voice.

"No, but you will be thinking seriously of doing so. I know you will do what's best for Wakeford, and for us all."

Davina left soon after, to talk to Hoby about the kitchen pipes. As soon as she had gone, Mrs Wakeford hurried to Lady Sophia's bedroom. She found her ladyship looking tired and wan, though no longer feverish.

Seating herself at the bedside, Eulalie delivered a report of her conversations with Roland and Davina. "I think," she said complacently, "that I have been able to hint them in the right direction. They will both be a little more circumspect in their dealings with the Rowans. Now we must put our heads together, Sophia, and see if we can coax them to come to London."

Lady Sophy did not trust herself to speak her true mind. Some day, she thought, she would give herself the felicity of pushing Eulalie off a high cliff; but for the present it was necessary to placate the woman. Reaching under her pillow, she drew out a folded sheet of paper.

"This came this morning," she said. "It's from Lady Holland. She writes that she has spoken to Mr Allen, who expresses himself most interested in the sale of Henry's books. Her ladyship suggests I bring Davina to Holland House on Monday ten days hence, to meet Allen, and also Lord Holland. *He* is acquainted with everyone, you know, and may help Davina to find the right sort of buyers."

Eulalie nodded shrewdly. "Excellent, but it gives us very little time to prepare. You will need to travel to town on Thursday, at the latest." She cast a dubious look at Lady Sophy's pallid face. "I hope you will be well enough, by then."

"I shall have to be. Will you travel with us, or take your own carriage?"

"Neither. As it happens I am already promised to go to

Tunbridge Wells for a fortnight. My dear friend Letitia Bracknell and I are to take the waters. It's all to the good. Roland is far more likely to visit London if he sees the chance to kick up his heels, without his mama clinging to his coat-tails!"

"As you choose." Lady Sophy raised herself higher on her pillows. "To come to details: I believe we shall require three carriages at least. Tredgold must take ours, and go by way of Luton to collect Jane—she has appointments with the mantua-maker, next week. Rebecca will take the chaise with all our baggage, and your Eliza shall bear her company. Davina and I will travel in your carriage with you and Roland. We will set you down at Mrs Bracknell's and the two of you may proceed to Tunbridge in her conveyance."

Though Mrs Wakeford very much disliked being addressed in this high-handed manner, something in her sister-in-law's eye warned her not to argue.

"Whatever you say, my dear," she agreed. "And now I wish you will have a word with Davina. I'm sure when she hears of the Hollands' offer, that will turn the trick."

Later that evening Davina sat in her room, struggling to compose her thoughts. Anger and humiliation contended with the conviction that her step-mama's poisonous warnings were justified.

She would never believe that Rigg was the sort of man who would flirt with one woman, simply to score a hit with another. Rake he might be. Popinjay he was not.

What was impossible to ignore was his affection for Amabel. What more likely than that he should love her? How could any man resist a woman so beautiful, so accomplished, so wise in the ways of the fashionable world?

Davina studied her reflection in the looking-glass. No beauty there, no style, not a touch of that town bronze the Corinthians were said to admire. A dowdy, a bluestocking, nothing at all to compare with Amabel Rowan.

She tried to recall what Rigg had said to her that afternoon. Surely nothing over-familiar, or improper. He had been friendly and kind. And she? Davina pressed the cold mirror to her face. Had she appeared forward, too eager? How dreadful if that should be so, and how odious to think people might be laughing at her behind her back, saying that poor Davina Wakeford was at her last prayers and ready to throw herself at the head of the first man to give her good-day.

Well, they should have no further chance to criticise her. There was no need to address Lord Rigg again, except in the way of common politeness. Soon, mercifully soon, she could escape to London. By the time she returned, Rigborough would have forgotten all about her foolish excursion into Jack Frost's goblin kingdom.

The next day was Sunday. Lord Rigg, emerging from church after Matins, glimpsed Miss Wakeford ahead of him, and hurried to come up with her. To his discomfiture, although she had seen him, she did not stop to greet him, but climbed quickly into the Tredgold carriage, and was whisked away up the hill.

That same afternoon, a large parcel was delivered to him at Rowanbeck. Opening it, he found it contained the painting of the Three Graces. He searched the wrappings for a letter, but found only Miss Wakeford's printed card. It bore no message.

"What's this?" enquired Mr Clintwood, who had at that moment entered the room.

The Earl handed over the card. "A snub I no doubt deserve," he said.

"Miss Wakeford? I thought you were in her good books."

"So did I, but obviously I mistook the matter."

Mr Clintwood looked unhappy. "You know, Lucas, it's probably nothing to do with the girl's own view of you. Mark my words, it's that mischief-making mama of hers that's to blame. Painted you pretty black, no doubt."

"And been believed!" Luke's voice was cold. "A foretaste of what I may expect from the ton. It's in my mind to leave for London tomorrow. Winkler says the road through Charlbury is passable. I shall drive myself. If you want to take the opportunity to try Talbot's greys, you're welcome to do so."

Edward Clare called at Wakeford Hall on Monday and asked to speak privately to Miss Wakeford. She invited him into the morning-room, sent for coffee which he preferred over tea or wine, and waited for him to explain the nature of his visit.

"A little bird has told me," he said, "that you are to go to London. Is it indeed the case?"

"For a short while only," she replied. "I must make arrangements to sell my father's books."

"There's a regular exodus from Rigborough," he said. "Jocelyn left yesterday, and Rigg at crack of dawn today. I'm fairly deserted! But I've not come to complain. Far from it. I'm the bearer of good news—good for me, and perhaps of some small interest to you." He gave her an arch smile. "I shall not after all be going to Bath. Rigg has asked me to manage Graydon for him, and as you know, that is only fifty miles from here."

"I'm happy for you. I'm sure you will make Graydon prosper."

"I mean to try, and I may say I have a great incentive." Edward reached over to take Davina's hand. "When I asked you to marry me, I had little to offer a bride. Now I can promise you will be mistress of a fine house, and a splendid estate . . . as well as of my heart."

And all, thought Davina wryly, in the gift of Lord Rigg! Am I never to be free of this tangle?

She turned to face Edward.

"Mr Clare, indeed I am grateful to you, and honoured by your offer, but my mind is not yet clear. I'm still confused. . . ."

"Of course. I have been too precipitate and you have grave matters to settle. But a man in love, you know, becomes impatient for his answer. How soon will you give me yours?"

"When . . . when I return from London. I should not be away above three weeks. By that time, in any case, Wakeford will be needing my attention."

"Don't trouble your head about Wakeford. I shall see to things in your absence. All will be well, and when you come home, I earnestly hope it will be to place your future in my care."

XII

LORD RIGG ARRIVED in Berkeley Square on Tuesday afternoon, having paused in Clarges Street to set down Robert Clintwood.

He found that pleasant transformations had taken place in Rowan House during his absence. Charles Turnbull was taking his post of secretary very seriously. He had already dispelled all trace of Hibberd's slovenly reign. He was on excellent terms with the housekeeper, Mrs Dubbleday, and between them they had engaged new staff and set them to work. Rooms had been cleaned, minor repairs effected, and Josh Nabob's warehouses ransacked for samples of brocade for new curtaining. The cellars had also been restocked, though here Charles entered a caveat.

"I've laid in enough for ordinary purposes," he said, "but if you mean to hold large assemblies, or a dress-ball, you will need far more."

The Earl gazed at him in mild astonishment. "My dear Charles, why in Heaven's name should I hold a ball?"

"You may wish to, my lord."

"Nothing could be farther from my thoughts. And don't call me 'my lord'."

"People will consider it very odd if I don't."

"That's of no interest to me. If it pleases your puritanical conscience to address me as 'sir' in company, so be it, but when we're alone it will be 'Luke', if you please. Tell me, did your father receive my letters?"

"He did, and will be here to dine tonight. He'll bring Shedley with him."

"Excellent. You'll be of the party, too, Charles. We've urgent family matters to discuss, and you'd best be *au fait* with them from the start."

Mr Shedley's mood, as the hackney cab deposited him at Rowan House that evening, was ambivalent.

As a man of egalitarian views, an admirer of the republican aims of the American States, and of the writings of Jean-Jacques

Rousseau, he held a low opinion of the aristocracy, whether French or English, and nothing he had so far learned of the Rowans had done anything to change it.

He had served as legal adviser to three former Earls of Rigg. Ranulph he categorised as a man of superior intellect, but loose morals; George as an uncertain-tempered dunce; and Talbot as a figure of pathos, feckless rather than bad.

Luke Rowan he knew only by reputation, and a very shameful one he thought it.

Mr Shedley's standards were rigid. He was quite clear in his mind what his attitude to Luke must be. He would offer his lordship the best of legal advice, and nothing more. He certainly did not propose to champion his cause, or become embroiled in the sordid emotional storms that seemed to rage forever about the heads of the Rowan clan.

This stern view was softened a little by Lord Rigg's latest letter, shown to him a day or so earlier by Joshua Turnbull.

Mr Shedley now knew that it was Lady Rigg who had turned the pistol on her husband, and though Luke Rowan might be suspected of adultery, he was innocent of attempted fratricide. Furthermore he had accepted exile and social ostracism to shield the woman he loved. One might think such action mawkishly sentimental, but one had to admit its generosity.

During dinner, Mr Shedley kept a watchful eye on Lord Rigg. He could find little to criticise in him. His figure was athletic, and showed no signs of a debauched way of life. His dress, while decidedly fashionable, avoided those extremes distasteful to a man of sense. The weskit was plain. Only one seal—the Rowan —dangled from the gold fob-chain. A single pearl was set in the folds of the exquisitely neat cravat.

Mr Shedley had to concede that Lord Rigg was the complete gentleman. His manners were unexceptionable, he was an attentive host, set a good table with superlative wines, and conversed with easy informality, never trying to force his own views on his guests.

It was clear that both Joshua and Charles Turnbull were deeply fond of this man, and that he returned the affection. Mr Shedley, for all his crusty bachelorhood, had the highest regard for family devotion.

He was inclined to think that in time, and with the proper

guidance, the sixth Earl might live down his unsavoury past, and attain a reputable position in society.

After dinner, when the four men withdrew to the library to discuss their business, Lord Rigg revealed another side to his character—one that nearly caused Mr Shedley to lose his temper.

The little lawyer had brought with him certain papers relating to the estate, which he felt Lord Rigg should examine. His lordship gave them only a cursory glance, and waved them away.

"We'll leave routine matters for another time," he said. "Tonight I want to talk of my brother Talbot, and in particular of his financial dealings while I was out of England."

Mr Shedley stiffened. "My lord, you were sent full details of everything connected with your late brother's estate."

"I was. The estate records are in perfect order, and I congratulate you on it. But what Talbot spent on the estate is only part of the story. Under our father's will, he couldn't touch Rowan capital, but he could spend the interest. He was also left a considerable fortune by our mother—as I was. In short, Tal had access to a very large sum of money. He appears to have spent the whole."

"He spent every sou he could lay hands on," said Mr Shedley grimly.

"Did you have no control over his private expenditures?"

"None whatsoever. The money was his, and he squandered it. He went through the income from the estate, and when that was gone, he spent the money left by your mama. He cashed bonds and sold moveable assets. In the last year of his life he even asked me to break the terms of your father's will, so that he could sell land. Naturally I told him that was impossible. We may thank God that Rowanbeck and the other properties are protected by entail."

"Did you remonstrate with him?"

"I argued, up hill and down dale. He took not a whit of notice."

"Was there nothing you could do, in law, to check him?"

"Nothing. He was not insane. A man who is legally sane may bury his fortune in his cabbage-patch, if he chooses."

Luke nodded. "I see. How much do you estimate Tal got through, in three years?"

Mr Shedley pursed his lips. "An enormous sum. So far as I can establish, something in the region of sixty thousand pounds."

"Sixty thousand pounds, disbursed by a man who was paralysed, who never left his house for months on end, whose only interest was in brandy! Mr Shedley, did it never occur to you to write and warn me what was afoot?"

"No, my lord, it did not. It was your brother who was my client, not you."

"But in his interest, couldn't you have written?"

"No." Mr Shedley's regard was frosty. "If you recall, at that time I believed you to be guilty of the attempted murder of your brother. Had I known the true facts, my decision might have been different."

The Earl's hard stare relaxed somewhat. "True enough," he said. "Did you consult any other member of my family? Lady Rigg, for example?"

Mr Shedley permitted himself a dusty chuckle. "Lady Rigg, my lord, is not noted for her financial acumen. It would have been a waste of time to talk to her. I did, however, speak to Sir Jocelyn Clare. I told him Talbot was spending far beyond what was wise, or in my view, proper."

"What was his answer?"

"He bade me mind my own business."

Josh Turnbull, who had been silent to this point, now exploded in wrath. "Aye, and we know why, don't we? Clare didn't want you nosing out how he was robbing Talbot. That's where the sixty thousand went, straight into that maw-worm's pocket."

"So I think. In fact, Jocelyn doesn't attempt to deny it. He thinks himself secure. He's told me that if I expose him, he'll tell the world it was Amabel shot Talbot."

"Let him," said Mr Shedley. "We'll roast him, at law!"

But Joshua shook his head. "Nay, that wouldn't do. We might win the lawsuit, but we'd drag Lady Rigg through t'mud in t'process. Reckon if we're to beat Clare, we mun fight him wi' his own weapons."

"What then do you suggest, sir?"

Joshua looked at the Earl. "Hawkins is here," he said. "He's summat to tell. But before we call him in, I want your word that whatever he says, you'll not fly into a passion."

Luke hesitated only a moment. "You have it," he said.

Mr Turnbull nodded, and signed to his son to pull the bellrope by the fireplace.

Silas Hawkins had been no more than ten years old when Josh Turnbull found him crouched behind a tombstone in the parish graveyard. Questioned, he said he was from St Giles, which Joshua knew to be a noisome slum where thieves, vagrants and harridans lived six or seven to a room, their only sanitation the kennel and the open cesspool. There children were trained from infancy in the arts of cly-faking and wipe-snitching. Hawkins admitted to being on the kinchin-lay—his task being to visit respectable suburbs and rob the children of the rich. Today he had taken nothing, and was too terrified to go back and face his master.

Joshua carried the boy home to Cheapside, dressed his sores and fed him. Thereafter attempts were made to train him as a stable-boy, a gardener, a kitchen-hand. He learned nothing and remained to all save Joshua surly and disobedient.

When the lad was fifteen, Joshua hit upon the notion of making him a back-street agent of Turnbull & Sons, a rôle Silas was to fill to perfection.

Set him down in a gin-shop in Seven Dials, a riverside tavern, a City coffee-house, and he would soak up an ocean of information. From it he would dredge the news of deals struck, cargoes shifted, alliances formed and broken, the stuff on which merchants thrive and grow fat.

Hawkins could tell you—if he chose—who cheated the exciseman and who his wife, who was willing to murder for a shilling, and whose price came higher. Oddly enough, he could not himself be bought. He was a genius, and took an inordinate pride in his skills.

He could assume many guises, many turns of speech. Tonight he appeared as the dandy on the strut, in a coat of plum-coloured superfine, very tight in the waist and broad on the shoulder. His pantaloons, of a shade between fawn and lavender, were cut fullish at the ankle in the French style. He wore his cravat in the *trône d'amour* knot, and his black curls in the careless disarray made popular by Lord Byron. There was about him an air of seediness, the look of a man a trifle down on his luck.

Mr Turnbull regarded him with a derisory eye. "Eh, me fine cockalorum, and where've you been?"

"With Mr Colman." Hawkins sketched a bow at Luke, and touched a temple to Mr Shedley before slipping into his chair. His impudent grin flashed out. "Could've landed a part, what's more. Second gravedigger, in 'Amlet."

Mr Turnbull glanced at his nephew. "George Colman is Manager of the Little Theatre in the Adelphi," he supplied. "Ran with Prinny's pack, for a while."

Hawkins laughed. "Aye, and it landed 'im in the King's Bench."

This was the prison where certain debtors were incarcerated, and a stir of interest went round the table.

"And what did Mr Colman have to say?" demanded Joshua.

"He told me that four year ago, Sir Jocelyn Clare was dipped to the tune o' fifty thousand."

"Fifty-three and a half," corrected Joshua. "What of it?"

Hawkins tilted his head. "Seems the gennelman paid 'is gamblin' debts. Had to, seein' as he played at Carlton House. But he stinted on all else. Mortgaged his Lunnon house, and kep' the tradesmen a-squealin' for their blunt. Bailiffs in, furniture out. And then . . . all on a sudden . . . 'e changed 'is tune, an' started to pay 'is dues. Word goes it was 'is fambly stood bail for 'im."

"No law agin that," said Joshua gruffly. "Come to the point, man."

Hawkins sniffed. "I asked Mr Colman, who was Sir Jocelyn's friends? He said, none a decent man could boast of. There was 'Monkey' Franchot that was sent to Bedlam, and Colonel McPhail that went to Ireland, which comes to the same thing. There was Beau Clevedon, that'd wear naught but silk next 'is 'ide, and died last year o' the French sickness. There was Gore-Evans. 'E married a rich widder-woman an' was carried orf to Glasgow for 'is sins. An' there was Mr Jonas Whitstaple. The loan-sharks got poor Jonas, an' 'e was put in the King's Bench." Hawkins smiled round, enjoying his effect. "'At's where 'e met up with Mr Colman, an' confided in 'im the sad tale of 'is betrayal an' downfall. Seems Mr Whitstaple loaned twelve thousand pound to Sir Jocelyn Clare, and 'as never been repaid —which if 'e was, 'e'd be a free man again."

"How does that help us?" demanded Joshua.

"Well sir, I don't need to tell you that when a cove is hincarcerated in a debtors' gaol—with nary a hope of seein' 'is 'ome and 'is loved ones again—then that cove is, as you might say, done to a turn. Ready for anythin'. Ready to consider offers. Ready, like as not, to set 'is name to a dociment."

Lord Rigg, who had been watching Hawkins closely, shook his head. "You've not told us the whole," he said. "Am I to understand that the twelve thousand pounds loaned to my cousin by this fellow Whitstaple, was for a dishonest purpose?"

"Aye." For the first time, Silas looked uncomfortable. "It was . . . kind of a bribe, like."

"And what service was Jocelyn to render in return?"

"You won't like it, my lord."

"Never mind about that, speak up."

"There was a lady," muttered Hawkins. "A lady as Mr Whitstaple wished for to tumble. Sir Jocelyn was to persuade 'er to be. . . ."

"More accommodating?"

Hawkins nodded. Joshua Turnbull, looking at his nephew's stony face, said anxiously, "Remember, Luke. You promised."

Luke turned to Mr Shedley. "Will it be possible for you to learn who are Jonas Whitstaple's creditors, aside from my cousin?"

"Certainly, my lord."

"Do so. Buy up the bills, and let me have the list of names as soon as you are able."

"Nay," said Joshua quickly, "let me have it. Sithee, Luke, you'd best act through me. Better if the Rowan name don't figure in this. Better for the lady."

Luke nodded. "Very well." He turned back to Shedley. "Once the bills are paid and in my uncle's possession, I wish you to visit Whitstaple. See if you can persuade him to sign an affidavit, setting out the facts of his transaction with my cousin."

Mr Shedley looked shocked. "Lord Rigg, that is tantamount to offering the man an inducement to sign. It would be highly unethical, and would render the document quite inadmissible in any legal action."

"There'll be no legal action. I plan to settle out of court, and in my own fashion. If you feel unable to do as I ask, I shall find some other intermediary. Of course, your decision will in no way affect your status as my legal adviser."

Mr Shedley was silent for a moment. "As a lawyer," he said, "I must refuse. As a private individual, I accept. You will hear from me as soon as I have anything to report."

The following morning, Lord Rigg rose late; consumed a leisurely breakfast; glanced at the newspaper; and was debating whether or not to order his curricle brought round, when his secretary appeared, demanding to know what Luke proposed to do about his correspondence.

"As little as possible," said his lordship equably.

Mr Turnbull's brow puckered.

"There are a great many bills," he said.

"Pay 'em, Charles."

"Begging letters."

"Use your discretion."

"Invitations."

Lord Rigg's eyebrows rose. "You amaze me. Let me see."

Charles handed over a pile of cards. His lordship flicked through them, a half-smile on his face, and returned all but one to the young man.

"Those are from shabsters," he said. "You may burn them. This one is different. I see Clint's hand in it. What do you think, Charles? Should I accept?"

"If you mean, should you go to Holland House, I'd say 'no'. All the smarts will be there, it'll be a regular lions' den."

"And I run the risk of being eaten alive—or worse still, spurned as unfit for feline consumption?" Luke sat for a moment turning the card in his fingers. Suddenly he smiled. "You may leave this one with me. I'll answer it. And my friend may call upon the angels to seal up the lions' mouths."

On Thursday afternoon, Mr Shedley paid a visit to the King's Bench.

As a man of the law, he was not ignorant of conditions in the city's prisons. He had several times visited Mr Leigh Hunt in the Horsemonger Lane Gaol, after Hunt was confined for the crime of calling the Prince Regent a 'fat Adonis of fifty'.

He had inspected the Marshalsea and Clink Prisons; and had joined with his friend Mrs Elizabeth Fry in speaking out against the terrible hardships endured by those incarcerated in Newgate Gaol.

But the King's Bench, situated at the corner of Newington Causeway and about a mile from the end of Westminster Bridge, he knew to be more like a small village than a prison. It was a street enclosed by a high wall, and contained its own shops, a stretch of open ground set aside for walking and exercise, a butcher's stand, a tap-house, and a public kitchen where prisoners could take provisions and have them dressed free of charge.

In the King's Bench the inmates were permitted to move around freely and mingle with their fellows. The poorer of them —if there could be any such distinction among those who owed all they had ever owned—occupied rooms on what was known as "the common side". For the better sort of Crown prisoner there were some dozen or so furnished apartments. The turnkey at the entrance gate informed Mr Shedley that Mr Whitstaple had one of these, and directed him to a house in a small paved court.

Mr Shedley climbed narrow stairs, and tapped on a door. There was the sound of movement within the room, and then a small trap in the upper part of the door was opened to show a pair of close-set eyes, a long pointed nose, and a peevish mouth.

"Who are you?" demanded a thin, querulous voice. "I say, who are you and what d'ye want?"

"I want to talk to you, Mr Whitstaple. My name is Thomas Shedley."

"Don't know you. Never saw you, never heard of you. Eh?"

"I'm a well-wisher."

The thin man took this in instant dislike. "Well-wisher?" he cried. "If that means preacher, then be off with you! I can't abide creepers and crawlers!"

"I'm a lawyer, sir, not a priest."

"Can't abide 'em, either. Lawyer and liar is all one. Go away, I say, go away!"

"Not until I've discharged my duty, which is to discuss with you the prospects of your release from this place."

"Release? What d'ye mean? Eh? Eh?"

"If you will allow me to come in, I will explain."

The round eyes stared for a moment. Then the peephole slammed shut, a chain rattled, a key turned, and the door opened. Mr Shedley advanced into the room.

It was hardly a gentleman's abode, he thought. A miserable fire smoked in the grate, and the curtains were faded. The room's occupant, too, was shabby, his once-fine clothes bearing the signs of long wear, and his cravat and shirt none too clean. He was watching Mr Shedley with unconcealed dislike, his mouth working convulsively.

"I tell you, sir," he burst out, "I don't know you and I don't trust you! Say what you came to say, and leave!"

"Very well." Mr Shedley laid aside hat and gloves, and sat down uninvited. "Let me first ask if you are Mr Jonas Whitstaple, that once resided at Number Seven, Albemarle Street?"

"And if I am?"

"If you are, then I offer you my commiserations, for you have debts totalling the sum of twenty-one thousand pounds, nine shillings and eight pence, debts you cannot meet, and never will meet so long as you are entombed in the King's Bench."

Mr Whitstaple suddenly plumped down in a chair. "That's it!" he said. "My tragic circumstance! Can't pay till I'm free, and can't be free till I pay. There's justice for you, there's fair play for you!"

"There is a mortgage on your house," pointed out Mr Shedley in a matter-of-fact tone, "that might be transferred from the present holder—Mr Horace Pudbury—to someone who might be less . . . importunate in his demands for repayment."

Mr Whitstaple sat very still, fear as well as suspicion in his eyes. After a moment he said huskily, "and how would such a transfer come about?"

"Such things happen, my dear sir."

"Not of their own accord! Who's behind this? Name me a name!"

"That I cannot do. You will have to trust me."

"Trust?" Mr Whitstaple laughed shrilly. "I trust no man, woman, or child, sir."

"A pity, for I might get you out of here."

Mr Whitstaple's mouth trembled. "It is all very well for you to say so, to make promises, to raise my hopes with empty words!"

For answer, Mr Shedley reached a hand into his pocket, drew out a small sheaf of papers and thrust them into the thin man's hand. Whitstaple fingered through them, slowly at first, then eagerly.

"My bills," he said, "my bills! How did you come by 'em?"

"By paying them," Shedley said. "You will see they are fully discharged. You may burn them if you wish."

Mr Whitstaple needed no prompting. Leaping up, he thrust the papers into the fireplace, where they quickly became ashes.

"That's not all," he said. "Where are the rest?"

"In my client's hands," returned Mr Shedley.

"Ah, yes. Mr Nobody. And why does he have 'em? What's he after? Eh?" Mr Whitstaple stepped closer. "God knows, I've nothing but the clothes I stand up in, I've nought to offer anyone."

"On the contrary, sir, you possess something of great value to my client."

"What's that, pray?"

"Information. Knowledge. You may supply, if you choose, the answers to certain questions."

Mr Whitstaple looked frightened. "I can't be made to answer."

"Certainly not. It's a matter of free choice, as I said. A token that you are prepared to return favour for favour."

"What are these . . . questions?"

Mr Shedley scratched his ear. "I believe, sir, you were once on friendly terms with Sir Jocelyn Clare?"

Mr Whitstaple's countenance turned purple.

"No friend of mine," he cried. "Clare's a traitor, a bilking hound, a lying, cheating, pinchbeck swine! I'd not be rotting here, but for him!"

"Twelve thousand pounds," agreed Mr Shedley, "would certainly earn you some measure of parole. Does Clare admit the debt?"

"No, he does not."

"And you never took him to court for it?"

Mr Whitstaple's only answer was a scowl, and the lawyer shook his head. "Dear me, can it be that you loaned Clare so large a sum as twelve thousand pounds, without any written note to cover it? No guarantee? I think that very strange!"

"Think what you please," said Whitstaple, his expression both sullen and shifty.

"Perhaps," continued Mr Shedley, "the reason you did not secure the loan was that you could not? Was it dirty business, sir? Something you didn't dare put in writing? Something no gentleman would care to record?"

"Damn you," shouted Whitstaple, "how dare you come here to insult me? If I were a free man, I swear I'd call you to account for it, damned if I wouldn't."

"Tut, sir, this won't bring you out of debt! However, if you choose to languish here, that is your affair. I shall tell my client you decline to accept his help."

He started to rise and reach for his hat; but before he gained his feet, Whitstaple suddenly collapsed into a chair, covered his face with his hands, and broke into sobs.

Mr Shedley made no move to comfort him, but waited until the thin man raised a tear-streaked face.

"Well, sir, shall I leave?"

Mr Whitstaple mopped his eyes with a grubby kerchief. "You don't know what it is to be brought so low," he mourned. "My name is dragged in the mire, my friends have deserted me. Nothing remains of all I had. Nothing."

"A high price to pay for a woman, however beautiful."

Whitstaple regarded him closely. "What do you know of that?" he whispered.

"I know Clare took you for a green fool. You paid him to procure the favours of a lady."

"I did not pay him, I loaned him the money. Favour for favour. . . ."

"A nice distinction. A loan, which would be repaid by the lady's compliance. . . ."

"I got nothing. She would not even meet me."

"Ah! So you were gulled. Hornswoggled. And here you are in a debtors' prison, for your pains. Mind, you may be safer here."

Mr Whitstaple looked up nervously. "What d'ye mean?"

"Merely that I wonder at your audacity, in attempting such a deal! Had you succeeded in seducing the lady, her husband would certainly have killed you."

"There was no danger. He was beyond caring. Nothing but a tosspot, drunk before noon most days."

"He was not so far gone that he couldn't have put a bullet through you, before breakfast."

"He's dead now."

"Yes, but his brother is very much alive, and back in England. A quick-tempered man, and an excellent shot. I think we must keep this sorry tale from his ears."

"You would not tell him?" Mr Whitstaple seemed likely to fall on his knees, and Mr Shedley contemplated him with distaste.

"It is not my tongue you should worry about, but your own. If my client is able to secure your release, he will expect silence. No word must leak out. Not one."

"I will be discreet. Oh, sir, I will be the very soul of discretion, I assure you. Only tell me what you want of me!"

"Your signature," said Mr Shedley, "to a statement of the facts."

"You shall have it. How will it be done?"

"I will prepare an affidavit, and bring it to you to sign. You will be relieved of your debts, and your return to the world will be facilitated."

"My blessings on you, sir, and on my kind deliverer!" Mr Whitstaple hurried to the door after Mr Shedley. "I will do my part, never fear! Word of a gentleman!"

Mr Shedley smiled coldly. "Give me your word as a debtor, Mr Whitstaple, for that I know you to be."

XIII

THE MONDAY OF Lady Holland's At Home dawned so wet and cold that Lord Rigg decided against driving himself. He left Rowan House at three that afternoon in a closed carriage, with Winkler and a groom on the box, and Mr Clintwood as his fellow-passenger.

The weather worsened as they travelled through the green fields of Kensington, and by the time they reached their destination they could barely discern the façade of the old Jacobean mansion from the lurid sky behind it. Despite these inclement conditions, they found a great many coaches jostling for place in the driveway, while the courtyard was filled with shouting coachmen, tigers and linkboys.

"Might have guessed it," said Clintwood gloomily. "The Hollands always invite more guests than they've room for. It'll be a confounded squeeze in the drawing-rooms, and catch-as-catch-can at the buffet."

They made their way into the house. The entrance hall was crowded, and the hubbub considerable. As Luke came through the door, he was conscious of a sudden lull, and of numerous inquisitive stares directed his way. He allowed a lackey to divest him of hat, coat and gloves, and stood looking quietly about him.

One or two people, catching his eye, ostentatiously turned their backs on him. Others ventured a nervous smile or bow. The majority affected indifference and resumed their talk, while casting sly glances at his lordship, and one another.

"We've run slap bang into the Devonshire faction," said Clintwood. "We'd best seek neutral ground."

They began to edge towards the door of the main salon, but had taken only a step or two when a voice hailed them from the far side of the hallway.

"Rigg! I say, Rigg! Over here!"

"It's Godfrey Webster," murmured Clintwood. "Let's hope he won't give us the kiss of death!"

Sir Godfrey was Lady Holland's son by her first marriage.

Though handsome in a coarse-grained way, he was not well-liked, being less than scrupulous in sporting matters, and inclined to boast of his conquests in the bedchamber. Moreover, he had put himself in the bad books of both the Devonshires and the Melbournes by engaging in a much-publicised flirtation with Lady Caroline Lamb.

Luckily Sir Godfrey appeared to be no more anxious to fraternise with the new arrivals than they with him, for he greeted Luke with the sketchiest of bows, and said bluntly, "Sarvant, Rigg! M' mother desires a word with you in private, if you please. Clintwood, you'll excuse us."

So saying, he swung off along a side corridor, leaving Luke to follow as best he might.

Mr Clintwood, though annoyed at being so neatly cut from the herd, was not at a loss. He moved into the drawing-rooms, and presently met with a group of army-officers with whom he was acquainted. One of them, Arthur Upton, drew him aside and said in a low voice, "I saw you come in with Lucas Rowan. Don't tell me you're sponsoring him?"

Clintwood looked mildly surprised. "Lord save us, Rigg don't need a sponsor."

"I mean, you take his part?"

"Why yes. Don't you?"

Upton frowned. "Not if it's true he's turned Lady Rigg out of her home. Poor little soul, as if she hadn't suffered enough at his hands."

"Who fed you that Banbury tale?" demanded Clintwood. "No, let me guess! It was Jocelyn Clare, wasn't it?"

"Well yes, as a matter of fact it was. We were with Kangaroo Cooke last night—playing macao for demmed high stakes, 'way above my touch—when Clare said Lady Rigg was to be sent to live in the Dower House, and was in great distress because of it."

"Nothing's settled. Rigg will give her the house she wants, but it can't be Rowanbeck. You must see that."

"I do, of course. But. . . ."

"But you prefer to think ill of Rigg, despite the fact that Bow Street brings no charge against him, and that he's acted more than generously to the Clares?"

"Has he so?"

"Yes. Edward's to manage Graydon, and Jocelyn is to keep a whole skin, which is more than he deserves. Amabel will be well provided for. If you don't believe me, Arthur, speak to the lady yourself. She'll be in London before the end of April."

"Staying at Rowan House?"

"Yes, with her companion, Miss Finch."

Mr Clintwood, having set the score right with Upton, then looked about for a fresh challenge. He spotted Lord Althorp, talking to Lord Grey. Althorp was large, red, and weatherbeaten, and looked like a farmer, but he was likely to be Chancellor of the Exchequer, some day. Grey was cut out for even higher things. These two men, with Lord Holland, formed the chief power of the Whig party, and exercised enormous influence in society. Mr Clintwood touched a finger to his cravat, gave the points of his weskit a tug, and forged his way towards them.

Sir Godfrey made no attempt to converse with Lord Rigg as they made their way through the house, but merely led him to a closed door, tapped upon it, threw it open, and at once withdrew. Luke entered the room alone.

He had never been on terms with Lady Holland, but had heard much of her eccentricities. She was said to be the supreme egotist, and to indulge in all manner of foibles, cramming her guests elbow-to-elbow round her dinner-table, moving their places in the midst of the meal, forbidding anyone to wear scent in her presence, and becoming hysterical at the onset of a thunderstorm.

Yet Charlotte Turnbull had advised Luke to do all he could to win her ladyship's approval, for she was not only a famous hostess, but an extremely clever woman, and quite ruthless in gaining her own ends. "If she likes you," Charlotte said, "she will do all she can for you, and that is no mean thing."

The sitting-room to which Luke had been brought was both cold and stuffy, the casements being tightly shut, and the fire on the hearth meagre, and inclined to smoke.

Opposite the fireplace, in a heavily-carven oak chair, sat an imperious figure in a purple gown, with a silk turban wrapped about her head. Before her knelt a youth in the uniform of a page. His hands were thrust beneath the lady's skirts, and he was busy massaging her stockinged feet and ankles. After a moment he apparently touched some sensitive spot, for she emitted a sharp cry, and struck him impatiently on the shoulder.

"Oh, go away, Edgar! You're as clumsy as a bear!"

The page departed quietly through a second door, and the lady leaned across the arm of her chair.

"Lucas Rowan, is that you? Come into the light, man, where I may see you."

Luke advanced to make his bow and shake the hand stretched out to him. "Your ladyship's humble servant," he murmured.

"Humble?" She gave him a mocking smile. "No Rowan was ever humble, least of all the black-a-vised ones like yourself. Sit down, Lord Rigg. I take it you know that it was Robert Clintwood's father asked me to invite you here?"

"Yes, ma'am, I do."

"Good. You'll forgive my bluntness, but no purpose will be served by the making of pretty speeches. I was not at first inclined to accede to John Clintwood's request. I dislike taking part in a family feud, it is like being the meat in the middle of the pasty, exposed to teeth on either side."

"I don't bite," Luke said, smiling.

"My dear sir, you will! Don't delude yourself on that score! Jocelyn Clare is already at work, inciting people against you, and he won't give up on it, this side of the grave." She leaned back in her chair, surveying him with a critical eye. "Tell me, please, why I should interest myself in your unseemly squabbles?"

Luke sat for a moment considering her question. He saw, by the challenging gleam in her eyes, that she was not one to be won by flattery and soft soap.

"I can think of no immediate reason," he said at last. "After all, I'm hardly known to you."

"True. I knew your brother Talbot better. Despite his glaring faults, I confess I rather liked him."

Luke nodded. "Yes. So did I."

"Yet you put a bullet in him, my lord."

"Purely by accident."

"Liar. I have always believed it was Amabel that fired that pistol. Am I right?" As Luke made no answer, Lady Holland waved a hand. "Not that it makes much difference. Scandal attaches to the affair, and I have had enough of scandal. My husband plays a leading rôle in public circles. I won't have him tarnished, by association. You understand me?"

"Perfectly. If it eases your mind, Sir Nathanial Conant assures me no charge will be preferred. The case is closed."

Lady Holland seemed satisfied with this answer. "Tell me," she said, "now you are home, what will you do with your time?"

"There's a great deal to occupy me at Rowanbeck. I hope as well to open Rowan House for the summer."

"Tush, that's not enough! A man should do more than farm his acres and waltz at Almack's. I suppose you mean to take your seat in the Lords?"

"Very likely," said Luke. "I may also purchase one or two steamboats."

"Steamboats!" Lady Holland stared, then burst out laughing. "Why in the world would you do such a freakish thing?"

"To amuse myself, and to make a great deal of money. In a year or so, steamships will travel to America and India—so my Uncle Joshua Turnbull informs me."

Her ladyship's smile became edged. "Mr Turnbull is an estimable man, I'm sure, but he cuts no ice with the ton."

"I know it."

"I hope you do not think of going into Trade, my lord."

"I may do."

"That will not be acceptable to people of quality."

Luke gave a faint shrug.

"Lord Rigg," said her ladyship, sitting up straighter in her chair, "you are here to seek favours, you wish to be taken back into society, yet you won't make the least push to conform with society's rules."

"Seeking favour is one thing, ma'am, and grovelling another. Society must take me, and my relations, as it finds us."

"By heaven, you're as stiff-necked, in your fashion, as your grandfather Ranulph, and he had the pride of Lucifer."

Luke bowed his head. "A hopeless case, ma'am. Only your consummate skill can bring me safe home."

There was a short pause, then she laughed again, but on a kinder note.

"Very well, my lord, I will do what I can for you. Do you play whist?"

"Yes."

"How well?"

"Tolerably well."

She nodded briskly. "My husband dines at Brooks's on Wednesday, to play whist with Lord Fleet and Mr Osbaldeston. He will, if he can contrive it, invite you to join their table. Osbaldeston is bosom bows with the Devonshires at the moment. He also likes to win at cards. I suggest you lose enough to satisfy his avarice, but not enough to arouse his contempt."

"I'll do my best, ma'am."

"Good." She rose to her feet. "Before you leave, you must pay your respects to my husband; but first, you and I will parade together a little. Lend me your arm, if you please. My rheumaticky bones plague me like the devil in this wet weather."

For the next twenty minutes, Luke moved through the reception-rooms of Holland House at his hostess's side. It was not an elevating experience. Too many one-time friends, seeing him approach, turned aside, and found an urgent need to speak to someone at the far end of the room; and though he derived a certain sardonic amusement from these antics, he also felt the sting of them. Only the fact that a few people made a point of welcoming him prevented his quitting the scene and calling for his carriage.

At last Lady Holland released him. "It went well enough," she said. "The gauntlet has been thrown down. Now we must see who is brave enough to pick it up."

"I imagine my Cousin Jocelyn will lead the challenge," Luke said.

"Yes, and that means that the Regent's clique will oppose you. Still, no need to weep over that!"

"None. And thank you most sincerely for your support. I'm deeply grateful to you."

"Lud, don't thank me yet! It's early days. Now go and see if you can find my husband."

Luke, having first secured a much-needed glass of claret from a passing footman, set off in search of the library. Lady Holland had said it was "at the far end of the house," a singularly unhelpful instruction to one situated at its middle. Should it be left, or right? Luke decided to turn right along what seemed to be a main corridor.

Like the rest of the building, this was panelled in painted oak, and though numerous branches of candles had been placed along its length, they did little to dispel the general gloom. There were several doors on each side of the passage, all of them shut. Luke walked slowly, sipping his claret as he went.

It was at the gloomiest turn of the corridor that he came into violent collision with a person emerging pell-mell from one of the anterooms. He was very nearly knocked off his feet. The wineglass he carried was slammed painfully against his teeth, while its contents splashed into his face, temporarily blinding him.

He groped for a handkerchief and mopped at his eyes. When he could see again, he found himself face to face with a figure dressed in a coat of extravagant design, a satin waistcoat with broad red and white stripes, a cravat tied in a sad travesty of the Mathematical, and a starched collar so high its wearer was quite unable to turn his head. Framed between the points of this collar were the flushed and perspiring features of Mr Roland Foote. It was abundantly clear that he was not only extremely drunk, but in an uncompromising mood.

"Rigg," he said thickly, brandishing an empty winebottle under the Earl's nose. "What th' devil are you doin' here? Why'n't you look where you're going?"

The last thing Luke desired at this moment was to be involved in bucolic farce. Long experience told him that his only salvation lay in instant retreat, and he started to back away. Unfortunately Mr Foote saw this as a sign of weakness, and blocked the attempt, prancing round to face his lordship, both fists raised in the boxer's stance.

"Stay where you are, sir! I say, stound your grand like a man!"

"Mr Foote," said the Earl firmly. "Be a good fellow, and go and put your head under the kitchen pump."

Mr Foote took instant affront. "D'you s'ggest I'm drunk, sir? Is tha' wha' you s'ggest? By God, I sh'll call you out f'rit. Swear I shall!"

He lurched dangerously. Luke caught his arm to steady him. Roland took this for aggression and began to mill about, ducking and weaving and aiming wild blows at Luke's head. Luke, fending them off with ease, was debating whether he should land the silly fellow a facer to sober him, when without warning

Roland rolled up his eyes, buckled at the knees, and pitched forward into Luke's unwilling arms.

It was at this precise moment that a door on the opposite side of the corridor swung open and Miss Davina Wakeford stepped through it. She was wearing, Luke had time to notice, a very ugly gown of snuff-coloured poplin, and a bonnet trimmed with cerise velvet. Confronted with the tableau presented by her brother and his lordship, she froze rigid for an instant, and then hurried towards them.

"Lord Rigg," she said, "where did you find him?"

"I didn't. He ... er ... found me."

"I should have locked him in," said Miss Wakeford despairingly.

"You should indeed. But since he's out, what do you wish done with him?"

"Oh ... if you will be so good ... put him back where he came from. In there."

She gestured at the anteroom from which Roland had sprung, and the Earl, with a feeling of resignation, lugged his burden over the threshold.

The room was a small parlour, currently in use as a depository for hats, coats and pelisses. Casting about, Luke discerned a divan to the left of the doorway, and placed Mr Foote on it. Mr Foote neither stirred nor made a sound, lying with jaw dropped.

"Thank you," said Miss Wakeford. She advanced to stare down at her brother's form. "Do you think it would help," she enquired, "if we doused him with cold water?"

"No," said Lord Rigg coldly. He found his kerchief and began to mop the dregs of wine from his person. His cravat was sodden, his new coat almost certainly ruined, and his temper extremely brittle. There could be no point in approaching Lord Holland dishevelled and smelling like a vintner's shop. Suppressing a longing to slap the unconscious Mr Foote about the chops, he said, "All you can do is leave him to sleep it off."

"How ... how long will that take?"

"Several hours, I expect. He's dead away."

Miss Wakeford turned to face him. "In that case, sir, I need not trouble you further. Pray accept my apologies for the discomfort you've been caused. I shall see to it that Roland makes full reparation for the damage to your clothes."

Luke looked directly at her for the first time. Under her deplorable bonnet he saw a white, tense face, the chin lifted at a defiant angle, the large grey eyes shining with unshed tears.

He sighed. "May I ask, Miss Wakeford, what you propose to do until your brother wakes?"

"Nothing. I mean, I shall just sit here quietly with him."

"That won't answer, I fear." Luke glanced about him. "This is a cloakroom, by the look of it. In a short while people will come to collect their coats. There will be servants in and out. I think it will be preferable to order your carriage brought round to the back door. I'll convey Mr Foote to it. Your coachman will lend a hand. What is his name?"

"Micklejohn," said Miss Wakeford. She took a deep breath. "It's no use having him called for, though, because he's not here."

Lord Rigg experienced a sinking of the stomach. "And your groom?"

Miss Wakeford silently shook her head.

"Do I understand," said the Earl, "that it was Roland that drove you here?"

"Yes. He was not so very drunk when we left Park Street. That is, he was a little in alt, and refused to allow Micklejohn or Jevons—Jevons is my uncle's groom—to mount the box. He said he wished to drive."

"No doubt," said his lordship, clutching at straws, "you brought a female companion? Your maid? A friend?"

"I'm afraid not. Roly and I came alone. I know you must think I sadly lack conduct. . . ."

"I think your brother lacks it, to drive you when he is drunk, and to allow you to wander about London unattended!"

"It is not Roland's fault," she said quickly. "I insisted he must accompany me, though he didn't wish to. Oh, what use is it to talk! You do not understand the situation!"

"I'm doing my poor best, ma'am."

Miss Wakeford sank down into a chair. "I did not know what else to do," she said. "The whole house was at sixes and sevens. I speak of my Uncle Tredgold's house in Park Street, where we are to spend a week or two. Roly and I came to London only yesterday, you see, with my Aunt Sophia. I know now that I should never have allowed her to leave Rigborough. She has had the influenza, and a high fever, but she swore she was cured, so I let her overrule me. You see, she had arranged the appointment for me to come here today, to meet Mr Allen, who is Lord Holland's librarian. Aunt Sophy was so anxious that nothing should cause me to break it."

"And your Uncle Murray Tredgold? Where is he?"

"He went to Luton, to fetch my cousin, Jane. It was all settled that Aunt Sophy and I were to come to Holland House together, but this morning when she woke she was so unwell that I felt obliged to send for Dr Kentridge, and *he* said that Aunt must on no account leave her bed for at least a week.

"Of course, that made her fret on my behalf, and fretting made her fever rise even higher. To quiet her, I said I would persuade Roly to accompany me. How was I to know he'd passed the morning in some horrid, low place, drinking something called Blue Ruin?" Miss Wakeford frowned slightly. "What precisely is that, do you know?"

"Backstreet gin," said Luke.

"Oh. Well, I can only think it has a delayed effect. Roland seemed all right when we set out—except, that is, for not allowing Micklejohn and Jevons to come. And . . . and I'm afraid I let him have his way because he doesn't like to be crossed, you know, and my one thought was to keep my appointment with Mr Allen."

"You're lucky you didn't end in the ditch!"

"We did not, however. Once or twice it was a near thing, and by the time we reached this place, I could see that Roland was very much the worse for wear. I brought him in by the back door, and found this room. I thought that the . . . the evil effects might dissipate. But I'm afraid that while I was talking to Lord Holland and Mr Allen, Roland must have located the wine servery, with the results you see."

"The fact remains that we can't leave him here. I'd best find the steward, and ask if we may have your brother moved to one of the bedrooms. It will be less public than this."

"Oh no, please!" Davina sprang up and came towards him. "I cannot embarrass others with my . . . my problem."

"My dear child, if we leave your problem as he is, he's likely to come to, and cast up his accounts all over someone's pelisse. That will be far more embarrassing to everyone."

"Lord Rigg, I am not well acquainted with the Hollands. I am already under an obligation to them. I cannot, will not, impose further on their hospitality."

"It won't be the first time they've lent a bed to a guest that's a trifle below par."

"But . . . you see . . . we are not guests. At least, not in the same sense as yourself. I came to Holland House on a matter of business. Lord Holland and Mr Allen are to help me find a buyer for the Rigborough Missal. It could destroy everything if I were to place too great a strain on their good nature."

Miss Wakeford paused, for Lord Rigg was staring blankly, as if he did not quite grasp what she had said. She placed a hand on his sleeve.

"If you please, sir, leave us here. You've been most kind, most forbearing, but from now on we'll contrive to . . ."

"One moment!" He interrupted brusquely. "Did you say you are going to sell the Rigborough Missal?"

"Yes, if I'm able. Mr Allen seems to think it won't be difficult. Indeed he says he has several likely buyers in his eye, already."

"You're mad!" The Earl was shaking his head in disbelief. "It's unthinkable! The Missal has been in Rigborough for four centuries. It belongs to the people of Rigborough."

Miss Wakeford removed her hand from his wrist. "There you mistake," she said coldly. "It belongs to me."

"You know quite well what I mean, madam. I'm not talking of the law. In God's name how can you, a Wakeford, your father's daughter . . . how can you ever think of parting with something so precious and unique? What's prompted you to do such a thing?"

Miss Wakeford had had a long and trying day. Throughout all its trials and tribulations, she had managed to preserve her temper, but now she lost it utterly.

"I will tell you what prompts me," she snapped. "It is financial necessity, which you know nothing about. I am selling the Missal to save Wakeford from bankruptcy, and more than that I'm selling it to give the people who live there a decent way of life. Let me tell you something else. There is a picture in the book you'd do well to study. It shows the riverside cottages—on my property, and yours. Do you take my meaning? Those cottages were there four hundred years ago when Geoffrey of

Wakeford made his paintings, and they are there still, and by now they are leaky, damp, rotten, unfit to house pigs! I take shame to house human beings in them, and if you cannot understand that, then all I can say is that you are as arrogant and harsh and penny-pinching as all the rest of your m-miserable ancestors! And now sir, you may go to the Devil, and leave me alone!"

Luke stared at her. A number of crushing retorts raced through his mind. He had had enough of this cranky girl and her loutish brother. They had ruined his afternoon, not to mention his coat. The proper course would be to summon the steward, and leave him to sort out the whole tangle.

But instead of reaching for the bell-rope, he found himself placing a hand on Miss Wakeford's shoulder, and saying in the bracing voice he would employ to an overtired child:

"Come now, don't cry. Sit down for a moment in this chair. I am going to call for your carriage at once, and my coachman shall drive you and Roland safe home in it."

XIV

Rebecca Bracket had spent a miserable afternoon. From the moment a hangdog Coachman Micklejohn confessed to her that Mr Roland had kicked him and Jevons off the box, and druv off alone with Miss Davina, Becky's mind had been filled with horrid images of the carriage overturned in a ditch, and both its occupants lying fatally injured.

She could be glad of only one thing—that Lady Sophia had swallowed the physic prescribed by Dr Kentridge, and fallen into a heavy sleep.

Becky sent Micklejohn after the truants on horseback, but being unfamiliar with the lanes of Kensington, he only succeeded in losing his way, and returned home empty-handed and drenched to the skin.

It was past seven o'clock, pitch dark, and raining heavily when at last she heard the rumble of wheels in the mews, and thankfully beheld the Tredgold carriage turn in through the archway of the yard. So great was her relief that she did not so much as question the strange coachman on the box, but rushed to attend to his passengers. Grim-faced she watched while two footmen carried Roland unconscious into the house; and as soon as the young man was laid on his bed, she made her way along the corridor, to ring a full peal over Davina's head.

"How could you have done such a thing?" she cried. "So worritted as I've been, wonderin' if you were dead or alive! I shall have something to say to that fine brother of yours tomorrow, I promise! And as for you, Miss, whatever was you thinkin' of, to jaunter about alone, like a hoyden? Don't you know what's proper in a lady? Why didn't you take me with you?"

"You were needed to look after Aunt Sophy."

"Then you should have took Annie, or one of the other maids. Lady Holland will be sayin' you was dragged up all anyhow, and never taught better!"

"I did not meet Lady Holland," said Davina tiredly. "She is

suffering from the rheumatics, and only appeared when all the guests were assembled."

"Thank the Lord for that," said Becky uncharitably. She suddenly remembered the coachman. "Who was it druv you home? I never saw him before."

"His name is Winkler. He's coachman to Lord Rigg."

"Rigg, did you say?" Becky's tone suggested fears of rapine, at least. "You never come all that way alone with *him*, did you, Miss?"

"You know quite well I did not! Rigg chanced to be at Holland House, he saw that Roly was in no fit state to drive, and he directed his coachman to bring us home."

"He did, did he? And what became of his own carriage?"

"He and his friend Mr Clintwood brought it back."

"In all this rain? Well, I will say that was kind in his lordship."

"No, it wasn't. Rigg did it to salve his own pride, which I assure you is excessive."

Becky stared at Davina's stony profile. "Now see here, Miss, his lordship did you a kindness, and all I can say is, I hope you thanked him as you ought. I hope you didn't shame us all, by acting rude, or pert?"

"I was extremely rude!" Davina tore off her bonnet and flung it on a chair. "I called him unfeeling, and stingy, and I don't know what else, and what is more I don't regret a word of it. Rigg is an ass, a pompous, arrogant ass! He had the effrontery to prose at me for selling the Missal. Me, a Wakeford! As if he could suffer one tenth of what I do, at having to part with it! He is a stupid puffed-up nincompoop, and I hate him!"

Having got this off her chest, Miss Wakeford burst into tears. Becky was at once all sympathy. "There, there, my poor lambie," she crooned. "You're overwrought, and no wonder. All the problems you have to bear, and as brave as a soldier about 'em. Enough is enough, I say. I'll tell you what I'm going to do, I'm going to bid Annie fetch up a hot bath for you, here by the fire, and when you've took it you're to climb straight into your bed and I'll bring you your supper on a tray. Hot victuals and a good night's sleep will soon set you to rights."

She adjured Davina to take off her wet clothes right away, and bustled off to the kitchen.

Davina was glad enough to follow orders. It was pleasant, for once, to be soothed and cosseted, and to leave everything in someone else's hands.

When she had eaten her supper, she lay for some time, watching the firelight, and thinking over the events of the day. The interview with Lord Holland had been far less terrifying than she feared. Odd-looking he might be, with his vast stomach and narrow head—like a turbot standing on its tail—but his manner had been so sunny and jovial that she had quite overcome her shyness, and her dislike of having to sue for favours.

Mr Allen, too, had been most reassuring. Neat and knowledgeable, he had expressed the view that the Book of Hours would find ready bidders. He had urged Davina not to leave London, but to remain within easy reach, so that transactions might be made expeditiously; and he had named a starting-price that exceeded Davina's wildest dreams. Such a sum would be enough to repair the cottages, re-roof all the barns, and buy new farm implements. There would even be a handsome amount over for seed and breeding-stock. If the rest of the collection sold as profitably, by next year she might see her estate on its way back to prosperity.

At this point she allowed herself to indulge in a fantasy in which Lord Rigg, suitably clad in sackcloth and ashes, was forced to witness Wakeford's renascence, and to withdraw all criticism of her actions.

Unfortunately, this delightful vision was speedily replaced by others. There rose before her the picture of Lord Rigg, drenched in claret, hauling Roly into the antechamber; Lord Rigg enduring in gentlemanly silence her unmaidenly and shrewish tirade; Lord Rigg, maddeningly polite, handing her up into the carriage and directing Winkler to take great care of her.

There was no getting away from it, she had been rude and ungracious, and she found herself wishing passionately for a chance to apologise. But she was filled with the depressing conviction that if at any time Lord Rigg should happen to cross her path, he would treat her with the disdain she deserved.

The next morning was cold, with heavy mist swirling beneath the trees in Hyde Park. Looking from her window, Davina thought the prospect as grey and flat as her own mood.

She dressed and went to her aunt's bedroom, to enquire how she did. Lady Sophy insisted that she was feeling much more the thing, but she still looked wan and tired, and Davina gave her only an edited description of the visit to Holland House, leaving out Roland's escapade, and the role played in it by Lord Rigg.

After breakfast she settled herself at the desk in the morning-room, and spent over an hour trying to compose a letter to his lordship. The right phrases proved elusive. When she allowed herself to write as she felt, her step-mother's warnings rose to mind. Would Rigg think her just another scheming female, anxious to ingratiate herself with him? When she tried for a more formal tone, the result seemed to add insult to the injury she'd already done.

At length she achieved a brief note that did not please her, but was not altogether repellent. She sealed it, and gave it to a footman to deliver in Berkeley Square.

Her despondency was not helped by Roland, who appeared as she was giving the footman his directions.

"What do you want to apologise for?" he demanded, as soon as the man had left the room. "I shan't do so! I must say, I don't know how you came to allow him to interfere in our affairs. Rigg, of all people! You know how shabby he's behaved to our friends the Clares. I should think you'd resent the loss of Edward Clare, at least. Once he's left Rowanbeck, I doubt you'll ever clap eyes on him again. If I was you, I shouldn't let him slip through my fingers so easily. Husbands ain't so easy to find at your age!"

Just what might have been Miss Wakeford's response to this very ungallant speech is not known, for at that moment the peal of the front doorbell, and a flurry of greetings in the hallway announced that Sir Murray and Miss Jane Tredgold had arrived from Bedfordshire. Both were in high spirits, and greeted the Wakeford pair with enthusiasm, the whole party then repairing to Lady Sophy's bedside to report news of the Buccleughs, to enjoy anecdotes of Luton high life, and to marvel at the exquisitely witty sayings of Meg's three young hopefuls.

Jane lost no time in speaking to Davina about the coming Season. "Mama has told me you may consent to be presented at Court with me," she said. "I must say, Dav, I wish you will.

I shall find it the dreariest thing imaginable, if I have no one to laugh and cose with."

This was something less than the truth, for Jane expected to enjoy every moment of her come-out. Through the circumstance of having inherited her mama's fair prettiness, and her papa's cheerful disposition, she had never had the least difficulty in securing partners at parties. She knew that London society was far more exacting than that of the shires, but she had been schooled to comport herself with ease in any company. Finally, she was aware that her papa, besides being well-born, was the possessor of a handsome fortune, which would allow him to launch his daughter in impeccable style.

Still, Jane was sincere in wishing for Davina's company. Despite the three years that separated them, they had been close friends since childhood, and as Jane confided to her mother when they were alone together: "Davina may say what she likes, but I know she longs above everything to see London. Why, when Papa offered to take us to the play tomorrow night, her eyes fairly sparkled. She has never had pretty things to wear, or been shown any fun. At Wakeford all they do is lecture her about her duty, and grouse at whatever she tries to do. It has given her such a conscience that she honestly believes she can't cut line, but must sit at home, and work, and pander to Aunt Eulalie's wishes. She's no better than Cinderella, I swear."

"Yes, but the thing is, how do we persuade her to stay? I've tried all I know. I thought arranging for her to meet Mr Allen might turn the trick, but she still talks of going back to Rigborough as soon as that wretched book is sold, and that could be next week."

"John Buccleugh says," remarked Jane, "that when the fish won't bite, one must try different bait. How will it be if we appeal to Davina's frivolous side?"

"My dear child, she has none."

"Oh yes, Mama, indeed she has, only it's hidden under all the duty, and responsibility. I have been thinking—why don't I take her to Madame Cluny with me? I'm to go there tomorrow, to fit my court dress."

"The very thing!" Lady Sophy pulled herself higher on her pillows. "My dear Jane, positively a stroke of genius!"

"There's one snag, though. Davina is sure to say she can't afford a fashionable modiste."

"Money need not trouble us. I shall speak to your father. Let me see. . . . Davina must be asked to accompany you, in my place. Becky must go, also. Be so good as to fetch me my writing-case, my love. I must pen a little line to Madame, she must be forewarned of our plan, and she must have Davina's measurements, and colouring. I shall drop her a hint or two, on how things must be handled."

Jane scurried to the bureau, returning with the writing materials. Taking them, Lady Sophia said in a firm voice, "Now remember, Jane. Davina is not to buy anything in the least hardwearing, or *useful*. Indeed I rely upon you and Becky to prevent her doing so. Take as your guide to taste, your Aunt Eulalie. If anything is brought forward that would remotely appeal to her—you are to reject it out of hand!"

The shopping expedition took place as planned, the party leaving Park Street at ten o'clock next morning. Sir Murray strolled to the front door to see the young ladies off, and as each passed him, pressed a folded bill into her hand, with the stern injunction that it was all to be spent, or he'd know the reason why.

Not till the carriage was bowling along Grosvenor Street was Davina able to examine the paper more closely, and when she did, she was for the moment bereft of speech.

"Jane," she stammered at last, "there must be some mistake. Uncle Murray can't have realised. This is a bill for fifty pounds!"

"I know," agreed Jane composedly.

"But . . . I cannot possibly accept it! I wouldn't know how to spend so much money!"

Jane gave her impish smile. "You'll find, dearest coz, that practice makes perfect. You must spend it, Dav. Papa will be so hurt if you don't. Am I not right, Becky?"

Miss Brackett agreed that she was, and as the carriage had already turned into Bond Street and was drawing up at Madame Cluny's door, there was no time to pursue the argument.

Although Davina had visited London on several occasions, she had never before crossed the threshold of a top-ranking modiste. The shops in Oxford, where her mama usually took her to buy gowns, were apt to be dark, poky, and crowded with wares on which the prices were clearly marked.

Madame Cluny's establishment was of quite another order. It resembled a polite drawing-room, rather than a sales-place. There was a handsome Turkey carpet on the floor, a crystal chandelier overhead, and a few delicate, gilt chairs ranged along the walls. Of merchandise there was no sign, and the lady who presently advanced to greet them was so faultlessly groomed, and of so imposing a bearing, that Davina could not think she would stoop to discuss mere money.

Here she was mistaken. Louise Cluny was of the Paris bourgeoisie. She had fled to escape The Terror, arriving in England with only the clothes on her back. Thanks to a clever pair of hands, an ability to predict the trends of fashion, and an extremely hard head, she now owned a flourishing business, her own carriage, and a neat villa in Harley Street.

As she greeted Miss Tredgold, and enquired tenderly after Lady Sophia's health, her sharp black eyes were making a lightning assessment of Miss Wakeford.

Lady Sophia had explained in the note sent round the day before, that the girl was the only child of her dead brother, and that there was "some slight hope" of her being presented at Court this year. Madame Cluny would oblige Lady Sophia by showing her niece one or two gowns, of the sort that would be convenable for a young female making her come-out. Nothing too insipid or ingenue should be offered, as Mademoiselle was one-and-twenty, and accustomed to mix with people rather older than herself.

The phrasing of this missive was not lost on Madame. *En effet*, one saw that Lady Sophia wished to bring Miss Wakeford into society, but that Miss Wakeford (a free agent, *évidemment*), had not yet consented to the scheme. Madame's part, *sans doute*, was to convince Mademoiselle how important it was (and also how very pleasant), for a lady of quality to be at all times correctly and elegantly attired.

Surveying Davina with a practised eye, Madame became aware of certain difficulties.

First there was the question of the girl's situation. Lady Sophy had made no mention of a mama. Did that imply that Miss Wakeford chose her own clothes? Could one believe she had deliberately gone out and purchased that abominable dress, that bad joke of a bonnet? If so, there was little hope for her. Not even the most brilliant modiste could prevail over a client who combined lack of taste with a strong will.

Perhaps, though, the poor child had been victimised by some unscrupulous female. One knew, *hélas*, what cruelties could be perpetrated by a spiteful older sister, a prudish aunt, a jealous step-mama. One should, at least, give Miss Wakeford the benefit of the doubt.

One came, next, to considerations of payment. If there was one thing Madame could not abide, it was customers who were tardy in paying. Debating within herself, she decided that one should not refine upon that score, here. One remembered the admirable Sir Murray Tredgold, so wealthy, so pleased to see his womenfolk prettily clad, and so unfailingly quick to meet his obligations.

It would be well, in this case, to make a discreet arrangement —even to cut one's prices quite significantly—should Miss Wakeford see something that took her fancy.

Finally, one could set Mademoiselle's own person to the credit side. Madame noted with approval the graceful figure, a little taller than the average, yet softly rounded, absolutely a couturière's dream! The visage . . . not beautiful, but vastly appealing. The eyes very large and fine—so many of the English had small eyes—and the smile, frank and delightful. Yes, there was good material here. Given time, one could make something of distinction from it.

But one must move carefully. No haste and no overinsistence, or the strong will one saw there would resist all one could do. *Eh bien*, one used a little finesse!

For the first hour, Madame Cluny addressed herself exclusively to Miss Tredgold's needs. The white court dress being made for her was fitted, and a number of muslin gowns paraded for her consideration. A Spanish shawl with a knotted fringe was discarded as being a thought too dark in colour, and the proper size for a fur muff seriously debated.

Only when it was clear that Miss Wakeford had been lulled into a sense of security, and was gazing with undisguised interest at each new article produced, did Madame make an almost imperceptible sign to her assistant. The sprigged muslins and simple lawns so appropriate for seventeen-and-a-half-year-old Jane, began to be supplemented by rather more sophisticated garments.

There was, for example, an afternoon-dress of pale green cambric, delicately tucked across the bosom and finished with small jade buttons, which Madame said (purely in passing), would suit someone of Miss Wakeford's colouring. A little later there appeared a dashing pelisse in the deep soft blue known as mignonne, and a ravishing bonnet trimmed with ribbons of the same hue. (It was when Davina was persuaded to slip the bonnet on that Becky contrived, she could not tell how, to step heavily on Davina's own hat.)

Madame's assistant now entered into the spirit of things, and brought out in quick succession a day-dress of gossamer lilac wool; a bronze-green walking-dress; a half-gown of Italian grosgrain; an afternoon gown of jonquil-yellow crape and another of straw-coloured silk trimmed with blonde lace; and two evening gowns, one of cream satin and the other of rose silk with an overdress of matching lace.

Miss Wakeford, without knowing quite how it came about, found herself trying on first one and then another of these confections. She saw herself transformed, not only in the long pier-glasses but in the shining eyes of her beholders.

Madame, in ecstasies, lost her senses and suggested prices so low they made her assistant blink; and when at last the Tredgold carriage rolled back to Park Street, not only was the whole of Sir Murray's gift disbursed, but Madame had agreed to place a reserve on one or two items that, Jane said, might have been designed for Davina.

Sir Murray made good his promise to take Jane and Davina to the play that night.

Lady Sophy could not, of course, go with them, and Roland begged to be excused, saying that he had already engaged to play cards with some friends. By happy chance Mr Mortimer Foote, who had that day returned from visiting relatives in Sussex, dropped in to pay his respects, and was persuaded without difficulty to stay for dinner and join the theatre party.

Davina dressed early, unsure which of her new gowns she should wear. Her choice fell on the cream Berlin silk. Annie, the little maid deputed to attend on Davina during her stay, arranged her hair in a high knot with short curls bunched over the ears, a style that showed off Davina's slender neck to perfection. The string of pearls bequeathed to her by her mother, a silk shawl draped casually over her elbows, and a small beaded reticule, completed what she felt was a truly elegant toilette, an opinion confirmed warmly by Lady Sophy. Davina floated downstairs feeling like Venus on the wings of Zephyr.

The evening that followed was a delight. What could be more delightful than to dine in congenial company, in one of the most beautiful houses in all London; to drive to Drury Lane in a well-sprung carriage, with a fur rug over one's knees and a hot brick at one's feet; and to admire the brilliance of the new gas-lamps that illuminated Piccadilly and the fashionable shops?

Once at the theatre, Davina found something to fascinate or entertain everywhere she looked. At the doors were the vendors of flowers, hot cakes, and bills of the play, and the crowd of flashily-dressed young bucks who, Mortimer confided, would not stay for the drama, but would soon rush off to box the watch, or engage in some other street devilry. Most compelling sight of all, was the fashionables ascending the staircase, or strolling in the passageways behind the auditorium.

It all seemed like a vast pantomime staged for her peculiar edification, and her cup overflowed when, moments after they had taken their place in the Tredgold box, the entire audience surged to its feet and broke into spontaneous applause as the popular Duke of Sussex appeared in the Royal box, and stood beaming and bowing to all and sundry.

Sir Murray warned that the first piece to be performed—a farcical comedy—had won scant praise from the critics, and that many people would elect to arrive after it was over. Davina hardly cared. For the first time in her life she was a pretty girl in a pretty gown, conscious of admiring glances flung her way, and free of all duties save that of enjoying herself.

When the lights went up at the first interval, Sir Murray suggested they leave their seats and stretch their legs a little in the corridor.

Tucking Davina's hand through his arm, he steered her through the throng, with Jane and Mortimer following behind. From time to time he would identify some well-known personage, and more than once when one of these notables greeted him, he stopped to present his young companions.

It seemed to Davina that the gentlemen thus presented were most affable, but the matrons less so. They directed very searching glances at herself and Jane. ("As if," she later told her aunt, "they were measuring us for our coffins!") One high-nosed lady eyed them so sternly, and addressed them in such a cold, snubbing way, that the girls felt ready to sink. Sir Murray, however, merely chuckled as he moved them along. "Don't worry about Mrs Drummond-Burrell," he said. "She's rude to everyone. Imagines it increases her consequence, which it don't."

"She will never allow us vouchers for Almack's," mourned Jane.

"She wouldn't be able to keep you out, if she tried. Lady Sefton, Sally Jersey and the Princess Lieven are all prepared to speak for you."

They had completed their perambulation and were making their way back to the box, when they came upon a group of latecomers, standing chatting at the head of the stairs. Davina saw with dismay that Lord Rigg was among them. He had his back to her, and was talking to a soberly clad young man, and a strikingly handsome woman in dark red silk. The fourth member of the party was Mr Robert Clintwood, and as soon as he saw Davina approaching, he smiled, bowed, and touched the Earl's arm, signalling him to move aside.

The Earl turned. His glance, at first one of polite indifference, sharpened as it fell on Davina. For a moment he seemed at a loss, but he made a quick recovery and bowed, saying in an undertone, "Good evening, Miss Wakeford. Thank you for your letter. It was generous in you to write, after my very presumptuous behaviour."

She curtsied, stealing a look at him under her lashes. She could not be sure if he was serious. Though his voice was bland, there was a glint in his eye that she found unnerving. She had the feeling that she was not going to be allowed to forget her outburst at Holland House, but would be reminded of it at some quite inappropriate moment in the future. Furthermore, his lordship's lazy gaze was taking in her new gown and hair-style, and his smile expressing candid approval, in a way that made her feel suddenly shy.

She was grateful that the ringing of the bells in the foyer precluded further conversation. People began to crowd back towards the auditorium. The Earl turned to address a few words to Sir Murray, then sauntered away to join the handsome lady, who was chatting to friends further along the passage.

Later, at home in Park Street, Jane and Davina relived the excitements of the day. Both agreed that while the play had been affecting, and the performance of the principals most creditable, it was the audience that had provided the chief entertainment.

"We were very lucky to have seen Sussex," said Jane. "Pa says he is the best of the Royals, and very kind and charitable. He is not handsome, though. I thought the handsomest man present tonight was Mr Clintwood. Rigg is too dark and piratical, and he does not smile enough. Mr Clintwood's manner is just what must please, friendly, but not encroaching. And he has such a fine bearing, such beautiful military whiskers! What is his first name, Davina?"

"Robert. He was a Captain of Hussars, but is retired from the army now."

"I think Robert a very reliable sort of name." Jane finished plaiting her hair and tied a ribbon on it. "I warn you now, I intend to do all I can to encourage Mr Clintwood's addresses!"

"How do you know you will even meet again? London is such a vast place!"

"Of course we'll meet. The Clintwoods are invited everywhere and so are we. Besides, he noticed me. One can always tell, when a man has that warm look in his eyes, that he means to pursue the acquaintance. Lord Rigg," she added pensively, "looked very warmly at you."

"I expect he was thinking how nice it would be to wring my neck. When we met at Holland House yesterday, I called him arrogant and parsimonious."

"Did you?" Jane stared at her cousin with new respect. "I own I could never have been so bold. It seems to have had a very good effect on him. No doubt it was the novelty of the experience. In general, you know, people don't speak their minds to an earl." She climbed into bed and sat hugging her knees. "Who was the tall lady with Rigg? Mortimer seemed to know her, and I could not help thinking I have seen her before."

"You've seen her portrait, at Wakeford. She's Mrs Turnbull, that was Lady Charlotte Rowan—Rigg's aunt."

"Of course! Now I recall! She ran away from home and married to spite her family. Mr Turnbull is a merchant. Very rich, but not at all the thing, Mama says. You won't see *them* at the ton parties. I'm surprised Rigg chooses to cultivate them, when he is trying to win acceptance for himself. Perhaps he's ignorant of what people think."

"I don't believe he cares what they think. He's sincerely attached to the Turnbulls."

"Yes, and I suppose he's doing the pretty to them, before Amabel comes to town. She'll never invite them to Rowan House. She's a terrible snob, and won't allow anyone who smells of the shop to cross her threshold." Jane lay back on her pillows. "I don't expect Mama to invite the Rowans here, either. She says they are fast and bad ton. On the other hand, Papa may invite them."

"Why do you say so?"

"Because I heard Lord Rigg invite him to shoot pheasant at Rowanbeck in the autumn. Pa will never pass up such a chance. And you must admit, Davina, that Rigg wouldn't have extended the invitation if he'd taken you in strong dislike. That would be to run his head into a noose. I shall be surprised if we do not see his lordship in Park Street quite soon."

Davina made no answer. She was not sure that she wished to see Lord Rigg again. He was a disturbing influence in her life. She had come to London to arrange for the sale of the Missal. That done, she would return to Rigborough, and rural obscurity.

It would be foolish to ignore the warnings issued by all who knew the Rowan history. Scandal, and dissension, and being constantly in the limelight were not what she enjoyed. As for that gleam in his lordship's eye, it was probably directed at any passably presentable female he met.

Sighing a little wistfully, Miss Wakeford snuffed out the candles, and climbed into bed.

XV

Miss Tredgold was right in her assessment of Lord Rigg's sentiments.

Far from taking Davina in dislike, he was strongly drawn to her.

At their first encounter on Hagg Hill, he had thought her a quiz, with her shabby, muddied garb and quaint opinions; but as time went on, he had come to admire her courage, intelligence, and sense of humour.

These were qualities to be valued in a friend, but he had never judged them to be the basis for a passionate attachment between a man and a woman.

Then had come the afternoon on the canal-cut. Skating with Miss Wakeford, Luke had felt in complete harmony with her, and the world about them. He would have laid odds she felt the same. It had come as a bitter disappointment when she repulsed him next day, and many times on the journey to London he had been tempted to turn back to Rigborough, to insist upon talking to her, and to discover the reason for her changed attitude.

The débâcle at Holland House had been, he realised, a turning-point for them both. If he had walked out, and left Miss Wakeford and her obnoxious brother to find their own way home, there would have been the end of it. But he had not walked out. He had chosen to sacrifice his chance of a tête-à-tête with Lord Holland, and to tool a carriage through the streets in pouring rain. What was more, these actions had not caused him a moment's regret.

Instead of being repelled by the lady's display of temper, he found himself admiring her the more. By God, she was right to rate the welfare of her dependants above mere property, and to consign him to the devil for questioning it! She had ten times the spirit, ten times the character, of any female he'd so far encountered.

When her brief letter of thanks was delivered to him next day, he found himself as pleased as a stripling engaged in his first love-affair. Miss Wakeford was not, after all, indifferent to him. In a few days—next week, or the week after—it would be pleasant to call in Park Street, and renew the acquaintance.

This complacency was severely jolted that night at Drury Lane. Brought face to face with Miss Wakeford, he saw that what he had once taken for a pebble, had been transformed into a diamond of the first water. Here was a young woman who, while not precisely beautiful, was vastly appealing, and drawing admiring stares from every man present. Here, moreover, was a lady of quality, Miss Wakeford of Wakeford Hall, surrounded by the barriers of respectability, and protected by a family who would not encourage the advances of a man without standing in society.

Lord Rigg perceived, in short, that his urgent task was to regain his good name.

On Tuesday morning he rose betimes, ate a rapid breakfast, and drove round to Mr Shedley's offices in Lincoln's Inn.

Mr Shedley was able to give an encouraging report of his meeting with Jonas Whitstaple. It had taken a little time, he said, to persuade the man to sign the affidavit he had drawn up, but he had finally consented.

"I have the document here," the lawyer concluded. "I'm of the opinion that for safekeeping, it should remain in your deed-box, but I've had a fair copy made which you may use in any dealings with your cousin."

The Earl nodded, studying the paper with a look of frowning distaste.

Beneath its legal flourishes, its meaning was plain enough. Mr Whitstaple stated on oath that he had loaned the sum of twelve thousand pounds to Sir Jocelyn Clare. In return, the latter had promised to arrange a rendezvous between Whitstaple and the Countess of Rigg. He had failed to keep his side of the bargain, and had informed Mr Whitstaple after months of delay that the lady would have none of him. He had also failed to repay the loan, even when Whitstaple was forced into bankruptcy and a debtors' prison. Whitstaple, though in dire straits, had so far kept silence, out of respect for the lady's feelings. Now, however, having succeeded in discharging all his debts, he felt at liberty to put on record the facts of Sir Jocelyn's duplicity.

"A disgusting document," said the Earl at last. "I wish there was no need to use it, but I see no other way, short of calling Jocelyn out."

"There must be no duelling, my lord. That would bring the whole story into the open, and make Lady Rigg the target of much distasteful gossip."

"Can Whitstaple be relied on to hold his tongue?"

"He can. If shame at his own behaviour does not suffice, then fear will. The man's too terrified to utter a squeak! No sooner was he sprung from the King's Bench, than he bolted out of London. I'm told he's gone to earth at his father's home in Dorset."

"Amen to that! I've no quarrel with the worm. Only with Jocelyn."

He handed the affidavit back to the lawyer. "Give me the fair copy, if you please."

Complying, Mr Shedley was moved to sound a warning. "Have a care, my lord. Your cousin is vindictive and tenacious. He'll strike back at you, if he can."

"I'll bear it in mind."

"What do you mean to do?"

Luke smiled. "Invite Jocelyn to my house, to discuss Mr Whitstaple's timely release from gaol."

That evening the Earl elected to dine alone, refusing to allow Mr Clintwood to remain at Rowan House.

"We blackmailers," he said, "prefer to conduct our business without witnesses. Why else do you imagine I sent Charles out?"

"Clare's a treacherous creature," Clintwood answered. "He may attempt violence."

"Do you know, I almost hope he will? But I fear I won't be allowed the pleasure of thrashing him. He's craven at heart."

"And if he comes armed?"

"No, Robert, there's too much to incriminate him if my body is found floating in the Thames. Go home, if you please."

Mr Clintwood left, albeit unwillingly. The Earl enjoyed a leisurely meal, ordered a bottle of port brought to the library, and settled down with a book of critical essays.

The hours ticked by.

It was not until after one in the morning that there came the sound of carriage wheels, and a ring at the front door bell. A short while later, Sir Jocelyn strolled into the room.

He was, as always, dressed in the height of fashion, but his manner was less urbane than usual, and there was a glitter in his pale eyes that suggested that he had drunk more than was good for him. He made no attempt to shake hands, but came to sit in a chair by the fire.

"Well, Rigg," he said, "what the devil is this about Jonas Whitstaple? It was damned inconvenient, having to break up my game to come here. Could you not have waited till tomorrow?"

"I could," said Luke equably, "but you, it seems, could not." He drew the affidavit from his pocket and handed it over. "Read that, then we'll talk."

Sir Jocelyn read the document through once, and then a second time. His pettish expression gave way to a look at once bland, and wary.

"May I ask who drew up this rigmarole?"

"Thomas Shedley. It's legally sound."

"I assume you bought Whitstaple's signature by paying his debts for him? Very pretty, I must say!"

"As pretty as acting the pimp to procure a woman of your own family, for a lecherous toad like Whitstaple!"

"My dear cousin, I did no such thing. Whitstaple must have mistaken the matter. This statement is a tissue of lies, and of course I deny it totally."

"That won't profit you, Jocelyn. You forget, the facts can be corroborated by one person whose word will not be doubted."

Sir Jocelyn dropped the paper to the floor. "If by that you mean Amabel, surely you realise she will say nothing? She can hardly accuse me without involving herself. If you attempt to use that affidavit, you will damage her past recall. I'm quite safe, I think."

Luke stood up abruptly, towering over the thin man. "You are safe only as long as you do my bidding," he said. "From this time on you will have nothing to do with Amabel. You will not attempt to see her, to threaten her in any way, or to extort money from her. You will not speak a single word against her, or do anything to sully her reputation. If you do, then be sure I will destroy you in those circles you prize. The Prince Regent is none too nice in his morals, but he will draw the line at associating with a man that meets his gambling debts by blackmailing a defenceless woman, cheating his friends, and fleecing a member of his family of sixty thousand pounds. That money I intend to write off as an irrecoverable debt. It's a small price to pay to be rid of you. Now get out of this house!"

Sir Jocelyn sprang up and began to protest, but Luke cut him short. "There's no more to be said. Don't try me too far. If you value your skin, leave at once!"

For a moment the two men stared at each other. Then Sir Jocelyn turned on his heel and hurried from the room.

Luke waited till he heard the carriage wheels die away along the street. Then he stooped, picked up the paper from the floor, tore it across and across, and dropped the pieces into the fire.

The following morning, when he came down to breakfast, he found a letter from Amabel beside his plate. He read it, and smiling a little, addressed his secretary.

"You were right, Charles. There will be a ball at Rowan House. My sister-in-law is set on the idea."

"Oh? Does Lady Rigg come to London?"

"She writes that she will leave Rowanbeck in a few days' time with Cornelia Finch. They are to travel by easy stages. She says that once settled in London, she plans to entertain—on a small scale at first—but she adds that towards the end of the Season, a ball may be considered admissible. Prepare for some heavy campaigning, my friend!"

"I have never before undertaken to arrange a ball," said Mr Turnbull nervously. "It's not quite in my line."

"It will be! Don't worry, Amabel is an old hand at such things. Try to prevent her from staging any major event during the Newmarket race-meetings. Impress upon her that I will not have the ballroom hung with pink silk, and that I refuse under any circumstances to assume fancy costume. Apart from that, she has *carte blanche* to do as she pleases."

Lady Rigg and Miss Finch arrived at Rowan House on the following Wednesday.

Though they had travelled only from Barnet, having spent the night there with friends, Miss Finch was so much afflicted by travel-sickness that she had to be packed off to bed with cold cloths on her forehead, and her vinaigrette to hand.

Lady Rigg, as fresh as a daisy, expressed herself not altogether sorry about her companion's low state. "It's so much easier to talk when Cornelia's not present," she told Luke. "I've a great deal to tell you that is of a private nature. Come, let us have tea, and a comfortable chat."

His lordship ordered a tray of tea to be brought to the drawing-room, and settled down to hear all the Rigborough *on-dits*. Amabel, being interested only in people, was not able to report on his estate, except to confirm that Edward Clare was as busy as a bee in a bottle. "He can do nothing but prate of winter feed, and turnip tops, and the best way to treat mawworm in cattle," she complained. "Lord, Luke, what a dull stick he is! I pity poor Davina when she marries him."

"If she does," said the Earl.

"Of course she will! Edward is confident she'll accept him, and I must say I don't know who else she will get. Men don't favour clever females, you know, and there's no denying that Davina is the complete bluestocking, as well as being incurably dowdy."

Lord Rigg gave an involuntary smile at this, and Amabel, who was watching him closely, wondered what it signified, but he offered no comment.

Changing the subject, she announced that she had inspected the Dower House from cellar to attic, and was of the opinion that with certain alterations, a wall or two knocked down, the plumbing overhauled, and a new roof put on, it might be made quite tolerable. "It's not Rowanbeck, of course, but those days are over. From now on, I must cut my coat to suit my cloth."

Lord Rigg refrained from pointing out that it was his cloth that was to be cut, and said mildly that he would engage an architect, and Amabel must tell him exactly what she had in view.

"You're very kind to me, Luke," she said, her blue eyes misty. "Although we're not destined to find happiness together, I shall always cherish a deep affection for you. We are true friends, are we not?"

"True friends," he agreed, smiling.

"And you, what have you been about, since last I saw you?"

"I've been very dull. I've visited Holland House—played whist at Brooks's with Lord Holland—driven in the Park—visited Jackson's Parlour for some sparring practice."

Amabel unerringly picked the plum from the pudding.

"If the Hollands are with you, you'll be out of the woods in no time."

"Oh, there are a few thickets to pass yet. But leave that, for the moment. There is something I must tell you in confidence, while we have the chance."

"Oh, what is that?"

"It concerns Jocelyn Clare." He saw the alarm in her face, and added quickly, "No, don't be disturbed. He won't trouble you, ever again."

She sat silently scanning his face, and then said haltingly, "Luke . . . I fear you don't know the whole of it. . . ."

"I know as much as I need to. Whatever has happened, is over and done with. Whatever threats Jocelyn has used against you, are at an end. You are free of him, I promise."

She gave a deep sigh. "Oh, if I could believe that. . . ."

"Believe it, Amabel."

She looked at him searchingly. "Luke, Jocelyn is a very dangerous person. I thought, when he first came to live at Rowanbeck, that he had our interests at heart, but I learned that he never considers anyone but himself, and will do anything—anything at all—to get what he wants. He is vile! He doesn't know the meaning of the word 'pity'. He led me to do things—condone things—that I'm deeply ashamed of."

"Forget all that. You are to start afresh. You're to be happy. That's my wish, my command!" He rose and stretched down a hand to her. "Come. Mrs Dubbleday is anxious to see you, and you must meet my secretary, Charles Turnbull. I think you are going to deal extremely together."

XVI

The Season was now in full swing. Each day, more houses in the fashionable part of town were thrown open, their shutters taken down and their knockers re-hung. Carriages rolled in from the country, mud to the axles, to set down the rich, the titled and the famous. Every hotel was full. Naval officers put up at Fladong's in Oxford Street, the Army at Stephens's in Bond Street, Ibbetson's was favoured by undergraduates and the impoverished clergy, while at the other end of the scale was the Clarendon, where rich gourmets were ready to pay as much as three or four pounds for a French dinner. Even grubby Limmer's, with its dark, fusty rooms, was packed with country squires and racecourse aficionados, come to London to buy horses, drink port wine, and see a little high life.

A glittering programme of events was promised for the summer, which was to see the festivities surrounding the marriage of the Regent's daughter, Princess Charlotte, to Prince Leopold of Saxe-Coburg-Saalfeld. A galaxy of routs, balls and assemblies lay ahead, and the ladies of the ton spoke shudderingly of "sad squeezes", and affected a drawling ennui about the whole. This deceived no one. Competition for invitations to the leading events was as acute as ever, and nothing could exceed the smugness of those lucky enough to be included, and the mortification of those left out.

The news that the beautiful Countess of Rigg was in residence at Berkeley Square soon spread, and while a few were inclined to censure her for putting so prompt an end to her period of mourning, most agreed that she had suffered greatly, had shown herself a devoted wife to Talbot Rowan throughout his long illness, and was entitled to take up the threads of her life once more.

It amused Luke to see how smoothly Amabel slipped into the exacting rôle of young and lovely widow. She behaved with the utmost circumspection, eschewing all public pageants and the livelier sort of parties, and attending only small, select gatherings. Her manner in company was perfect—a little wistful, a little tremulous at the prospect of facing the harsh world, yet trusting in her dear, good friends to protect her.

Within a week of her return she had begun to attract a court of admirers, who haunted Rowan House and vied for a chance to act as her escort. "Amabel's Circus", was Mr Clintwood's inelegant phrase for these gentlemen, whom he had met when he took Lady Rigg driving in Hyde Park one afternoon.

"There must have been half a dozen of 'em," he said, "riding alongside my phaeton and frightening my cattle! There was young Jerviss if you please, tossing rosebuds into Amabel's lap and spoutin' some verses he's dashed off in her honour! I soon sent him to the rightabout. I swear I don't know why you let such a set of mooncalves dangle after her."

"I can think of no better way to silence the rumours of an *affaire* between Amabel and me," replied Luke. "Besides, it will let me out of squiring her to all sorts of damn dull parties."

"Oh no, it won't," said Clintwood briskly. "Here I've been working myself to a shadow, setting up invitations for you, and you're looking to cry off! You'll oblige me by showing willing, my lad, or I wash my hands of you!"

Luke laughed, but did not argue. He knew he could not hope to be rehabilitated in polite society without the good graces of certain highly respected and excessively dull people.

It was not enough that men of his own age-group welcomed him back, declared him a capital fellow, a first-rate whipster, a man that Gentleman Jackson was pleased to go a few rounds with.

It was not enough that older men like Lord Holland and Lord Althorp should appear to accept him, that Marcus Sherborne had strolled the length of Bond Street arm in arm with him, or that Willoughby d'Eresby had asked his opinion of a horse on sale at Tattersall's.

In the long run it was not the gentlemen who must be won over, but those well-born ladies who were still implacably opposed to him—the middle-aged mamas of budding débutantes, who saw Lord Rigg as a ruiner of reputations, the high sticklers who never forgot or forgave any infringement of their rigid code, the ambitious hostesses, who cultivated the goodwill of the Regent, and would do nothing to affront him.

Sighing, Luke obeyed Mr Clintwood's dictums. He became

the very model of dull respectability. He even ordered a set of formal evening-clothes, satin knee-breeches, black coat and silk stockings, in case the patronesses of Almack's should suddenly lose their sanity, and invite him to one of their assemblies.

Davina's ideas of concluding a rapid sale of the Rigborough Book of Hours proved over-optimistic.

Mr Allen came to Park Street two days after the interview at Holland House. He examined the book and pronounced it to be a masterpiece, and in an excellent state of preservation.

"A sale of this nature must be very carefully negotiated," he said. "We must cast our net as wide as possible, without attracting the scaff and raff of dealers. One thinks of certain names in Paris, one thinks of the Vatican, as purchasers. There are great patrons of the arts, like the Rothschilds, and John Julius Angerstein. I have also consulted Sir John Fleming Leicester, who naturally hopes that such a treasure may be kept in England."

"Oh, so do I," said Davina earnestly. "I shall feel a traitor if it goes abroad. Do you think that perhaps the Prince Regent . . . ?"

"He will certainly be interested," said Mr Allen, "but one must face the fact that he is, at present, so deep in debt that he is harrying Parliament to give him new loans. Still, we must not despair. We will do our very best to find an English buyer. To come to practical matters—you have said you wish to keep the Missal here in this house. Are you sure it is secure?"

"Why, yes! It's locked in my uncle's strongroom, along with my aunt's jewellery and important papers. But if you feel it should go to the bank. . . ."

"Not yet, perhaps, and not necessarily to the bank. But when the time comes for prospective bidders to inspect the book, or have their agents do so, then perhaps we must find some other venue. It will inconvenience Sir Murray and Lady Sophia to have folk tramping in and out all the time, will it not?"

"I suppose so. Oh dear, everything is so much more complicated than one foresees."

Mr Allen rose. "No matter, Miss Wakeford, we have made a start. Leave things to me, for the moment. When I have a clear picture of buyers' interest, we must meet again. If all goes well, that should be before the end of April."

"Only then?" Davina sounded dismayed, and Mr Allen tilted his head.

"These things take time. I trust you're not in need of a hasty settlement?"

"No, not that."

"One must never let a collector feel that time is on his side . . . that he can beat one down. Of course, if I receive any exceptionally promising bids, I'll let you know at once. In the meantime I urge you to keep your own counsel, and be patient. You'll be rewarded, in the long run."

Davina thanked him for his kindness, and he hurried away, leaving her to inform the Tredgolds that her stay in Park Street might be somewhat prolonged.

"Exactly what we have been hoping for," said Lady Sophia. "Now there can be no objection to your being presented, and you can't pretend that we are holding you here against your wishes."

"It was never against my wishes. There's nothing I like better than being here with you, and London is . . . a dream of delight. But you see. . . ."

"There's no 'but' about it," said Sir Murray. "The thing is settled, puss, and I'm mightily pleased it's turned out this way."

Further argument would have been churlish, so Davina could only express her gratitude, and settle in to enjoy her good luck.

Lady Sophy's plans for launching Jane had been laid months earlier. They were now stretched to include her niece. All the Tredgolds' friends were informed that Miss Wakeford, of Wakeford Hall, was to make her come-out. Since Lady Sophy was a famous hostess, and everyone wished to be invited to her parties, Davina found her name added to the Tredgolds' on all the cards sent to Park Street.

Lady Sophy also took her on an alarming number of shopping forays, until she declared herself quite overwhelmed at the flood of gowns, hats, shoes, silk stockings, gloves, shawls, muffs and bonnets that were apparently essential to a young lady spending three months in town.

One of the first to see Davina in her new finery was her stepmother. Mrs Wakeford, arriving from the country in the last week of March, did not at first recognise the elegant creature running downstairs to greet her; and when recognition dawned, she was not well-pleased.

"That dress, Davina! It's silk. Silk is only for married females. I'm surprised Sophia didn't tell you so."

"It's cambric, not silk," said Davina. "Feel it, and you'll see."

"It looks outrageously expensive! How much did it cost, pray?"

"I don't know. Aunt Sophy wouldn't tell me."

"Where is Sophia? I thought that at least she'd be on hand to receive me."

"She asked me to apologise for her. She's gone to Devonshire House, to collect vouchers for Almack's."

"Hoity-toity! How grand you've become."

Davina signed to a footman to carry Mrs Wakeford's trunk upstairs. "How was your stay at Tunbridge, Mama? Did you find the waters beneficial?"

"Not in the least. In fact, I wished to come here last week, but Letitia would not budge. She's selfish beyond belief. Imagine, she allowed herself to be taken in by the flatteries of a most encroaching person. I hope he may not follow her to London, for I certainly never wish to see him again."

Mrs Wakeford continued to complain all the way up to her bedroom, and remarked, as a parting shot, that Davina must remember that fine feathers did not make fine birds, and that gentlemen much preferred a modest girl in a simple gown to one dressed up like a French doll.

When Roland Foote arrived home some hours later, and lounged in to greet his mother, he annoyed her by taking Davina's part. "I don't see anything against Dav getting a few fal-lals," he said. "The more Aunt Sophy buys for her, the less weight on our purse. 'Sides, I shouldn't care to have my sister going about London, dressed like a scarecrow. Might give people a bad impression of the family."

Eulalie stared at him coldly. "I suppose, Roland, it has not struck you that if Davina marries, then Wakeford and what you are pleased to refer to as 'our' purse, will go beyond our reach for ever?"

"They've done so, already. And if you don't wish to marry Dav off," continued Roland with maddening logic, "then all I can say is, you shouldn't have jostled her into coming to town."

"I did not jostle her. She came of her own will, on a matter of business. I did not expect her to prink herself out in expensive gowns like this!"

Roland shrugged. "Yes, she's bang up to the nines, now. But Lord, Mama, you don't need to fall into the sullens about it. Dav ain't the marrying kind. She can talk of nothing but that dashed Book of Hours. Not another thought in her head."

Mrs Wakeford was in no way convinced, and her fears intensified when she spoke to her hostess that evening. Lady Sophy was in raptures about Davina, and said she had every hope of seeing the dear child engaged to be married before the end of the summer.

"She has taken extremely well," she said. "Everyone has remarked what a charming, unaffected girl she is, and the fact that she's a trifle bookish hasn't counted against her at all. Lord Holland told me he found it a pleasure to converse with her, and he is very witty, you know, and dislikes dull females. He said Davina will make an ideal wife for a young man anxious to enter public life. As to the younger set, Mortimer says they like her very well, because she is a good dancer, and chats easily, and looks very pretty, too."

Lady Sophy paused for a moment, then said, with the air of one placing the cherry atop the cake, "I have reason to hope, my dear Eulalie, that Davina has caught Lord Pangbourne's eye. He saw her for the first time at the Foleys' assembly, and called the very next morning. Then, at the Seftons', he never left her side, and I heard him request his mama to be sure to include Miss Wakeford in the invitations to their dress ball. You know, if Pangbourne is interested, our worries are over. He is a pleasant, sensible young man, and to receive his addresses must make any girl happy. His family is well-to-do, and won't be put off by Wakeford's temporary set-back. What a triumph if he speaks for her! Don't you agree?"

"And Davina? What does she think of this paragon?"

"Naturally, she will need time to get to know him."

"She doesn't encourage him?"

"She doesn't flirt with him. That is not her style."

Eulalie missed the stiffness in her sister-in-law's voice, and answered with a toss of the head, "I expect she means to have that lummox, Edward Clare. Sophia, I do hope I shan't be called upon to accompany Davina to too many parties? You know how crowds fatigue me, and bring on my attacks!"

"You need not put yourself out at all. I'm bound to chaperone Jane. There's no need for two of us to suffer."

As she spoke, Lady Sophy was debating whether or not to tell Eulalie of the much thornier problem that confronted them.

Among the first callers at Park Street had been Lucas and Amabel Rowan. During most of their short visit, his lordship's attention had been engaged by Sir Murray, who wished to discuss salmon-fishing on the Severn. Amabel had devoted her time to chatting to the ladies, and had ended by begging that Davina and Jane be allowed to join a party of young people who planned to drive out to Richmond Park as soon as the weather was a little warmer.

"We are to take a basket luncheon, and picnic by the water," Amabel said. "My cousin Cornelia Finch will be of the party, and so will Roland and Mortimer Foote, and Mr James Tunmer and his sister. Mr Tunmer is neighbour to my parents in Yorkshire, you know. It will be all old friends together. Do say yes, dear Lady Sophia."

Her ladyship found herself in a dilemma. While she had no wish to see her girls involved with the Rowans, they were Davina's closest neighbours. To refuse an open invitation for which no date was yet set, would be to offer an insult which might have long-lasting effects. Lady Sophy could only smile and offer a general assent, in the hopes that Lord Rigg at least would not take it into his head to join the expedition.

She did not miss the glow of pleasure that suffused Davina's face, nor the fact that when Lord Rigg took his leave some ten minutes later, he held Davina's hand for rather longer than was proper.

Lady Sophy had raised two sons and three daughters. She recognised the signs of burgeoning affection when she saw them. Clearly it was her duty to warn Eulalie of what was in the wind. On the other hand, she knew that Eulalie cared not a groat for Davina's happiness, and would cheerfully wreck it, to suit her own pocket. The important thing was to retain Davina's trust, and that couldn't be done by betraying her to Eulalie's avarice.

The Season, after all, had just begun. Much could happen in a few weeks. Lady Sophy made no mention of her fears, but sending up a fervent prayer that Lord Pangbourne might quickly be brought to hand, led Mrs Wakeford downstairs to dinner.

Mrs Wakeford would have been well advised to question her son's behaviour, rather than that of her step-daughter.

Roland, intoxicated by the thought of having £500 a year, to spend as he pleased, had plunged headlong into London's high life.

His first move was to visit Schultz's establishment, where he bespoke a new coat of superfine cloth, dark grey and single-breasted, with wide lapels and silver buttons. He also ordered several pairs of pantaloons, one plain waistcoat and two fancy, and a drab overcoat with ten shoulder-capes.

The price Schultz quoted made him blink a little, but Roland had set his heart on being ranked among the swells, and scorned to patronise the lesser tailors in Clifford Street. Besides, his friends assured him that he should buy on tick, as no one dreamed of paying bills on the dot.

Within a day or so he purchased such things as hats, boots, and undergarments; several dozen shirts; a cane with an amber knob, said to be all the crack; and a diamond tie-pin.

Satisfied that he presented a stylish appearance, he then threw himself into the social round. He paid an early visit to Tattersall's, where a number of unsound animals were paraded for his inspection. Roland, being an excellent judge of horseflesh, rejected these out of hand and after some bargaining bought a thoroughbred chestnut with a fine head, solid shoulders, and long sloping pasterns. The auctioneer accepted a low bid only because the prad, in his view, was unmanageable. Roland knew otherwise, and proved his point by riding Crack O' Dawn home.

It was while he was out riding, next day, in Rotten Row, that he ran across Mr Toby Dalbiggin. Toby was an old school-friend and drinking companion . . . the same that had persuaded Roland to drink Blue Ruin on the morning of the Hollands' At Home.

It was not long before the two young bloods had agreed that routs and assemblies were all very well for females, but a dead bore for a man of athletic tastes. By the time they had made a circuit of the Park, they had laid plans to engage in far more diverting pastimes.

Roland did give a passing thought to what all this would cost; but he believed Mr Dalbiggin to be very plump in the pocket, since his grandfather was a wealthy corn-merchant who doted upon Toby, and kept him well-supplied with funds.

Mr Dalbiggin, for his part, said that he had been on the town long enough to know what was what, and urged Roland to cut line and enjoy life.

They visited Jackson's Saloon at Number 13, Bond Street, where the followers of The Fancy gathered daily. The great champion did not offer either Roland or Toby any praise as boxers, but he watched Roland engage in a bout of single-stick with one of his assistants, and was good enough to say that with application Mr Foote might become expert in the art.

They attended the Opera, not because they liked music, but for the amusement of strolling in Fops' Alley with other young exquisites, and of ogling the women in the lowest boxes.

On warm evenings, they visited the public-houses on the fringe of Tothill Fields, where Nuns and Abbesses were always on the prowl for custom, pick-pockets abounded, and the liquor sold went by such names as Nelson's Blood, Sudden Death, and Flash o' Lightning.

One Sunday morning they even drove out to Copenhagen House, beyond Battle Bridge, to watch the bull-mastiffs fight. It was a bloody business and Roland, who loved dogs, disliked it so much that he spent no more than ten minutes at the ringside, and passed the hours in dalliance with a young serving-wench named Polly Odgers. Polly was a country girl, homesick for the farm, and less grasping and hard-eyed than her London sisters. Roland formed the habit of driving out to see her, once or twice a week, and always remembered to bring her some trinket.

He did not attempt to conceal these pastimes from his mother, nor did she show any displeasure at them. They were natural to young-men-about-town, and as she had foreseen, they cured Roland of his hopeless passion for Amabel Rowan.

What Roland did not reveal, however, was the fact that his friend Mr Dalbiggin had one very dangerous fault. He was a compulsive gambler, and he quickly infected Roland with the same disease. If they had confined themselves to betting on the turf, all might have been well, but Toby preferred to hang about the gaming-tables, and play faro, macao, or quinze.

Roland was an inexpert card-player. He could not readily recall which cards were discarded, and which still in play. He was reckless when he should be cautious, and vice versa. Worst of all, he was no judge of his fellow-men, and couldn't distinguish a straight from a leg. The stakes at those clubs patronised by Toby might not be as high as at Almack's, or Watier's, but they were high enough. In a very short time, Roland had lost a good deal more than he could afford.

Of course he had occasional runs of luck. These convinced him that once he caught the hang of things, he would begin to show a handsome profit.

Mortimer Foote, who spotted Roland one night as he was about to enter the house of a notorious gamester, took the trouble to call in Park Street next morning, and take his cousin to task.

"Keep away from Wrackham, Roly," he said. "The man's an out-and-out scoundrel. Not allowed on the Great Go. Blackballed at Brooks's too, since poor young Gower blew out his brains. Boy wasn't yet sixteen, and Wrackham had no right to accept his bets, let alone call 'em in. Nasty fellow. Shouldn't like to see you in his clutches."

Roland, who had reached much the same conclusion, nevertheless resented being lectured by Mortimer. "I shall do as I please," he said hotly, "and I hope you won't go carrying tales to Mama."

"Of course I won't. You may go to the devil, if you wish. Only thought to put you on your guard."

"Don't prate, man. I went to Wrackham's for a lark, to watch, not to play. Dalbiggin won't let me exceed my possible. Very fly customer, Dalbiggin."

"No, he ain't," said Mortimer flatly. "Wears a pink neckcloth, with a checked weskit. Jumped-up counter-clerk, nothing more. He's always in some fix or another. Grandfather has to bail him out, but you don't have a grandfather, and if you want to steer clear of the doldrums, you'd best not play cards with Wrackham's set."

It was good advice, and like most good advice, was ignored. Roland continued to lose at the tables, and was soon carrying a load of debt far beyond his capacity to repay.

Mortimer said nothing to Mrs Wakeford. If he had, she would

have paid no attention, for she herself was an inveterate gambler. Most of her time was spent at the whist-parties of her friends. The stakes set were moderate, and Eulalie an habitual winner. "We Footes," she would say complacently, "are natural card-players." She forgot that the skill lay on her side of the family, and that Roland took after his papa, who had ruined himself by gaming.

XVII

THE PANGBOURNES' BALL took place on the first Monday in May. As it was one of the most prestigious of the Season, and likely to be attended by people a great deal older and more august than her two protégées, Lady Sophy arranged for a few young people and their parents to dine at Park Street.

"It will allow you to become acquainted," she declared. "Nothing is more daunting than to arrive at one's first large assembly, and recognise not a single face. Mortimer and Roland will of course take good care of you, and Eulalie and I will see that suitable partners are presented to you. I have invited the Millwards to dinner—their girls are amiable and pretty—and Mr Garth Trevor and Captain James Frimley will complete the party. You may be sure that you will start the evening with several dances already spoken for."

Despite this foresight, Davina found herself quite tense with apprehension when the Tredgold party entered Pangbourne House. Mrs Wakeford might say that the hallway was not half so large and fine as their own at Wakeford, but to Davina it seemed enormous. At the head of the staircase stood the Dowager Lady Pangbourne, clad in heliotrope silk, rubies at her throat and wrists, and a tiara like a Viking helmet on her head. She was, at the moment, hob-nobbing with the Duke of Wellington, who looked to be in considerable awe of her.

Moving slowly up the stairs was a long line of fashionables. As she studied the ladies, their magnificent gowns, their glittering parures, their tall ostrich plumes, Davina wondered how she could ever have thought her rose-coloured silk and single string of pearls grand enough for such an occasion.

The gentlemen were as splendid as the ladies. Some wore dress regimentals, some old-fashioned knee-breeches, some the black pantaloons, white waistcoats, and swallow-tailed coats of ordinary evening dress. Everywhere glittered the ribbons and stars of Orders, and it seemed to Davina that if any of these splendid beings should invite her to dance, she would lose all power of speech or movement.

By degrees their group attained the upper landing. Lady Pangbourne welcomed them in tones of booming geniality, and young Lord Pangbourne, who until then had been completely obscured by his mother's gigantic form, emerged to take Davina's hand in a friendly clasp, and beg her to form part of his set in the first quadrille.

This mark of favour did much to restore her spirits, and she was able to follow her elders into the first reception-room with something like composure.

There the press of guests was so great that it seemed impossible to make progress, but Sir Murray forged slowly on, like a flagship with the small craft of his fleet sailing after.

Mortimer Foote offered Davina his arm, and entertained her with murmured remarks about the notabilities present. The tall man to their left was the brilliant advocate Lord Erskine, talking to dark and enigmatic Lord Granville. (Mr Foote did not think it proper to add that Granville had been Lady Bessborough's lover for years, and had broken her heart by his recent marriage to her niece.) The thin man on their right was Lord Foley, known as "Number 11" because of his skinny legs. Over by the centre window was the dashing officer and noted whip, "Kangaroo" Cooke. He was talking to Lord Alvanley, close friend of the now-disgraced and bankrupt Beau Brummell.

A little further on, they passed Sir Jocelyn Clare. He caught Davina's eye and bowed slightly, then turned back with a bored air to his companion. This was a plump young man wearing a dandified coat with heavily padded shoulders and a nipped-in waist. His round, snub-nosed face was familiar to Davina, and she asked Mortimer who he might be.

"I've seen him quite often," she said. "He comes to Park Street to collect Roly, but I can't remember ever to have been introduced to him."

"That's Toby Dalbiggin." Mortimer frowned slightly as he spoke, and Davina looked at him enquiringly.

"Do you dislike him?"

"Lord no! Fellow's a lightweight. Nothing in him to dislike. I was wondering what Clare can want of him, that's all."

"It looks to me as if Sir Jocelyn's being held against his will!"

"Then it's the first time I've known it happen. Clare pleases himself. He'd ditch Toby soon enough, if it suited him."

At this point their conversation was interrupted by Lady Sophia, who bade them come and meet some of her friends. Davina made her curtsey to kind Lady Sefton; to ugly, vociferous Madame de Staël; and to lovely, garrulous Lady Jersey, who kept their entire party kicking its heels while she repeated all the latest *on-dits*.

By now the noise in the room was deafening, and the air, laden with the heavy scent used by men and women alike, fairly trembled with heat under the great chandeliers. Davina sighed with relief when at last they were able to edge through a double doorway to a second and much more spacious salon.

This too was crowded, though not with such terrifying swells and notables. Davina descried a great many young girls, some pretty, some plain, all dressed in modest white or pastel colours, and all studiously minding their manners; their mamas and chaperones, chatting earnestly on the chairs ranged along the walls; and gentlemen, handsome young officers with splendid mustachios, town exquisites with their hair cut and pomaded in the Brutus style, even a few older gallants, but each of them very much on the lookout for likely beauties. This was the antechamber to the ballroom, but it might also be the antechamber to a happy and profitable marriage. Whether it was for the quadrille, or for life, the need to find a suitable partner was uppermost in every mind.

As the Tredgold party entered the room, dozens of pairs of eyes swivelled towards it, appraising Jane and Davina and the Millward girls with deadly thoroughness. There was neither the casual ease that obtained at Rigborough parties, nor the sublime indifference Davina had expected of this lofty peak of society. "Why", she thought, "Uncle Murray is quite right in calling it a marriage-mart! One might just as well be a heifer, up for auction on market-day!"

She had come in the expectation of being a wallflower, thinking herself too old to compete in such company as would be present tonight. But to her surprise several of the gentlemen presented to her by her Aunt Sophia, solicited her for a dance, and she found that her card filled as rapidly as did Jane's. She put this down to a wish to oblige the Tredgolds, and would have been astonished to learn that she was already regarded as a front-runner in the matrimonial stakes. The company was aware of the marked attention Lord Pangbourne was paying Miss Wakeford. Her name was an old and distinguished one, her property extensive. And she had a poise and elegance that commended itself to a world that set high value on such qualities.

At ten-thirty, Lord Pangbourne moved through the antechamber, escorting the charming Duchess of Rutland, whose rank gave her precedence over the other ladies. Behind came Lady Pangbourne, leaning on the Duke's arm. As they reached the ballroom, the orchestra at once struck up for the first country-dance. Other couples hurried onto the floor, and in no time at all they were all turning and skipping through its measures.

Davina loved to dance. She was familiar with her steps and did not, like many of the débutantes present, have to watch her feet, but could keep up a conversation with her partner. This was Mr Trevor, a young man who danced with more enthusiasm than skill, but whose wit was lively, keeping her giggling at his sallies as they met, parted and met again.

The country-dance was followed by a polonaise, which she danced with Mortimer, a polished exponent. After that, the first quadrille was announced, and John Pangbourne appeared to claim Davina's hand. As an officer of the Duke of Wellington's command, he was an excellent dancer, and led her through the difficult figures with ease, so that she accomplished even the *grande ronde* and the *pas d'été* without fault.

Lady Sophy, watching them from her seat among the matrons, decided that they made an extremely handsome couple, and noticed that when his lordship escorted Davina back to her place he did not at once move away, as a busy host was entitled to do, but took the chair next to hers, and sat laughing and joking for quite ten minutes.

Happy in the conviction that Davina was safely launched, Lady Sophy felt free to concentrate on her own Jane, who was flirting rather too openly with the dashing Captain Frimley, and who must be taken aside and gently checked before word got round that the youngest Miss Tredgold was a trifle fast.

There now being a short interval, the gentlemen of the party moved off to procure lemonade for the young ladies, and something stronger for themselves. The Millwards became engrossed in conversation with friends who had recently come to town from Dorset, and Mrs Wakeford, who disliked balls, announced that she was tired of watching grown people caper like grasshoppers, and might from now on be found downstairs in the card-rooms.

For a few minutes Davina was left alone. She sat quietly, watching the world go by, and was studying the antics of an enormously fat man who minced to and fro, flaunting a lace handkerchief in one hand and a quizzing-glass in the other, when a voice spoke at her side.

"Admiring Mr Molyneux, Miss Wakeford?"

She looked up, startled, to find Lord Rigg smiling down at her.

"Jealousy prompts me," he continued, "to warn you that the fellow wears corsets. If he comes any closer, you will hear them creak. May I sit down?"

"Pray do!" Davina moved to make room for him on the sofa. "I beg your pardon, but you see, I did not expect to see you here tonight."

"You nearly did not. Amabel took it into her head to call at Melbourne House on the way here. So, alas, did the Prince Regent. His carriage blocked ours for almost two hours."

"How very inconsiderate in him. I'm surprised you did not ask him to move it."

Rigg's eyes glinted. "Would you have done so?"

"Yes, why not?"

"Why not, indeed?" He turned a little so that he faced her more directly. "Miss Wakeford, am I too late to beg a chance to stand up with you?"

"I'm afraid my card is already filled, sir."

"As I feared. I must learn to be quicker off the mark. Tell me how you've fared so far. Has it been very dreadful, meeting the ton?"

"No, not at all. At first, I thought it might be, but everyone has been so kind. I've enjoyed myself immensely."

"It's not kindness that has made them fill your card, I assure you. You look delightfully tonight. If you continue like this, you'll be taking the town by storm."

Davina glanced up at him quickly. She had no wish to be numbered among his lordship's casual flirts. But meeting his eyes, she saw in them an expression that was almost a caress.

186

The funning retort died on her lips, and she blushed and turned her head away in confusion.

At just that moment, the music for the waltz burst out. Couples started to move towards the ballroom. Those girls whose mamas disapproved of the new dance, remained disconsolately in their places, while their luckier friends swept by wearing smug or pitying looks. Davina could see that most of her party had already taken the floor. She peeped at the card in her lap. Roland's name was scrawled alongside this number, but of Roland there was no sign. She folded her hands, trying to look as if she cared not a jot about being left unpartnered, but beneath her skirt one foot tapped irresistibly to the beat of the music.

"It seems," Lord Rigg said kindly, "that your partner is detained."

"It seems so."

"Some unavoidable accident, I collect? Locked in the cloak-room, for instance. Struck down by a passing dinner-wagon, and left for dead. Kidnapped by the Dowager for some unspeakable purpose."

"You've been reading too many novels," said Davina severely. "It's Roly who's defaulted. I shouldn't wonder if he's talking horseflesh to some crony, and has forgotten all about me."

Lord Rigg assumed a downtrodden air. "I see what it is. You don't care to stand up with me, and are inventing excuses."

She laughed. "You know that isn't so."

"In that case," said his lordship, rising and holding out his hand, "why are we wasting time?"

Davina looked at him uncertainly. Across the room she perceived her aunt and uncle, advancing towards her in a purposeful manner. She said a little breathlessly, "I believe, my lord, we should not. . . ." But even as she spoke, she was standing up, tucking her hand through Rigg's arm, and hurrying with him towards the ballroom.

Miss Wakeford was no stranger to the waltz. She had danced it at numerous parties, with various gentlemen, and had never understood why the Mother Grundies should condemn it as dangerous to the virtue of young females.

Now though, as Rigg placed an arm about her waist, and took her right hand in a firm grasp, she perceived her error. She wanted nothing so much as to move closer into his embrace, to reach up and touch his cheek, to feel his lips on hers. As the music whirled them away, it seemed to her that the mirrored walls, the other dancers, the musicians in the gallery, all vanished, and that only Luke and herself were left, spinning together outside of time.

Lady Sophy, meanwhile, was giving vent to her feelings. "When I find Roland," she said through her teeth, "I am going to dismember him with my bare hands!"

Sir Murray looked startled. "Why, what's poor Roly done?"

"It's what he hasn't done. He should be here, waltzing with Davina. I expect he's sneaked off to the card-tables. As for Eulalie, how can she be so dead to her responsibilities? One would have thought she would stand guard for the brief moment I was absent, but no, she must needs abandon Davina to her fate!" Lady Sophia smiled brilliantly at a passerby, and then muttered savagely, "Mrs Letherby-Simms has noticed. I can tell by that cat-got-cream look on her face. It will be all round the town in a few hours."

"What will?" demanded Sir Murray, feeling he'd lost the thread of things.

"Why, that they are falling in love. Cannot you see what's under your very nose, Tredgold?"

Sir Murray raised his quizzing-glass, but the kaleidoscope of waltzing couples made him dizzy. "No. Who?"

"Davina and Lord Rigg! Oh, it is too provoking of them!" Lady Sophy seized a glass of Tokay from a passing tray and drained it at a draught. "That isn't the worst of it, either. There's that odious Jocelyn Clare, gloating like a spider! He'll write to his brother you may be sure, and we shall have Edward posting up to London and making a nuisance of himself. What are you going to do about it? Don't just stand there, like a gapeseed!"

Sir Murray realised that the time had come to make the supreme sacrifice. Removing the empty glass from his wife's hand, he set it down, and extended his arm to her.

"Come, my love," he said. "It is far too long since I danced the waltz with you. Come, and we'll show these young sprigs just how the thing should be done."

Jocelyn Clare went home from the Pangbournes' Ball in a pensive frame of mind.

His sharp eyes had not missed the encounter between his cousin and Miss Wakeford, and he drew precisely the same conclusions from it as did Lady Sophy. The pair were in a fair way to become besotted with each other.

Jocelyn wasted not a thought on what this might mean to his brother's hopes. Edward had never stood much chance with the Wakeford chit, and any man fool enough to allow his intended to jaunter off to London, ran the risk of losing her to someone richer and more attractive.

Still, it might be politic to pen a line to Edward. If he were to retire from the lists, the field would be open to Rigg. It was imperative that Rigg give this girl his whole heart. A man deeply in love, was a man deeply vulnerable.

By now all Jocelyn's energies were concentrated on one aim, to destroy Rigg. The hatred he had felt all his life for the Rowans —their superior rank, their wealth, their possessions, their status as leaders of society—was now narrowed down and focussed on the person of this one man. Ever since the humiliating confrontation at Rowan House, Jocelyn had done little but scheme up ways to level the score. At first there had seemed some prospect that the ton would do his work for him, by ostracising Rigg. That prospect had faded. Though a few great houses still closed their doors, far more were throwing them wide. The Hollands, the Lambs, the Seftons, the Rutlands, had all declared for Luke. It could not be long before the generality followed suit, and crawled to lick the new Earl's boots.

Now at last a new weapon had come to hand. To wreck Rigg's personal happiness, to contrive that for the second time in his life he should lose the woman he desired—that would be a revenge sweet beyond words.

Jocelyn did not rush into hasty action. Instead, he set himself to make discreet enquiries about the Wakeford and Tredgold families.

He already knew that the Wakeford estates were encumbered, and that Davina Wakeford had come to London to sell part of her father's collection of books. He quickly learned of her visit to Holland House, and her agreement to employ Mr Allen as her agent in the sales.

A few casual questions in the clubs, established that the lady's step-brother, Roland Foote, was bitten by the gamblers' bug, and spent most of his nights playing cards or dice. Mr Foote's allowance, the pundits said, was small, and his skill at the tables even smaller.

All these facts Jocelyn found absorbing, but not of any immediate use.

What he was searching for, was information of a more intimate nature. Not to put too fine a point on it, he needed backstairs gossip. He had little hope of gleaning any from Rowan House. Rigg picked his servants carefully and paid them handsomely. Gooden, brought from Rowanbeck, watched them like a hawk and would make short shrift of anyone carrying tales to an outsider, while Rigg's secretary, young Turnbull, could neither be bought, nor bullied. In short, the Berkeley Square establishment could not be breached.

Park Street was a different kettle of fish. Its occupants were not expecting attack, and therefore not on their guard. It should be easy enough to bribe some housemaid or valet to bring reports of what went on above-stairs.

Sir Jocelyn had no intention of playing any overt part in the drama. A go-between was essential—someone who could obey orders, and keep a still tongue in his head.

Pondering the problem, Jocelyn remembered the ex-butler, Hibberd. The fellow had come crawling for favours after Rigg dismissed him, and only a week ago had written a whining sort of letter, begging Sir Jocelyn to help him find employment.

Here was a man with a grievance, and one that was acquainted with the staffs of many of the large houses in this part of town.

Going to his bureau, Sir Jocelyn found the letter and read it through. Hibberd gave as his direction, his sister's house in Clerkenwell. A message sent there, he said, would always reach him.

Sitting down, Sir Jocelyn drew paper and pen towards him, and began to write.

The tavern that Hibberd suggested as a suitable meeting-place lay in a small lane behind Bedford Square. Sir Jocelyn, alighting from the hackney cab that had brought him there, decided it was a good choice. The place had just the right sort of drab respectability. It was unlikely that he would encounter anyone he knew in it, but if he did, he would not attract suspicion.

He found the ex-butler already seated at a table, with a tankard of porter before him. Sir Jocelyn ordered a bottle of wine, waited till it was opened and set at his elbow, and then turned to Hibberd.

"You wrote that you are in need of work," he said. "I think I may be able to supply it."

Hibberd remained silent, his small eyes scanning the thin man's face.

"It is work," continued Sir Jocelyn, "that will demand a high degree of discretion."

Hibberd's smile became sly. "Ah, now, sir, you know I'm not one to blab."

"Very well, then. Do you know Sir Murray Tredgold's house in Park Street?"

"Yes, I do."

"Do you know anyone who works there?"

Hibberd tilted his head. "There's Jenkins," he said, after a while. "Roger Jenkins, Sir Murray's valet. Him and me, we used to break a bottle sometimes."

"My revered cousin's wine, no doubt! Let that pass, though. How approachable is this Jenkins?"

"Depends, sir."

"On what?"

"On what you want doing, and how much blunt you're prepared to sport. Sir Murray pays better than most. Hundred a year, I dare swear."

Sir Jocelyn shrugged. "Tell your friend that I'll advance him a year's salary. Say that if I receive what I want, he'll be paid as much again."

"Two hundred!" Hibberd's eyes shone. "And may I ask, what would he have to do to earn it?"

"I need information about the Tredgold household—its comings and goings, its little squabbles, its loves and hates. Come, Hibberd, I don't need to teach you the art of eavesdropping for profit!"

"What if Jenkins don't choose to risk his place?"

"Then the deal falls away, and I must look for someone less lily-livered. What risk is involved, man? Jenkins has nothing to do but look, and listen, and make his report to you. You will rehearse the details to me. It's common practice, God knows."

This was true enough. In most great houses, a servant could be found who would sell his master's secrets. Brummell's man had been offered a fortune for the secret of the Beau's boot-polish. Lovers paid good money to know when husbands would be from home. Gamblers constantly sought to learn the system favoured by luckier players.

Hibberd agreed to speak to Jenkins, and reported within twelve hours that the bargain had been struck.

Each night thereafter, Jenkins crept from the Tredgolds' home to meet his paymaster, and each night Hibberd carried his load of gossip to Grafton Street.

Sir Jocelyn seldom offered any comment on what he was told, although he seemed to take a peculiar interest in the sayings and actions of Miss Wakeford and Mr Foote. Once or twice he asked a question about Mr Foote's financial situation. Did he, for example, leave unpaid bills in his bureau, and if so, what did these bills total?

Occasionally Hibberd caught a gleam of satisfaction in his interrogator's eyes, and when that happened it sent a shiver down Hibberd's spine. There was something downright wicked in that look, he thought. As soon as this job was done, it'd be best to cut line, and quit, and let the Devil take care of his own.

XVIII

During the whole of May, Lord Rigg was a regular caller at Park Street.

He never arrived except by appointment, and he behaved at all times with the utmost punctilio. He was careful to send in his card before setting foot in the Tredgolds' house, and once inside, always enquired first for Sir Murray, or Lady Sophia. If he offered to take Miss Wakeford driving in the Park at the fashionable hour of five, he invariably included Miss Jane in the invitation. He never drove through the rougher streets, where there might be sights distressful to maiden eyes, and he avoided using the cant terms popular in Corinthian circles. He attended dreary exhibitions, drank tea at afternoon assemblies, and startled his friend Mr Clintwood by strolling in, one evening, wearing knee-breeches.

"I thought," said Mr Clintwood accusingly, "that you said you'd not be seen dead in half-masters!"

Lord Rigg sighed. "I very likely shall be, Robert, if I have to endure another evening like this. I attended a concert. A lady of uncertain years sang, just a shade off-key, for what seemed an eternity."

"Why did you stay?"

"The lady is known to Miss Wakeford, who felt obliged to attend the début." Seeing the look on Clintwood's face, the Earl grinned. "She didn't like it any more than I did, Clint. She may be blue, but she's not tone-deaf."

"Taken with her, ain't you, Luke?"

"An understatement," said his lordship calmly.

"Then I wish you happy. She's a charming girl, and you'll suit admirably. Likes you, too, or I'm no judge."

"You think so?" Lord Rigg sounded anxious. "Sometimes I feel sure she returns my affections, yet at other times she seems to withdraw from me utterly."

"Leading you on, my dear fellow. Shows she's interested."

"Those tricks are out of her ken. She's as transparent as crystal. It's one of the things I particularly admire in her."

"Know what I think?" said Clintwood. "It's that Gorgon, Mrs Wakeford, warning her off you. She's been dead against you from the start."

"If that were all, I'd feel a deal happier! No, I fear it's Lady Sophia's dislike of me that's the obstacle. Miss Wakeford is extremely fond of her aunt, as well as being beholden to her for this visit to London. She'll never do anything to hurt the Tredgolds, and what's more, I won't encourage her to. I've known too much family discord to wish to inflict it on others."

"Lady Sophy will see reason in time."

"There's no sign of it, Clint. She strongly favours Pangbourne's suit."

"Miss Wakeford, though, does not," said Mr Clintwood, "and when all's said and done, that's the only thing that matters."

Despite Clintwood's bracing phrases, he was concerned for Luke, the more so as Miss Tredgold, with whom he was now on excellent terms, confirmed her mother's opposition to the match.

"It isn't that she dislikes Lord Rigg," Jane said, "but she fears he's only trifling with Davina, and will soon turn to some new flirtation. He has that reputation, you know."

"He's not flirting, he's serious in his intentions."

"Then why doesn't he speak, to Davina or to Papa?"

"Because he feels he must establish himself in society first—and because he don't wish to offend your parents. Luke's been a rakehell in his day, but on some points, he's a high stickler."

"Oh dear, what a tangle it is! I shall try and coax Mama a little, but I doubt if it will do any good!"

Jane kept her word, seeking out Lady Sophia in the course of the next morning. She began by asking whether she might invite Lord Rigg to join them for supper on Sunday. "It will please Davina so much, Mama. I know she feels it, when we treat him snubbingly."

"Snubbingly! What nonsense! I'll thank you not to be pert!"

"I don't wish to be, Mama, it is only that I can't help seeing that John Pangourne, and Mortimer, and Mr Clintwood are made to feel so much at home, here—invited to take pot-luck with us, or drop in as they please. . . ."

"One does not invite the Earl of Rigg to take pot-luck, my child."

"If it's all right for Lord Pangbourne...."

"The Pangbournes are very old friends, and I feel no need to stand on ceremony with them."

"Well, the Rowans are Davina's neighbours, and besides, she's in love with Rigg. She only cultivates the others to please you, but truly, her heart isn't in it."

"That is enough, Jane!" Lady Sophy's tone was quelling. "Allow me to know a little better than you, what is in Davina's best interests. She may fancy herself to be 'in love', as you call it, but I assure you such fancies pass. Marriage is built upon far more lasting elements. A woman marries not only a husband, but that husband's family, and if it's a set of dirty dishes like the Rowans, then happiness can never result. You'll understand, when you're a little older, that I'm right. And that's the last we will say on the matter, if you please! Run along now, my love, and change your gown. We're due to meet the Hemsons within the hour, to witness the balloon ascent!"

When her daughter had gone dolefully away, Lady Sophy rang the bell to summon Becky Brackett, invited her to sit down, and asked her without roundaboutation what were Miss Wakeford's feelings for Lord Rigg.

Becky sighed. "She's head over heels, my lady. And so's his lordship, what's more."

"Becky, you know young people fall in and out of love in a trice."

"Rigg's six-and-twenty, ma'am, and our Miss is of age. They're old enough to know their own minds, and those minds is made up."

"Don't you agree that John Pangbourne is a most attractive gentleman? Davina does not dislike him, I know. Perhaps if we are patient...."

"We're not talking of like or mislike, here, my lady. We're talking of love."

"Fustian, Becky! You sound like a street ballad-singer! Don't tell me you wish to see Davina married to Rigg?"

Rebecca looked straight at her mistress. "I don't wish it. The Rowans spell trouble, I reckon. But mebbe this one's a cut above the rest of the breed. Miss Davina thinks so, and she's a girl that's not easily gulled by sweet talk and kickshaws. All I can say is that if his lordship asks her to wed with him—and who can be sure he will?—then she'll give him her own answer, and there'll be naught you and I will do to change it. She's had to hoe her own row for a long time, my lady, and it's made her that strong-willed you'd never believe."

With this Lady Sophy had to agree, but it did not alter her view. What she could not tell Jane or Rebecca was that malicious tongues were at work. Only yesterday, Alfreda Banks had hinted that Lord Rigg had brought Amabel Rowan to London as his mistress, and that his flirtation with Davina was only a cover for his real amours. Needless to say, Lady Sophy had made short work of Mrs Banks, but the sour taste of the slander remained.

Davina herself was making no attempt to conceal the fact that she enjoyed Rigg's company. Though she happily attended those assemblies and balls recommended by her aunt, and acted as though she thoroughly enjoyed them, there was no mistaking how her eyes lit up at Rigg's approach. Though she took care never to dance with him more than twice in an evening, the waltz was always his, and more often than not it was Rigg who took her in to supper.

Lady Sophy found herself in a dilemma. She had brought Davina to town to secure her happiness. Davina was blissfully happy. How could one now complain at it? What right had one to interfere?

So Lady Sophy argued the case back and forth in her mind, and could come to no conclusion. As it turned out, the tangle was resolved not by her action, but by Roland's, and in a way that was well-nigh disastrous to the peace and unity of the family.

It was in the first week of June that Davina received a letter from Mr Allen, saying that he had excellent news about the Rigborough Missal. He had received an offer which, he said, "exceeds all expectations". Without wishing to raise Miss Wakeford's hopes too far, he believed that a meeting with the buyers' agents might be arranged within a few weeks. Might he do himself the honour to call at Park Street when he came to town on Friday, and present the details for her consideration?

The letter arrived just as the family was rising from the breakfast table. Davina's first reaction to it was one of panic.

Why did Mr Allen not name the buyers, in his letter? And why must there be such a long delay before the principals met? It must be that the offer came from abroad, and that if the sale were concluded, the Book of Hours would be lost to England.

And Mr Allen's talk of a vast sum—how could she ever hope to comprehend such a transaction? She had no experience whatsoever in such things.

Her uncle, seeing her dismay, took her hand and said comfortably that she mustn't fret, because with her permission he intended being present at the discussion with Mr Allen, and would keep a weather-eye on the Wakeford interest.

Mrs Wakeford and Roland, meanwhile, were preparing to snatch a share of what they saw as a windfall from heaven. "With thousands in the kitty," Roland said, "we can make an end of penny-pinching, and live as we ought."

"May I point out," said Sir Murray acidly, "that the book belongs to Davina, and any profits are hers, and hers alone?"

"They'll go to Wakeford," Davina said. "Mr Shedley has explained to us that we must restore the estate, to survive." She then excused herself, saying she must write to Mr Allen at once. As she made her way to the morning-room at the back of the house, she could hear the wrangling voices of her step-mother and step-brother, and the steady drone of her uncle's replies. "Like kites over a carcase" she thought angrily, as she sat down at the desk.

She composed a suitable letter and sent it off to the post. That done, she sat for some time trying to accustom herself to the idea that the Book of Hours would soon pass to a new owner. It was more painful than she could have thought possible; but she fortified herself with the picture of a Wakeford flourishing and vigorous once more.

Twice in the days that followed, Roland came to her with demands for an increase in his allowance. She told him that there was no chance of one, that neither she nor Mr Shedley had such funds to disburse.

Later she blamed herself for missing the desperation in Roland's pleas. But she had her own problems to face, and felt no need to shoulder Roland's as well.

XIX

Since the June weather was halcyon, the Countess of Rigg's picnic to Richmond Park proved an unqualified success.

A party of thirteen guests, three coachmen, five grooms, and Lord Rigg's French chef, Gaston, assembled at Hyde Park, and set out from there in convoy at eleven o'clock.

Amabel herself travelled with Jane Tredgold, Mr James Tunmer, and his ten-year-old son Timothy, in the Tunmers' glossy landaulet, drawn by four staid bay horses. After them came Lord Rigg driving his curricle with Miss Wakeford as passenger, and a groom perched on the rear step. Mortimer Foote followed in his phaeton with Mr Tunmer's sister, Lucy. Then came the large old-fashioned barouche which Lady Sophia had lent, to convey the watch-dragons Miss Cornelia Finch and Miss Becky Bracket.

Three members of the party—Roland Foote, Robert Clintwood, and his lordship's secretary, Charles Turnbull—elected to go on horseback, while at the tail of the cortège lumbered the Rowans' baggage-chaise, laden with baskets of food, crates of wine, a small barrel of ice, folding chairs, rugs, cushions, a portable telescope, and Gaston. This caravan prompted Mr Clintwood to remark that with proper generalship and a little luck, the expedition might survive in the wilderness for as much as a whole day.

The route was through Hammersmith, Barnes and Mortlake. For the first few miles Lord Rigg was occupied in keeping a firm check on his greys, which found the pace set by the Tunmer team something tedious. Once past Kensington, however, they settled down, and as there was little traffic on the road, Luke was able to give more attention to his companion.

She looked charmingly today, he thought, in a muslin gown sprigged with green-leaf motifs, and a wide hat of chip-straw, tied on by long green ribbons. A white parasol trimmed with green completed the ensemble.

Miss Wakeford, unaware of his lordship's gaze, was absorbed

in her own thoughts, her attention apparently on the fields they were passing. Lord Rigg cleared his throat deprecatingly.

"Remarkably fine turnips, are they not?" he said. "Or should I say mangold-wurzels? I fear I'm no expert."

Davina turned to smile at him. "I beg pardon. I didn't think I should prattle while you were busy with the horses."

"You were miles away," he said.

"Yes, at Wakeford."

"Homesick, already?"

"Oh no, I'm enjoying myself too much to be homesick. I own that, though I wouldn't like to live in London, for a visit it's exciting beyond words."

"How long do you plan to remain in town?"

"Until Mr Allen has concluded the sale of the Missal. He . . . he told me yesterday he has received a firm offer, and the sum he mentioned . . . well, I found it staggering, but he assures me it is fair to both sides."

The Earl studied her. "Yet you're not happy?"

Davina sighed. "I should be, I know. But you see the offer is from the Vatican, and I had hoped so much to keep the book in England."

"I see."

Miss Wakeford quickly changed the subject, and his lordship did not return to it. For the rest of the journey they discussed such things as Luke's travels in America, the recent riots among factory-workers in Manchester, a race-meeting at Chevely at which his lordship had lost all but his boots, and the massive levee held at the Queen's House to celebrate the recent nuptials of the Princess Charlotte.

Time seemed to fly past, for the two were in that stage of attraction when each longs to know the nature and opinions of the other, so that even the most trivial piece of information is treasured. They were, in short, enchanted with each other, and finding themselves in complete harmony on all important subjects, reached their destination very well pleased with themselves and the world.

Davina, who had never before visited Richmond, thought it a delightful village. They drove past the green with its ancient houses, Maids of Honour Row, and the ruins of the palace where Queen Elizabeth had died—couched on the floor, Lord

Rigg said, and propped up with cushions to ease her labouring heart. On the way up Richmond Hill they paused to admire the splendid prospect over the Thames valley, and at the crest, entered the Park through the gate opposite the Star and Garter Inn. A grassy, undulating plain opened before them, well-wooded and with herds of fallow and red deer browsing among its thickets.

The other carriages having joined them, a suitable spot was chosen for the picnic, in a shady grove that led down to a little lake. As Lord Rigg was busy instructing the servants how best to set out the tables, and tether the horses, Davina left him and strolled across to join the rest of the guests, who were preparing to take a stroll round the water.

She was greeted effusively by Cornelia Finch, who begged her to thank kind Lady Sophia for lending her carriage for the day. "I cannot tell you how grateful I am," she said, "for you know I am a poor traveller, and cannot grow used to the new style of going in an open vehicle. In my day, ladies went by coach, driven by a coachman. Now it seems to be the fashion for every gentleman to play the rôle of a Jarvis, and even to dress like one! As to these horrid phaetons, and curricles, I detest being perched so high above the ground, with nothing but air on either side. I live in constant dread of finding myself in the ditch. Do you not agree, Miss Wakeford?"

"I must say I never enjoyed driving in the phaeton with my brother," admitted Davina, "but somehow with Lord Rigg, I feel differently. He is always in complete control of his team, and never takes foolish risks."

"Cousin Lucas," said Miss Finch with conviction, "is exceptional in every way. I would never speak of this to just anyone, but I can tell you he's been generosity itself to me. Do you know, he's fixed for me to have a competence? Money of my very own, for the rest of my days! I shall never again be forced to seek employment as a governess or paid companion. I am to live in the Dower House with dear Amabel, and if she marries and does not need me, I am to have my own set of rooms at Rowanbeck, and Rowan House too. You can't imagine what that means, to a spinster like me, to be given security and ... respect! It is not only I that must be grateful to him. Amabel is a changed person, these last few weeks. She was used to be so nervous and moody, I feared she might sink into a decline. Now, she's as happy as the day is long." Miss Finch lowered her voice a little. "And so much sought after, Miss Wakeford! Well, she is a great beauty, so it's not surprising the gentlemen adore her. I hope she will choose Mr Tunmer. He's the perfect match for her. He's known her since she was a child—his estates march with the Sears', you know, in Yorkshire. He was married before, but his dear wife died when the boy was born. That is ten years ago, and they say he is on the lookout for a second. He seems devoted to Amabel, don't you think?"

A short while later, when they reached the edge of the lake, Davina was able to make the acquaintance of the Tunmer family. Miss Lucy Tunmer, it appeared, had been at the same dame-school as Jane Tredgold. She was a plain girl, rather stout and red-complexioned, but with a twinkle in her bright blue eyes, and a sharp sense of humour, that made her instantly likeable.

Young Timothy Tunmer, a likely lad with a shock of red hair, was clearly set upon a career as an officer of Hussars. He very quickly cut Mr Clintwood from the herd, and led him off to set up a model of the field at Waterloo, using pebbles for guns and sticks for battalions. Reminded by his papa of his manners, he stood up to make his bow to Davina, but at once returned to the battle. In fairness it must be said that Mr Clintwood seemed to be enjoying himself as keenly as his young admirer.

Mr Tunmer himself proved to be worthy, but dull. Chatting to him, Davina reflected that years of marriage to the dashing but profligate Talbot Rowan might well condition a woman to look for more sober traits in her second husband.

This put her in mind of Edward Clare, who was kind, courteous, and hardworking, like Mr Tunmer. She had received a letter from Edward only yesterday, in which he reported that he had visited Wakeford Hall and found all well. Blight, he said, had been found in one of her potato-fields, but it had not spread. Her wheat was in good heart, and two more of her dairy herd were in calf. He concluded with the news that he was suffering from a heavy chest cold, but was finding oil of wintergreen, well rubbed in, most efficacious.

It was as she recalled this missive that Davina realised she had not the slightest intention of marrying Edward. She glanced back up the slope, to where Lucas stood. He had taken off his coat, and with shirtsleeves rolled to the elbows, was engaged in lowering bottles of wine into the stream to cool. Mortimer Foote and Charles Turnbull were with him, and as she watched, some remark set them all laughing. The sound filled her with happiness, and she turned back to Mr Tunmer with such a blinding smile that he later remarked to his sister that, aside from Lady Rigg, he counted Miss Wakeford the most attractive female he had met in many years.

Only one member of the company was not in high spirits. Roland Foote, having unsaddled his chestnut and leg-haltered him, had walked off alone, and was now to be seen sitting on a tree-stump, tossing pebbles into the lake. Luke, who made an attempt to draw him into conversation, was met by a surly scowl and a turned shoulder.

In ordinary circumstances, that would have been the end of it, but Luke was in love with Davina, and wished to be on good terms with every member of her family.

Sir Murray and Jane he felt had already accepted him. Lady Sophia had not, but she might in time be won over. Roland was openly hostile. No doubt the young chub's antagonism had begun with jealousy over Amabel, but Roland seemed to have fallen out of love with her the moment he reached London. He was perfectly civil with Tunmer, and Amabel's other flirts.

Looking at Roland's hunched and lonely figure, Luke pitied him. His mother was a vulgarian who thought of no one but herself. His own father had died without making provision for his son. His step-father, lost in scholarly clouds, had probably ignored him. He had some reason to resent those more fortunate than himself. The problem was, how to get past the barriers he erected, and help him.

At this point in his reflections, Luke heard an apologetic cough, and turned to find Mortimer Foote staring at him with the intent air of a puppy at a rabbit-hole. Luke smiled, and Mr Foote, taking courage, approached and sat down on the grass, his back against the bole of a tree.

"Roly's blue-devilled," he said.

"So it seems." His lordship also sat down.

"Not a bad fellow, you know," said Mortimer earnestly. "Has this unfortunate disposition. Own worst enemy."

"You think so?" Luke gave a rueful shrug. "I thought I was cast in that rôle."

"No, no. Admires you, though he'll never admit it. Finds you all he'd wish to be himself. Address, you know. Polish. Air of well-bred ease. Nonpareil, in fact."

"Thank you," said his lordship, much moved.

"Not at all." Mortimer plucked a blade of grass and nibbled it. "Not to mince matters," he said, "you're rich and Roly ain't. Never had anything but debts in his basket. Father's, mother's, and now his own."

Luke stretched out his legs. "Is he in debt?"

"Yes, he is. Been playing too deep. Shouldn't have told you, I suppose. Roly wouldn't like it."

"I'm glad you did. I'm the Wakefords' nearest neighbour, and . . . well . . . I admire his sister greatly."

"That's what I thought."

"That being so, tell me, how deep is he in?"

"I'm not sure. Tell you this much, though. I bumped into him, t'other night, when he was coming from Jack Wrackham's house. That's a gambling hell, case you didn't know. When I tried to tell him to steer clear of Wrackham, he told me to go to the devil."

"From what I recall, Wrackham is crookeder than a cricket's leg."

"Far crookeder. Sets up the little country lambs to be shorn by his regular customers—and takes his cut, too. Wouldn't be surprised if he sold doctored wine, what's more. Friend of mine took some of it, a few nights ago, and woke up twenty-four hours later with a head full of tinsmiths!" Mortimer sighed. "Don't know what you can do for Roly, Rigg, but I felt you should know the score."

"I'm very much obliged to you." Luke regarded Roland, who was still gazing moodily across the lake. "Tell me, what do you imagine he hopes to do with his life? Would he like to go to Oxford or Cambridge?"

"No. He's not one for books. Had enough of 'em at Wakeford."

"What about the estate? Has he any taste for farming, or management? Would he like to run the place?"

"Not at all."

"Then what does he want?"

Mortimer considered the direct question in silence. At last he said simply, "Horses."

"Horses?"

"Yes. Roly likes horses." After a further pause, Mortimer added, "Horses like him."

"I see. Should I purchase him a set of colours? I believe my friend Clintwood could help there, although it's hard to join a Hussar regiment."

"Don't think he fancies the cavalry."

"What then?"

"Stud farm," said Mr Foote earnestly. "Breed racers, jumpers, and so on. Roly'd be good at that, and he'd make a respectable living from it. Hope you don't mind my mentioning it."

"On the contrary, I'm extremely grateful. I'm sure we can achieve something on those lines. As to his gambling—if you hear he's in dun territory, let me know, will you? He mustn't be allowed to fall into the hands of the Greeks."

"I'll do my best." Mortimer's smile was anxious. "Not sure he'll talk to me, even if he's in trouble, but I'll do my possible."

XX

It was on the day after the visit to Richmond that Roland Foote began to suspect he was being spied upon. Going to his wardrobe to take out a clean handkerchief, he noticed that the coats in it had been shifted. At first he felt no concern, thinking that the valet Jenkins had taken away some article to be pressed. Then he saw that a pile of cravats had been moved. He crossed to the bureau and checked that it was locked. Unlocking it, he examined the contents of the drawer where he kept his valuables. A small roll of money was intact, but the pile of unpaid accounts which he'd crammed to one side, seemed to be not quite as he remembered to have left it.

Jenkins was summoned and questioned. He protested innocence, denied that there was a second set of keys for this room, and was inclined to take umbrage at Roland's inquisition.

Since nothing had been stolen, Roland could do no more than send Jenkins back to his work, and resolve to keep a closer watch on him in future.

The details of this episode were quickly carried by Jenkins to Hibberd, and thence to Sir Jocelyn Clare.

"It's time to cry off," Hibberd said. "The young pup's smelled a rat."

"Bid Jenkins steer clear of the bedrooms," Sir Jocelyn replied. "I'm in any case more interested in Sir Murray's strongroom. Does Jenkins know what's in it?"

"Yes, for the old man called him to lend a hand last week, when Lady Sophia's emeralds were sent to be cleaned. Besides her ladyship's jewels, there's a roll of blunt as thick as your arm, Jenkins says."

"What else is in the safe?"

"Legal papers, and that old book they set such store by. Done up in a wooden casket, not very large."

An unholy light shone in Jocelyn's eyes. "The Rigborough Book of Hours," he said softly.

"That's right. Jenkins said two gentlemen called yesterday. Mr Thomas Shedley, who's in the Law, and Mr Allen who isn't."

The two of 'em went upstairs with Sir Murray and Miss Wakeford, and they had the book out of the safe. Carried it like gold, Jenkins says."

"Better than fine gold," murmured Sir Jocelyn, "and more than the price of rubies." He remained in brooding thought for a while, then looked up. "The key to the safe? Does Sir Murray keep it on his person?"

"He does, sir, on his fob-chain. You won't get it off him, I can tell you."

"He must take it off when he disrobes?"

"Of course. But he never lets it out of his sight. At night it's lodged beneath his pillow, and when he takes his bath, why, he sets it on the chimney-piece where he can keep his glims on it."

"And if some other member of the family wishes to take something from the safe?"

"Then Sir Murray will be present. He'll unlock the safe, stand by while it's opened, and lock it again after. A cagey old brock, is Sir Murray."

Sir Jocelyn nodded. "Did Jenkins hear what was said by Allen or Shedley?"

"He heard Mr Allen speak of receiving a handsome offer for the book—from Rome."

"Indeed! Did he name the amount?"

"He was about to, when Shedley, that's a weaselly-eyed old codger if ever there was one, caught sight of Jenkins standing by the door, and gave Sir Murray the nudge. Sir Murray sent Jenkins away. But later, Jenkins heard the young Miss talking to her uncle, and saying it was a plummier bid than any they'd get from an Englishman, and she feared she must accept it."

Sir Jocelyn nodded. "I doubt if anyone, anywhere, can outbid the Vatican."

"You think that's who's after it?"

"Oh, certainly! A huge sum, offered from Rome, for a book of exceptional religious interest? Tell me, how do Miss Wakeford's mother and brother react to the proposition?"

"Already snarling for their share of the spoils."

"Excellent. Does my Cousin Rigg know of the offer?"

"Sure to. By all reports, Miss Wakeford's nutty upon him. Stands to reason she'll have told him what's afoot."

"I agree. Hibberd, the situation has possibilities! I wish to be fully informed about the negotiations for the sale of the book. Everything, mind, no matter how trivial."

Hibberd sniggered. "Thinking of putting in a bid yourself, are you?"

"Perhaps. One last question. Does Jenkins know how to take an impression of a key?"

"Course he does. How else would he have been able to search the drawers in Mr Foote's room? All he needs is a bar of tallow soap, and a few minutes' privacy." Hibberd suddenly blanched. "Here, you're not thinking of robbing that safe, are you? Because if so, you can count me out! I've no wish to rot in clink for the rest of my days!"

Sir Jocelyn regarded him lazily. "Hibberd, do you know how much Rome is prepared to pay for that little volume?"

"No, I don't."

"Something over forty thousand pounds. I heard it from the Regent, in the strictest confidence, of course! And I happen to know that there are other would-be purchasers in France, and in Germany. Collectors who are less illustrious than his Holiness the Pope, but not so quick to ask embarrassing questions, if you follow me?"

"You're mad!" Hibberd was gaping like a fish. "You'll end on the gallows, if you don't watch out!"

"Not at all. With a little good management and forethought, I shall end a rich man, living comfortably in some country where the manners are less barbarous, and the winters a great deal less hard, than in England. You could share in that pleasant existence, Hibberd. After all, what is left for you here, with no employment, and your character quite discredited?"

"I'll not listen to you!"

"I don't wish for your answer at once, but brood upon the matter. Consider your present unhappy lot, and compare it with the future you might enjoy. In the meantime, inform Jenkins that I will pay him one hundred guineas for the impression of the key to Sir Murray's strongroom."

Sir Jocelyn leaned back in his chair and closed his eyes. Hibberd stared at him for a moment with an expression of mingled fear and fascination. Then he picked up his hat and hurried from the room.

*

A day or so after Mr Allen's visit, Miss Wakeford and Miss Tredgold, driving home from a visit to the lending library in Bond Street, saw Roland emerge from a jeweller's shop, and stopped to take him up.

As he climbed into the carriage, their gaze was drawn to the handsome pearl pin tucked into the folds of his cravat, and the set of gold seals glinting on his fob-chain. Jane began to quiz him, wanting to know if he had robbed a counting-house, to be able to afford such finery. He grinned at her in high good humour.

"No, Miss Sauce-pot, I have not. The dibs happen to be in tune at the moment, that's all."

"I suppose you mean that Flybynight won at Newmarket? I heard you tell Papa she would."

"Flybynight, and Random Tandem too! They've turned my fifty guineas into five hundred. What do you say to that?"

"I know what Pa will say. That you're mad to risk so much on a horse, and he washes his hands of you."

"Oh, there's no risk," said Roland airily. "I know prads. I study the form, and only put down my blunt on a cert. A man must play his luck, and I'm on a winning streak."

"You weren't a week ago."

"No, but I'm right as a trivet again. If I could but build up to a round four thousand, then I could buy those match bays of Leaming's. Prime tits, real sweet goers. Lord, what wouldn't I give to own 'em!"

In her corner of the carriage, Davina sat silent. She had the feeling Roland was living far beyond his means, yet she could think of nothing to say to him. She could hardly accuse him of extravagance, when she herself was spending what seemed a fortune on trivial things like clothes, and parties.

She wished very much that she could ask Mortimer's advice, but he had gone out of town to visit a great-aunt in Brighton. She could only hope that Roly would have the sense to quit gaming if his luck changed.

Her own calendar was crowded to the limit, and as the Season's roundabout spun faster and faster, she seemed to be in Park Street only to sleep. Her step-mother, too, was engaged in a heavy social programme, and their paths seldom crossed.

In mid-June, the Tredgolds held their own dress-ball, and it was during this that Lord Pangbourne asked Davina to marry him. She refused his offer, and was considerably distressed when he would not take her answer as final.

"I wish he wouldn't persist," she said to her aunt, when in the early hours of the morning the last guest had departed. "I like him so well, and wouldn't hurt him for the world."

"I'd think poorly of any man who gave up after one rebuff," retorted Lady Sophy, "and I think you've been much too hasty in refusing him."

"What else can I do, when I know I'll never marry him?"

"Never is a big word, my dear. How can you be sure what your sentiments may be in a few weeks' time? Be reasonable!"

"This isn't a matter of reason. It's what I feel in my heart."

"You mean you've already bestowed your affections elsewhere!"

"Yes. I hadn't quite realised it, until John Pangbourne declared himself, but I realise it now."

"Lord Rigg, I suppose?"

"Yes."

"Has he made you an offer? He has certainly not asked your uncle's permission to do so!"

"He hasn't spoken."

Lady Sophy came to sit beside her niece. "My love," she said, "do try to be practical. A female has only a limited time to make her choice, and despite what you may read in romantic novels, there are not so many good fish in the sea. If you lose Pangbourne, what will you do? Dwindle into genteel spinsterhood, or end by taking some suitor you like a good deal less? It can't be that you mean to go home and marry Edward Clare!"

"No." Davina sounded woeful. "I wrote to him two days ago, saying I cannot accept him."

Lady Sophy was tired, and bitterly disappointed, but she knew better than to say so. "We'll talk again tomorrow," she said cheerfully. "You know how much clearer things become after a good night's rest."

Davina looked at her anxiously. "You won't tell Mama what I've said?"

"No." Lady Sophy unhesitatingly added another guilty secret to her store. "It shall be between you and me. And now, let's go upstairs to our beds, or the maids will be sweeping us out with the cinders."

While Lady Sophia was still pondering how to overcome Davina's foolish *tendre* for Lord Rigg, an invitation arrived which considerably heightened her concern. It was addressed to Miss Wakeford alone, and requested the pleasure of her company at Sunday luncheon, at the home of Mr and Mrs Joshua Turnbull. Lady Sophy carried the news straight to her husband.

"It's most provoking," she said. "Charlotte Turnbull has done this at Rigg's prompting, you may be sure."

"And why not? The Turnbulls are his kin, after all—and a dashed sight more presentable than those Clare shabsters."

"You don't know the Turnbulls."

"Yes I do. Know the Nabob, at any rate. Worked on the Anti-slavery League with him, and liked him well. He's a thought rough, to be sure, but a more generous man I've yet to meet, and he sets a damn good table. Best wines in London. These Cits always know where to lay hands on a bottle."

"We're not discussing the fleshpots, Tredgold! Can't you see that if Rigg's inviting Davina to meet his family—shabby or no —his intentions must be serious?"

"I should hope they are," said her husband maddeningly. "If he cries off, I shan't get my pheasant-shooting."

"That seems to be your chief consideration!"

Sir Murray looked at her over his spectacles. "I'm blessed if I know why you dislike the invitation. If I remember aright, you were once bosom bows with Charlotte Turnbull."

"Yes, but that was before . . . before. . . ."

"Before she went down in the world? Well, I'll tell you something. I wish Josh Turnbull had invited us as well. Might give us the chance to redeem our long neglect of them."

Lady Sophy bit her lip. She had often felt a stab of conscience about Charlotte, and had several times formed the intention of healing the breach; but somehow, in the hustle and bustle of raising a family and launching its members on the world, the reconciliation had never come about.

Now she sighed. "You're right, of course," she said. "Davina must go, and we must put a good face on it. But don't imagine

I'm any the happier about Rigg's suit, for I'm not! I disapprove of him entirely."

Lady Sophy would have been chagrined to know that Davina's chief fear was that the Turnbulls might disapprove of her. Luke always spoke of this family in terms that showed his deep affection for it. She had had many chats with Charles Turnbull, and was beginning to understand that the Turnbulls, in their way, were quite as high in the instep as any member of the ton. A new force was arising in England, one spawned by trade and industry, and the fortunes these produced. The City merchants already exercised enormous power, and were gaining more every day. In a decade or so, they would not need the patronage of the aristocracy to achieve social recognition.

Davina was well aware of the snubbing treatment Charlotte had endured at the hands of the fashionable world—in particular Lady Sophia. Might she not show her resentment by treating Davina with coldness, and advising Luke to have nothing to do with the Tredgold clan?

It was a distinctly nervous Miss Wakeford who descended from his lordship's curricle, and advanced up the steps of the house in Russell Square. Her first sight of Josh Nabob did little to calm her apprehensions. He looked, she thought, exactly like the cartoon drawings of John Bull, ready to gobble up anyone who dared to cross him. But the next moment he smiled, and led her indoors with an old-fashioned, flourishing bow, and spoke to her so kindly that she regained her confidence, and was able to face her hostess with something like composure.

Her immediate impression was that Lady Charlotte, besides being exceptionally handsome, was very much a Rowan. She had the dark colouring and high-bridged nose one saw in all the Rowan portraits; and although her manner was gracious, one caught that hint of reserve, of detachment, that Lord Rigg displayed on occasion.

Several of the young members of the family now came crowding into the drawing-room—Charles, his younger sister Emily, Amanda who was not yet past the schoolroom stage, and the two hearty boys, Herbert and Frederic. They all seemed blessed with their papa's outgoing ways, came up with broad smiles to be presented to Miss Wakeford, and made it plain that anyone in Luke's good books must be regarded as a friend.

Davina had not much experience of large family gatherings, and for a while the Turnbulls' boisterous exchanges and constant raillery made her feel shy; but she soon caught the general good humour, and began to chat and laugh with the rest. Charles Turnbull made a point of sitting beside her at the long dining-board, and fended off the questions showered on her by the boys, while Lord Rigg was at her other hand, watching her with quiet pleasure, and ensuring that she was never allowed to feel at all the outsider.

Still, it was an ordeal to feel herself on probation, her least word or gesture closely observed, especially by the dark and enigmatic lady at the foot of the table.

As soon as the meal came to an end, Mr Turnbull carried off Luke and Charles to the library, "to smoke a pipe or two". The younger scions dispersed in a way that suggested they'd been warned to make themselves scarce, and Davina found herself accompanying her hostess on a stroll about the garden.

This was quite large, by London standards, with well-tended rose-beds, lavender bushes, and even a grotto that sheltered the carved figure of a faun, playing on a set of reed pipes. Davina exclaimed when she saw this.

"Why, how beautiful," she said. "It looks to be very old. Where did you acquire it?"

"We found it when we dug the foundations for the house," said Lady Charlotte, sitting down on a shady bench and gesturing to Davina to do the same. "Joshua believes it must have stood in the garden of a Roman villa built on this site."

Davina glanced about her. "One would never think you have been here less than two years, ma'am. You must have a green thumb, to make plants flourish so."

"I love my garden. I've never grown used to living in a city."

Davina turned to her with quick sympathy. "Oh, I know just what you mean! I've been in town only a few weeks, yet I miss Rigborough sadly. "You . . . you will be visiting Rowanbeck often, now, I expect?"

"I hope so. Luke has invited us all for Christmas, and I own I look forward to introducing the children to all my old haunts." Charlotte began to speak about Rigborough and the people she had known there, including of course the Wakefords. It seemed the most natural thing in the world for Davina to describe the

Hall's financial predicament, the plans laid for its rehabilitation, and her hopes of selling the Rigborough Missal.

By the end of an hour, when Lord Rigg appeared to say it was time to return to Park Street, Davina felt she had known Lady Charlotte all her life. That lady, on her part, was tolerably well pleased with what she'd learned of Miss Wakeford.

"A pleasant, intelligent girl, and much in love with Luke," she told her husband. "A pity that Sophia is so opposed to the match."

"Did Miss Wakeford tell you that?"

"Certainly not. She is by far too loyal to mention such a thing to a comparative stranger. I had it from Luke."

"Umh. There's a look in your eye that says you mean to beard Lady S. in her den!"

"I will if I must," responded Charlotte calmly. "Sophy was always a great deal too hidebound in her views. It's plain as a pikestaff those two were made for each other. They mustn't miss their chance of happiness. And don't tell me not to meddle, for I shan't pay any heed."

Joshua chuckled. "When did you ever do so? A self-willed wench, if ever there was one." He gave her a sly grin. "Come to that, I'm not above doing a bit o' meddlin' meself."

"Oh? To what end?"

Mr Turnbull settled himself on the sofa beside his wife.

"That Missal o' their'n," he said. "Luke told me night before last there'd been a firm offer from t' Vatican. He said the lass was fair downcast to think of it goin' out of England. So I got to thinkin', what's to stop us formin' a consortium, same as we'd do to buy tea, or spices, or some such? I'd a word with Angerstein, and Leicester, and Luke himself. The long and the short is, we're to put in an offer. Luke will speak to Mr Allen, first off, tomorrow."

Charlotte regarded him with respect. "Do you think you can outbid the Vatican?"

"Aye, I do."

"And if you purchase the book, what will you do with it?"

"It'll rest in the British Museum, likely. Angerstein's forever sayin' us City men must lay down our blunt to benefit t' common herd. I'll be honest, buying books ain't my style, but I won't complain if it's for Luke and his lass. Who knows, some day folks may raise a statue to me, as a patron o' the arts."

"As a champion meddler, more like."

Joshua's eyes twinkled. "Nay, love, nay. When it comes to meddlin', tha knows I can't hold a candle to thee, any road."

On Monday afternoon Miss Wakeford and Sir Murray Tredgold, out driving in the Park, were overtaken and hailed by Mr Allen in a hired hackney carriage.

"Great news," cried the little librarian, when he had paid off the hackney and scrambled up into the Tredgold landau. "I've been searching everywhere for you! I've received a fresh offer for the Missal—a quarter as much again as we had from Rome —and from an English principal."

"English?" said Davina, with a beaming smile. "Oh, but that is wonderful! What is his name, sir?"

Mr Allen shook his head. "That I am not at liberty to reveal. It is not a single individual, you understand, but a consortium, and certain of the members prefer, for reasons of . . . er . . . diplomacy, to remain anonymous."

"The Regent, is it?" said Sir Murray, interestedly. "I've been hoping he'd come up to scratch. Always known him to be a liberal patron of the arts."

"He's certainly a liberal spender of the national funds," said Mr Allen drily, "but it is not His Highness who is involved here."

"Reputable people, though, I trust?"

"Oh, eminently. Though I'm not permitted to name the shareholders, I am able to say the chief negotiator is Julius Angerstein. You can be comfortable in your minds about anything he sponsors, both from the financial and the artistic points of view."

"How long will the arrangements take?"

"Angerstein suggests June 18th as a transfer date. It will take that amount of time for your lawyers and theirs to settle the terms of payment, and to draw up the necessary papers."

"If it's bought by a consortium," said Davina, "where will it be housed? In a private collection?"

"No. They hope to place it in the British Museum—the

foundation, perhaps, of a great national library. But I must tell you this offer may persuade the Vatican to go even higher."

"I don't wish for more," said Davina decisively. "Pray close the deal, Mr Allen."

They made another circuit of the Park to discuss the details of the sale, before setting down Mr Allen at his hotel. On the way back to Park Street, Sir Murray remarked confidingly that he'd be damned if he didn't think the consortium was Rigg's idea.

"Done it to please you," he said with a knowing smile.

Miss Wakeford begged him not to say such a thing. "Think if it came to his ears, and he had nothing to do with the offer. It would put him in disgust of me."

"No danger of that, puss! But there, I was only funning. If Rigg's responsible, he'll tell you soon enough, else where would be the point of it?"

Davina glanced at the coachman's rigid back, and shook her head warningly.

Sir Murray was unabashed. "Micklejohn's no gabster," he said. "He won't carry tales."

In this he was over-optimistic. The normally taciturn Micklejohn happened to be on drinking terms with Sir Murray's valet. Later, over a tankard of ale, he rehearsed the afternoon's events to Mr Jenkins, and the full story reached Sir Jocelyn Clare within the hour.

Sir Jocelyn received the news of the fresh bid with a glee that his jackal Hibberd found both puzzling and frightening.

"Why do you want to steal an old book?" he demanded. "There's jewels in the safe worth ten times as much."

"They'd not serve my purpose. It's Rigg I want, and I have him, now. I have him!" Sir Jocelyn snatched up a wine-glass, filled it, and thrust it into Hibberd's hand. "Drink up, man! We've a fortune in our grasp. Your share shall be five thousand, if you carry your part! Five thousand pounds, Hibberd. Think of that!"

"I'd as lief take what you owe me, and quit. I don't trust you, and that's a fact."

"Chicken-hearted, my dear fellow. Come, brace up! You need only follow my instructions. The first is this. Tell Jenkins that on the night of June 17th, he is to leave Park Street as early as he can contrive, and remain until dawn in the company of honest folk—I hope he numbers one or two such among his acquaintance?"

"Why June 17th?" said Hibberd. "What's it betoken?"

Sir Jocelyn chuckled. "On that night, the Countess of Rigg is to hold a dress-ball at Rowan House. My name is not on the guest-list, Hibberd—and like all wicked sprites, I intend to exact the heaviest possible penalty for the omission."

When Hibberd had left, Sir Jocelyn went upstairs to exchange his olive-green coat for a black one. He added a dark hat and gloves, picked an ebony cane from the stand in the hall, and quietly let himself out of the house.

XXI

A STRANGER VISITING Wrackham's Club for the first time could not be blamed for mistaking it for the residence of a gentleman of means, who chose to live in comfortable seclusion.

In a sense the description fitted Mr Wrackham. His birth was perfectly respectable. He had been educated at Eton and had served for a while in a regiment of excellent repute. In the army he conceived an aversion to putting his skin at risk, and at the age of twenty-five he bought out, and came to London to seek his fortune.

During the next five years he insinuated himself into the Dandy Set, where he learned that steady profits may be made from gambling. Again, it was not his own money he put at risk. Rather, he gave others the opportunity of losing theirs.

When he was thirty, his elder brother died, leaving Jack the house in Jermyn Street, and a moderate capital sum. Jack saw his chance. He set up an establishment where the pinks of modality could come to play faro, hazard, baccarat or macao. The stakes were enormously high. Fine food and wines were served. Women were barred from the premises, and there was an inflexible rule that debts must be promptly met.

Wrackham built up a small but select clientele, and when Mr Brummell gave the club his nod, success was assured. Not a night passed but one might find some person of note at the tables. Wrackham, if not precisely admired, was widely accepted.

It is hard to say just how this happy state of affairs came to alter. Perhaps the Dandies, always fickle, found some new place of entertainment. Perhaps the patrons found that they lost more often, and more heavily, at Wrackham's than at other clubs. Whatever the cause, a decline set it. The men around the tables were increasingly of the sort that makes its living by gaming. There were unseemly brawls on the premises. It began to be said that Wrackham never touched a card, unless it was to mark it, and a young gallant who accused him of sharping was later found lying in a back alley, beaten half to death. Rumour had it that Wrackham's touts prowled the polite drawing rooms of

London, on the hunt for young chubs with more money than sense. There was the tragic case of young Gower, a lad of sixteen who, having lost a hundred or so at the club, went into St James's Park and blew out his brains.

What Wrackham now owned was a gaming-hell. The quietness of the building, its close-drawn curtains, were furtive rather than discreet, and the owners of good hotels in the area warned their clients against going there.

Sir Jocelyn did not approach the front entrance, but strolled along the narrow path at the side of the house, and tapped gently at a plain door. An eye glared at him through a peephole in the panel. Chains and bolts were released, and the door swung open.

Sir Jocelyn handed his card to the burly individual facing him.

"Tell Mr Wrackham I wish to speak to him," he said.

The burly man scowled, shrugged, and went away up the back stairs. In a short while he reappeared at their head, and beckoned.

"Master's in the counting-house," he said, as Sir Jocelyn drew level with him. "'Nother flight up, back o' the buildin'."

Sir Jocelyn mounted the second stairway, and turned left along a corridor. On the way he passed a room in which could be seen five men seated round a baize-topped table. One of them glanced up and saw him, but made no sign of greeting.

At the end of the passage, a door stood ajar, showing a bar of light. Sir Jocelyn pushed it open without knocking, and stepped into Jack Wrackham's sanctum.

Wrackham was seated at the far side of a large desk, reading. A decanter of brandy stood at his elbow, a half-empty glass was in his hand. As Sir Jocelyn entered, he raised the glass to his lips and drank, watching the thin man over its rim. His eyes, the only lively feature about him, were small, and of an opaque, pale green. His hair was black and straight, brushed back from a remarkably high forehead. His chin was rather small and his mouth small and plump. He had the pallor of a man who sleeps all day and seldom sees the sun. He seemed neither pleased nor displeased at the sight of his visitor, but waved him unsmilingly to a chair.

"In funds again, Jocelyn?"

"Yes. A happy situation which you, I'm told, don't share."

Wrackham shrugged. "Now up, now down, it's the way of life."

"I saw Pavey in the green room. For shame, Jack. Watier's showed him the door years since."

"And would have done the same to you, my dear, had you not found your Cousin Talbot so remarkably open-handed."

Jocelyn laughed softly. "Well, well, let's not rip up at each other! I am here on business. You may pour me a glass of brandy. I'm sure it's superlative."

The dark man complied, pushing the glass across the desk without a word. Jocelyn sipped at it, nodded appreciatively, and set it aside.

"At the Pangbournes' ball, some weeks ago," he said, "I met a young man named Toby Dalbiggin. I found him a tedious bore, save in one respect. He mentioned your name—in the most flattering terms. One of your bird-dogs, is he, Jack?"

Still Wrackham remained silent, and Sir Jocelyn tilted his head knowingly. "I suppose that he owes you a great deal of money? His grandfather is reputed to pay all his run-of-the-mill expenses, so young Toby must be in exceptionally deep water. It occurs to me that you are his creditor, and that he's found this way of working off what he owes you. Not that I blame you for using him. In these hard times, a man must live as he may. To return to Mr Dalbiggin. I led him on a little—it was such a very dull party—and he happened to let fall the name of Roland Foote, who is known to me. Has he been patronising your establishment, Jack?"

"That's none of your concern." Wrackham spoke with perfect calmness, and Sir Jocelyn nodded.

"Normally I would agree. But just at this present I have a certain interest in Foote."

Wrackham's small green eyes sharpened. "Why?" he said bluntly.

"To borrow your phrase, that's none of your concern. Let's just say that Mr Foote may be a source of profit to us both, if we do but bend our minds to it."

Wrackham hesitated, but not for long. "How?" he demanded.

"You must allow him to win money from you. Seven or eight

hundred should suffice to convince him he's . . . er . . . the very Prince of Macao!"

Wrackham laughed. "I've no money to burn, my friend."

"I will provide the initial stake." Sir Jocelyn tossed a roll of bills across the desk. "Eight hundred. Count it if you wish."

Wrackham made no move to touch the money. "And if he takes your bait, what then?"

"Then he must lose five thousand, quite quickly."

Wrackham's mouth curved downward. "I can't regulate the fall of the cards!"

"Possibly not, but I'm very sure that Pavey can, and there are others of the same stamp among your customers."

"Do you tell me you are ready to put up five thousand to cover my losses?"

"I will redeem young Foote's notes, which you will allow him to sign, and which you will hand to me."

The dark man stared, half-disbelieving, half-fascinated. "How do I know you have five thousand?"

"The sum will be lodged at Drummond's Bank. As soon as I have Foote's signed chits, you will get your money."

"Why are you doing this?"

"For reasons I don't intend to share with you. Come now, Jack, five thousand is not to be sneezed at, is it? It will at least allow you to light your stairways better!"

"I'm not sure I like it," said Wrackham simply. "I don't trust you, Jocelyn."

"Dear me, you are the second to say so tonight! But who speaks of trust, here? I offer you the guaranteed sum of five thousand pounds, plus the original eight hundred. Of course, if what I ask is beyond you, I shall go elsewhere." Sir Jocelyn made as if to retrieve the roll of bills, but Wrackham quickly moved it out of reach.

"All right," he said. "I'll see what can be done."

"Good. It must be soon, mind. I'm in some haste." Sir Jocelyn stood up. "You'll bear it in mind, of course, that I am not in any way involved? I count on your discretion. It's your sole remaining virtue." He chuckled, and surprisingly the dark man laughed with him, his eyes vanishing in rolls of pallid flesh.

"I'll speak to Dalbiggin tomorrow," he said.

*

Some ten days later, Roland Foote and his friend Dalbiggin met at a public house on the fringe of Shepherd Market, to decide where they should seek the evening's entertainment.

Roland expressed himself in favour of going to Sadler's Wells to view the Grand Aquatic Spectacle. "They pump water, you know, from the New River into a vast tank, and stage the most splendid naval battles on it. I'm told the ships are set afire and the sailors plunge into the waves. There's even an Heroic Rescue of a Drowning Infant."

Mr Dalbiggin protested that he had no taste for tableaux, and urged a visit to Wrackham's Club. "One more night such as we enjoyed last week," he said, "and our fortunes are made!"

Roland demurred. "I'm seven hundred to the good already. That's enough for me."

He continued to sing the praises of the Wells, but somehow time wore on, and he consumed a great many brandies which Mr Dalbiggin generously paid for, until at ten o'clock the two of them set off on foot for Wrackham's Club.

On previous visits they had been led straight to one of the ground-floor gaming-rooms, but tonight Mr Wrackham met them at the door and explained that these were all engaged. He went on to say that if they cared to wait a moment or two, he would see if they might be accommodated in one of the private card parties in progress upstairs.

"It's an honour," whispered Mr Dalbiggin, as their host disappeared up the stairway. "It's only the big guns that are allowed above. It shows Jack thinks well of us."

Though Roland felt a pang of unease at the thought of playing cards with strangers, he was far too proud to admit it.

When Wrackham returned with the news that Mr Adrian Pavey's school was short of two players who had been suddenly called away to attend a father's sickbed, Roland agreed without demur to help fill the gap.

He was relieved to find that the room to which he and Mr Dalbiggin were conducted was brightly lit, and contained no mirrors such as card-sharps were reputed to employ. He was further cheered to recognise one of the men already seated at the table as an acquaintance of Toby's who had once or twice ridden with them in the Park.

Mr Pavey seemed completely the gentleman, welcomed the

two newcomers in a pleasant voice, introduced them to his companions, and set out clearly the rules and stakes applying in the school.

Roland took his seat between Toby and a bluff, roaring country-squire named Pargiter, who confessed that he was not in general a gambling man, but wished to see a little sport before returning to his farm in Sussex.

The game, which was faro, began. Roland had always had a good head for figures, and tonight he seemed to be able to predict with incredible accuracy in what order the cards would emerge from the pack. At first he played cautiously, and watched his opponents with a keen eye. Later, becoming bold, he made larger bets, and by midnight he had a considerable pile of ivory chips before him.

It was at this point that Mr Pavey ordered a new bottle of Tokay to be opened. The wine had a flowery potency, and no doubt it accorded ill with the brandy Roland had already swallowed. He began to be gripped by euphoria. Moreover his eyes played him tricks. The faces of the other players appeared to swell and then to shrink in the most amusing fashion. He was convinced he was still playing with exceptional skill, even though his winnings were evaporating like dew on the grass. And when Mr Dalbiggin announced that he'd had enough of this lark, and tried to persuade Roland to leave, Roland merely broke into gales of giggles, and swore that wild horses would not drag him from such amiable company.

The night wore on. Dalbiggin's young friend departed, but Mr Pavey magically produced another to replace him. Numerous more bottles were opened and emptied. Roland discovered he had no more chips on the table or guineas in his purse, but jolly Squire Pargiter waved a massive hand.

"Don't let it concern you, Foote, my dear fellow. Damned if I don't accept your notes. No harm in it. Y'r name's known to me. Friend of my friend Pavey, here. Sign away, sir, sign away!"

Roland signed. The candles burned lower, the cards flickered back and forth on the baize, but now they were malicious. Roland lost, and signed notes, and lost again. At last, as the greasy dawn light showed through the cracks in the blinds, the wine overcame him altogether, and he fell forward senseless across the table.

Hours later he awoke on a sofa in Mr Dalbiggin's lodgings. He was in sad case, his head feeling as if it were split by an axe, his eyes pierced by red-hot needles, his tongue shrivelled to ash. He had almost decided that he was dead and in hell when Mr Dalbiggin's face floated into sight.

"Feeling more the thing, old man?" enquired Dalbiggin. "Thought you'd never wake, by God! It's five in the afternoon!"

Roland cursed him roundly. For answer, Dalbiggin pushed a glass into his hand. "Drink up," he advised. "Hock and soda-water. Nothing to beat it, for a man in your condition."

Roland drained the potion, and sat up. The ceiling revolved giddily, and he groaned. "Last night," he said thickly. "I lost to that yokel from Sussex, didn't I?"

"Squire Pargiter," supplied Toby. "Yes, you lost to him. He was leaving town, and couldn't wait to redeem your notes, so Jack Wrackham went bail for you. Only thing possible, with you dead to the world."

"Notes," said Roland, staring. A hideous fear assailed him. He could scarcely breathe. "Do you tell me I signed promissory notes?"

"'Fraid you did, yes. I tried to prevent you, but you'd have none of my advice. Weren't yourself, at all. In fact, not to put too fine a point on it, you were drunk, Roly. *Non compos mentis.*"

Roland lurched to his feet, catching hold of Dalbiggin's arm to steady himself. "How much?" he said hoarsely. "How much did I lose?"

"A considerable sum."

"How much, damn you?"

"To be precise . . . four thousand, nine hundred and eighty-seven pounds."

Roland turned green. "Four thousand . . . No! You're bamming me, ain't you, Toby? Don't rib me, man, it ain't fair!"

"No word of a lie, Roly. That's the sum." Mr Dalbiggin's face creased suddenly in genuine emotion. "It's a damnable place, and they're all damnable people."

"You can say that, now? Yet you took me there. You persuaded me!" Roland checked as the truth began to pierce through the clouds in his brain. "By Heaven, I see it now! You're one of 'em, aren't you? One of Wrackham's touts! You set me up to be fleeced!"

He caught hold of Dalbiggin's shoulders, spun him round, and was about to drive a fist into his face, when a wave of nausea overcame him. Letting go he reeled to the window, flung up the sash, and vomited into the alley below. Some minutes later he turned weakly back towards the room. It was empty. Mr Dalbiggin had left, and though Roland waited almost an hour, he did not return.

Somehow Roland managed to pull on his shoes and his coat. His pockets he found to contain only a few pence, not enough for the price of a hackney carriage. He was forced to limp back to Park Street. He entered the house from the mews, slipped up the back stairs, made his way to his bedroom and locked the door. Exhausted, he threw himself down on the bed. All about him, the house stirred with the comings and goings of its occupants. Once someone tapped quietly on his door, but he made no answer. At last, late in the night, he fell into uneasy, dream-haunted sleep.

Whatever Roland's faults, he did not lack courage. On Wednesday morning he woke early, washed, shaved, dressed himself in formal clothes, and rode round to Wrackham's Club. Seen in daylight, it had a seedy look, and he wondered how he could ever have been fool enough to patronise it.

He had some difficulty in gaining admittance, and more in rousing Mr Wrackham, who disliked the daylight hours; but at last he was permitted a brief interview.

Mr Wrackham confirmed the amount of the debt. Roland asked to be shown his notes, and Mr Wrackham produced them from his safe. Roland examined the signatures, checked the total of the amounts, and nodded.

"Very well, I accept the obligation. You'll be paid in full, I promise."

Wrackham examined his nails. "Promises are cheap, Mr Foote."

"I said you'll get every penny! Only I may n-need a little time."

"A gentleman is expected to pay his gambling debts when he incurs them, you know."

"I am aware of that. I will return here tomorrow afternoon, and bring the money with me."

Roland left with as much dignity as he could muster, and for the next few hours paced the streets, trying to conjure up some way of meeting his debt. The more he racked his brains, the more impossible did the task appear. Nigh on £5,000! There was no way he could find it, not even if he sold everything he owned, including his horse.

There was only one way out. He'd have to borrow the blunt. But when he came to consider who might lend it, his spirits sank to the depths. His Uncle Tredgold would certainly not like to see his nephew in a debtors' prison, but Roland's whole being shrank from approaching Sir Murray. There'd be no end to the old devil's prosing and moralising. All chance of remaining in London, or even coming up for a night's fun and gig, would vanish. One would be condemned to rot in Rigborough with the bucolics until the end of time! It was not to be thought of.

The same arguments applied to his mother, with the added consideration that she would be quite unable to raise as much as five thousand, even if she wished to.

His cousin Mortimer, who might have been relied upon to cough up a few hundred, was still visiting his relations in Brighton, and would not be home for a week.

Throughout that night, tossing in tangled sheets, Roland agonised, and in the cold dawn decided that his only hope lay with the Greeks.

He knew, of course, that these backstreet money-lenders gave loans only on the most ruinous interest, but he clung to the pipedream that some miracle would occur—that he would win a vast sum on the horses, or somehow persuade Mr Shedley to advance him a capital amount.

When he visited the loan-sharks, fresh shocks awaited him. The shrewd gentry told him flatly that they did not lend a sou to a young man who could offer neither present security, nor the expectation of future wealth.

Weary and heartsick, Roland considered leaving quietly for France, as poor Brummell had done, but some small spark of pride sustained him, and he doggedly made his way back to Wrackham's club to confess failure.

Wrackham took the news calmly, and cut short Roland's stumbling explanations with the remark that it was all one to him, since he no longer possessed the chits.

Roland stared at him in disbelief. "What do you mean sir? What have you done with them?"

"Sold 'em," said Wrackham indifferently. "I can't afford to carry a debt of that size, you know."

"Sold?! You can't mean that! It's beyond what's permissible, to hedge a debt of honour!"

"Honour doesn't trouble me overmuch. Money does."

"Who holds my notes?" Roland leaned threateningly over his tormentor. "Answer me, sir! I demand to know!"

"By all means. They were redeemed last night by Sir Jocelyn Clare. He's your creditor, now."

"Sir Jocelyn?" Roland shook his head. "I don't understand. Why should he do such a thing?"

"You'd best ask him."

"I shall, and at once!"

Roland reached Sir Jocelyn's house in Grafton Street soon after six o'clock. His arrival was observed, from behind drawn curtains, by Sir Jocelyn and Hibberd.

"Go down, Hibberd," ordered the thin man. "Tell him I'm from home—that I've gone into the country and am not expected back before Monday or Tuesday."

Hibberd was away for some time, and returned shaking his head. "The young man's powerfully upset," he said. "He tried to worm it out of me, where you might be found. Said it was a matter of life and death."

"How sad that you could give him no answer!"

Hibberd looked narrowly at his employer. "What if he does himself an injury?" he demanded. "He looks half-crazed, to me."

"Foote isn't the suicidal type. A few more days of fevered imagining will bring him pat to my hand."

"You're a demon from hell, you know that?"

Sir Jocelyn's only reply was to bow his head, as one acknowledging a compliment.

XXII

ALL THAT WEEK, Roland fretted over his problem. He haunted Grafton Street in case he might bump into Jocelyn Clare, hurried round to Mortimer's lodgings to see if the knocker was yet on the door, and badgered the seedier loan-merchants in the City.

His erratic behaviour passed unnoticed by his family. Mrs Wakeford was laid low by an attack of the colic, Lady Sophy was occupied in ministering to her needs, and Sir Murray and Davina were taken up with the sale of the Missal.

Mr Julius Angerstein duly came with two of his experts to view the book, and thereafter there were interminable discussions with Mr Allen, Mr Shedley and Davina's bankers. She would have liked to conclude the deal at once, but Mr Allen told her that the consortium was quite specific in its terms. The purchase money was to be paid over on the morning of June 17th, and the book handed to its new owners the following day.

It was unfortunate that Roland chose to approach his sister at the end of a particularly demanding day, and ask her to lend him £5,000.

"The sale's almost through," he said with an attempt at nonchalance. "In a day or so you'll be damned plump in the pocket. Come on, Dav, what harm will it do to lend me a little? I'll pay it back, I swear."

Miss Wakeford regarded him with cold fury. "I will not be plump in the pocket," she said. "Every penny of that money must be ploughed back into the estate. You know that as well as I do."

"You don't understand," he said. "I'm desperate! How do you think a man can squeak through on what I have?"

"Roly, I didn't sell the Missal so that you could live high on the hoof. Can't you get it through your head that without careful management, we shall be bankrupt?"

The resentment that had been smouldering in Roland ever since he learned the terms of his step-father's will, now burst into flame. "Oh yes," he said in a sneering tone, "I can see how hard-pressed you are! Not a stitch of clothing to put on your back! Living from hand to mouth, forced to beg your bread! No wonder you're angling for a rich husband, to keep you from the poorhouse!"

"Be quiet!" Miss Wakeford sprang to her feet. "How dare you speak so to me."

"It's true, every word of it! You go in silks and satins, you are to be seen at every ton party, yet you deny me a pittance!"

"You call five thousand a pittance? Good God, how come you to think I have so much to give away? What do you mean to spend it on, I'd like to know?"

"It's none of your business!" Roland recklessly tossed away any chance of gaining sympathy. "I was a dolt to come to you in the first place. I know what a pinchpenny you are. I shan't trouble you again!"

He flung out of the house, leaving Davina on the edge of tears. The Tredgolds, coming in a short while later, were left to guess the reason for her mood. Sir Murray said it was ever thus when one was engaged in an important transaction. Lady Sophy was inclined to blame the heat, which had become oppressive, while Jane said knowingly that poor Dav was pining for Lord Rigg.

This made Miss Wakeford even crosser. "No such thing," she declared. "I told Rigg not to call, as my time would be taken up with business matters. In any case, he's out of town, visiting Graydon with Edward Clare."

"Gone to earth," approved Sir Murray. "Sensible fellow. I can imagine what it must be like at Rowan House, with a dress-ball in the offing! The whole place in a turmoil, nowhere for a man to sit down, and nothing to eat but cold cuts and pickles!"

This was less than just. Lady Rigg and Charles Turnbull together made a formidable team, and the preparations for the ball had gone without a hitch. The invitations, sent out well in advance, had brought in such a gratifying crop of acceptances that Amabel looked forward to seeing her reception-rooms full to bursting-point. Miss Finch had personally supervised the lowering of the great chandeliers, and the cleaning of their crystal drops. Charles, planning on a scale that would have satisfied even Josh Nabob, felt able to promise that the music, the wines, and the supper dishes would excite nothing but praise. He had engaged extra staff and coached them in the duties they were to perform on the great night. He had made arrangements for flowers to be brought to London, packed in ice, the day before the party, and had even had a stretch of the garden dug over and planted with flowering shrubs, so that the vista from the ballroom windows should enchant every eye.

No detail was too small to escape the planners' attention. Amabel was able to tell Lord Rigg, when he returned from his visit to Graydon, that she expected their ball to prove the peak and pinnacle of the Season. And she informed him, and Mr Clintwood, that in case they should be wishful to send posies, she had ascertained that Miss Wakeford would be wearing cream satin with an overskirt of Chantilly lace, and Miss Tredgold, ice-blue faille.

On the afternoon of June 16th, Roland Foote at last found Sir Jocelyn Clare at home. A man-servant admitted him to the house, and conducted him to the salon on the first floor where Sir Jocelyn sat at ease, his feet on a padded stool, a decanter at his elbow, and a book of verse in his hand. He glanced up as Roland approached, and said in tones of faint surprise, "Ah, Mr Foote! I have been expecting you hourly. Porritt tells me you've been more or less encamped on my doorstep this week past!"

Roland had spent a good deal of time rehearsing what he would say when he came face to face with Sir Jocelyn; but the malice in the thin man's tone, and the mocking smile on his face, drove out these careful speeches. Instead, he said in a shaking voice:

"Sir! Jack Wrackham informs me you have redeemed my notes, and I demand to know the meaning of it!"

"Meaning? Why, it means you owe me, instead of Wrackham. Have you come to make payment? I do hope so, for I confess I'm a trifle pressed for funds, just at the moment."

"I'll pay in full, don't worry! But first, why did you buy my notes?"

Sir Jocelyn raised his brows. "Out of friendship, and concern for a neighbour, of course. Don't tell me you prefer to remain in Wrackham's clutches! I promise you, when it comes down to brass tacks, he's worse than any Greek. Pray sit down, Mr Foote, and let me give you a glass of claret."

Roland perched uneasily on the edge of a chair, waving away the offer of wine.

"Sir Jocelyn, I must be plain with you. When I pledged those notes, I fear I was . . . I was in my cups, sir!"

"Alas, how often that is the case! To look upon the wine when it is red has been the cause of many a man's downfall."

"I mean that had I b-been sober, I would n-never have signed my name . . . I would never have got in so deep. . . ."

"But you did sign, Mr Foote. You signed for four thousand nine hundred and eighty-seven pounds."

"I don't argue the amount. . . ."

"And, sir, you are of age, and therefore responsible for your gaming debts."

"Yes." Roland's face was scarlet. "I'm not trying to wriggle out of the net. I owe the money, and I'll pay up, but I m-must ask you for a little time. Since you've been so kind as to stand my friend . . . perhaps your g-generosity will stretch to a few days more?"

Sir Jocelyn leaned over to pour himself a glass of claret, took an appreciative sip, and settled back in his chair. "A few days? I wonder what makes you name that particular interval?"

"It will give me the chance to . . . to make arrangements."

"Do you expect your financial circumstances to improve so suddenly?"

"They might."

"By what means?"

Roland hesitated. "My family," he mumbled. "Funds may become available."

Sir Jocelyn nodded. "No doubt you refer to the sale of the Rigborough Missal. That should certainly replenish the Wakeford coffers, but do you think that that niggardly creature, Thomas Shedley, will suffer you to borrow from them to repay a gaming debt?" As Roland made no answer, Sir Jocelyn cocked his head. "You're counting on the fact that your relations won't wish to see you disgraced? You will be, once word of your default gets about. Welshing at the tables is the one sin Society can't condone."

"I've said I'll pay!"

"But how, my dear fellow? I'm forced to remind you that the effect of debt is cumulative. It gathers weight. It becomes the millstone that crushes out a man's energy and self-respect, that sinks him in the nethermost part of the sea. Your future is disgrace, penury, and prison, Mr Foote. I take it you have considered that last possibility? Yes, I see you have. So the long and the short of it is that you must find five thousand pounds, without delay. The question remains . . . how?"

"M-my sister. She'll help me."

Sir Jocelyn smiled into Roland's frightened eyes. "But that's not so, is it? I'm afraid she cares nothing for you and your embarrassments. Why, only last week, when you went to her cap in hand, she refused to lend you a sou."

"How the devil do you know that?"

"Servants prattle, sir, and so do clerks and agents. One gleans a grain here, a grain there, until the harvest is in. It would surprise you, how much I've learned about the sale of the Missal. For instance, I know that the purchase money will be paid into your sister's bank at ten o'clock tomorrow morning, and that on June 18th, the book will be delivered to Julius Angerstein. What happens next is a topic for debate. Some say it will be resold at once, at a handsome profit, to the Vatican or some dealer in Paris."

"That's a lie, anyway. It's to lodge in the British Museum."

"Flummery!"

"I tell you it's in the agreement! Davina insisted."

"Miss Wakeford is certainly too honest to see through the stratagems of a man as devious as my cousin Rigg."

Roland glanced up quickly. "You think Rigg's one of the principals?"

"I'm sure of it. This is precisely the sort of sly trick he likes to turn . . . to ingratiate himself with a trusting female, to play upon her affections and hoax her into selling for far less than she need. I warn you that once this deal is closed, that's the last your sister will see of him. He will go back to his paramour, and they will laugh together over the way they've deceived you all.

"I won't attempt to deny that I detest my cousin. I hold him a liar and a cheat, the man who has kept me from my ancestral home, the creature who was ready to murder his own brother, for the sake of his lands and title. Rigg escaped justice on that occasion. I pray he may not do so again, but I'm not over-sanguine. No doubt he'll end by having both book and money

—for of course, if the Missal is stolen, the money must be refunded."

"Stolen?" Roland's protuberant eyes almost bulged from his head. "What do you mean, 'stolen'?"

"The idea hasn't occurred to you? I must say it's been uppermost in my thoughts ever since I learned the peculiar terms of the sale. The money to be paid tomorrow, but the book not to be handed over until the following day. I've puzzled over the reason for that delay. One answer springs to mind. The Missal will lie overnight in Park Street, unprotected, while you and the rest of your household disport yourselves at Rigg's dress party. Pray tell me, what's to prevent his hiring a brace of villains to break into your uncle's home, and steal the book?"

"That won't fadge," said Roland impatiently. "The thing's locked in the strongroom. No one could breach such a door."

"Dear me, I see you're as naïf as the rest of the world! Don't you know that half the ton buys its safes from Barrable's?" Sir Jocelyn felt in the pocket of his coat and drew out a bunch of keys. Detaching one, he laid it on the table beside him. "That my friend, unlocks the safe in the corner of this room. It also unlocks several safes at the Admiralty, one at Carlton House, and, I have no doubt, your Uncle Murray's strongroom. If Rigg doesn't possess a key of similar pattern, I shall be astonished."

Roland surveyed his host in silence for some minutes. At last he shook his head. "Rigg don't intend to jilt Davina," he said. "I can't abide the fellow, but any fool can see he's nutty on her."

"He has always been an excellent actor."

"No. He means to marry her. Take my word for it."

Sir Jocelyn gave a faint sigh. "In that case, sir, you're lost. Once they're married, Wakeford and all its assets will pass into Rigg's hands. You will be left with nothing."

"I have nothing now." Roland's tone was bitter, which seemed to please Sir Jocelyn, for he nodded in sympathy.

"Indeed, you were sadly abused by the terms of Henry Wakeford's will, and you are right to expect redress. A man in your position must . . . look for pickings, shall we say? He must seize such opportunities as come his way."

"What do you mean?" Roland's expression, though guarded, was by no means unreceptive.

Sir Jocelyn answered at a tangent. "Do you know what the consortium is offering for the Missal?" he said.

"No, only that it's a vast sum."

"Rather more than forty thousand pounds. And I can assure you that there are other interested parties who would go even higher—and ask no awkward questions. Do you understand me?"

"Of course I do! You're saying there are collectors who don't mind buying stolen goods."

"Exactly so. My next point is this. In the circumstances, are we not entitled to seek our own advantage? To retrieve a little of what has been denied us by our greedy and self-centred relations?"

Roland saw quite clearly where the conversation was leading, and began to shake his head, but Sir Jocelyn held up a thin hand. "Please, I beg, don't be too hasty. Face the facts, Mr Foote. Your choice of action is not wide. You have a debt you can't meet, with the shadow of public contempt and a prison sentence hanging over you; a family that cares nothing for your suffering, that denies your cry for help; and the prospect of very soon being ejected from Wakeford and forced to live on a meagre five hundred a year.

"It's a bleak picture, is it not, but there's one gleam of light in it. Tomorrow night you will have the chance to put an end to all your difficulties. All you have to do is slip away from Rigg's party. Walk the short distance from Berkeley Square to Park Street. Let yourself into your uncle's house, go to the strongroom, unlock it with that key, and take out the box containing the Rigborough Missal. Bring the box to the closed carriage which will be waiting at the corner of Park and South Street, and hand it over. In return, you will receive your chits, and an additional payment of five thousand pounds. A handsome reward, don't you think, for so little effort? Why, on such a foundation, you may build a fortune."

Roland was staring as if mesmerised. "It wouldn't answer," he muttered. "I'd be seen."

"By whom? At Rowan House, all attention will be on the ballroom, and the antics of the guests. No one will notice if you leave the scene for half an hour. Guests will be arriving and departing throughout the evening. You will wait until midnight

". . . slip out through the garden—you may wear a cloak to cover your appearance, if you see fit—and take the back alleys to Park Street. Your uncle's house will be almost without light, the servants fast asleep."

"No, they won't," Roland objected. "My uncle's valet will wait up, he always does. And there's my aunt's abigail, as well."

"I will undertake to see that Jenkins is not on the premises. Lady Sophia never asks the Bracket woman to wait up for her."

"My family . . ."

". . . deserves no consideration whatsoever. After all, what have they ever done for you?"

". . . but if they suspect me?"

". . . they will say nothing. That's the beauty of the scheme, don't you see? They will hardly wish to brand you a criminal. As for Rigg, if he's as devoted to your sister as you make out, he'll not damage his cause by accusing you."

"He'll kill you," said Roland with conviction. "He'll know it's your doing, and hunt you down."

"I shall be far from here, my dear sir. My property is already sold, the proceeds safely out of England. With what I make from the Missal, I shall live very comfortably in Paris, or Rome."

"The hue and cry. If I'm caught. . . ."

"There will be no hue and cry. Immediately after handing over the book, you will return to Rowan House and mingle with the guests. Your absence will never be remarked. As for me, I have laid my plans. I don't fear arrest."

Roland sank his head in his hands. "I need time to think."

"Time, I fear, is a luxury neither of us can afford. Come, sir! One throw of the dice and you're free of all your troubles, and five thousand in your pocket besides."

"And if I refuse?"

"Then I shall reluctantly be compelled to call in your debt at once, and your career as a man of fashion will be over before it's begun." Sir Jocelyn's tone was matter-of-fact. "The choice is yours."

"Very well," said Roland miserably. "I'll do as you ask."

XXIII

June 17th dawned hot and sunny. Lady Sophia, surveying a cloudless sky from the breakfast-room window, announced that it was going to be a perfect day, words which seemed to Miss Wakeford to be tempting fate. Her nerves were still very much on edge, and would be until the sale of the Missal was settled.

She did not go out driving that morning with her aunt and cousin, as she was awaiting a visit from Mr Shedley. He arrived at eleven o'clock, wreathed in smiles, to tell her that the sum of £41,000 had been paid into her bankers' hands an hour earlier.

"I congratulate you, my dear lady," he said, warmly shaking her hand. "You've saved your patrimony. Wakeford will flourish for another thousand years."

"If so, the credit goes to you, my uncle, Mr Allen—in fact to all my generous supporters." Davina sighed. "Though it's excessively pleasant to feel so rich, I confess I'll not be happy till we've handed over the book. I lay awake half the night, listening for thieves on the stair."

"That at least you needn't dread," said Mr Shedley. "The Missal is safe in the strongroom, and in any case, your uncle has taken peculiar measures to protect it. He dropped a word in Sir Nathanial Conant's ear, last week. There'll be a couple of Robin Redbreasts posted in Park Street tonight, and you may be sure that anyone attempting a mischief will soon find himself under arrest."

"He's engaged the Runners? Then I shall certainly be easy in my mind."

"Just so, but don't speak of it to anyone. The fewer people who know of it, the better."

Davina promised to be discreet, and turned to a subject that was very much on her conscience, namely Roland's request for a loan.

"I was horridly unkind to him when he approached me," she said. "He's been avoiding me ever since. I know he resents the fact that Papa left me so much, and him so little."

"Your father," said Mr Shedley severely, "left you a load of debt and responsibility. I see no signs of Master Roland wishing to take his share of that."

"Roly's too young to see things in that light. He feels he's been victimised—and frankly, I don't care to be at odds with him all my life. Perhaps now that we're in funds, you may see your way to advance him a few hundreds?"

Predictably, Mr Shedley refused point-blank to hand over a lump sum, saying the young chub would only squander it; but he did agree, albeit grudgingly, that Roland's allowance might be increased.

When Davina searched for Roland to tell him this news, she was told he'd left the house at seven o'clock that morning, without saying where he was bound. He failed to reappear for the whole of that day, a fact that caused his mama grave concern.

"The poor boy is not himself," she declared, with a darkling look at Davina. "He's hardly eaten for days. He's not as robust as Some People seem to think, his spirits are easily overthrown. I've tried to coax him to take a course of Velno's Vegetable Syrup, but he won't. I only hope he may not be working himself into a *crise des nerfs*."

"No such thing," retorted Sir Murray. "Roly's suffering from liver, same as the rest of us. A dose of calomel will soon set him to rights."

This homespun advice did not please Mrs Wakeford. She shook her head, and expressed the hope that they might not all live to regret their shocking neglect of her son.

After an early luncheon, the ladies of the household retired to their rooms to rest. Davina was roused from a half-doze by one of the house-maids, who told her in a conspiratorial whisper that there was a fine gennelman downstairs, that was wishful to talk to her.

"What is his name?" said Davina, climbing off her bed, and searching in the wardrobe for a fresh gown.

"It's Mr Edward Clare, Miss. I did say as' you was laid down on your bed, but 'e wouldn't take no for an answer. He axed me to bring you the message, so I brung it. I hope I did right?"

"Quite right, Annie. Please go and tell him I'll be down immediately."

Having dressed and run a comb through her hair, Davina hurried to the drawing-room. Mr Clare was standing at the bow window, but turned as she entered, and came to shake her hand.

Her fear that he meant to enact some tender scene was dispelled by his first words, for he said with a smile that he'd not come to pester her.

"I won't pretend that your last letter didn't cause me pain," he added, "but though my hopes are dashed, I accept that your answer is 'no'. It is a matter of regret to me, for your character is such that any man must count himself lucky to be your husband. I for my part would have done all in my power to make you happy. But there! One cannot dictate to the heart. We must close the book of love. I need only add that I remain your true friend, as I trust you are mine."

"Indeed I am." Davina freed her hand, which he still clasped. "Pray, won't you sit down, and take some refreshment? Tea, or a glass of wine?"

"Nothing, I thank you. Mine must be a short visit." He took the seat she indicated, and lapsed for a time into silence, his gaze lowered. At last he sighed, and said, "The question I wish to raise is very delicate. After all, say what you like, blood is thicker than water."

Miss Wakeford agreed that this was very true.

"Ordinarily," continued Mr Clare, "my lips would be sealed. But in view of our friendship . . . the very special affection in which I hold you, ma'am . . . I feel I must speak out."

Miss Wakeford nodded gravely.

"I know that what I tell you will be treated as confidential?"

"It shall go no further than these four walls."

He nodded, apparently satisfied. "You are probably aware that I've spent these past few days at Graydon, with my cousin Lord Rigg?"

"Yes, he told me he was to meet you there."

"Quite so. It was, I may say, a highly rewarding sojourn. Lucas and I were able to decide what's to be done for the property, and also to resolve certain misunderstandings. I'm glad to say we are now on an amicable footing with each other."

"I'm happy to hear it, sir."

"Yes, but this brings me to the difficult stretch." Edward cleared his throat. "You will forgive me for saying that I'm aware of my cousin's high regard for you. What I mean to say is, even a clodpole like me can't miss it. But the fact is, I've known for some time that he was paying court to you."

Davina looked up, startled.

"Yes," said Edward. "My brother Jocelyn wrote to me—it must have been in the first week of May. It was not the sort of letter a man likes to receive, Miss Wakeford. In fact it was a lot of damnable, mischief-making nonsense."

"What did he say?"

"I hardly like to tell you, but . . . not to put too fine a point on it . . . he suggested you were anxious to secure a rich husband, and the clubs were laying bets whether you'd have Pangbourne, or Rigg."

As Davina stared in indignation, Edward shook his head. "I'm making a hash of this. You'll be wishing me at Jericho, I expect."

"No. I'm grateful to you. Please go on."

"Well, you may imagine how Jocelyn's news upset me. Fairly bowled me over, truth to tell. Of course, when your own letter arrived some fortnight later, it explained all. I realised you'd never sought to mislead me. I stopped hating you, but I'm afraid I still hated my cousin. In fact, I was within inches of posting up to town, to call Luke out!" He smiled wryly. "Just as well I didn't, eh? Luke would have put a bullet through me without any difficulty. He's a better shot than I'll ever be."

"Mr Clare," said Davina in exasperation, "I am sure that Lord Rigg would never have let it come to a duel. He told me once he thinks such affairs both brutal and archaic. Besides, how would it profit him to blow a hole through the man he depends on to run Graydon?"

"Very true." Edward's face relaxed. "Dear Miss Wakeford, ever reasonable. But still, like it or not, it's my duty to warn you against my brother. It's hard for ordinary, decent folk to understand Jocelyn. He's eaten up with envy and spite. Show him happiness, and he feels bound to set his heel on it. For most of my life, I've done nothing to check him. Turned a blind eye when he schemed against Luke and Talbot. Never spoke up when he played the tyrant to Amabel. But I'll not allow him to harm you, and that's flat."

"Truly, I doubt if he could. I hardly know your brother. Our paths never cross."

"They will," said Edward grimly. "Anyone close to Luke becomes the target for Jocelyn's malice. If he can serve you ill, he will, because he knows that's the best way to strike at Luke." He rose to his feet. "I must leave now. I promised I'd be on parade at Rowan House by six. I look forward to seeing you later. Perhaps, for old time's sake, you'll stand up with me in the polka?"

"I shall like that, and thank you."

When Mr Clare's hackney carriage had driven away, Miss Tredgold came dancing down the stairs to join Davina. She brandished two nosegays, one of cream roses, the other of rosebuds and forget-me-nots.

"Yours is from Rigg," she announced. "His note reads: 'To my very dear Miss Wakeford. The waltz is mine, always. L. R.' If he doesn't propose to you tonight, then you may bite me." She took a deep sniff of the rosebuds. "Now, if I can only bring Clintwood up to scratch, we may both be betrothed before the week is out."

The Tredgolds had decided to dine *en famille* before driving over to Rowan House. Davina dressed early, and was tucking one of Rigg's roses into the bodice of her gown when Becky appeared in the doorway.

"Beautiful," she declared. "You look like a bride, so you do."

"Don't, Becky. It's ill luck!"

The abigail came forward with a smile. "As if luck could change his lordship's mind about you. And you, my lamb? You're happy, aren't you?"

"Too happy." Davina turned away from the glass. She did not wish to talk about the ball, or Lord Rigg, even to Rebecca. "Is Roland home yet?"

"No. I've been on the lookout for him. Worritts your Ma, he does, with his gadabout ways." Becky moved to the window, which overlooked Aldford Street, the narrow lane that led to the mews behind the house. "Why, speak of the devil! There he comes now."

Davina went to join Becky. She could see Roland on the

street-corner. He was deep in conversation with a short, dark man in black.

"Who's that with him?" she asked.

"Never clapped eyes on him. Drat that boy, I do believe he'll be late for his own funeral."

As they watched, the short man turned and hurried away towards Mount Street. Roland came along the lane at a brisk trot, and passed their window without looking up. Next moment he disappeared through the archway to the stables.

Davina would have forgotten the incident had not Mortimer Foote taken her aside when they met, a little later, in the drawing-room.

"What's Roly up to?" he demanded. "Came round to see me at eight o'clock this morning. Eight, mark you. Dash it, a man's not fit to be seen before ten."

"What did he want?"

"Money. Asked me to lend him five thousand."

Davina's pulse lurched.

"I told him not to be a clunch-head," continued Mortimer. "Said if I'd five thousand, I'd know of better ways to spend it. Then he said a hundred or so would do to be going on with. I gave him that, but I'd like to know what the devil he's planning to do with five thousand."

Davina shook her head. "I don't know, unless it's to buy Mr Leaming's bays."

"Did he tell you so?"

"No, but he's been talking of them forever, and saying how much he'd like to own them. Last week he asked me for the same amount—five thousand."

"Well, if it's Leaming's prads he's after, at least he won't waste his blunt. Prime blood and bone. Though as I recall, Leaming was asking four, not five. And it don't explain what Roly said about Calais."

Mr Foote fell into a brooding silence, and Miss Wakeford, perceiving she must let him tell his story in his own way, sat down and folded her hands.

"I gave him black coffee," Mortimer said at last. "He looked so dashed pale, and he was shaking like an aspen. He drank it off, and then out of the blue, he started quizzing me about Calais. Wanted to know on what days the packet sails from

Dover, and where one may book a passage, and the price of a berth. Struck me as odd. Don't it strike you as odd?"

Miss Wakeford nodded dumbly.

"Next thing was even odder. He asked if I could lend him a domino."

"A what?"

"Domino. Cloak, you know, with a hood?"

"I know what it is, you gudgeon, but who wears such a thing, these days?"

"Nobody. At least, I suppose one might do so for a *bal masqué*, or a night at Vauxhall, particularly if one was in dubious company. But the company at Rowan House won't be dubious."

"Morty, you can't think he'll wear it tonight?"

"Make a cake of himself, if he does. Told him, folk will think he's rats in the rafters." Mr Foote's long nose twitched. "Thing is, Dav, putting it all together—the money, the passage to France, the domino—I don't like the smell of it. Puts me in mind of that Scottish fellow my Aunt Clara's always quoting at me."

Miss Wakeford shook her head, mystified.

"Fellow that came out of the west," supplied Mortimer. "Snatched up some female in the middle of dinner, and rode off with her."

"You mean Young Lochinvar?"

"That's the one. Shocking bad form, I always thought, to break into a supper-party like that. Might be all right for Glasgow, but it won't go down in London. Still, when I think how Roly feels about Amabel Rowan, I must say it puts me in a bit of a pucker."

Davina burst out laughing. "Morty, you don't seriously suggest Roland would try to . . . to abduct Amabel?"

"Might. Romantic notion, and Roly's a romantic fellow. Might think it would fix Lady Rigg's attention to be swept off to France."

"I should just think it would, but the idea's totally absurd. I promise you Roland hasn't spared Amabel a thought in weeks, and if he did wish to do something dramatic, it wouldn't include a Channel crossing. You know how seasick he gets. He can't even take a boat on the canal, at home."

"That's true," said Mortimer brightening. "But it still don't explain what he's up to."

"I daresay," said Davina, "he's making enquiries on behalf of some friend who plans to visit Paris. And the domino is for . . . for some other enterprise. There'll be a simple explanation, I'm sure."

"I expect you're right." Mr Foote, the most chivalrous of souls, had caught the anxiety in Davina's eyes, and quickly turned the subject by describing the alterations the Regent was presently making to the Pavilion at Brighton.

His doubts, however, remained. He knew, far better than Davina, how easily a man may fall into debt in London, and he very much feared his erratic cousin had landed in the suds. He resolved that the next day he would have a quiet word with Sir Murray, and for tonight he would keep a very sharp eye on Roland.

Rowan House was now gripped by the tension felt by a regiment about to undergo attack. Everyone was, in Robert Clintwood's phrase, standing to stations: butler and wine-steward, cooks and flunkeys, parlour maids and abigails, stable-lads poised to jump to the heads of carriage-horses, and link-boys brandishing torches ready-kindled.

At precisely nine-thirty, Charles Turnbull gave the nod to the musicians in the gallery to strike up a tune, and the welcoming-party assembled in the hallway. Lady Rigg, exquisite in silver lace, her shining hair cut and curled in the new shorter way, stood next to Lord Rigg, who in swallow-tail coat and black pantaloons was the epitome of quiet elegance.

A little to one side, Mr Clintwood waited with Edward Clare and Cornelia Finch. Miss Finch had honoured the occasion by acquiring a brand new gown of lilac satin, elaborately beaded round the hem. A garnet parure of old-fashioned design glittered on her narrow chest, and as a dashing note she carried a very large chickenskin fan, handpainted with medallions of the Royal family at Kew.

Farther off, in the anteroom leading to the ballroom, the Turnbulls were chatting to Amabel's Yorkshire friends, the Tunmers. Lady Charlotte looked as handsome as ever in a gown of the soft colour known as rose-dorée, matching French kid gloves, and the pearls Luke had brought her from India. Beside her, her husband was complete to a shade in satin knee breeches, black coat, striped silk stockings, and slippers trimmed with silver buckles. A fine diamond shone in the lace at his throat, and his kerchief was perfumed with sandalwood. As he told Miss Lucy Tunmer (whom he categorised a very good sort of wench with no nonsense about her), if he had to dress up like the Grand Panjandrum, then he might as well smell like him, too.

Shortly before ten, the streets in the neighbourhood began to echo with the rumble of wheels, and in no time at all the line of smart conveyances stretched right round the Square. Carriage after carriage drew up at the steps to discharge its passengers. Group after group of guests advanced, laughing and chatting, through the wide front doors. Footmen scurried to gather up coats and wraps, and Amabel, listening to the names that rolled off her major-domo's tongue, knew with a full heart that her party would be counted a triumph.

The Tredgolds and Wakefords arrived when the press was at its height, and joined the queue moving slowly across the hall. Davina was glad of the delay. Despite her best efforts, she could not calm her thoughts. She was plagued by anxiety about the Book of Hours. Roland's strange conduct perturbed her. Above all, she was nervous of meeting Lord Rigg.

In the week he had been absent from London, she had tried to think about him in a detached, and logical way. She had reminded herself as much as a hundred times that he had never spoken of love, let alone marriage. She had called to mind the warnings of those well-meaning friends who said he was a libertine, not the marrying sort, a trifler famous for ruining the hopes of respectable females.

She had told herself sternly that once the Book of Hours was handed over to its new owners, she had best forget his lordship, and go home to Rigborough.

All these sensible resolutions vanished in smoke the instant she glimpsed Rigg's tall figure on the far side of the hall. It struck her with blinding force that she had no intention of leaving town before the end of the Season. She would remain in London, she would stick like a burr to Rigg's side for as long as he would permit, and if in the end it turned out he wanted no more than a casual flirtation, then so be it. At least she would have decided her own fate. No one, friend or foe, was going to dictate to her how to conduct her life.

The decision filled her with elation. She put up her chin, her large eyes sparkled, and Lord Rigg, turning at her approach, encountered the full radiance of her smile. His own face lit up in response, and he took her hand and raised it quickly to his lips. The gesture was fleeting, but the sharp eyes of London's ton never missed such signs of an affair of the heart. Within minutes, Emily Cowper was telling Lady Melbourne that Rigg and the Wakeford chit would make a match of it.

"Smelling of April and May," she opined. "Heavens, though, if you could but have seen the look on Sophia Tredgold's face. Thunder and lightning. I hear she's been hoping young Pangbourne would come up to scratch, but I suppose he's cried off."

"No, he hasn't," said Lady Melbourne. "Dorian Pangbourne told me herself that John proposed to Miss Wakeford, but she refused him. A pity, in my view. He's a better prospect than Rigg. Too many dirty dishes in the Rowan cupboard."

"If you're thinking of Jocelyn Clare," said the Countess Lieven, who had joined the group, "his star's set. I have it on excellent authority that the Cits have blacklisted him, and as Prinny's anxious to raise new loans from them, Clare's *persona non grata* at Carlton House."

The gaze of all three ladies shifted to the far side of the antechamber, where Mr Joshua Turnbull was in conversation with several other men.

"Things have come to a pretty pass," remarked Lady Melbourne, "when people of refinement must depend upon the goodwill of vulgarians like Josh Nabob."

Countess Lieven, who thought Lady Melbourne herself something of a parvenu, smiled thinly. "I am not sure that I would describe our Regent as a person of refinement," she said.

"You know quite well what I mean. Rigg one can stomach, but not his uncle. I hope you don't consider sending him vouchers for Almack's."

"Certainly not," returned the other. "He wouldn't accept them if I did. But I shall certainly ask him to become patron of my fund for orphan waifs. That will please him, and fill our coffers nicely. There is never any point in cutting off one's nose to spite one's face."

By eleven-thirty, the ball was in full swing. Lady Sophy, surveying the scene from the sidelines, found in it naught for her comfort. It seemed that the whole world had gone over to the enemy.

Lord Rigg, having welcomed the last of the latecomers, was now entering the ballroom with Amabel on his arm, and it was clear to the meanest intelligence that the ton was opening its heart to them both.

Eulalie Wakeford, who should have known better, had gone off with Cornelia Finch, to play whist. Sir Murray was arguing with Mr Tunmer over the rival merits of the Severn and Wye fishing. Davina was dancing with Edward Clare, and Jane with Robert Clintwood. Even Joshua Turnbull was leading a slightly bemused Lady Holland through the rousing paces of the polka. Mortimer and Roland were nowhere to be seen, and one could only hope they had not lost all sense of duty to their partners.

Lady Sophy's head ached. The thump of the music was intolerable. She bethought herself of a small salon she had passed on the way in. It was tucked away behind palms and banks of flowers, and might provide a little peace and quiet. She made her way to it, and was sinking down onto a sofa when she saw that she was not alone. Standing in the doorway, and smiling as if they had parted only yesterday, was Lady Charlotte Turnbull.

"May I come in, Sophia?"

Lady Sophy nodded wearily. "Of course, Charlotte. You've a far better right to move about this house than I."

"I suppose that's true, though of recent years, I've had little occasion to." Lady Charlotte came in and sat down facing Lady Sophy. "Are you quite well, my dear? You look very white."

"I'm quite all right, thank you. Merely seeking a respite from . . . from everything."

Charlotte regarded her composedly. "May an old friend advise you not to refine too much upon things that can't be altered? Luke and Davina will make up their own minds."

"At least," flashed Sophia, "I will speak mine, first!"

Charlotte tilted her head. "Why do you oppose the match? What has Luke done to make you dislike him?"

"You know as well as I do."

"Past scandals, you mean? Dear Sophy, look about you, tonight. Surely you can see that society has decided to bury the past?"

"Easy enough, since society has nothing at stake. Davina is as dear to me as my own daughter. I won't see her thrown away on a man whose moral character is in serious doubt."

"Luke's character is sound as a bell. Some members of my clan leave much to be desired, but he's not one of them. Indeed I believe you've reason to be grateful to him—on more than one score."

"Have I so? Must I thank him for ruining Davina's chances of achieving an eligible marriage? For making her the target of idle gossip? No doubt you are about to remind me that Rigg's money has saved Wakeford from bankruptcy?" Sophy sat upright. "Let me tell you that though he may buy the Missal, he will not succeed in buying my niece."

Anger showed in Charlotte's eyes. "I remember," she said levelly, "that my father once told me that the reason the Wakefords refuse ennoblement, is that the position of God is already spoken for. You are a great snob, Sophia, and it's very unbecoming in you."

"I am not a snob! I won't be spoken to so! All I wish is Davina's happiness."

"Then give her your blessing, and let her marry Luke. He's deep in love with her, and she with him." Charlotte rose and stooping, dropped a kiss on Lady Sophy's cheek. "It has been good to talk to you. I hope very much we'll meet again, but if not, remember all I've said."

She started towards the door. Sophia called out as she was about to pass through it.

"Charlotte? I have often wished . . . I wish you to know . . ." The words would not come, and she shook her head. "It's no use."

Charlotte's look became compassionate. "You may rely upon Luke," she said, and went out of the room.

XXIV

LADY SOPHY'S MIGRAINE would have worsened could she have witnessed the actions of her step-nephew at that moment.

Throughout the evening Roland had behaved in exemplary fashion. He had greeted Lord Rigg with polite formality, and Lady Rigg with easy friendliness. He had stood up with his sister in the first set of country-dances, and with Miss Tredgold in the second. He had visited the card-room on the floor above, to see how his mama did.

He had taken no more than four or five glasses of hock, and even to the critical eye of Mortimer Foote, appeared quite sober. He was, however, in an extremely nervous state, unable to concentrate on what was said to him, and referring constantly to the watch on his fob.

Mortimer was convinced that his cousin was about to commit some indiscretion, though what it was, he could not imagine. He would dearly have liked to confide in his seniors, but Sir Murray seemed always to be engaged with persons too august to be interrupted, and Lady Sophy was nowhere to be seen. Lord Rigg, as host, had his hands full, and it was unthinkable that he should be further burdened.

There was only one thing to be done, and Mortimer did it. He stuck like a leech to Roland, joined the same set in the dancing, and remained within earshot of him at all times.

Even so, he nearly allowed his quarry to escape him. It happened at midnight, just as the musicians broke into the strains of "Ah, du Lieber Augustin", and Lord Rigg was seen to enter the ballroom with Miss Wakeford on his arm. A frisson of interest ran round the watching guests. Mortimer's attention was temporarily distracted, and when he looked round again, he was just in time to see Roland disappear through one of the wide doors leading to the garden.

His reaction was purely instinctive. He followed his cousin silently and at a discreet distance, across the lawn, through the garden gate, and out into the narrow confines of Farm Street.

At this hour the lane was deserted, and the lights so few and dim that Mortimer could barely descry Roland's hurrying figure. He set off in pursuit, doing his best to tread softly over the cobbles.

Along Farm Street they went, turned right-hand into South Audley Street, and left into Aldford. Clearly they were headed for the Tredgold residence and the Park Street mews. By the time Mortimer reached the stable-yard, Roland had already climbed the shallow steps to the terrace behind the house, and was circling round towards the side entrance.

Mortimer paused at the entrance to the coach-house, uncertain what his next move should be. If Roly was merely deserting a party that bored him, that was his own business—but surely, in that case, he would have warned someone of his intention?

The Tredgold mansion seemed unnaturally dark. There was no light in the servants' rooms above, and the curtains at the lower levels were all close-drawn. Mortimer waited for light to blossom as Roland entered the building, but none showed. He shook his head, puzzled. A man didn't creep about his home without so much as a taper to light his way. And where was the valet? He at least should be up and about.

"Dashed havey-cavey," said Mortimer aloud. "Shall have to go and see for myself."

He started forward, but had taken no more than a step when a hand closed over his right wrist, another over his mouth, and he was hauled bodily backwards into the darkness of the coach-house.

"Don't you make a sound, cully," muttered a voice in his ear. "Not a peep outer yer, or it'll be yer last."

Mortimer had no penchant for martyrdom. He stood perfectly still, raising his hand in a signal of compliance.

"That's the ticket," continued the voice. "I'm a friend, see? Just you do as you're bid, and you'll come to no 'arm. Understand?"

Mortimer managed to nod his head.

His assailant grunted. The iron fingers dropped from his mouth to his throat, lingered there for a moment of horrid indecision, then fell away. Mortimer edged round slowly, trying to peer through the gloom.

"Who the devil are you?" he said hoarsely.

"Why, sir, I'm a friend of Mr Roland Foote. And you'll be

Mr Mortimer Foote, I've no doubt. Followed 'im from Rowan 'ouse, if I don't mistake?"

"It's nothing to do with you."

"Well, there's two opinions about that." The man chuckled softly, and a shiver went down Mortimer's spine. As his eyes grew accustomed to the dark, he could see that the stranger wore black clothing, a black hat pulled low over his eyes, a black muffler wound high about his chin. His build was light and lean, and he moved from one foot to another in a restless weaving pattern that put Mortimer in mind of a cat, needling its claws for the kill.

"Look now," the whisper came. "Up there."

Mortimer turned towards the house. A small glimmer of light had appeared. It moved upwards past the uncurtained windows on the main stairway, checked a moment, then faded.

"Young gennelman's bound for the study."

"How do you know where the study is?" demanded Mortimer.

"I told you, I'm acquainted with yer cousin." The purring chuckle came again. "Some might say, 'is accomplice. Aidin' and abettin' the pore young man to steal into an 'ouse at dead o' night; to creep past sleeping doors; to tiptoe to a certain lock, and turn a certain key, and find . . . summink o' value. Eh? What d'ye think o' that?"

"I think you're a liar! My cousin's no thief."

"No? Then if 'e's not, why, no more am I. Innocent babes, the pair on us." The dark figure moved suddenly, and Mortimer, starting back in alarm, tripped and almost went sprawling on the cobbles.

"Steady." Once more the hand gripped his arm. "Watch the window. If 'e's got it, 'e'll give us the sign."

"Got what?" said Mortimer, and as he spoke knew the answer. "The Missal! No! He'd never touch that. Take your hands off me, you blackguard!"

Surprisingly, the man did as he was bid. His eyes were fixed unwaveringly on the study window, and after a moment the curtain parted to emit a bar of light, remained so for the count of ten, then closed again.

The dark man turned to Mortimer. "Time's short now," he said, "so mark what I say. The two of us will nip round to the front o' the 'ouse. We'll wait there, nice and quiet. If you spoil my lay, Mr Foote, I'll 'ave yer liver an' lights."

Something cold brushed Mortimer's cheek. He saw it was a horse-pistol.

"You'll not succeed in this plan," he said wildly. "You'll be caught, and I very much hope you'll be hanged."

The dark man grinned. "Reckon I'll cheat the gallows, cully. Come, quit gabbing, and stir your stumps."

The pistol nudged Mortimer's ribs. He found himself hustled from the mews, along Aldford Street and round the corner to the Tredgolds' front portico. In the shadow of this his kidnapper halted.

"Watch," he ordered, "an' keep yer gob shut."

Mortimer gazed about him. Under the watery gleam of the lamps, the roadway showed almost empty. Some way along, where Park and South Streets converged, a single carriage was drawn in to the kerb, its driver apparently asleep on the box. The windows of the mansion were all in darkness, but a single lamp burned over the front door.

"Here 'e comes," breathed the dark man. "Follow 'im, but not too close. Keep well into the railings."

Mortimer nodded dumbly. He felt in a daze. He found himself praying that Roland would not appear, that somehow he could be saved from what must be accounted the onset of lunacy. But the front door swung gently open, and there emerged a figure wrapped in what Mortimer recognised as his own domino. The wearer glanced up and down the street. Mortimer glimpsed Roland's white face and staring eyes. He was tempted to cry out, but a sharp jab of the horse-pistol silenced him.

"Now!" muttered the dark man.

Roland came quickly down the steps, and strode away towards the carriage at the corner. Mortimer and his incubus, sneaking along behind, saw him lean towards the window of the vehicle, and address the occupant. Who this was, it was impossible to tell. Mortimer could see only a white hand resting on the window's edge.

Now Roland was gesturing vehemently, as if in argument. The hand withdrew and reappeared, holding a leather pouch. Roland seized it, glanced briefly at its contents, and thrust it beneath his cloak. He then drew out a small, squarish object and handed it to the occupant of the carriage.

It was too much for Mortimer. Starting forward, he shouted "No Roly! Don't, man!"

It was the signal for Hell to loose its cohorts.

At Mortimer's shout, an upper window was thrown up and a female head emerged, yelling blue murder. Two men in the scarlet jackets of Bow Street Officers, burst from a neighbouring basement and pounded towards Roland. The dark man, sprinting forward, crashed straight into them. Mortimer, standing slack-jawed, perceived that the owner of the carriage had drawn a pistol and was pointing it straight at Roland. He yelled a warning. The driver of the carriage jerked upright and cracked his whip. The pistol cracked, and Roland, with a cry of pain, spun like a teetotum into the gutter. The carriage lurched away from the kerb, and thundered at full gallop towards Hyde Park Corner, with one of the Runners in desperate pursuit.

Mortimer dropped on his knees beside Roland. The shot had struck him in the left thigh, and though the wound was bleeding profusely, it was not the dreadful pumping of a severed artery. Mortimer pressed his handkerchief to the wound, snatched off his cravat and bound the pad in place.

The dark man, meanwhile, was shouting abuse at the second Runner, who was answering in kind. He now broke off the altercation, and came over to Mortimer. "Carry 'im indoors," he directed, "and send for Dr Kentridge, Mount Street, Number 34. I'll get word to yer uncle at Rowan 'Ouse." He turned to the Runner. "Lend a 'and, will yer? Do summink to earn yer keep!" So saying, he turned on his heel and hurried off along South Street.

Mortimer was outraged. "Stop that man," he commanded. "Who is he? Why don't you arrest him?"

The Runner shrugged. "The devil will look arter 'is own," he said. He gazed down at Roland. "Fainted, and better so. Best move 'im now, 'e'll suffer less. I'll take 'is shoulders, sir, and you 'is 'eels. That's the bully! Up we goes, an' steady, back to the 'ouse."

At the moment Roland was approaching the carriage in Park Street, his sister was spinning through the closing bars of the waltz in Lord Rigg's embrace. As the music died, his lordship retained his grip on her hand.

"I've ordered an interval of fifteen minutes," he said. "Do you care to stroll in the garden with me? There's much I wish to say to you."

She nodded, and allowed him to lead her through the nearest of the French doors, which a footman immediately closed after them. The air outside was pleasantly cool after the heat of the ballroom, and though there was no moon, soft light from the windows of the great mansion lit the grass, the scented rosebuds and the neatly raked paths.

No other couple was in sight. Miss Wakeford's thoughts were as erratic as her pulse. She made a token attempt to free her fingers from Lord Rigg's grasp and found them clasped the more tightly. Smiling down at her, he said, "A week is too long to be apart from you, Davina. I've missed you abominably."

It was the first time he had used her given name, and it made her feel giddy. She said confusedly, "Indeed, I've missed you too, my lord."

"Lucas," prompted his lordship.

"Lucas." The word pleased her so much that she repeated it. "Lucas?"

"Yes, my love?"

"What . . . what did you, at Graydon?"

"Worked, far harder than I care to. Walked miles, rode miles. Talked to Edward Clare. We solved some problems, made some plans. One of them concerns your brother."

"Roland? In what way?"

"I hope to set up a stud-farm at Graydon, to breed racehorses. I intend to ask Roland to manage it."

"Oh, that will be famous! The best thing in the world for him, and you'd not regret it. He's excellent with horses." Davina's face clouded. "If only he'll accept."

"Why should he not?"

"I . . . I don't know. He acts foolishly at times."

His lordship glanced at her thoughtfully. "Yes, but which of us does not, particularly at that age? I expect I may make him see reason."

"Thank you," she said warmly. "I think you are the kindest, most generous man in the world."

"I'm not kind at all. It's simply that I'll do anything to get in your good graces—anything, that is, except attend another of your aunt's musical soirées. My last appearance didn't seem to raise me one jot in her estimation."

Davina could think of no tactful reply, and swtiched to a less thorny topic.

"Amabel must be pleased with the success of the party? Half the ton seems to be here."

"Yes, she's in alt. Did you know, by the way, that she's to marry James Tunmer? Not immediately, of course. She'll go north to visit her parents when the Season ends. Tunmer's lands march with the Sears'. They'll announce their betrothal next spring."

"I'm glad. He seems a very dependable sort of man."

"Personally I find him a dead bore, but I expect they'll suit admirably. At least James will be able to support Amabel's extravagancies." Luke placed an arm round Davina's shoulders. "And you, my lass? How have you gone on, in my absence?"

"I've been very busy, and bustling, and ill-tempered, I thank you. The Missal's sold, thank God, and the money paid. By noon tomorrow it will be settled once for all."

He nodded without speaking. His silence piqued her, and she said challengingly, "I would give a great deal to know the names of the buyers."

He smiled at her abstractedly. Clearly he was not anxious to discuss the matter, but the curiosity that had been growing in her for weeks could no longer be contained.

"Lucas," she said roundly, "are you, or are you not, one of them?"

"I am." He was watching her closely, now, "but I hadn't meant to admit it, quite yet."

"Why not?"

"Because," he said, turning to face her and drawing her closer, "I have this curious desire to be loved for myself, and not for my investment in Wakeford Hall. Still, since the secret's out, I'll be plain with you. I'm happy to own a fifth share in one of our greatest national treasures, but it will count for nothing if I don't possess your love, my dear, dearest Miss Wakeford."

He then pulled her to him and kissed her with a tenderness and attention to detail that she found eminently laudable. It was some minutes before he released her, and raised his hand to stroke back a tendril of her hair.

"I trust," he said, "that this means you'll marry me? I hope you're not merely toying with my affections?"

Davina took his hand and pressed it to her cheek. "If you hadn't spoken," she said simply, "I think I should have died."

"In that case, we've only to fix on a date. I suppose you'll need time to buy your bride-clothes, and so forth. Shall we say, a month from now?"

Davina opened her mouth to reply, but before she could do so the peace of the garden, and indeed of the entire neighbourhood, was shattered by a series of ear-splitting shrieks. Lord Rigg jerked round to survey his house in shocked dismay.

"Good God, what's that?"

Davina shook her head. She was already hurrying back towards the door. By long experience she knew that the disturbance was caused by her step-mama, indulging in a fit of strong hysterics.

XXV

By the time Luke and Davina reached the card-room on the first floor of the house, it had been deserted by all save the members of the Wakeford family.

Eulalie Wakeford literally held the centre of the floor. She lay on the Savonnerie carpet, surrounded by cards and spilled counters. Her shrieks had mercifully sunk to a muted whimper, and her eyes were rolled up in a very alarming way. Lady Sophia kneeled beside her, chafing her wrists. Jane Tredgold wafted a bottle of salts of ammonia under her nose. Sir Murray stood to one side, looking on helplessly, a glass of brandy in one hand. Seeing Lord Rigg in the doorway, he hurried across.

"Rigg, the most shocking thing. Davina, my child, your poor mama. . . ."

"What is it," said Davina, "what's provoked her?"

"No, no, it's not temper, this time." Sir Murray rubbed his kerchief over his face. "It's Roly. There's been an accident."

Davina went cold. "What sort of accident? Uncle?"

"He's been shot. Not a fatal wound, thank God. Mortimer's with him."

"Mortimer? How comes he to be with Roly, where did this happen?"

"Park Street." Something in Sir Murray's expression warned Davina to say no more. He placed the glass of brandy in her hand. "Try and persuade your mother to swallow it," he said. "Go along. Do as I say."

Davina moved off. Sir Murray turned dazedly to Lord Rigg. "It was a fellow named Hawkins brought the news," he said. "I . . . it seems he knows you, my lord."

His lordship ignored the implied question. "How much did he tell you?" he enquired.

"He said Roly was hit in the thigh, a surface wound. They've carried him into my home, and the doctor has been sent for. Mortimer and two Bow Street Runners are with him."

"Who was his attacker?"

"No one can tell. The shot was fired from a carriage."

"Was Hawkins the only one to bring you news?"

"No. My coachman, Micklejohn, came, sent by Becky. But the man's a numskull. I could get no sense out of him. Rigg, I must get home at once."

"Of course. Has your carriage been sent for?"

"Yes, Robert Clintwood is seeing to that."

"You'll need more than one conveyance, sir. I suggest you send Mrs Wakeford, your wife and daughter, in your own coach. You and Miss Wakeford shall go in mine. I'll order the horses put to at once." He paused. "It will give you time to arrange your thoughts."

Sir Murray did not seem surprised at this rather odd remark, and Lord Rigg, giving him a friendly clap on the shoulder, moved off to give orders to a footman. As soon as he was out of earshot, Miss Wakeford hurried to her uncle's side.

"The Missal," she said urgently. "Is it safe?"

Sir Murray took her cold hands in his own. "I'm afraid not, child. Becky sent word with Micklejohn. She says the book has been stolen." Sir Murray checked, at a loss for words. At last he said simply, "I fear we must face the fact that it was Roly who stole it."

Ten minutes later Eulalie Wakeford, still in a half-swooning condition, was carried down to the Tredgold coach and lifted tenderly to a nest of cushions. Lady Sophia and Jane climbed in after her, the steps were raised and the door closed, and the vehicle set off at a sober pace for Park Street.

Some few minutes later, Lord Rigg's carriage was brought round, and Lord Rigg assisted first Sir Murray and then Davina to enter it. As he handed her in, Luke bent his head and murmured, "Remember, love, nothing has changed. I'll come to you as soon as I'm able."

She shook her head silently, tears on her cheeks. Luke kissed her fingers, then released her. As soon as the horses began to move off, he hurried back into the house. He found Robert Clintwood and Joshua waiting for him in the hallway.

"Clint," he said, "find Edward for me, if you will, and tell him he must take my place as host. Amabel will help him to fob off the questions."

As Clintwood went away towards the ballroom, Luke turned to his uncle.

"A fine mess we've made of things, between the lot of us. I suppose we may count ourselves lucky Jocelyn didn't kill young Foote outright."

"Hawkins reckons he never meant to shoot t'lad," Joshua said. "When Mortimer Foote shouted, the carriage jerked forward, like, and t'pistol went off."

"One must hope the Runners hold the same view. In any event, it will make small difference if Jocelyn is caught—as he's like to be. The hunt will be up, by now. They'll be watching the roads, and the ports."

"Then we must make sure we reach him before the Law does," said Joshua calmly. "Charles has done his work well. We've agents posted every village from here to Dover. Jocelyn won't escape us."

"How long before we hear?"

"Four or five hours. Not more. Reckon he won't get so far as Lewisham." Joshua studied Luke thoughtfully. "And when you have him, what will ye do with him?"

"That decision," Luke answered, "we'll make when the time comes."

When Miss Wakeford entered her uncle's house, she found it in confusion. Light blazed in every room, and maids rushed from room to room, carrying blankets and hot water. From the kitchen regions issued a steady keening, very distressful to the ear. Only Becky seemed in full command of her wits. She came to meet Davina in the hall.

"Your mama is upstairs," she said. "laid down on her bed. We've put poor Master Roly in the morning-room. It'll be easier to tend to him there, than upstairs. We're shorthanded, what with Letty and Cook in conniptions, and that good-for-nothin' Jenkins gone missing." She turned to her employer. "Those two from Bow Street has been asking for you, sir. They were wishful to speak to Master Roly, but the doctor sent them to the rightabout, I'm glad to say. I've put 'em in the bookroom, which is good enough for such a rare pair o' busybodies."

"I'll go and talk to them," Sir Murray said. "But please tell me exactly what happened here tonight."

"Well, sir, I sleep light, and around midnight it was, something waked me, for I found meself sitting up in my bed, certain sure something was amiss. I lit my candle, and went down the stairs, treading as light as I could . . . and there I saw the door of your study standing wide, and a light burning and the strongroom door open. I went and looked into it, sir, and I could tell at a glance the box with the book was gone."

"What did you do then?"

"I went to the front window, sir, and flung it up, and cried out 'Stop, thief!' at the top o' me lungs. That's when the men in the street started to run wild, and the horses bolted off, and Master Roly fell. I didn't know it was him, till Mr Mortimer come up and pulled back the hood of that cloak he was wearin'. So then, I ran down, and helped the men carry him back in the house. I sent Frant for the doctor, and Micklejohn to give you the news." Becky's voice faltered and tears began to roll down her face. "Oh, sir, if I'd known it was Master Roly, I'd have cut out my tongue rather than cry thief, but how was I to guess, sir? How was I to guess?"

"There, there." Sir Murray patted Rebecca's shoulder. "You're in no way to blame. Don't cry. I shall explain to the Runners that this is a misunderstanding—that Roland acted quite innocently. You must tell the staff to say the same, and warn them not to gossip to anyone till we've set the matter straight."

Becky gave him a tearful nod, and went off, dabbing at her eyes with her apron. Sir Murray turned to his niece.

"Davina, can you think of any reason Roland might have for stealing the Missal?"

She nodded. "I think he's run into debt. He came to me last week, asking for a loan of five thousand pounds. He asked the same of Mortimer, only yesterday. Oh God, if only I'd been less blind, less smug, less stupid!"

"Why didn't you tell me of this?"

"Because at the time I thought he wanted the money to buy a team of horses. I did speak to Mr Shedley . . . asked him to increase Roly's allowance. It never occurred to me that he might be desperate enough to steal. Uncle, how are we to get him out of this? What if the Runners arrest him?"

"They won't risk that, while he's so ill. I'll find a way to stave them off till we can recover the Missal."

"How can we do that, without capturing the other creatures, the ones in the carriage? And if we do, they'll incriminate him. I believe we must cut our losses . . . tell the consortium the book's been stolen, and repay the money. That way at least we may be able to save Roland."

"And what's to become of Wakeford?"

"We'll find some other way of raising the money."

"We might arrange terms with the consortium," said Sir Murray. "Repay the money over a period of time. I could speak to Angerstein."

"No." Davina was adamant. "There are reasons I can't indulge in special pleading." She stripped off her long gloves and dropped them on the hall table. "I . . . I learned last night that Rigg is a member of the consortium."

"What of that?"

"He asked me, at the same time, to marry him."

"In that case, he'll wish to do what he can for Roland."

"But don't you see, that's exactly what I can't allow? The only way Luke can help, is to keep silent about Roland's part in the theft. To do that, he would have to lie to his partners in the consortium. I won't ask it of him. It's better that I forget him. I shan't see him again."

"My dearest child. . . ."

"No, please, Uncle. Don't say any more. I can't bear it, just at present. Invent what story you like, say what's best for Roly. I'll support you in it. But it mustn't compromise Luke Rowan. And if he calls here, you will oblige me by saying I . . . I don't wish to see him. Please."

Sir Murray regarded her sadly for a moment, then said, "Don't despair yet, Davina. We'll work something out, between us. It's not the end of the world, my dear."

Davina made no reply, because to her, it was.

Upstairs she changed her ball-dress for a cotton gown, and went to her mother's room. She met Lady Sophia on the point of leaving it.

"Your mama's asleep," Lady Sophy said. "I gave her a

soporific, on Dr Kentridge's advice. Jane will sit with her. We'd best go and see how Roland does."

They met Mortimer Foote and the doctor in the lower hallway. The latter said bracingly that Roland was as well as could be expected. "He's lost a lot of blood, but the bullet wasn't deep-lodged. He's suffering from concussion . . . wandering in his mind a trifle, but that'll pass. Keep him warm and quiet. In particular, keep those pesky Redcoats away from him. Any shock could start the bleeding again. That woman of yours . . . Bracket, is it? Sensible female, let her stay with him."

"He will recover, won't he?" said Davina anxiously.

Dr Kentridge patted her arm. "Bless you, ma'am, of course he will. He's strong as a bull. Infection's always a threat, of course, but it's a clean wound. If he shows signs of fever, give him a saline draught. I'll send round a paregoric, for the pain. In the meantime, no food, and only water to drink. I'll call again in a few hours' time." He turned at the door. "I advise you good people to get some rest. Won't do the boy any good, wearing yourselves to shreds."

Mortimer was the only one to heed this advice, going off to his lodgings with the promise that he'd be back by seven. Davina went to Roland's room. He was only half-conscious, and his dazed eyes did not seem to recognise her. His right hand tugged fretfully at the counterpane, and he muttered something she couldn't catch.

"He keeps talking of a key," said Becky in a low voice. "It worritts him sorely."

Davina went to the discarded clothes that lay on a chair nearby. The black domino was there, and Roland's coat, and the blood-stained trousers they'd cut off him. She found the key in his fob-pocket and carried it over to the light. It exactly matched the key she'd seen so often on her uncle's chain—the key to the strongroom. She slipped it into the bosom of her gown and went back to the bed.

"Roly," she said, in a slow, clear voice, "I have the key. You'll be safe. I have the key."

Though she repeated the words several times, he appeared not to understand, and continued to toss and mutter. At last she took his hand and stroked it gently. Comforted, he fell into a fitful sleep.

Davina looked at Becky.

"Where did he get it, do you think?"

"Jenkins, I'd say. I never did care for that piece of mouldy cheese!"

"Don't speak of it to anyone."

"That I won't." Becky's eyes were tender. "And don't you fret, my lamb. We'll come about, see if we don't."

Davina nodded wearily. A trick of the night breeze carried a faint thread of music to the room. Rigg's party was still in full swing. She put the thought from her. There was no time for repining, no time even for remorse. That could come later.

Now she must think. A story must be concocted, and the members of the household briefed. A search must be set up for the Missal. One would have to offer a substantial reward. The money paid by Angerstein must be refunded. Thank God none of it had been spent.

The night dragged on. Becky's head nodded and drooped. Davina sat wide awake, still holding Roland's hand, and planning, planning.

Lady Sophia sat in the drawing-room, where a fire had been lit against the early morning chill. Sir Murray came in, closed the door, and crossed to stand beside her chair.

"Have those men gone?" she asked.

"No."

"Will Dr Kentridge let them question Roly?"

"I hope not. I've told them Roly took the box at my bidding. They haven't yet summoned up the courage to call me a liar."

"They will, unless we can produce the Book of Hours." Lady Sophy ran her fingers through her tumbled hair. "You must persuade Davina to change her mind. If she marries Rigg, Roly will be safe."

Sir Murray smiled lop-sidedly. "A few hours ago, you were saying Rigg should only have her over your dead body."

"That was different. You know it was."

"I doubt I'll be able to change Davina's mind."

"You must make her do so! Rigg will never stand by and let his wife's brother go to gaol."

"And Davina won't trade upon his affection for her. It would

261

be dishonest, in her view, and I tend to agree with her. We've been over this ground ten times, Sophia, and I suggest...."

He was interrupted by the sound of a carriage drawing up at the front door. At the same time, the clock on the mantel began to strike five.

Lady Sophy sprang up and ran to peer through the curtains.

"It's Rigg. Clintwood is with him. Rigg is getting out, but not Clintwood." She glanced round to see her husband moving towards the door. "Tredgold, where do you imagine you are going?"

"To tell his lordship that Davina won't see him."

Lady Sophy whirled to the door to block his path.

"If you do any such thing," she said ominously, "I swear I shall obtain a bill of divorcement."

"Don't be ridiculous, Sophia. Let me pass, if you please."

"I shall do no such thing!" Lady Sophy's voice had risen so that the butler, Frant, who had appeared in answer to the ring of the front doorbell, stopped in his tracks and regarded her enquiringly.

Lady Sophy gave him a curt nod. "The door, Frant!"

He moved to obey. Sir Murray said quietly. "This is on your head, Sophy, not mine."

Next moment, Lord Rigg entered the hall and came towards them.

XXVI

No one could have guessed, to look at his lordship, that he had shared in the alarums and excursions of the past few hours. He had exchanged his formal evening dress for dove-grey pantaloons and a coat of Bath suiting. He was freshly-shaven, his Hessians gleamed and his cravat was a work of art. He might, by his appearance, be making a morning call on respected friends, rather than visiting a house of doom, and his first words showed nothing more than polite concern.

"Forgive this early call, Lady Tredgold," he said, "but I'm anxious to know how Roland does."

"He's asleep. Dr Kentridge says the leg-wound is not serious, but he has a concussion that must be watched. He's allowed no visitors, as yet."

She shot an involuntary glance at the library door, behind which voices could be heard in altercation. His lordship nodded lazily. "Quite so," he said. He turned to Sir Murray, who was standing close by, frowning at his wife. "May I come in for a moment, sir? I believe there are matters we should discuss."

After a brief pause, Sir Murray nodded. "Yes, come in, Rigg. It can do no harm to talk."

When they were settled, Luke came straight to the point. "I'm here," he said, "to make a confession. A few hours ago, I asked your niece to marry me. I should of course have asked your permission—and Mrs Wakeford's—to pay my addresses. I hope I will be forgiven for the oversight."

Lady Sophy gave him her most charming smile. "Of course you are, my lord. We're not so old-cattish that we've forgotten what it is to be in love, and to act on impulse."

"You're very kind, ma'am."

Lady Sophy waved an airy hand. "Dare one ask, sir, what was Davina's answer to this very gratifying offer?"

"She accepted me," said Luke, "but in the light of certain events, I fear she may have changed her mind."

Lady Sophy seemed astonished. "Good heavens, no! Why should she?"

263

"Sophia!" said Sir Murray warningly, but she took no notice. "There can be no doubt," she said, "that Davina is devoted to you, and I could not conceive of anything more delightful than to see you two betrothed. You have our blessing."

Luke bowed. "Thank you. Nevertheless, I believe I must have Miss Wakeford's own assurance."

"Of course you must, but just at present she is sitting with her brother. I can hardly call her away. Later, when she is rested, you must call again."

"Later will be too late. I will see her now, ma'am, if you will be so kind as to ask her to come here?"

Sir Murray gave a quiet chuckle. His wife faced Lord Rigg stare for stare, but her gaze fell first. She rose and gave the bellrope a sharp tug.

Frant appeared almost at once, and Lady Sophy said flatly, "Request Miss Davina to come to me immediately, if you please."

They waited in silence for a minute or two. Then they heard the sound of running footsteps, and Davina appeared in the doorway.

"What is it?" she said, hurrying towards her aunt, "Has something . . . ?" She checked as Lord Rigg rose to his feet. "You!" She swung to face Sir Murray. "Uncle, I asked you not to allow this."

Sir Murray lifted a pipe from the mantelpiece and began to fill it. "I am growing very tired," he said, "of being told how to behave in my own house. Rigg here has done us the courtesy of coming to call. He has asked permission to pay you his addresses. Your aunt has given it. I now await the next move—yours, I think, my lord."

"By all means, sir. Miss Wakeford, in the presence of witnesses, I beg you will do me the honour to marry me."

"I cannot." She turned desperately to Lady Sophia. "You must excuse me."

She started for the door, but Luke caught her wrist. "My love, don't tell me your feelings have changed so drastically, in five hours."

"They have. That is, I must ask you n-not to pursue the matter, for my mind is made up."

"Would it help to unmake it again, if I told you that the

Rigborough Book of Hours is at this moment safely lodged in the bank?"

"What?"

"Safe in the bank," repeated his lordship. "If you will but sit down a moment, and listen?"

Davina plumped down on the nearest chair. Lord Rigg remained standing, facing three accusing stares.

"I must apologise," he said, "for leaving you in ignorance so long, but it was unavoidable. I had, you see, given my word that I would say nothing."

"To whom, I'd like to know?" demanded Sir Murray.

"To Roland," returned his lordship. "I did try to persuade him that it would be best to take you into his confidence, but he said you would interfere with his plans, and bound me to silence."

Lady Sophy shook her head. "I don't understand. Why should Roly apply to you?"

"Because I was, in a sense, already involved. The fact is, my cousin Jocelyn Clare contrived to buy up gambling debts incurred by Roland, to the tune of five thousand pounds."

"Good God!" said Lady Sophy faintly.

"Jocelyn then offered to surrender the chits and pay Roland an additional five thousand pounds, if he would steal the Missal."

"How did he breach my strongroom, I'd like to know?" said Sir Murray.

"Jocelyn provided him with a key—an impression, I imagine, taken from your own. Does anyone in your employ have access to your fob-chain?"

"Yes, by Jupiter, Jenkins does, and the rogue's been missing since last evening."

"Never mind Jenkins," said Lady Sophy. "What about Roland?"

"He had, of course, tried to raise the money to meet his debts, and failed." His lordship looked thoughtfully at Davina. "When my cousin threatened foreclosure, Roland pretended to agree to stealing the book. Then he came to me and told me the whole. He'd devised a plan by which he hoped to trap Jocelyn...."

"And do you mean to tell me," interrupted Davina, "that you encouraged him in it? You let him run that dreadful risk?"

"I didn't encourage him. In fact, I urged him to make a clean breast of it to you, sir, but he refused. He said it was through his fault Jocelyn was in a position to threaten us all, and he meant to settle the matter himself."

"You should have stopped him," insisted Davina.

Luke looked at her. "My dearest, that would have been quite the wrong thing to do. What Roland needs is a chance to prove himself a man—to think and act for himself."

"Quite right," said Sir Murray. "The boy's been mollycoddled for too long. Time he cut the apron-strings." He turned to Lord Rigg. "Go on, my lord. What happened next?"

"Roland's plan was simple . . . to stage a fake burglary. I had a word with the Chief Magistrate, and found you'd employed Runners. It was agreed that between them, and my uncle's agent Silas Hawkins, my cousin was to be caught red-handed, and placed under arrest. Unfortunately, Mortimer became involved in the action, and things went awry. For that, I am deeply sorry."

"But the Missal," Davina said. "You said it was safe?"

"Yes. Roland removed it from the strongroom yesterday, very early, and brought it to me."

"Then what did he give your cousin?"

"A bound copy of the collected sermons of the Dean of Tewkesbury," said Luke. "It was the right size, you know. One must hope that Jocelyn finds it improving reading."

Sir Murray looked thoughtful. "Where is your cousin, my lord? Has he got clean away?"

"No, he's in custody. I took the liberty of confiding Roland's plan to my Uncle Joshua Turnbull. His man Hawkins was able to discover that Jocelyn had booked a berth on the packet sailing from Dover tonight. My uncle's agents watched the Dover road, and arrested Jocelyn before he'd gone twenty miles."

"Do you mean to hand him over to the Law?"

"I will if that's your wish," Luke said. "He's guilty of shooting your nephew, if nothing else. But I can't help feeling it would be wiser to let him use that berth to Calais. It will save us all a great deal of unpleasantness."

Sir Murray nodded. "I agree. Send him packing."

"Thank you. There's time to see he catches his ship."

Luke stood up. "And now, I expect you'll wish to be rid of me. Lady Sophia, your servant!"